aise for *On Swift Horses*:

'A story so vivid, so hauntingly told, you can almost feel its complex, conflicted characters appearing in front of you as you read' *iNews*

'Worth reading for the poetry alone … The prose is unexpectedly graceful: quietly lyrical and self-assured … But in these characters' cautious balancing of desire and self-restraint, the novel also has something universal to say about the necessary risk of love' *Sunday Times*

'A marvel, a beautifully written novel that traces its raw, guarded characters from California to Las Vegas to Mexico with grace and inevitability. Shannon Pufahl's mid-century West is dead-on right, as recognisable as a box of old photos and yet completely original in voice and scope'
JESS WALTER, author of *Beautiful Ruins*

'Pufahl paints her characters with remarkable compassion and decency … Her lyrical prose depicts an American West that is both desolate and beautiful and inspires a sense of individuality that can apply to much more of the human experience than we've previously been led to believe'
San Francisco Chronicle

'A beautifully written debut' *Psychologies Magazine*

'With gorge… …netimes dangerous w… BBC

'Once in a rare while you come across a novel of such transfixing beauty that it enlarges your faith in the medium itself. *On Swift Horses* is, for me, one of those books. As an exploration of life lived in the outer distances of plain sight, it is suffused with hazard and touched by grace, furnished with the longevity of a postwar classic and the immediacy of the present tense. It is, simply put, a masterpiece'

ANTHONY MARRA, author of *A Constellation of Vital Phenomena*

'Odyssean ... Pufahl's voice is strikingly solid, timeworn but not nostalgic, as she unravels a cinematic story that avoids genre clichés or sentimentality ... The spaces she creates for her characters – San Diego's languid Chester Hotel hiding in plain sight, Tijuana rendered as an underworld – have the aura of realms' *New York Times Book Review*

'Pufahl limns the borders of the prodigal and the moral, and there – among the seedy hotels, the off-duty sailors, the noise and dust of the horse races, in Tijuana and in Vegas – she finds new forms of fidelity and care. Read this book for the adventure, for the keening lyricism of the lost and searching, but mostly read this book because no one writes like Shannon Pufahl. Her voice is muscular, awesome and pure. This book knocked me flat on my back' JUSTIN TORRES, author of *We the Animals*

'[An] engrossing, melancholy debut novel [with] echoes of Don Carpenter's *Hard Rain Falling*, Leonard Gardner's *Fat City* and Patricia Highsmith's *The Price of Salt* ... Pufahl's prose is consistently lyrical and deeply observant ... She evokes the fear and possibility of life in a new place, with new emotions. She writes with a grace and force that's rare even among seasoned writers' *Los Angeles Times*

'Each gorgeous sentence of this epic, set in the American West in 1956, should be savoured' *Refinery29*

On Swift Horses

SHANNON PUFAHL

4th ESTATE • *London*

Fi... 2019

A catalogue record for this book is
available from the British Library

ISBN 978-0-00-829400-7

Printed and bound in Great Britain by
CPI Group (UK) Ltd, Croydon

MIX
Paper from
responsible sources
FSC™ C007454

This book is produced from independently certified FSC™ paper
to ensure responsible forest management.

For more information visit: www.harpercollins.co.uk/green

For Dorthy Figgs—

my grandmother and a first-rate card player

The declaration of love marks the transition from chance to destiny, and that's why it is so perilous and so burdened.

—ALAIN BADIOU, *In Praise of Love*

An honest game has always been a great rarity.

—HERBERT ASBURY,
Sucker's Progress: An Informal History of Gambling in America

I.

ONE

The sea

At the Heyday Lounge the horsemen think they are the only gamblers. They file in each morning, their shoes dusty and their pockets jangling with coins, like parishioners. They sit in a dark corner under a single blade fan, a plantation relic hauled from the lounge owner's Southern home to this coastal city thirty miles from Mexico. Above them the fan has the look of salvage but it makes no sound, and though it keeps the flies from their faces and necks and midmorning cocktails they do not notice it.

Every weekday the men come. They speak openly because they believe the lounge owner to be simple—which is true—and Muriel, their waitress these long mornings, to be a woman and therefore incapable of both memory and complex reasoning. It does not help that she is young, that she looks like the empty plains she comes from, flat and open and sad. She and Lee, newly married, have been in San Diego only a few months and are learning slowly how to be modern, and though she has always worked it is fair that the horsemen take her for a housewife forced into labor by circumstance. They could not know from her wide shoulders and square waist and rural modesty that she had taken the bus from Kansas on her own, that she could play cards and drive a car, or that she'd left behind a house she owned outright, to come here.

So they wave their hands at her and call her sweetheart from across the room and order their drinks with pointed enunciation as if she were hard of hearing. Though she remembers not only their drinks but the clip of their mustaches, the red-rimmed dimness of their eyes, she writes the orders down on a notepad and hands the paper to the bartender. The horsemen are retired trainers from the furlongs at Del Mar or bookmakers for rich men in the coastal hills. A few are ex-jockeys, burned out and overweight, unsure what else life might have to offer them. They talk as men do, confident and gently adversarial, about the coming race day, the horses off their feed, the jockeys with tapeworm, the cup and feel of the track. They set long odds and argue over them.

For a few months Muriel listens. She writes down their private speculations and begins to join their language to its objects. When her shift ends at two she walks toward the sea and takes a late lunch at a restaurant where she works a second job on the dinner shift. She sits in a booth in the corner and studies her notes and the previous day's racing form. She might rise and walk then, along the rolling line of surf. She thinks of horses, and her mother, and the day she was married. As she walks she collects shells and beach glass and slips them in the pocket of her sweater. Before she returns to work she unfolds the pocket and dumps these same items back onto the beach, so all that's left is a rim of sand in the pocket hem. At ten Lee walks to the restaurant from the factory a few blocks away and they go home together, arms linked like young lovers and not like married people, because they do not know each other very well.

THEN, IN EARLY DECEMBER, Muriel has a night off from the restaurant but tells Lee she's working. In the drugstore across the street from the Heyday

Lounge she buys a pair of sunglasses she considers ridiculous. They cover her eyebrows and half of her nose and make her look much older, like a woman in possession of a fortune or a married lover. She buys a sunhat and a thin scarf printed with flowers. She removes her sweater though her arms show and she worries they will burn in the low winter sun and make her sleep difficult. She takes a twenty-minute bus ride to the Del Mar Fairgrounds. The bus winds around Jimmy Durante Boulevard and from the windows of the bus she can see the grand entrance to the track, the high hedges and the waving flags. A statue of Bing Crosby, the track's founder and financier, gleams hard and gold in the afternoon light. In San Diego in those days it was said that Crosby used the track to impress Grace Kelly, who hated horses but loved men. Muriel lets the bus wind back around to Camino del Mar and gets out to have a coffee in a diner along the beach. She smokes and looks around as if she is waiting for someone. Her shoulders are warm and the bridge of her nose sweats under the sunglasses. The sea is soft and cold-looking. From the beach several others watch as a woman wades out to the breakers and stops. Muriel thinks of her mother, who had told her about the shore at Galveston, where she had been once with a man Muriel knew was not her father. Her mother said the sea was smooth as a lake and brown, and that someone told her it was filled with jellyfish. Muriel watches as the woman at sea turns and lifts a hand to her forehead and seems to regard the shore in contemplation of some final leaving. It is a curious thing, being married, how Muriel must think of this odd afternoon errand as something done for both of them, an adventure Lee will share in one way or another. She had thought it would be difficult to lie to him but she found it easier than their daily recitations of the truth. She had expected for herself the same power her mother found in men. But she often finds her husband's gaze embarrassing.

Finally she stands and walks up the seaside street and back across Durante. She passes the high hedges and the tall gates and walks past the turf club and the runs. At the turnstile she crowds in with another woman and two men. The warden in the booth waves them through.

She climbs the stairs behind the three others and lets them break off in the stands. From this height she looks around. She is surprised by how many people are at the track and how many of them are drunk. The sailors clump together and slap each other's backs. Their heavy white pants hang to their heels and they laugh and push back their vigorous hair. There are men in ripped shoes and young boys in bow ties and there are many other women too, Muriel is glad to see. She sits under the second-floor balcony in the shade and covers her hair with the scarf.

From the stands the horses are not what she imagined. They are tall and obdurate and only lightly controlled. A dozen of them are paced out and lined behind the gates. The field is looped first in grass then dirt, a third smaller track built for harness racing and unused. Across the field the stables are lined in courtly rows, and from this height Muriel can see the sharp shadows thrown by the palms, over the hot-walkers and the low-roofed stalls. The smell of the dirt and the stables and the wheaty smell of the grass are familiar to her, though from the sea comes a punkish wind. She has a gimlet and studies the racing form, thinking of the words she's heard the horsemen use, the names of trainers and jockeys. She watches the men file to the betting windows along the aisle. For a long time she watches without seeing any woman approach the glass and she begins to worry that perhaps she is not allowed to bet at all. The horses rear in their gates. Their bridles clang against the gates and sound like vespers. Then the gunshot and the race begins. The men in the stands yell instructions at the huge dark horses in a language of violence rolled in with endearment—summer up, take it, ride that, brake baby. The dust and the noise are thrilling, and Muriel stands without thinking and watches the horses turn the track, the pounding of their hooves at odds with their agile speed. When the race ends the men rise and punch the air, then tear their tickets in half and throw them to the ground.

After the race the crowd calms. Muriel moves to the windows and the cashier does not look up and when she speaks he is not surprised. She plays two dollars on the next race, on a horse named Pastoral, whom the men at the bar called canny and somber. The odds are six-to-one and when the horse crosses a length ahead she is up twelve dollars. She can hardly believe it. She takes her ticket back to the man behind the glass, who smiles this time and counts out the bills. She drinks another gimlet and no one notices. She lets the next race pass and then she rises and leaves through the tunnel. She takes the bus back downtown, her money folded away in her purse. Lee comes to collect her at ten and they walk home together. By then the drink has come out of her and she is tired, her dress dirty with sea air and car exhaust. The wind off the ocean blows down the alleyways and makes her shiver.

Lee says, "You should have worn a sweater."

She leans into him and his solidity is a fact that seems weighed against possession. He puts an arm around her and she considers the scarf in her bag, which would warm her. Though he would make nothing of it, she does not want him to see it, it is too much a part of the day.

Across the street a barbershop is closed but still lighted, a man sweeping up, his silent figure inside the fluorescence like an image on a screen. By the door of the shop a boy of seven or eight is still out at this late hour, throwing rocks across the empty street in some game of his own devising. When he sees them he comes forward with his hand out. Lee looks at her and then at the boy and makes a gesture meant to indicate penury. The boy turns to Muriel and she sees the fox in him and he knows she sees it. He starts to sway back and forth and then to dance. His pockets are full of rocks and they make a sound like dice. Then the sweeping man disappears into a back room and the shop lights go out and they are suddenly alone with the boy. In the dark street he lifts his knees high and slaps his little palms against them, and though he does not sing he seems about to. He holds Muriel's gaze and she laughs and pulls her purse up and brings out a quarter and hands it to him. Lee reaches out for her arm but does not stop her. The boy takes the coin and gives a look to Lee, who says to Muriel, "Oh for heaven's sake," in the embarrassed way his Lutheran mother might have said it, if he'd ever known her. The boy turns from them and dances back to his post at the curb; Muriel thinks she will remember him a long time, as the recipient of her good fortune.

In the hallway of their boardinghouse Lee stops to call his brother from the shared telephone. Most often Lee does not reach his brother but tonight he does. Muriel listens to his quiet voice on the phone, laughing and then pleading, the way he is even when Julius is merely mentioned now, an older sibling's curse, to envy the freedom of the younger man and also believe he will suffer from it. It is the same voice he used in the street and he would use this voice on her again, if he knew. And if she took him to the track he would not understand, he would scowl at the dirty men and the fragrant, snorting horses.

THE MORNINGS in San Diego have a particular tang, the ocean air sweetened by the drift of tanker fumes. Muriel and Lee are among the many thousands arriving each month, husbands and wives but mostly just men, bright with Western promise and their own survival, back from the Pacific. In general a masculine city, Muriel thinks, sailors and black ships and swirls of oil in the ports. The coastal hills cut a jagged line at the horizon. The great fig tree in Balboa Park spreads its roots like an apron of snakes.

At night when it is dim and she is tired she often mistakes the waving surface of the bay for wheat, and this she prefers to the sea, the low intimation of the Plains glimpsed sidelong. Days when they are both off work they walk together through town and along the thoroughfares, collecting cans and bottles for the junkman. South of Balboa Park the interstate is being pulled through by cranes and paddle scrapers and a hundred men a day on the iron trusses. Often the two of them stand watching for long moments as Lee narrates the freeway's path, through La Jolla and Oceanside and all the way to Oregon. A second highway crosses the first and runs east all the way to Ohio, passing through the open country they left behind. These routes will isolate the naval station and the ports, and the dark district by the railyard where the sailors take their leave, and the locals speak of this as a blessing, a cross over something vague and unseen that the future will not accommodate.

Inside this new grid the city widens up and out, over the coastal hills and north to the mesas, networks of tract housing all the way to Birdland. Lee wants a half-acre in Mission Valley, on the San Diego River, where they can build a three-bedroom and plant fruit trees. He has pinned the advertisement above the window in their kitchenette. When he and Muriel sit up late smoking and playing cards he tells her about the narrow valley, once settled by missionaries and then by nut and dairy farmers, now divided into lots graded flat and grassless. Sometimes he stands and goes to the little window and touches the pastel houses and the long furrows of cypress trees, and though he sighs dramatically and smiles Muriel knows he is not joking. She knows that he imagines her there in a real kitchen and a real bed. He believes the great future will meet them, in the new suburban landscape. They could prod that future along if they sold her mother's house in Kansas, but Muriel will not yet consent to it. When Lee asks she says she isn't ready, and if he worries why that might be he doesn't say so. The truth is he doesn't need her permission but he wants it.

It is 1956 and Muriel is twenty-one years old. Old to be starting a family, but she had waited almost a year to marry Lee and refused for a year before that. She had thought she could live as her mother had and then her mother died. Her mother had been the first woman in Marshall County to own a car, an eight-hundred-dollar Chevrolet she won in a department store raffle. She was Catholic but would not attend any Mass where the women weren't allowed to wear pants, which left one church on the north side of Topeka. Every weekend they left Muriel's stepfather in Marshall County and drove a hundred miles to hear the Mass in slacks. They stayed Saturday night in a motel by the highway and washed their faces and their scarves in the sink and rose early the next morning. After church they ate at a seafood restaurant across the street called Lucky's. When rain filled the gutters they jumped from the street to the curb in their flat church shoes and stayed another night while the weather passed. Later, Muriel's mother was the first woman in Marshall County to get a college degree and then a divorce. She died at thirty-six, a month before Muriel's nineteenth birthday. When the paper reported her death they said that she was married and that she'd died at home, neither of which was true.

That Christmas Lee came home and brought his brother, whom she had never met. Both men owed another year to the navy and they'd agreed to pool their discharge pay and build a house in California when it was all over, but Lee took the leave when she asked. She hadn't written him in months though she had received letters almost weekly. She wasn't sure what she wanted from him. He and his brother hauled in to Long Beach and spent five days on a bus through the snowy mountains and arrived on the last Sunday in Advent. It had been just four months since her mother died.

The day the men arrived Muriel and Lee made love on top of the covers with the weather radio on. It was a balmy winter, rainy and with little snow, and even with the radiator off and fingers of steam reaching across the windows they sweated in their underwear. She asked him to wear a condom—a tube of lambskin she'd bought the week before, both weighty and soft, like an elbow glove—and he'd asked her again to marry him, this unsuperstitious Catholic girl living alone in her dead mother's house.

While they lay together Julius returned from an errand in town and came into the yard and saw the pulled curtains and the fogged glass. He took off his heavy jacket and boots and his shirt and he lay down in the damp grass under their window. When Muriel opened it to smoke, as Lee wet his face and hair in the bathroom down the hall, she saw Julius lying there, bare-chested, staring at the window above. She startled, but being a woman generally unafraid of men, she cocked her head curiously at him. He raised one hand from the ground in a funny little wave.

"Toss one of those down to me," he said.

Muriel hesitated but sensed in his receptive pose someone merely curious. The cigarette fell limply and landed on his shoulder. He reached across and took the cigarette without sitting up and placed it between his lips, then feigned checking his coat pockets by patting the sides of his bare chest.

"And now a match," he said.

Muriel began to laugh, then covered her mouth so Lee would not hear. She dropped the matchbook out the window and Julius caught it and lit his cigarette and his smoke began to wind along the side of the house. He lay smoking and smiling and then with one prone hand he tried to toss the matches back up to her. Each time they fell back to the ground comically.

"I guess I'll have to return these later," he said.

They looked at each other a long moment and then Muriel became embarrassed and stubbed her cigarette out on the window sash and ducked back inside.

That night they stayed up with a bottle of rice liquor and Julius told jokes about Eisenhower and Protestants. Neither he nor Muriel mentioned his bare chest or the rain on his skin. He told them about Korea, about the landscape paintings he had seen burning there, stacked so that mountains burned through mountains, rivers melted onto ocean waves curling up like hair, and he said it must be like how the world began. When they were very drunk they went out and walked into the shaved wheatfield and lay under the winter sky. It was Christmas Eve. The men talked of their father and California and between them Muriel felt included in a deep understanding. Later, as Lee slept, she and Julius played cards and talked and though soon they were too drunk to make much sense she remembers the snap of the cards on the table and an alertness to her dead mother's proximity. Julius told her about a man he knew years ago, before the navy and the war, who sold rabbits in town. The man bred them in a hutch lashed to the bed of his pickup, Julius said, each night stopping somewhere near a park or a wooded lot so as the rabbits slept they might hear the sounds of their brethren, of their own country.

Curled in the cab of the truck the man slept under blankets made of rabbit fur. *He was the rabbit man,* Julius said, *he wanted to be one of them. He had the thickest hair you ever saw, and a little nose like a rabbit, and big brown eyes.*

The man drove all over town, to fairgrounds and schoolyards and to the flea market downtown, offering everywhere some different price for the rabbits, depending on how he felt about them. *One day you'd see him,* Julius said, *and a three-pound rabbit he was snuggling in his arms would cost fifteen cents, then the next day it'd be up to fifty, because the thing had held his gaze for a full minute in a way he thought of as romantic, then that same unsold rabbit would do something terrible, like scratch his arm all up or fight with another rabbit, and the price would drop again to almost nothing. You see, it was his affection that drove that particular economy, and for that reason he made so little he had to sell his truck and all his rabbits, and I heard he wound up working in a gas station, like anybody else. But oh, he was still handsome as all get-out.*

Julius leaned across the table in feigned amusement and showed his missing tooth when he smiled and Muriel smiled back at him. In the look held between them was some acknowledgment though Muriel did not know what the story meant. She had never heard a man talk this way about another man. She felt she was hearing a riddle.

"He didn't live anywhere?" she asked.

"He lived in that truck."

"So how did you know him then?"

Julius did not answer. Instead he reached out and held her hand for a moment and turned it over palm up then dropped it. She thought about his chest rising and falling and the rain on his skin and the way he'd looked up at her. Then he picked up the cards and shuffled them and dealt and did not say much after that.

In the morning Lee banged coffee cups in the kitchen and mended things in the house that she did not know how to mend and she agreed to marry him after all. Because she was orphaned and alone, but also because of Julius, who had made her feel that the world was bigger than she had imagined and because Lee, in loving his brother, became both more interesting and more bracing. She knew her mother would not approve but her mother was not around to say so. She sold first the car and then the furniture. Her mother's clothes she left boxed on the porch for the Lions Club. She bought the bus ticket and paid the tax board for the year and with what little was left she paid the Carter boy down the road to insulate the pipes and till up the lawn and cover it over with gravel to keep the grass from overgrowing. She sent the same boy home with her mother's houseplants and hoped for the best. She told Lee they'd keep the house because that's what her mother would have wanted and Lee did not argue with her. That she would get to California and find Julius gone was not something she considered.

THE FIRST TIME is a transgression. The second is a strategy. After work, Muriel takes a quick lunch down the street and emerges from the café transformed, her dress balled in her purse, wearing now a pair of loose slacks and one of Lee's striped dress shirts, the low-brimmed hat over her hair and the big sunglasses. She gets off the bus a stop early and walks the last half-mile to Del Mar. She does this once a week, then twice. Depending on what she's heard that morning she bets a quinella or a box or a place, at first on just one race and then on three or four. She does not always win. Sometimes she deliberately lays money on a horse the men have said is lame or sick in the head, or on a jockey they'd seen drinking rum with young women the night before. When she loses those races she feels a sense of power she never gets from winning, because losing proves the accuracy of her judgment. It has the benefit, too, of concealment. As long as she is not seen by the men at the lounge—who, she thinks, have never actually looked her in the face and would not recognize her even if she introduced herself—she feels she may engender any speculation she wishes except that she is cheating.

It comes to her naturally. From the horsemen she learns a vocabulary built from idiom and double entendre—silks and shadow rolls, tongue straps and hand rides—and the rest she learns by instinct. She learns what it means when the track is cuppy, when a horse is washy or ridden out. She becomes familiar with the anatomy of horses, croup and neck, muzzle, cannon, hock, loin, as if she had run her hands along each and felt what they were made of. She begins to think of the landscape differently, as if the horses themselves have given it names. The hills and the lowtide terraces are sorrel, dapple-gray. The round, unburdened trunks of palm are chestnut in the coastal light, light that's blood bay or buckskin depending on the weather, cast high and cloudless over the roan sea.

She is stopped sometimes, at work or waking in the mornings, by a poignant feeling. The feeling is like happiness but it comes so slowly and is so austere she might easily mistake it for grief. She could not explain it but she knows this feeling has something to do with keeping a secret from Lee, which she had somehow always felt she was doing even before she had a secret to keep. It has something to do with wherever Julius is and what her mother would think of all this. If she were a different kind of person she might have wondered whether love was always this way, if it existed in the spaces between people, the parts they kept strange to each other. She tapes the money inside a white envelope, on the underside of the lazy Susan, a place her husband will never look and may not even know is there.

A FEW DAYS BEFORE Christmas they borrow a Lincoln from Lee's boss to see the lights at the Del Mar Fairgrounds. Neither has seen Christmas lights before. At the fairgrounds they go on for miles, roped lights in the shape of trees and hills of snow, illuminating the space around them and the horizon in each direction, like a city gone nuclear. The cars line up with their headlights off and wind through the new world. Those with radios tune to a station playing Christmas songs. Lee turns his broad face to her as they sit idling in the line of cars. His is a simple amazement, the way his eyes become bright and focused when something small and unmiraculous makes him happy. If she had not heard his stories of the war or the privation of his childhood she might think him a savant or an innocent, someone inured to pain or ignorant of it. He seems unchanged by the sea or the city. She knows that even strangers recognize this immutability in him, that they see it as heroic. For a moment she considers telling him about the horses, because she envies the smallness of his joy. She is able to imagine that he would not care how she came by the money, only that she had it.

"To think this time last year we were in Kansas," Lee says.

The racetrack lights are off but she can see the dark palms rising above the stables, just ahead. Lee leans across the bench seat and over Muriel's handbag to kiss her. She thinks how quickly it had all happened. On the radio the Jackie Gleason Orchestra plays "I'll Be Home for Christmas" like a dirge. Car horns bleat behind them and Lee laughs and pulls away from her and drives on. The palms move in gray contour against the winter sky. Of course there is no snow but the lights throw shadows on the ground in metallic circles that trick the eye. She hadn't known the trees would be so lovely in the dark or that the track would be so close.

"You know," he says then, "it ain't like we have to wait for him, if that's what you're thinking."

"You've said that before."

Lee shakes his head.

"It was your plan to come here. You two," she says.

"But it's just us now."

"He's just stretching his legs. It was a long time you were overseas."

"It ain't shore leave, now."

"It's only been a few months."

Lee sighs. The music snaps out and is replaced by static, then another station breaks through. That station plays a bandstand number too loud and ends the conversation. Lee reaches over and cups her knee and drives on.

Back home they kiss for a long time until Lee leans back and looks at her softly and lets his hands rest on her arms. He waits a moment. This part of lovemaking Muriel finds stifling and inelegant, though she could not say exactly why. She does not know if he wants her consent or her desire but either way she wants to refuse him, simply because he asked. She looks away and knows he will read this as demure. He kisses her neck and brings his arms around her again. Her secret makes her more aware of his deference. She thinks of what it will feel like in another few minutes when he is inside her and how straightforward this feeling is. She'd like to skip ahead to that moment. Beyond his shoulder the perfect flat wall of the bedroom catches their shadows. The window is open and the noise of traffic and other lovers and construction and children and cooking is the noise of a city breaking into itself. A man calls out the name of their street and another that crosses it and a second voice calls back. Of course the men are not in the room or even near enough to see, but like the cars and the birds and the backhoes their voices become part of lovemaking, and it occurs to Muriel that she might like this noise and the cover it offers.

Later, they lie together a long time. The supper hour has come and gone and the city has quieted. The phone in the hall rings a long time before Lee finally rises to answer it. Muriel hears him wish his brother a happy Christmas and say that they should be together, that Julius should come soon. Muriel stands and goes to the window that looks down into the alley between their building and its twin. She can feel the cold outside the window against her bare skin. She lights a cigarette and lifts the window. The streetlight falls into the alley and over the dry bricks and a few birds fly soft and quick across the entrance and toss small hand-shaped shadows against the alley wall. She recalls a boyfriend her mother had, sometime in the forties, who sold lightbulbs door-to-door. To persuade housewives and old widows, he cast against their walls the silhouettes of butterflies and rabbits and men in tall hats. After dinner, in those few months her mother loved him, that man taught her to twist her fingers into cheerful creatures. He had been kind, slimly built. The bulbs he sold made bluish light and glowed through the flesh of his hands. For a moment she thinks that man must be sitting somewhere against the wall of this alley, making birds with his fingers. In the hallway she hears Lee ask his brother if he needs any money and then his long sigh.

THE NEW YEAR comes and the weather hardens. Muriel adds more and more of the winnings to her tips and blames the extra money on holiday cheer, on the business brought in by the last of the men back from Korea. Lee folds the bills into eighths and stores them like hock in a coffee can. On Sunday nights he counts them out. Then, as the fairground lights on the racetrack's edge disappear, as spring comes, the horsemen begin to lose and Muriel does too. At the lounge the men sit grimly late into the day. They wonder if they've lost the touch. They worry they've misread all the signs. The feel of the track has left them, perhaps as punishment for their arrogance. They have no feel for jockeys and turf conditions, no joy for horses at all. They spit on the floor and smoke cigarettes until the fan above merely pushes the smoke back and forth, like a machine for making waves.

They have had all these conversations before but Muriel doesn't know that. In this new reality she becomes reckless, betting conspicuous amounts on odds-on favorites for little gain, just to remember the feeling of winning. She comforts herself by thinking she has solved the problem of her dishonesty. In the lazy Susan there is less than two hundred dollars; a few more weeks of padding her wages and it will be gone. She feels determined to lose the rest of it, as a kind of retribution or for the sake of some strange neatness. She thinks the word, *neatness,* as if she is tidying up the kitchen or ironing a dress.

Then the track is closed for two weeks. When it reopens, the turf is newly surfaced and smooth as hair. The horses have been traded out, some up from Santa Anita and others from the Canadian circuits, the jockeys rested and sweated out to make weight. On Fat Tuesday the races stretch through the afternoon and she drinks too much. She wins two races in a row and is flushed. Yet even with the drink she feels self-conscious and the crowd is tight around her. It is unusually warm and the track has been decorated with bunting and palm fronds tied into hearts and sprays like hands.

The last race is a special stakes and by evening the crowd has swelled. Women fan themselves with the palmhands and dab their temples with bits of ice. Muriel stands next to a woman from out of town, who tells her husband in an accented voice what to bet. Both Muriel and the woman have a decent bounty on a horse called Flood to win and they discuss his chances as the horses come to post. The horsemen have picked him, though they think he is too young and jumpy as a virgin. As the race begins, the foreign woman flicks Muriel's arm with her fingers and winks.

"This is us," she says, nodding to the track.

The horses burst free and the race comes together. Next to Muriel the woman bounces on tiptoe. When Flood wins by a length, the woman turns and puts a hand on Muriel's shoulder and kisses her lightly on the mouth. The strangeness of this kiss makes Muriel laugh. Her mouth opens around the sound and her teeth scrape the woman's big straight teeth—horse teeth, Muriel thinks, and laughs again. The woman laughs back at Muriel and Muriel can taste mint and whiskey on the woman's lips. Had Muriel said it out loud, *horse teeth*? They both pull away. For a moment the woman's eyes catch hers with a wince, then turn softer, turn down, and she raises her glass and jiggles the ice and mint and says, "Time to repent." She licks her lips, then wipes them with her fingers. The horses settle with their pit ponies, the air heavy with the heat of their bodies, and the noise of the track returns. The woman's husband fans his wife with his hat and asks if they have won. The woman does not answer him but looks again at Muriel and Muriel does not know how to look back at her. Then the woman turns to her husband and flashes her ticket and flicks Muriel's arm again as she walks away. Muriel is careful not to watch the woman though she wants to see her full height, the shape of her legs.

She carries this desire to the bus stop and downtown, then through the streets with Lee, past the oblate sea and the colorful houses, stopping in a pub for a drink and another at home. They leave the radio on as they make love, Lee's astonished face next to hers on the pillow, a soft fold in the dim light. Her tough man, undone. He says, *Muriel, we should have a child.* He whispers into her hair, *Muriel, don't ever leave me.* She knows after these months together to expect this as she expects his deference, and so she lets him murmur, touches his temples and his thick eyebrows with her fingertips until he falls asleep. She is like a parent then, not resentful but protective. The bedside clock ticks on the nightstand and the sheets scallop at the edge of the mattress.

When he is fully asleep she takes the money from the inside of her shoe and puts it in the envelope in the lazy Susan. Suddenly it seems there is too much of it. She'd won not a third of her money back, but she has a feeling of great prosperity. She knows this feeling would please the men at the lounge. That they would say she'd cut her teeth. That in gambling there is a plateau, a period of time when progression ceases, when exhaustion sets in, and then the odds shift. You win and you are alive again. She could play another month or longer if chance runs her way.

LATER, THE PHONE RINGS and wakes her and when no one picks it up Muriel rises from the bed and steps quietly into the hall to answer it.

When Julius hears her voice he laughs so sharply she has to pull the receiver from her ear. She brings the phone back and says Julius's name and finds she is grinning in the dark hallway. She asks him when he'll join them and he says, "Oh soon now, not long."

"You mean it?" she asks.

"You bet," he says.

She asks him what it's like in Santa Barbara or Ventura or wherever he is and he says, "Girl, you wouldn't believe it," and then he starts to sing a song about the badlands and how dark they are even in the morning. On his end of the line a siren spools out and when it stops she hears he's still singing and she listens until he can't remember the words and then she asks him if he's been eating and how the weather is and anyplace they might send a letter. He asks if she's been winning at cards and when she says she tried to teach Lee how to play hearts he says, "No trick-taking games, he's not brutal enough for it. You better stick to war."

Through the wall she can hear Lee snoring. In the kitchenette the radio plays the Grand Ole Opry. She slides down the wall smiling into her hand until she sits with her legs in front of her and her bare feet shooting into the hallway and disappearing into the dark. What a strange miracle to talk on the phone for no particular reason. They talk for ten minutes, then twenty, until Muriel begins to worry about the coins Julius is dropping for the line. She tells him he shouldn't waste his money and he says it's no waste at all but then he seems to remember his purpose and asks after his brother.

"He's asleep and I'm out here in the hallway with my hand over the receiver."

Silence on Julius's line and then a clank of freight and men's voices raised some distance away.

"We sure hoped you'd be here by now," Muriel says.

"My brother hopes a lot of things."

Muriel nods to the darkness.

"Don't you think it'd be strange?" he says. "All of us together?"

"That's what Lee wants though."

"True enough," Julius says, though she can tell he isn't sure.

"I want," she begins, but she worries she should not say the next thing. She is not sure what the next thing is. The dark hallway is silent and outside she can hear the traffic lights clicking. For a moment neither speaks.

Finally Julius says, "There's sometimes lots of ways of getting to a place."

She thinks of Christmas Eve and the story of the rabbits. His tone is the same, it seeks her approval for something. She wants again the feeling she'd had that night, of recognition. So she laughs. The line tosses back her laugh in delay and Julius says, "Well fine, what do you think then?"

"Oh now, Julius, it's just the way you said it."

"Maybe I will have to come there just to set you right."

His tone is lighter but not quite kind and when she laughs again he says, "You think I wouldn't."

"You haven't yet," she says, and then he laughs too. Her face is hot and she wants a drink. She thinks that no matter what else is true about Julius he loves his brother, and because he loves his brother he is also obliged to her. She had come all the way out west knowing this. And if he knew about her or about their life without him he might come along finally too. So she tells him about the horsemen and the notes she'd taken and how she'd run their advice both ways to see if it worked. For a moment he doesn't say anything. She worries the whole thing will lose its sweetness, in the open air between them. Then he laughs, asks her what her favorite kind of horse is, guesses geldings in a teasing voice. He means it cutely but she's disappointed. She can tell he doesn't believe her. Aloud it is hardly believable.

"No geldings there, Julius," she says.

"That's a nice racket for a gal, though," he says.

"Oh, but it's just a whim," she says, to take the sting out of the moment.

"Careful now. Might be one of them things you can't ever get enough of," he says, but he's still kidding her. The operator rings on and asks for another dime and Julius searches his pockets and comes up empty. The line goes dead and Muriel sits a long time with the receiver in her lap and the dial tone chiming. She hears Lee's snoring and the pipes laboring in the wall and the radio in the kitchen plays "Walking the Floor over You" and then "Goodnight Irene."

TWO

The Golden Nugget

A few days later Julius is in a back room in Torrance playing five-card. He draws so hot for so long that a crowd gathers, and in that crowd are men he knows and men he doesn't. All are good drinkers and quick to blame others and thrilled at the warm spring day.

"Hallelujah anyway," says one man, when Julius turns up a flush one card short of the royal.

He is playing two hardnosers and a novice and a young joe who bluffs too often. Along the walls the men are crowded together so close that ash from their upheld cigarettes drops onto their collars and into their shirt pockets. The smoke hangs above the crowd and drifts prettily. Outside the noise of jackhammers and asphalt trucks, and from the bar up front the low tones of the jukebox, so the back room sounds like a dentist's office. Julius is in this part of the city by mistake, forced onto Del Amo Boulevard by a girder collapsed across 190th Street which he'd been walking toward the sea, thinking about his brother. He hasn't found work in a week or more. But now he's got two hundred dollars and the game's big stack and there's nowhere he has to be and no one looking for him. He hasn't had this kind of luck since before the war or even earlier.

"You oughta take this game to the desert," says a man close to Julius.

Someone else hollers, "Get a little coin in your pocket and then we'll see what you're really about."

"I've been there and it ain't much," says another.

"Anything legit's bound to scrape you up, Freddy."

"Our Freddy here gets hives when even other people tell the truth."

"Even if you lose, you can watch them bombs for free."

"I just can't believe it, all night and no cops and twenty-dollar buy-ins."

"Sounds like Korea, the good parts anyway."

A voice from the back asks what they mean about the bombs and several men begin to explain at once but all Julius hears is the name of the place and several of its cheaper hotels and aspersions cast at the weather. The crowd drinks and cheers him but he's begun to sense the anxiety that accompanies good fortune. A few of the men know him to be a petty thief but never a card cheat, but most of them don't know either of these things. Along the back wall are three men talking and watching him. Another man by the door learns his name and calls it out. Before things get dangerously better, he takes five dollars from the plywood where they've laid the game and buys a round for the crowd. He wins two hands, then bluffs another just to lose and folds the next.

It hurts him to cheat luck this way but there is always a longer game. He's been in California just six months and already a man he knew was murdered outside a club in Rosewood. The police had raided two bars known for their friendliness to men and low lights. The raids changed the hustlers weekly, like the Sunday lettering on a church sign. He thinks about the nature of cheating and how it is tied to dignity, then pushes up his sleeves and buys another round and pockets for himself sixty dollars in ones and fives and lets the rest ride on a hopeless low straight that breaks the bank. He bows out and another man takes his place, but when he leaves the bar the three men by the wall follow him all the way to 203rd Street. It is just dusk and the city is sprayed in birdsong. To the west the blue ledge of twilight behind the buildings makes the city seem more important than it is. The men catch him in the alley and push him back and forth between them in a pinball fashion that means the thing they hate about him is also a thing they fear, and it is easy enough to hand over the cash and let that be the end of it and mercifully it is. Back in his little room he gets under the covers without undressing and he doesn't sleep all night.

A few days later he gets a letter from his brother's wife begging him south. Muriel has folded three crisp twenties in the envelope and signed off, *It's about time you got out of Los Angeles for a while.* Julius takes this as an omen. He thinks about her that Christmas in Kansas, coming down the porch steps with her skirt hem balled in a fist against the wind and raised halfway up her thigh, and about his brother's happiness. The story she's told him of the horses, which he might be willing to believe, but it's hard to imagine a woman alone in that way. He had promised to join them but that does not seem like what the letter and the money are telling him he ought to do. He waits a day and then he packs two rolled shirts and his knife in his good boots and carries each boot like a grocery sack under his arm and onto the train to Las Vegas.

FREMONT STREET BLINKS with men, lights, billets of paper, dropped coins, raised voices, and that afternoon's monsoon rain. Julius walks from the train station directly to Binion's and puts his name in for the poker room. He waits a long time to be called and when he is, the only open seat is at a table filled with young men in jackets and ties. He trades one of Muriel's twenties for a stack of chips and loses it in ten mercenary hands.

He walks back through the casino past the slot-lines and the craps tables and the crowds gathered for anyone hot. Outside on Fremont it could be ten o'clock or midnight or just before dawn. It is just like the men said: The sidewalks are full of Angelenos and old gangsters and showgirls in feathers from rump to neck. Julius walks awhile through this modern noise and the dry landscape, and no one wonders about him or even looks his way. Even carrying his boots and in his dusty jeans like a pauper against the lighted street he is just another fortune seeker in the West. He goes back to Binion's and sits at the bar and posts his boots upright on an empty stool and orders a drink. Behind him the slot-wheels clunk and the coins fall into the metal sleds. The craps tables beyond are full of suits and other legitimate men and the bar is open all night and drinking he has the sense of a deep rightness.

When a man sits next to him, Julius strikes up a conversation. The man is from Iowa, a salesman in Vegas for a trade convention, slight around the waist with blunt fingernails and thin white wrists. Julius shakes his hair and stretches one leg across to the rung of the man's barstool so their knees are touching and the man is hemmed in between the bar and Julius's body. The man tells Julius a story about a ranch just north of town, in Indian Springs, where for fifty dollars a Mexican with one eye would take men like them to a wild mustang roundup. He asks if Julius might like to go with him and Julius knows what kind of conversation this is. He says he knows next to nothing about horses but he could learn, and when he angles in the man turns toward the bar and into the fence of Julius's body.

When they are very drunk they stagger half a mile off Fremont to the neon fringe and pay cash for a two-bed room at the Squaw Motel. There they share another fifth of whiskey and talk a long time about the flat places they're from and how red the West is and from memory they catch bits of song and sing them out. Julius tells the man he's come from Los Angeles and how the place had shifted beneath him like a coin and the man says that's how things are now. Even in Iowa you'd be hard-pressed to get a job making anything but asphalt. They lie each to a bed and Julius asks across the distance whether the man is married and he says, "Sure."

"How long you been married?"

"Not long."

Julius holds the bottle over the gap between their beds and the man reaches out and takes the bottle and sits up a little and drains it. Then he hands the empty bottle back and turns on his side. He smiles but his smile is meant for someone other than Julius.

"My brother's married newly too," Julius says.

"That's nice."

"It is. Though it's strange too."

"I'm tired now, friend," the man says.

"We don't have to say nothing else."

"If that's all right."

Soon Julius is aware of the man's deep sleep and though the moment has passed he is not unhappy. Lee said that the best he ever slept was in Long Beach that last Christmas leave, when Muriel finally wrote and told him about her mother and asked him to come home. Lee and Julius had tendered in together on the *Bryce Canyon* and stayed at the Royal. They'd been at sea so long that even their boots were still serviceable, and though the war was over then and had been for some time, they both still owed a year to the navy. They sat in the hotel bar and Lee showed Julius the letter from Muriel and they talked about the plans they'd made together and Lee said it didn't change anything. The next morning they found the first bus and rode east.

A year later Julius walked out onto the same dock at Long Beach but everything felt different. A woman in a Quaker dress handed him a copy of Isaiah bound in blue paper. He cashed his half-pay and took a bus downtown and sat at a lunch counter and read the booklet. He had forgotten Isaiah and how in the Bible all men were singular, good or bad, and he decided not to join his brother in San Diego. Probably he had decided this some time ago. He walked all night through the city thinking about dragons and springs and stands of rushes, and about his brother's marriage, and he saw that the parks and the bars were filled with men. He felt absorbed into the great diffusion, as if he were dead. That afternoon he paid six bucks for a room with a window and slept all that day and into the next and that was the first time he slept the way he thought his brother had meant it.

AT DAWN JULIUS wakes to find the Iowan crying into the pillow, almost choking, his sobs forced out so hard his slight shoulders pull backward, bunched in the middle like a pleat. Julius rises and goes to his bed and places a hand on his back until the sobs fade, and as the harsh desert light comes through the motel window the man turns his face up to Julius and says, "I'm sorry. It's just the drink."

Julius says he's all right. For a while longer the man lies on his back looking up while Julius sits on the edge of the bed. Neither speaks and outside they can hear the swampcooler dripping onto the pavement. The man takes Julius's hand in his and waves it back and forth in a kind of comic handshake and then drops both their hands to the bedspread. Then he rises and enters the bathroom. Julius lies down where the man had been and falls back into hazy sleep. He wakes to find the man gone. Under a plastic motel cup is a hundred-dollar bill, a half-smoked cigarette in the ashtray, every towel in the bathroom wet and crumpled on the floor. It is a lot of money and Julius knows that he has been paid not for the room or the booze but for discretion. He says aloud to the room, "I wish you hadn't of done that," then folds the hundred into a tight square and puts it inside his boot. Should he see the man again he will return the bill, moist and reeking of his feet.

He steps out. The afternoon rinses the desert in brown light. He finds a cardroom dealing five-card, but the play is slow and stupid so he goes back to Binion's and tries his hand at faro. For a solid hour he wins more than he loses and while he's still in the black he cashes out and takes his winnings down the street to El Dorado. There he plays a game called high-low at a dollar a hand and cashes out well ahead. At the Lucky Strike the hotel's full, same at the Apache, and Binion's is ten bucks for a single, so Julius walks back through the fringe to the Squaw. The deskman takes him to the same room he'd had the night before. The sheets have not been changed, only tucked in at the corners, the bedspread tossed loosely over the pillows. He tries to sleep in one bed and then the other, and when he can't he lifts one bedspread and shakes the ash from it and drops it on the floor. He lies on half and pulls the other half over himself. When he wakes up in the morning he has seventy-five dollars and a stack of uncashed chips and the Iowan's bill. He showers and shaves and steps out into the bright day. He asks the deskman to switch him to a single room and pays for a week in advance.

FROM THE WINDOWS of their hotel rooms, visitors to booming Las Vegas may witness two competing wonders. On the desert floor Lake Mead accumulates, covering the brown valley. Two years of good snow in the mountains have swelled the banks, and in the afternoons tourists gather along the high ridge of Hoover Dam to watch the men sluice open the valves. Some say the walls of the dam are cemented with the bones of pack mules and men, probably rope too, Julius thinks, miles and miles of rope. And teeth. Empty carafes of coffee. Chewed and discarded fingernails.

But in the sky to the west of the dam is the real attraction. There mushroom clouds draw tourists in from less auspicious places, crowded cities in the east, farm towns north and west. On the rooftops men in tuxedos sip Atomic Cocktails with their sighing wives. They smoke smuggled cigars and ignore the news from Washington, the warnings of radioactive fallout, the strange, scraped feeling behind their eyes. These bombs, after all, are not meant to hurt them. Makeshift signs announce their names—Diablo, Hat Trick, Candy Boy—propped among the other dazzling junk of the city. On bomb days the pit bosses lure the gamblers outside, early morning before the desert sun appears and whites out the horizon where the bomb will lather, sometimes long into the day. On these mornings the casinos quiet, a spreading silence that echoes, inversely, the seismic gnash of the bomb outside.

In this setting Julius is not anyone in particular. He is not the tuxedoed men nor the lovers of those men and playing poker or twenty-one in the windowless rooms excites no one's suspicion and in the morning the street is still alive. Unlike in Los Angeles or Ventura or Long Beach he is not guilty of anything. In other cities where he's slept or turned cards or met men, he might have to slip out a side door or wait in an alley, but not here. To him, the neon and the money and the bombs are the marks of a city far ahead of the times. The tourists play poorly and Julius cleans them out and they shake his hand after and thank him and the cops sit with loosened ties at the same table. He sleeps during the day and eats when he wants to.

So he stays. Two weeks pass. He keeps his room at the Squaw a half-mile off Fremont Street. He plays faro until noon at a locals' casino run by Mormons and stashes his winnings in a rolled sock in the ceiling panel of his room. The Mormons run a nice joint though they themselves are merely rumors. Julius has heard they live out past the city limits in a compound with eight-foot-high fencing and a swimming pool treated with saline, to simulate the great stinking lake gifted to them by God. He stops sometimes at the train station and fishes out a dime and thinks of his brother and Muriel but he does not call them, and soon so much time has passed he worries they will resent or even forget him, and he dreads this imagined moment, the silence after he says his brother's name.

One morning he leaves the tables and steps into the dawn street and when he looks ahead to the horizon he sees a fist of fire reach up from the earth and soften into smoke. It is many miles away and the sound reaches him several moments later, a muted bang like a rock hurled against the side of a barn, and he thinks of how his brother, when they were children, would hook a thumb inside his cheek and pull it out to make a popping sound, to indicate that something had gone smoothly. Above him on the rooftops of the casinos a cheer goes up, peculiar, muffled, cautious even, and Julius looks above to see the tiny heads of men and women balanced against the easements, some even forcing their heads through the big looping letters of neon signs. The sky brightens suddenly then, as if the bomb has accelerated the dawn, and washes the buildings and the blinking signs in white until they seem almost to have disappeared. It is as if everything has frozen, as if they have all been returned to the desert unfettered by worry or language, base elements, the faces dissolving in the bright light until they are featureless, each face turned toward the horizon in the same astonished, straining way. He feels suddenly part of something, among these people for the first time.

That night he climbs to the Binion's roof and sits at the edge with his smoking hand out in the night. He's never really been on his own before and here it is easy. In the long western evening the booming city makes its careful transition. First the night birds and then the cars quieting and then the brief wind before sunset and the streetlights clicking on, until in a few silent spaces Julius can hear the peculiar hum of the desert. The bombcloud is still visible as a gray paste across the surface of the low moon, flattened now and stretching a hundred miles. He reaches his arm out across the alley and trails his hand through the air. He'd grown up in a shakeshingle ranch and had gone from there to the navy, where he'd never spent a night above the ground. From this height the city seems to belong only to him. He remembers an afternoon in childhood when he and Lee discovered an uncapped silo filled by years of rainwater. They had climbed the ladder and looked down into the hole from the rim, a hundred feet above the ground. The reflection of their own heads in the water was framed by the circle of light coming in, the circle turned black on the surface of the water like a negative and burnished around the edges, as if they stood inside an eclipse. For a moment he wishes for his brother and the future they'd imagined together. He looks out at the desert landscape and thinks of that silo and the memory covers the sight of the moon and the dispersing bomb so they are layered like bits of film, the dark of that water and the light inside it lifted through the bare mountains, so looking out he has a sense of boundless time. He flicks his cigarette up and out so it arcs into the alley. When he looks again the vision has dissolved. His brother has never been here and is not coming to take him home and if he walks through Las Vegas at dawn there is no one who cares to know it, no one waiting in a Torrance alleyway to steal back what they've lost. A man like Julius at the tables with his money in plain view. Here there are rules, and they are known, and you can win fifty bucks on a low-card straight fair and square, no hustle, just luck. What comfort in playing against the house and not against men.

A FEW DAYS later Julius walks into the Golden Nugget and sits next to two men smoking spiced cigarettes at the polished bar. For a while they make small talk until Julius learns their occupation. For weeks now he has watched the pitmen and the bosses run the casino floors and the sporting desks, men with quick eyes, and though they watch him and count out his chips he has never spoken to them. He asks the smoking men how a man might find such work. In turn they ask him what skills he has to offer. He is amazed they want to know.

He says, "I know how people steal. And I also know why they do."

The men look so much alike they could be twins. Each turns his head to the mirror behind the bar as if searching for some message in the glass and then turns back to him. They remind Julius of a pair of sister cats they'd had when he was a child, indistinguishably marked and moving as one body as only animals can, sitting under the oak tree by the bunkhouse snatching birds from the air. He recalls the long faces of those cats, their eyes bubbled and transparent from the side, as he looks at the two smoking men.

"But you yourself do not steal," says the man closest to him.

He places his fingertips together and looks at Julius over his tented hands. Julius leans toward him on the stool so his arm lies flat against the bar. He's had a few drinks and is flush with dollar chips.

"Partly I know how people steal because I have stolen, I'll be honest with you," he says. "But it seems to me that this ain't the place to steal, and I'd like to be on the right side of that."

The men consider this. They take in Julius's slim frame, his worn-down boots mud-splattered, the length of his hair. Julius has a warm feeling of acceptance, a sense that the men see not a thief or a sailor but someone born to a better fate.

"We've seen you around," one says.

"You play aboveboard, we like that," says the other.

They offer him a job running pit surveillance and he takes it, shaking each man's hand firmly but waiting until he is a few blocks off Fremont and nearly to the Squaw before he smiles.

He returns that night and climbs a set of narrow stairs to an attic above the floor of the Golden Nugget. The stairs lead out to catwalks along the walls and through the middle of the attic, touching just off-center above the casino pit below. The catwalks are scaffolded and set so close to the ceiling Julius feels his hair brush against it. Every ten feet a two-way mirror is set into the attic floor, so the man walking the catwalk can look through them and watch the players below. Large fans front and back send in a hot breeze. Julius walks to the center and looks down at a craps table. He sees only the players' hands, some fat-fingered and hairy, nails untrimmed, others slender and graceful. A man at the edge of the table leans forward to take the pot and for a moment looks up and Julius nearly turns away. But the wide shadowy sheet of glass bows down and out, convex, so the man looking up sees not Julius's silent gaze but his own face, arched and upside down, as if he is staring into the curved back of a spoon. Julius himself has seen these windows from below, and though he'd assumed he was being watched he had not really considered all this, that above him was a network of paths and railings, made for watching. The whole thing seems to him so ingenious he nearly laughs aloud.

For an hour he moves between the windows watching the action at craps and blackjack. He sees nothing unusual, though from above the character of each game is changed and made piecemeal, divided into possible cheats or cons, and these are different from the things a player would suss out, by virtue of being punishable. Watching the games this way impresses him. In Los Angeles a man like him would never be trusted with such a job.

When he moves toward the center of the scaffold he sees in the distance a dark figure. Julius stops and waits. The figure comes closer and in the light cast up through the windows Julius sees the man's boots, then his nubby trousers.

"You're new," the man says as he approaches.

Julius nods. They stand facing each other over the lighted window. The man is tall and dark-haired, Julius's age or a bit younger.

"Henry," says the man.

Julius says his own name and puts out his hand. The man's hand is rough but his handshake is light and quick. He holds his other arm against his waist and in the pale light Julius sees it is ripped in scars.

"First time?" the man asks.

"It is," Julius says.

"What do you think so far?"

Henry does not seem cruel to Julius though his appearance would suggest it, so Julius says what he thinks.

"You play?" Julius asks.

"Sometimes," says Henry.

"This sheds some light on that, huh."

"It does," Henry says. "Seeing it this way is like watching yourself make love."

Julius laughs and nods, then he reaches up to cover his mouth against the sound and because his missing tooth makes him suddenly sheepish.

"Instructive," he says, through his hand.

"But a little ruinous," says Henry.

"That's right," says Julius.

He drops his hand and looks at the man a long moment. The look goes on until Henry laughs and Julius laughs with him but then the laughter turns and stops. In this silence Julius becomes again self-conscious and looks away at the floor and then at his own hand on the railing. Henry says, "Welp," and goes on his way to the other side of the casino loft.

Every few hours Julius and Henry pass each other at the place where the scaffolds cross over the pit below. Henry raises a hand or makes a hasty salute. The breeze across the center cools and dies. Below the tables thin out. On the third pass Henry stops a moment and makes a joke about a woman at the corner craps table, and suggests Julius take a look down her dress, and Julius says he will.

At four A.M. Julius descends the stairway and punches a clock in a back room filled with bank bags and boxes of casino matches behind mesh cage. This room, too, is covered in two-way glass, and an iron door with a sliding bar lock leads to another room. As he marks his pay card, a man in a seersucker suit slips out and closes the door promptly and soundly. From inside the lock is turned again. The man in the suit catches Julius's gaze and holds it for a long moment, until his eyes begin to seem distant and opaque to Julius, like the two-way glass, as if somewhere inside the man there is another man who looks out, watching him. This must be the pit boss, Julius thinks. The man walks away without speaking.

Outside a yellow paring of sunrise. Julius walks all the way to the end of Fremont where the train station is busy with people. Beyond the station the brown scrubby plain rises into a rim of mountains. Julius steps into a phone booth, fishes out a nickel, and dials his brother's number. For a long time the phone rings and Julius listens to the jangling bell until the sound becomes the backdrop to a thought he's having. He thinks of the bomb he saw, and his new job. He wants to tell his brother these things but he isn't sure where to start. But the fact of his brother seems suddenly necessary, some confirmation that his voice is welcome and known. He recalls the last time he saw Lee, in Okinawa, and feels a hollow feeling of doubt, which passes, which turns to envy and then to fear. Julius hangs up before the call rings out again.

Back at the Squaw he lies awake a long time thinking of the games he's seen and the men's hands below him and their various shapes, the half-moons of nail beds catching the neon and the man Henry's scarred arm, until the daylight breaks fully through the curtains.

CASINOS MAKE SOME GAMBLERS forget the complications that attend money. As he walks the scaffold Julius considers the dark enclosure of the casinos, the money traded for chips and markers, the absence of clocks in any pit or cardroom, nothing closing or changing, breakfast buffets in the middle of the night. All the strategies for disrupting time, for breaking the link between cause and effect. But now it is Julius's job to resist these things. The peek gives him perspective. He paces the catwalk looking for drunks, card palmers and dice loaders, cheaters of all kinds. He spends the most time above the blackjack tables. Blackjack is the only casino game where the gambler can get an edge over the house and for this reason it attracts cheaters of all kinds. Card markers and sleeve-men, confederacies of slack players who fake dim-wittedness to pass good cards to their partners or bust out better players waiting for the drop. Of course they know he is watching. At the tables they listen for his boots above, trying to gauge the distance before palming an ace or passing a queen, and in this way he becomes a part of the games below and the methods of the cheating men.

Each night between eight and four Julius is their steward. He thinks of himself this way. His job is to watch the players and nothing more. He does not administer punishment, only speculation, only what he believes he sees. Mostly he watches the players' hands. Those with square or short or clumsy hands may mark but they do not palm. They are not built for it. The slender-fingered men, short nails buffed pale, no rings, wide cuffs touching the clefts of their palms—if those men start to lose, Julius will stay at the well above them past the time he is supposed to move on. Losing, for the best of them, is its own kind of strategy. He reports each suspicion with diligence to the two cat-faced men and collects his check at the end of each week. With the money he makes he pays for his room and his cash-ins and eats steak for breakfast and March starts to fade away. He sleeps through the warming afternoons and wakes with a feeling of purpose.

Then, at the beginning of April, the heat comes and covers the city in a shimmer. The casino attic is so hot Julius can feel his heart straining against his ribs. Sweat drips from his nose and brow and from his fingertips as he paces the catwalk. After an hour he takes off his boots and socks and unbuttons his shirt and wets a hotel towel and wraps it around his neck. He sips from a flask of whiskey and smokes to distract himself.

Before he and Henry are due to switch sides Julius rewets the towel with a cup of water already tepid. He leaves his shirt open and tucks the tails into the back of his jeans and walks to the other side. Henry walks slowly toward him and waves dully and does not call out. He is shirtless, covered in sweat, sheets of it over his face and neck. Julius watches him come. There is no breeze and the bowed glass is waxed by the heat. Henry pauses at the crossing to brace himself against the scaffold for a moment. He reaches out, one hand on the railing and the other pressed suddenly into Julius's bare chest, his palm squarely in the cleft of Julius's rib cage. Then he looks at Julius. "Oh," he says and sinks to his knees, his arms bent so his elbows press into Julius's thighs and his thumbs hook the flat bones in Julius's hips. Henry leans his head on Julius's waist, his cheek turned to the copper snap of Julius's jeans, and to keep him from falling Julius takes his shoulders and his fingers slide in the man's sweat. Julius leans as far as he can backward, the scaffold against him. He starts to say, "Now come on." Henry's hands fall away and he twists sideways to retch over the scaffold railing and Julius does not wait or offer comfort but turns back. As he walks along the catwalk to the other side he can feel Henry's palm still there in the center of his chest, like a footprint rising slowly from the stubble of a mown field.

When his shift ends he waits until he hears Henry's boots on the stairwell and keeps waiting long minutes after the door has banged shut below. It is a quarter past four when he finally collects his boots. He thumps them on the heels to evict mice or spiders and finds the Iowan's bill there. It's damp and when he unfolds it, it smells of sweat and cigarettes. He folds it again and puts it back. Downstairs he clocks out but makes a note in the margin that the last fifteen minutes should go unpaid.

Outside a cooling rain has come and gone and the streets reflect the neon in shallow pools at their edges. Julius turns toward the Squaw and is ducking down a side street when Henry catches him.

"Surely you ain't going home," Henry says.

"You mean my room or where I'm from?"

Henry laughs. "Home for the day, bud."

"Well, I was planning on it."

"Too hot to be cooped up."

"A lot cooler now."

"I owe you a drink, for before."

The man looks so earnest, so genuinely embarrassed by his own weakness in the heat, that Julius knows he cannot refuse without revealing something about himself. He remembers the shape of the man's shoulders where he'd touched him, square and ordinary now beneath his shirt. Together they walk down the wet streets and find a tourist bar and order the only kind of beer they have. Julius keeps an eye out for the bosses or any other men who might know them, who might think them in collusion or worse. For a while they talk about the weather and that night's gambling and the sad landscapes of their childhoods. Henry is from the Central Valley and spent many summers in the fields there.

"I settled for Henry because no one could say Javier," he says.

When Julius asks why he's come to Vegas and how long he's worked the peek, Henry says, "I guess they figure I can't be much of a cheat," and raises the injured arm.

"No, I guess you ain't no palmer," Julius says.

"Ain't much of anything."

Henry smiles and Julius sees something else about him.

"But I bet you play all right."

"If you mean playing the goat or maybe by ear, because that's all I've ever done till now."

"I sure wish there was more poker, and not just in them cardrooms," Julius says.

"House ain't got no motivation for it. You play it overseas?"

Julius nods.

"What's your game here?" he asks.

"Twenty-one," says Henry.

"That so."

Henry lowers his eyes.

"I know what people think about blackjack players."

"How many blackjack cheats have you seen from that attic, just this month?" Julius says.

"Blackjack gives a man the edge, that's true enough."

Henry looks at him a long moment and Julius looks back and each is reminded of the other's nakedness. Julius can feel this memory like a shape between them.

"You got people?" he asks.

"Oh, some," Henry says.

Julius nods. Behind the bar the long mirror snags the orange discs of overhead light.

"I'm supposed to be in San Diego," Julius says.

"How's that?"

"With my brother. We planned on it, when we was overseas. I think mostly he wants to keep an eye on me. Nice weather though, and in San Diego you can build a house in the river valley for a song."

"I know about California."

"I guess you do."

"How come you ain't there then?"

"Too hard to tell."

"But you could tell it to me."

Henry smiles at him and Julius smiles back. He thinks of Muriel's house in Kansas and his brother's happiness. That Christmas Eve in the winter wheat talking about everything. The last time they were all together on earth.

"Too hard to tell," Julius says again, and Henry laughs and shrugs and lets the mood change.

Soon they leave that bar for the Moulin Rouge. There Henry moves out onto the dance floor like he's at a wedding, a wedding long put off and finally consummated under duress, legs moving in an ecstatic shuffle surely picked up in the grange halls of his youth, but even in his joy and his relief Julius knows he is withholding. At first he is alone, but when a slow song begins he finds a woman on the edge of the crowd. Julius drinks and watches. Henry's cheek rubs against the forehead of the woman he holds, so close and so often that Julius can't help but imagine the feel of it, the smell in Henry's hair of tobacco, sweat, the raw wood of the attic catwalk. He knows what will happen next and he is not sure he wants it all again. He stands and steps outside. It is just past dawn, the heat already beginning to return. The streets are still crowded with men. The soggy bunch of the bill in his boot irritates him and to have something to do with his shaking hands he pulls the boot off to shift it. He worries that maybe all he's ever really liked are the moments in which love was uncertain, when he could arrange himself in postures of ready seduction, in bed or half-dressed or letting a button linger under his hand, or, before any of these, leaning inside a doorway or stepping off the curb to cross a street where a man stands waiting, the look between them as he walks, the moments when he could still turn away, the private, erotic knowledge that one is the object of another man's long gaze. He recalls other men from years or months before, men in the service or men who left the city in a rush or men who fell in love with women. He remembers the man from Iowa and his shaking back and the little snatches of song they sang. And his disgust is instructive, palliative. He does not have to worry over his own weakness then, when so many other weaknesses are apparent.

Finally Henry comes outside and looks up and down the street and sees him and waves. Julius pulls the boot back on, his sock bunched in the bottom and his jeans half-inside the shaft, and walks that way to his room at the Squaw, sending Henry through the parking lot ahead of him to wait in the alcove, then leaving the door unlocked while he takes off his shirt and jeans so Henry can scan the area before entering. But Henry does not wait, and before Julius can get his shirt undone Henry has banged through the unlocked door and turned Julius by the elbow and kissed him.

THREE

The valley

Muriel loves best those days when there are no races and the horsemen tell stories of fiasco and anomaly. At the lounge one afternoon she hears of a claiming race some years before, when a six-year-old broke a Del Mar track record and promptly dropped dead. Another, in which a redhaired boy from Montreal rode with his broken leg taped to the saddle girth. Or the story about the potbellied paint named Gingersnap who made such fast friends with an Angus bull that the two could not be separated and had to travel cheek by jowl in a special trailer widened for them.

Or, better: The horsemen in their leisure speak of things that cannot happen, that simply won't. There will never be another Seabiscuit, not because he was built by God, as the papers said, as the trainers claimed, but because the universe allows only so much improbability. Nor another corker like the half-bred filly Quashed, who beat a Triple Crown winner by a short head over two and a half endless miles. Likewise the storied beasts of another era, National Velvet and Sergeant Reckless, warhorses on the eastern front, creatures from a dream an entire culture had once shared and woken from.

Through March of 1957 Muriel plays the late afternoon races ten dollars at a time. The winnings are limited by the stakes, which are mean and provincial, and though she knows now the names of stables and jockeys and colts gone early to stud still each new detail excites her. Each new detail is a familiar shape in a dark room. The high stakes are coming when the spring season opens, and most days the men drink more and longer and sit with their knees spread wide and out from the tables, taking account of the odds.

"Hoo now, in a couple weeks we'll have some real money in play," says the man with the mustache.

"Just think about that Lakes and Flowers race last spring at Hollywood Park," says another.

"God that was gorgeous."

"Like watching a sunset, but faster."

"You got all the same riders as that race coming to Del Mar, and almost all the ponies, but no Misrule and no Porterhouse, so our field will be smooth as honey."

"We'll see where the odds end up. Eight races, I'll be damned if one of them doesn't come in double digits over the stilt."

The old jockey called Rosie, given to water metaphors, says, "Tide's coming in, bringing glad tidings."

"Since when do tides bring that?" says the mustache.

"It's called a pun, friend," Rosie says darkly, but all the men laugh because the future is so bright.

AT HOME Muriel is distracted. One night she burns the meat and then the bread and when Lee touches her arm she cries out because she had forgotten him in her speculations. Lee tilts his head but says nothing and together they walk to the diner around the corner. Muriel feels a restful invisibility there, among the other patrons, who eat and talk and worry not at all about horses or progress or the passage of time. Lee orders pie and when the woman brings it he cuts the piece down the middle and slides the smaller half onto his saucer and pushes the rest across the table and Muriel makes a show of eating it and then a show of being full. When he's finished his half and a third cup of coffee she pushes the plate back, barely touched. He winks at her and calls the waitress for the coffeepot and when she doesn't acknowledge him he takes the cup and stands at the counter for a long time. The radio behind the counter plays heartache music. He holds his cup out like a pauper and finally the woman fills it. When he sits to eat he says, "Can't have pie without coffee," as if he were apologizing for this mere fact, for both the waitress and himself.

After dinner they walk back to their building and as they cross the common foyer they can hear the ringing phone. Lee wings the door open and takes the hallway in three long steps and Muriel listens for his reaction. He waits only a moment before he hangs up and turns to her and threads his fingers behind his head. He says that some husky voice has offered him life everlasting.

"That's what she said." The hands behind his head like a man being marched somewhere terrible. "Over the telephone, no less."

Inside the apartment the smell of burned bread is chalky and unpleasant. Muriel opens the window above the sink.

"How long's it been?" she asks.

"A month now."

"Has it ever been this long before?"

"Not that I recall."

Through the open window come the sounds of the street below, cars idling at the curb and voices from the sidewalk and between these noises the high call of gulls making a last round before the full darkness. Lee cracks a beer and sits at the table and takes a drink.

"I guess he's doing fine on his own, wherever he is. Los Angeles or wherever."

He tips up the can and looks at her over the rim like a man making a point and when she doesn't answer he rises. He stands with his back to the counter.

"I guess you don't think so," he says.

"I don't know what I think," she says.

And she doesn't. She remembers Julius's voice down the line and what she'd told him about the races. She feels foolish, knowing she was not believed. Julius had not called since then. Lee looks at her as if he hopes she might speak again and explain away his worry or his bitterness but she says nothing more. Instead she goes to him and takes the beer and drinks and hands it back. It pleases him when she does things like this, simple things that suggest their shared lot in life, an easy intimacy.

"I told you he was always disappearing, even before our old dad was gone," he says. He hands the can back to her and she jigs it to judge its fill and drinks all but the last swallow.

"But it turned out all right before," she says.

"But it always happened again."

He crosses his arms and leans against the counter. Muriel cracks another beer and hands it to Lee and takes one for herself.

"We've been here nearly seven months," Lee says. "I'm not sure what else I can do."

He closes his eyes and opens them again. Muriel thinks of that Christmas Eve and the men's plans. How Lee had told her, as they lay together in her mother's room, that he would always take care of Julius. He'd said this the way any courting man might, as a stay against his own misfortune. She knows that Julius's absence changes what he's able to declare about himself.

"It isn't your fault," she says to him.

"You tell that to our old dad. Not that you could've even when he was alive."

Muriel nods remotely. She puts her head on his shoulder and sighs pleasantly, though his smell and this contact are at odds with her thoughts.

"Did I ever tell you about the time I caught Julius on Kansas Avenue in a bar the Del Monte guys used for faro?" Lee says.

"I don't think so."

"Our father was not dead but nearabouts. I guess I was eighteen then because it wasn't long after this that I signed us both up, though Julius was too young. I was out looking for him, down in the factory bars, and in the third or fourth one I tried there he was in a pair of overalls, cleaning the heads. You wouldn't believe the filth of that place. And it turned out he was working off a debt and he didn't want to tell me, because he'd stolen from that bar, right from the till, to play into their card game."

In the hallway the phone rings again but Lee does not move toward it. Soon someone else answers, speaking in a scolding voice.

"I'm not sure I realized it then, but I did soon after—my brother knew things I didn't, he had passions of his own," he says. He makes a face. She thinks of the story Julius told of the rabbit man and how he'd held her look for so long across the table. She does not share Lee's fraternal resentment but she does feel betrayed, and also that she has been the betrayer. She had told Julius her secret and sent him that money and after that he disappeared. She wonders if her confidence was a kind of permission, the way even bluffs could close the distance between people.

Lee finds a cigarette and lights it and blows the smoke hard toward the open window. He says, "You know, after I'd been let off here, in San Diego, I couldn't find him for two weeks. He'd been back himself already a month. I was sure of his date because I had a friend in the same crew and he told me they'd come back. Two weeks." Lee holds up two accusing fingers. "Then finally he got my number from somewhere and he called me. He'd spent all the money he had and he asked me to wire more to a motel in Palm Desert. This was before you got here, you was probably on that bus in Arizona or someplace."

For a moment Muriel looks at him without speaking. He holds out the cigarette for her and she shakes her head and reaches for the pack and lights her own.

"Why didn't you tell me that?" she says.

"I didn't see why it would matter to you."

"I thought you all got back at the same time," she says. She turns away and blows her smoke into the room.

"Well, we didn't."

She knows he wants to say more but she doesn't want him to say it. She doesn't want to know any more than she already does. She thinks of the time passing and Lee's worry. She sees him need her more because of all this. She steps forward and kisses him and before he can speak again she presses him toward the bedroom and unbuttons his top button and asks for his haste and his force.

THE NEXT DAY, Muriel stands at the end of the bar with a newspaper crossword folded neatly, jotting notes in the margins. In a week the season will open, and the undercard and then the Monday stakes are thick with good horses and riders known for putting on a show. For now the track is fast and the weather fine and the men speculate openly. Rosie is thinking through the chances of a newcomer named Willie Declan, who by all accounts will mount the favorite.

"You know the line, water everywhere and nothing to drink. That's how Declan is on that California Star," Rosie says.

"Hardly matters in that field. In with all those real riders, he'll be as lost as a girl," another man says, and drains his glass.

W. D., Muriel writes, *lost at sea*. But the horsemen are not done with Willie Declan.

"He's a cement brick," the mustache says. "Sure you can fit him in your hand, but you can hardly lift him." He gives the table a look.

"But the hunnerd-granner," says Rosie, who always stands up for the jocks.

"In the hundred-grander he ran on Whittleman's Bitty King, and that was a gift of a fine match. Bitty could've carried a Mark 7 and won on slop."

"But you can't say Declan isn't ready for a big race like this."

Rosie again, and at this a few of the men make kissing faces at him.

"Maybe not. But I can say that he's been a little light after that flu he had, and with Roustabout kicking up the way he is these last weeks no one will beat him who won't ride the rail for a halfie."

"I'll wait for positions. At six Declan could take two from the rail, especially if Sayonara gets anywhere under five, and Declan could squeeze in that way. That's how I'd run it, I'd sail the inner harbor," says Rosie, but his voice is lowering now. He is fifty years old and still fit but he carries some sorrow the other men find disquieting.

"I'm sure you would but that don't mean you *can*," the mustache says, and leans across the table and flicks Rosie on the chin.

The talk goes on this way. At this first stage the odds are fluctuating, and a late El Niño rain would bring a scratch or two, from the finer runners whose trainers won't race them on mud. Anyone glancing at Muriel's notes would see a set of names and numbers and track slang coded into her own shorthand: *'Nara if under five see W. D. Whittle on the wire if cuppy. Too Young 4–8. Roust at center post breaks 'Nara.*

The week goes on. The odds begin to calcify, then a horse falls ill and a jockey gets bumped and another disappears for two days downtown. The men grumble and reset their charts. The hot clear weather brings a strange nothingness: no moths against the screens, no hum of insects, neap tides quiet all night. Instead there is a permeating blueness like the inside of an eye. The heat brings people out of the houses and shops and back rooms. Along the narrow streets of Muriel's neighborhood, workmen cart flowers and crates and white heaps of ice. In the tiny front yards women dump wash water into short stemmy stands of geraniums. The children spill from stoops and curbs in overalls and short sleeves, the coastal sun catching them and turning them divine, in that instant freed by the sun from work and peril. Their mothers in dresses the color of unready peaches, sweating over the wash.

Downtown the dice players and cigarette men and men in tight pants, shirts unbuttoned to their navels. Walking from home to work is like passing between two worlds. Muriel finds herself one afternoon standing a long time in front of a shop window, thinking about the races. Behind her a newspaper vendor and two men in denim jackets are reflected in the window. The men are young and she can smell their cigarettes and their cologne. She looks up at the store window and draws herself away from their attention. She remembers her mother in the summer cooking chops and onions in her underwear while a man sat fully dressed at the table, watching her. The way this distinction between them, between nakedness and not, seemed to confirm something her mother believed about love: that vulnerability existed only in asymmetry, that two people could not be vulnerable together. Her mother believed if she gave men this small advantage she would not be harmed.

In the shop window a large television plays a game show. A man in a glass booth on a soundstage gazes outward in concentration while a clock ticks away in the corner. Muriel thinks of Julius and where he might be and why he hasn't come. The show gives way to an ad for Convair, a woman standing with a suitcase in her hand watching an airplane take off. Though she can't hear the TV Muriel realizes she is hearing an airplane and she looks up and sees a real airplane in the sky, reflected in the store window. She turns and tracks it as it flies over the city headed east. This confluence seems like luck or validation or something mystic. When she turns back to the television the plane is gone, but the other plane is still reflected in the window, as if it had flown off the screen and into the actual sky. She imagines the airplane flying past the rough buildings of this city, over the vendor and the smoking men and the mothers in their collared dresses. Out past the central mountains, then further east across the desert and into the scrub, rich and minty and full enough to hide a child, then over the irrigation circles and tired motels of her youth and down into the endless prairie and over her mother's house. The plane disappears in this direction and the sound goes and then it is just the men and the contrail, reflected in the glass.

That night, after Lee has fallen asleep, she peels open the envelope and counts the money there and thinks through the odds. She does a bit of math on the envelope flap. She thinks of Lee's story, of Julius in overalls working off a debt, and then about his discharge. She worries she's misunderstood them both. She thinks of Lee standing so long at the counter with his coffee cup, waiting for the woman to fill it. She studies the envelope and her arithmetic and she's not sure what she might need the money for, only that she does, only that winning would prove something vital that she cannot otherwise prove, and that no one else can see.

THAT WEEKEND Lee borrows again the boss's Lincoln and drives them through downtown and across the river to see the interstate. In another year it will be complete, running along the edge of Mission Valley; they can see its elevated form now, the men hanging overhead, the black dust from the columns. Lee stops the car along the curb and he and Muriel look up at the cranes and the skirts of rebar, the figures held by flat ropes. The general feeling of the time is that such a marvel is deserved, as marvels are deserved all over the West.

They drive on, past lemon and orange and avocado orchards, hidden inside the city as if cupped inside its palm. The orchards are surrounded on all sides by a network of cul-de-sacs and graveled lots and as they pass Muriel watches the rows of trees flare by the window, interrupted by patches of cleared land and glimpses of the river running low, gridded through with new roads not yet paved. She looks at Lee and in this light he has the chromed look of a photograph, peering ahead at the driveways and ghosted streets. They pass a cowfield, a roadside lean-to stacked with eggs, a sign offering jarred local olives, then again into the not-yet neighborhood.

Muriel knows where they are going and though she might have expected it still she feels deceived. In a half-mile the road turns back to gravel and curves south to the river. Lee stops the car and they get out to stand along the dirt margin. He turns to Muriel and smiles. He gestures across the lot in front of them, marked off by twine and stakes of wood, then marked off again by small flags stuck in the ground between the stakes. The back of the lot disappears in a tangle of blank ash and scrubby bushes, and below this hidden limit is a soft bluff that drops into the river, which they can hear from where they stand. Lee takes her hand in his.

"This tract is the best of them, two thousand for the land and the specs, then I bet we could build out for another six. Hardly anything, considering."

"Considering what?"

"Considering how fast all this land will go. What it will cost in another year."

Lee's voice lifts into insistence. He looks at her and she looks back. The fact of her mother's house in Kansas rises up between them.

Lee says, "We could get at least six grand for that house, you've got to know that's true. And we got a couple hundred bucks already."

She holds his gaze until he looks away and across the lot to the river beyond.

Finally she says, "But you promised your brother you'd do this together."

"And do you see my brother anywhere?"

His tone is wounded. He holds her hand just long enough to offer his forgiveness but not his surrender and then he lets go.

He says, "This place, California, it's indifferent to the past. All the people and the cities and the ocean and all of it." He waves an arm to indicate distance. "All the sailors coming back and the factories and the folks coming over the border. In another year there won't be nothing to buy and then where will we be, we'll have to go all the way backwards."

Muriel does not respond. The sunlight is muted inside the trees and the wind shakes them. She can see dust brought loose and drifting above the crowns of the trees. Lee puts an arm around her and when she stiffens he squeezes her lightly and drops his arm. As if to remediate this failed gesture he gathers himself and says, "You know, that last time me and Julius saw each other, on Okinawa. We had two days of R and R and we met in a village where all the men went, from the stations. This was last year, May, it's still so cold there in May we sat bundled head to toe even inside the bar, you could hear the wind outside. I thought he was being strange but I couldn't figure why and then we met this other fella from his station and things got real strange then."

Lee pauses and looks at her then looks away. Muriel has not heard this story before. He lowers his eyes against the vista and folds his hands across his beltline and toes the dirt and decides to say the next thing.

"Julius beat that fella pretty bad and we got eighty-sixed. Walked a mile in that cold afterward, just shaking and not talking. Then we sat in the train station and waited for morning, and it came out then that Julius was in trouble for something, he'd been caught in the barracks with some other man. I assumed smoking grass or gambling but then a few weeks later they put him on the *Saratoga*, even though he only had a few months left. In Long Beach they gave him a general discharge and half-pay and nothing for the leave he hadn't taken. I heard this from that same friend's cousin. Of course I don't know what he did but sure thing it was worse than poker."

"Why are you telling me this now?" she asks.

"You know what he said, when he finally called?" Lee says. "He said it was good I was marrying you. He said, that sad girl, she needs someone to tell her what to do."

Muriel crosses her arms and will not look at Lee, whose gaze is imploring. He wants to be forgiven right away for saying this, he wants her to understand he is only the messenger. Yet she catches in his tone a savage relief. He could not abandon his custodial role but it might be taken from him. He might be glad to have his brother disappeared. She hadn't known this before and it frightens her.

Muriel turns from him and walks to the road and waits. Lee walks down to the bluff and stands a moment looking out. He leans to touch the wooden stake and then the line of twine that runs out from it, his fingers light along the top like someone making a sense memory. He'd been a poor child and knew the value of things. For a moment she's not angry, thinking about how poor he'd been.

When he turns around he has summoned his dignity and he lifts one hand to wave it all away. They get in the car without speaking and Lee drives slowly along the road to keep the gravel from flying up and chipping the paint of his boss's Lincoln. When they pass the sign for olives Muriel asks to stop. Lee turns into the dusty yard and parks but does not cut the engine.

Muriel steps out of the car and climbs the porch and knocks but hears no movement; after a moment she knocks again, but still no one comes. She leaves the porch and shrugs to Lee but she's not yet ready to get back in the car, she wants first to succeed at something. She turns and walks around the house, toward a set of outbuildings and chicken coops in back. Behind an empty corral she spots a barn with an open door and a tidy interior, and as the light changes Muriel understands that someone is inside. She calls out.

In the doorway of the little barn appears a young woman in a man's striped overalls, cuffs pinched inside her boots. She raises one hand in the air without waving it, moving out of the doorway in quick steps like a child, into the dusty yard.

"You lost?" she says.

The chickens come clucking toward the fence and gather in a line and stare out at Muriel. Their sudden synchronous movement is comic. The woman in the overalls smiles and turns to shush the chickens.

"They're like watchdogs," Muriel says.

The woman says, "Dogs aren't so humorless."

Muriel takes another step toward the birds and they move back a fraction and as if a centerline had been drawn between them they part and peel off into their grainy little courtyard. As they totter away, they turn their small heads back suspiciously.

"I see what you mean," Muriel says. She thinks of the horses moving as a wall from the gate, then fraying off as the race finds its character. Animals were strange in this way, their sameness, their single-mindedness. The woman asks what Muriel needs.

"Your sign," Muriel says, and with her thumb points back toward the road.

The woman makes a noise of understanding. Muriel takes in her slight frame. She is dark-featured and short and surely native to this place, the kind of woman her mother might have known when she was cleaning offices downtown, with whom she might have had coffee or cold sandwiches.

"That's for García's, next house over."

Muriel thinks to apologize but the woman turns in a long stride toward the house and waves with one arm. Muriel follows, and though she is confused there is some pleasure in this, the casual submission to a stranger's command, after the conversation with Lee. On the back step the woman heels her boots off and holds the screen door for Muriel to enter. Inside the house Muriel sees no sign of another person. The walls are bare and the rooms divided by thin curtains like bedsheets and along the floor are books stacked at various heights. A lamp lights a corner where an armchair sits though the rest of the room is without furniture. She cannot see past the curtains to the rooms in the back, though she feels by some intuition that they are empty.

"Not much of a decorator," the woman says, a wave of her arm taking in the bare room and the perimeter of the house and the dry mums along the porch. For a moment Muriel sees herself as she imagines this woman does, as Julius apparently does, as someone simple and apologetic and easily led. They walk into a bright kitchen that faces the road. Through the window Muriel can see Lee in the car, his eyes closed against the sun, and beyond him to the river and the fields and the marked-off lots below. The woman looks out the window, over her shoulder, and Muriel sees her see the idling car and the square shape of her husband.

"Looking at land," the woman says. Her voice is deep and softly accented, Muriel notices now that they're inside.

"We are," Muriel says.

"Now's the time, I hear."

Muriel catches in the woman's tone a light resentment and understands then that she has been read as something else, that the woman sees not a Midwesterner or a waitress but a different kind of foreigner, a nice dress and a wide car coming in from town. She feels a refusal, a sense of herself as changed by the woman's presumption.

"My husband wishes it was," she says.

The woman turns from the pantry to look at Muriel.

"He's out there pouting now."

The woman registers no shock. Instead she collects a jar and hands it to Muriel.

"Is it land he's upset over or some other reason?" she asks. She puts both hands inside the bib of the overalls.

Muriel tries the lid and can't budge it. "He's got all sorts of problems," she says, and holds the jar out.

The woman regards it. "You think you can solve them with olives?"

"I've never had an olive, so I don't know, but I thought I'd give it a shot."

The woman drops the bib and takes the jar from Muriel. "That's big of you," she says.

She works at the jar lid with some force. A stalling quiet then, as they stand in the bright kitchen. Muriel has never learned polite talk. Her mother knew that people walked into the conversations you left open for them, that a small silence could change the course of a life. *Never ask a man about his day,* she often said. And because she never did, men told her all manner of other things, their secrets, their terrible fears.

Next to the sink is a small pair of scissors. A single coffee cup on the pine table next to a hand mirror. The woman's hair is in two braids and the ends are as straight and dark as the edge of a nailbrush. It is easy somehow to imagine her leaned against the counter, the bite of the scissors and the hairs falling along the lip of the sink. Muriel feels a shift in her perception, a sudden longing for woman's solitary act. Though Lee has not opened his eyes, she moves to one side of the window where she can't be seen.

"There's a story about this valley," the woman says finally. She waits for Muriel's interested look and Muriel gives it. "I'm sure you saw the fruit orchards. Was oranges and lemons and walnuts, get shipped out to Ohio and whatnot. But those are going too, for the tracts, but that's neither here nor there. Because what I mean to say is that not that long ago you'd have seen olive trees too. And olive trees have thin leaves like fingers, bright green on one side and pale on the bottom, seeming too small for how the trunks grow, which is twisted and thick, so an olive tree is like two things put together. I say this because if you haven't had an olive probably you've never seen an olive tree either, or you didn't know you had."

The woman pauses. Muriel remembers with pleasure the effusive, sudden talk of country people, after so long in the city. She nods to keep the woman going.

"So. Used to be this valley was full of them," the woman says. "They say when the Spanish came they looked down into the valley from the Lagunas and saw the leaves blowing and they thought the ground was changing color. And though they knew olives, it still took them a while to come down here, the sight was so strange."

She removes the lid and fishes one finger along the inside of the jar and flicks an olive into her palm. "If only they'd stayed up there looking down, but then I wouldn't be here I guess," she says. She holds the olive out to Muriel. Muriel takes it and puts it in her mouth. The taste is salty and the texture is fleshy, disorienting, but under the saltiness something plummy, rich as jam.

"There's a pit," the woman says.

Muriel finds it and spits it into her palm.

"What do I do with it?"

"I usually toss mine in the yard."

"But then it might grow a tree."

The woman laughs as if Muriel has finally surprised her. "But that's not the end of the world," she says.

Lee's voice on the porch, then, and the women turn from each other. The woman hands the jar of olives to Muriel without replacing the lid, then hands the lid to her. She opens the door and moves out onto the porch in her bare feet and Muriel follows. Lee moves back to stand on the steps.

"We could also use some eggs, if you're going to shop," he says to Muriel.

"I've got those. Laid this morning and warm yet," the woman answers. She leans her shoulder neatly against the porch rail. Muriel hides the jar behind her back. In her closed hand the olive pit feels like a pressed thumb. Lee nods and the woman moves past him into the sunny yard. She takes a container of eggs from the small hut by the fence and walks back toward them.

"What do we owe you, then?" Lee asks.

"Oh. I can't sell the olives to you, surely. It wasn't really me you wanted," she says.

She stands now below them in the yard and raises her hand to her forehead against the sun.

"Then we'll have to overpay you for the eggs," Muriel says.

Lee takes the eggs and heads back to the car, and once he's past the woman she looks at Muriel and makes a condoling face. Muriel dips into the jar and takes another olive and eats it. She spits the pit over the porch rail. The woman says, very quietly, "You've got it now."

Muriel lids the jar and hands the woman a dollar, then ducks into the idling car. The woman watches them back out of the drive and turn away.

BY THE TIME they've returned the car and walked back to the apartment the sun has lowered in the sky, throwing the buildings and the power lines into ashy shadow. Muriel makes a quick dinner and hard-boils half the eggs. Once they've finished eating and put out the next day's work clothes the mood has softened between them, and Lee turns on the radio and pours them each a glass of beer. They play three hands of gin and Muriel lets Lee win them all.

Later, as she lies sleepless, Muriel thinks of the woman and her tidy house. She thinks of the trees, grown so tall by the river. She remembers the story Julius told that Christmas, of the burned paintings in Korea, and then she thinks of her mother's funeral. Her mother had been buried without service in the Protestant cemetery a mile from their house. There was no bidding prayer and no eulogy, just the two pallbearers and a few of her mother's friends. It was almost September but the long heat of that summer carried through the season without ease. Nothing would settle. No rain, and the dust gathered in the air and hung there. The machines in the fields nearby turned up contrails of dust that lingered in lines a half-mile long. The heat collected in the bright spaces between the trees and birds and squirrels dodged through them as if through barnfire. While the casket was lowered Muriel looked out at the blazing landscape. Through the hanging dust the sun was setting, and the red light cast up and caught in the dust and waved like flame, and that was the end of things.

Next to her now Lee sleeps soundly and she can feel his heat in the room. She remembers Julius's serious look as he told them about those paintings, his fingers tented together. *What's the harm in landscapes?* he said. *That's what I can't get over.* Then his wide grin. When he finally calls, she thinks, I will ask him to tell that story again.

A FEW DAYS later Muriel leaves the Heyday in a loose dress, a sweater over her shoulders and her hair pushed back by sunglasses. She takes the bus as far as Twelfth Street and walks the rest of the way, nearly all her money folded in a piece of brown paper and pressed inside the elastic waistband of her dress. She imagines the odds will change one more time but not by much. Judging from the clear weather and the positions and the horsemen's last details she has a good number for the bay in the seventh race, and several others in the earlier stakes races. A chancy amount to win in the first five, plus a little luck on a series of boxes in the later runs would end the day well ahead, if the odds hold and the win pool clocks out where the horsemen predict. She has calculated each possible win to pay out below the tax limit. What she might do with the winnings she hasn't considered. The money has been abstracted into something else, something terrifically unlike her. Carrying it inside her dress she feels the way she imagines a saint might feel, with a secret that is also a piety, a kind of goodness that holds its own in the world. She could lose every race this season and still have enough to start over.

The track is crowded with the better class of gamblers, the fine-hatted women and men in linen suits, those for whom the horses carry history and status. These people will know the names of owners and foals and which stallions have come to stud. Among this crowd she will not be noticed because she is no one important. She wins the first two races and this does not surprise her, so before the third race she buys a drink and bets both the winner and the perfecta, which leaves more to chance but also more to gain. When these come through she feels the prickly blood in her ears and the drink falling quietly through her and she takes one ticket to the south windows and the second to the east so no single cashier will know how much she's won. She keeps out half the bills and folds the others into a tight square and closes it in the brown paper. Then she buys another drink and bets less than planned on a win-place-show, but she wins this race, too. This last-minute change, determined by an unlikely win in the previous race, makes Muriel feel conspicuous. She considers sitting out the fifth race. The day is warm and the crowd raucous and changeable, the clear feeling of the day is hazardous. Beside her in the upper section a man and a woman who is too young to be his wife lean into the shade with their legs entwined. Below them a fist of sailors with their hair undone and falling into their eyes. All around the track are postures of similar intemperance. Yet she is calmed by a sense of isolation from any other world. There is only now the heat of the day and the smell of the horses and the lived fact of her presence here. Suddenly she can do anything she likes. She stands and bets a win and another exacta, then moves quickly to an empty seat along a row of couples. Among them she will be invisible, and any seat next to her will be presumed to belong to her husband, off at concessions or at the mutuel window.

She wins that race and the race after. Now the square of bills is too large to be folded again, so she peels away a quarter of it and holds it without counting, because she can guess how much is there. The next race is the one she's waited for. With this stack of money she rethinks her strategy. To bet the whole amount would produce too big a win, so she takes a third of it to the east windows, a third to the south, and the rest downstairs to the front, and in that way makes three separate bets, all according to the horsemen's talk and her interpretation of it. All in all a two-thousand-dollar stake. She knows this caution is its own kind of risk, that anyone watching would find such behavior suspicious, or that another gambler with the same tactic could take notice of her. But she cannot bring herself to name the full number for a cashier. To tell a stranger such an amount seems to her less an act of hubris than an admission of startling freedom. That she could hand that kind of money to improbability.

She waits another fifteen minutes for the post. The crowd bristles and the breeze has whipped in from the ocean and brings with it the intricate, living smell of the offing. Finally there's Willie Declan on the big bay called California Star, coming to post in the sixth position with Sayonara looking grim in the third. She checks the odds one last time though she knows them. Around her the crowd has quieted and as the horses enter the stalls she has a strange feeling of doubling, the horses and their riders lined neatly behind the starting gate, the crowd lined in their rows to watch. A sensation like the tremor of a cask. The horses break in a wall and move toward the inside track and as the horsemen have predicted Declan finds the rail and squeezes Sayonara out and behind him. The field stretches wide, Declan keeping Sayonara at a length, then a half-length, then holding, and then a surge and Sayonara falling back again. The race continues without change or spectacle and when Declan takes the race by two lengths she doesn't move. Sayonara is second, and the clip-legged roan is third, behind the other two by a distance. She's won each bet she made.

Across the finish line the horses cool at a trot, then the pit ponies are led out and the horses become mere animals again, snorting and tightly controlled and walking along the outside rails. She thinks suddenly and for no reason she can name of the chickens at the woman's house in the valley and their coordinated movement, then of the moment she has imagined but not seen, of the woman leaned back, her braid brought in front of her shoulder to be trimmed. Something in this image makes her furious and light-headed. A quick calculation of the winnings alarms her and she looks around at the loosening crowd, some people leaping and some sitting resolute, a group of old men turned toward each other and away from the track, and waits for someone to notice her. As she waits she finds the inside seam of her purse with her fingernails and starts to work it, scraping at the thin lining until she breaks a hole. Without looking down she rips away at the seam until she's made a pocket in the side of her purse. She places the fold of money in it and hides the bulge with the newspaper she's brought and then the ball of her sweater pressed against it. Her face and arms are cold though she is sweating openly. None of the races has been remarkable. They will not enter legend or be spoken of in any way except personally, when years from now someone here remembers the afternoon at Del Mar in 1957, when he was on leave, or before there were children, or because it was his birthday.

Finally, when the crowd's energy has lessened and people have turned back toward the turf or their companions, she makes again her careful rounds to the separate banks of windows and puts half of the winnings in the hole in her purse and the other half down the front of her dress. Now the trouble is in getting home. Certainly she will not stay for the last races. Though she's made no outward sign she knows that any woman leaving alone on a day like today is an easy mark, and anyone might have been watching her. She crowds in behind a married couple pressing through the turnstiles and follows them out to the parking lot, then at a distance through it. When they peel away to find their car she moves swiftly forward, where another group of people is halted at the crosswalk, which clears for them to cross the turf road and onto Via de la Valle.

Then she is alone. With the scarf she wipes her brow and neck and brings it to her eyes as if she might cry into it though she does not feel like crying. She is not the type to search the peculiar for signs or omens but she cannot help the feeling now that some veil between worlds has been very slightly lifted, that she stands exposed on the weedy street corner. Across La Valle she can see the crowds of people outside the bars, everywhere in the coastal wind are halves of tickets and racing forms. It is seven o'clock in the evening. She knows she should move toward the bus station before she misses the seven-fifteen through downtown and is stranded for an hour among the crowds.

She turns toward the stop but walks slowly and only when she sees the bus does she move all the way under the metal shade. For twenty minutes she rides in a state of watchful anticipation. Through the windows the city goes by. Housing grids and cleared ground breaking open the late daylight. The heavy flicker of palm trees. She thinks back to the bus ride from Kansas, five days across the Plains and then the Rockies, down into the great valleys of the West, the young men on their way to the naval yards and on to Japan, retching out the slits of the bus windows, sick before they'd even seen the ocean. Then the day she was married, witnessed only by the court clerk, because Julius had not come. She should have known then—she might have changed her mind. The progress of things like a pitcher tipped downward to fill a glass. How quickly it had all happened.

She gets off a few stops early and stands under an awning not knowing what to do. Though she is far from the track now, she still has the feeling that anyone can look at her and know exactly what's happened. Across the street and down another block she sees the Radford Hotel, four stories high and unfancy, but decent, and in this decent neighborhood. She walks to the light and crosses at the crosswalk, then down the next block, keeping to the storefronts and in the shade thrown by the buildings. The sun is low now and falling away. At the desk she signs her maiden name in the log and is given a key for a room on the third floor. Once in the room she closes the door and turns over the dead bolt and the brass hook.

She lifts the skirt of her dress and pulls out the money there, then takes the rest from the lining of her purse and drops the pile on the bed. Nearly ten thousand dollars—she knows it to the cent. She lights a cigarette and looks from the bed to the window facing the street, then back along the wall, as if she is searching for some rent or weakness. She is surprised to see a telephone on the nightstand. She could call Lee and tell him she's taken an extra shift and then she could sleep or stay well past dark, but he might want to come by for her. On the bed and away from her the money is frightening and actual. She should have stopped after the third or fourth race. She sits on the edge of the bed and finishes her cigarette, then lights another. She lifts the receiver and asks the front desk for a line out, and when the tone comes she dials the number in Los Angeles, where they'd last reached Julius. After a dozen rings a man answers.

"Julius?" she says, though she knows already that it isn't him.

"Maybe so," says the man in the menacing voice men use to charm women. "Depends what you're after."

She thinks suddenly that what has spooked her is not good luck but the vivid fact of luck itself. Even with all her preparation and the long knowledge of the horsemen, her account of the weather and the odds, only preposterous chance could have led to this result. And if there was such good luck in the world, and if it could outpace her own agency and her own knowledge, then bad luck must be the same, and no luck, too. She has been seen and accommodated by luck, and she wants out of its sight line.

"What gives, sweetheart, you need some kind of advice?" the stupid man on the phone says.

She hangs up without speaking and lies on her side facing the curtained window. Her mother's house and her mother's grave are five days' drive and if she called the Carter boy she is sure he'd open the windows and sweep out the eaves, though what she would do after that she can't say. She could do anything she wanted now but she doesn't know what that might be. She cannot describe her disappointment and can imagine no one to whom it would matter.

She closes her eyes and lies still a long time. She thinks of her mother's house that Christmas Eve. In her memory the night deepens over the wheatfield as she and Julius sit turning cards in the kitchen. They have drunk all the wine in the house and Julius is turning up cards and explaining them. He says he once knew a man who sang so beautifully that other men wept even many days afterward. He tells her about the rabbit man and another man he knew who memorized the scientific names of flowers and all of these men seem to her unlike any she has known before. Like him they are receptive and lovely and out of place, not her mother's men or her mother's romance but something altogether else.

"Where do you find such people?" she asks.

"Oh everywhere, everywhere," he says, and raises his arms above his head and opens them out as if marshalling a symphony. She wants a better answer but she does not know what question will prompt it. In his conducting motion she sees the basic contours of another world.

Julius shuffles the cards and lays them out. He says, "This is the bedpost queen," and shows her the queen of spades with the jeweled scepter upraised and amative. He turns up the king of hearts and says, "And this is the suicide king," and when he asks her what it feels like to be in love she says she wouldn't know then realizes what she's said. But he laughs simply, then he lets his face sallow and says very seriously, "If the next card I turn up is a diamond or a seven we'll build the house on a hill so we can see the sea." He reveals the eight of clubs and they both look at it on the table and then he flicks it with his fingernail so it sails off the edge and he turns the next card and the next until they have the jack of diamonds.

When she woke the next morning he was still at the kitchen table playing solitaire with the radio on low and she stood a long time in the next room listening to him sing along. For months she had risen from her mother's bed and bathed and made coffee and gone to work and waited on the mail. She woke often from dreams about birds. And still she was no closer to understanding what she might do next. When finally she entered the kitchen Julius smiled and wished her a Merry Christmas but there was no indication on his face of what they'd shared. She'd thought then that he was trying on propriety, that the drink had turned and muted the feeling between them, and that was all. But now she knows he thought her sad and aimless, and too innocent for what he'd told her. The next evening the men left and sailed back to Japan and since then she had talked to Julius only once and he had never answered her letter. When she'd told him about the horses, he hadn't even believed her.

Now, beyond the wall of the hotel, the sounds of the city are muffled and blank and what life exists there is expressed only as a tapping, a constant interval of noise, undifferentiated. She presses up on her elbows. Then she turns to sit cross-legged and takes up the pile of money and begins to arrange the bills by denomination. As she does she rotates each and stacks it so it matches the corners of the bill below. Then she counts it out, first the big bills then the small. She finds a sheaf of hotel paper and rips off three sheets and divides the bills into two big stacks and a smaller third and folds them inside, creasing the edges of each sheet to make an envelope. She slips these into the pocket she's made in her purse and presses the edge of the ripped lining up and under the seam. Then she leaves the room and takes a narrow stairway back down and out a side door that leads to an alley. She walks the eight blocks home, catching with soft eyes the shapes of men and shopkeepers in her periphery, feeling the weight of the money the way one feels the imminent coming of rain.

At home she meets Lee's fretting look at the door and tells him a story about a missed bus, about having to walk several blocks from the restaurant to take another line, one that wound through the Stingaree at summer dusk and from whose windows she could see the men playing dice against the brick fronts. She knows he'd worry about her in that neighborhood, but now that she's home safe they can laugh about it, and she wants this laughter, this after-danger easing, to calm her. It does not occur to her that she wants to hurt Julius but his absence has turned into a justification, and she wants this day and what she will do next to stay the way a secret should, unavowed, and belonging only to her.

THE NEXT DAY the horsemen gather at the lounge later than usual, in black suits too big or small, depending on each man's age and density. Someone they know has died—Gerald, they say, though Muriel does not recognize the name—and rather than the previous day's big races they speak of the man's funeral, where they have just been. Three nights ago a vice raid over by the railyard cleared the streets and sent men to jail or worse. The man they're mourning was involved in some way, though no one says how. She sees that the jockey Rosie is missing.

"That's what men like that can expect," someone says.

Above them the plantation fan presses the air through the unseasonably warm day.

"Some asshole will always say *Well now at least he didn't suffer.* And I'd say, then you didn't know Gerald, because if there was ever a sufferer it was him—and it's not like I'm speaking ill of the dead when we all talked this way about him when he was alive."

The men speak quietly, as if this loss is a secret unlike the other secrets they tell.

"I hate to imagine Rosie's sorrow, though he brought it on himself. So did Gerald. *And whosoever is deceived thereby, is not wise,*" says the man with the mustache.

"What will happen to the Chester Hotel, you think?" says someone else.

"Same as any of those degenerate places. It'll come back or it won't."

"You suppose all them boys ran into the sea, to get away?"

"Is the Chester down by the sea?" one of the younger men asks.

Dark and cautious laughter, and then the man with the mustache says, "You're saying you'd like to know, huh?"

The young man lifts his chin and narrows his eyes and says nothing more. Another man says, "It'll come back. That building's a hundred years old and I bet them type of boys have been there just as long or longer."

The tables at the front of the lounge are empty; three men at the bar each sit one stool apart from the next, like strangers in a movie theater. One reads the paper and the two others talk about politics with their stools turned in toward the empty seat between them. Muriel's purse is tucked under the bar and hidden. She wishes the horsemen would speak of the races and say if they'd won as she had, but she is also relieved when they don't. She tears out the racing form and writes down the man's name and the name of the hotel, and then Rosie's name and then *one hundred* and *by the sea*, as if she were taking notes for the next day's post. The morning has drawn slowly and the men show no signs of leaving and Muriel waits. She feels like waiting might be the only thing left for her to do.

She considers the man's funeral and wonders if there had been horses there pulling the funeral cart, the coastal cypress decked in lace bunting, to make death seem like what it is, a return to the past, and in her mind the coffin holds the stranger Gerald as he might have been in his youth, lean and quick and ready. She folds the racing form into fourths and slips it into the pocket of her purse, with the money, as if for posterity.

When her lunch break comes she takes the bus ten blocks north and gets off near a service station perched just back from the street. Inside she buys a candy bar and then walks around the back of the station to a dim restroom and steps softly in. She dons again the slacks and striped shirt and broad-brimmed hat, careful not to touch the walls or the grimy sink of the restroom. There is some thrill in this that is almost erotic, parts of her body bared a bit at a time yet held away from the parameters of the room, as if she is undressing for someone she hopes will look but whom she won't allow to.

At the bank she waits in line with the other men and women missing lunch for their small errands. When it's her turn she slides two of the folded sheets of hotel paper through the window and asks for a cashier's check for seven thousand dollars, made out to George Lee Sims and Muriel Sims, and says she'd like the check postdated, ten days from now. When the teller complies Muriel lets her hands drop from the strap of her purse and relaxes. She sees the check is as she'd hoped, printed in the corner only with the bank's name and the address of its headquarters. Then she asks for another, made out to the property tax board of Kansas, and fans a dozen twenties on the counter, thinking that this young teller cannot know what she wants or why she is here or that her mother died in the undignified middle of the day.

She puts the two checks in her purse along with the receipts and turns to leave the bank. She waits until she is outside and several feet past the bank windows to walk more swiftly, down two more blocks to a post office, thinking that she was right about cash, that there are no real questions to ask about it, since it might come from anywhere but only ever means what it means. Inside the post office she buys three security envelopes and a plate of stamps. She writes a quick note to the tax board explaining that the check is prepayment for this year and next. Then another note to the Carters, asking them to tape the windows and drip the taps, along with four twenties folded tight, to cover another year of maintenance. She addresses the envelopes and stamps them. Then she places the seven-thousand-dollar check inside the torn lining of her purse, careful not to fold or crease it. She fills the last envelope with the rest of the cash and the racing form and the receipt from the post office and conceals this, too. Later she will sew the seam closed again and when all is settled she will find a hiding place.

Outside she removes her sweater and sits at a bus stop. From her purse she takes the last hard-boiled egg and rolls it gently against the bench to crack the shell and then peels it. In a few weeks the receipt from the tax board will arrive, and she'll use this envelope for the big check, to make it all seem authentic. She imagines the moment she hands the check to Lee, and the relief he will feel. Now there would be a fine lawn and Sunday dinner and gracious talk about the meal and she and her husband would have the quiet life they had never been afforded when they were younger and unmarried, still living with their parents in those forgotten towns. Maybe they came out west only to claim a past denied to them, and not, after all, a future free from such notions.

She tries to imagine what her mother might think of this deception and she can't. She'll still have the house and her own money but she is giving up something more crucial and her mother would have seen that. Muriel has been so lucky and now she is beholden to luck and that leaves her utterly alone. If she gets away with this she will never go to Del Mar again. She promises this to herself. And if finally Julius does call, she would say nothing of paintings or horses or even say his name.

FOUR

The meadows

Henry in the hem of neon between the alley and the street. At night in the dim light of the peek, hair and eyes so dark they disappear, so that Julius sees only the bright buttons of Henry's shirt and a flash of fingernail as he approaches the place where the catwalks cross. Henry in the morning at the Squaw Motel, curled inside the weather of some dream, Julius awake and watching him, knowing he must leave soon before daylight finds them together. Some nights a tenderness so great there is no way to touch Henry softly enough, other nights coarse and silent and sleepless.

Each morning Julius leaves the room with a telling joy he must tamp before the day begins. Once outside the room and through the lines of parked cars he turns onto Second Street and walks along the treeless grid of empty lots, taking the long way downtown. He feels wonderfully alone. That is what love feels like to him. As if finally he's touching the very outside of himself, pressed against the limits of his body, singular, replete. The early dawn milled down to the low horizon is a blasted white; years from now, whenever he thinks of that view or sees it again, he will be rushed back to this moment in his life, and forever it will feel like love to him, that kind of bright sky.

Their affair stretches through the end of the spring and then the monsoon season. At night, the peek cools so fast that the chill sometimes catches them in shirtsleeves, skin pricked against it. Then the bitter summer comes, and they walk between the glass windows barefoot, their hair drenched with sweat. One night, early in July, Julius stands at the window watching a man below win every other hand of blackjack, sometimes losing two in a row but rarely. He watches the man a long time. As he watches, he tries to find the one piece that gives the pattern away. There is always one thing that people fail to conceal. He's seen a man rise from the table after a profitable night only to see him again an hour later splitting chips with the dealer. He's seen men lean back in their chairs and reveal aces tucked into their belts. Once, two cowboys—so fresh from the train they sat at twenty-one with their duffels under their feet—played for an hour before Julius saw the thing he needed: not the pattern of their cheat but the interruption in it, one cowboy marking wrong and busting his friend, who snaked his eyes so briefly at the first man that Julius knew exactly the game they were running.

Below him now he studies the man's gestures for any of the cheats he knows to expect, palms and sleeves and marks, but also for surprises. Cheats are always evolving. At one hand the dealer turns up a nine and the man stands; at another the dealer shows queen and the man hits recklessly and wins. Then, as the dealer shuffles, the man leans back and Julius sees it, the flick of his eyes to another man at the table directly behind the dealer. That man wears a turquoise ring turned sideways so the stone leans off his pinkie and onto the felt. When the next hand goes around, Julius watches the dealer and sees him lift the corner of his hole card and flash the man with the ring. The dealer is new and Julius knows this is sloppiness and not a larger con. New dealers often needed practice at checking hole cards. Another deal goes around and the first man waits. When the dealer lifts his card the second man sees it and turns his ring halfway around and the first man doubles down and hits a hardy seven. He wins that round. On the next the man with the ring makes no move and the first man stands and loses. Partners, Julius thinks. A novel but volatile trick. For another few hands Julius studies the confederacy to confirm his thinking. A nod from the second man and the first man splits, then at the next deal the ring is turned again, and the first man hits a sixteen with the four of clubs and takes the pot.

It occurs to Julius, as it often does, that he could find the ringed man later, slide in next to him and whisper his role here. That in a dawn alley the man could slip him a bill for his silence and he'd have another enterprise, one in which his risk and investment are returned twice. But he isn't after risk now. Or rather, he is only in the business of spotting it. So he leaves the dark glass, descends the stairs to the room of bank bags and cages, and knocks on the thick door. When the door opens Julius stands several feet back from the door and quickly describes the confederacy to one of the cat-faced men inside, then returns to the casino attic. Such a con is hard to prove and the men are allowed to keep playing, but a few hours later, when his shift ends, the pit boss in the seersucker suit meets him at the door and presses two ten-dollar bills into his palm and thanks him for his diligence.

That night Julius tells Henry of the ruse he saw on the casino floor and the bills the pit boss gave him. They are twisted together in the sheet like a bouquet, the late hour lighting the room grayly from behind the drawn curtains.

"You think of tipping them off, though, those blackjack players?" Henry says.

He reaches from inside the sheet toward the nightstand where a cigarette sits smoldering. He brings it to his lips in the quaint way Julius loves, as if he is touching a soft place where he'd been kissed or struck.

"I might've," Julius says.

He reaches out two fingers to have the cigarette passed.

"I always do. Think of it, I mean. Have you ever done it?"

"Naw, naw," Julius says. "Too much to worry over."

"It'd be easy enough."

"Don't shit where you eat, is what I think," Julius says.

He had never been a philosophical thief. That is, he did not have a philosophy, nor did he believe in some set of rules that made the thieving legitimate, that elevated it above mere commerce. Opportunities presented themselves inside some other enterprise and the trick was to recognize them. Once in L.A. he had lifted a man's wallet and still spent the whole night drinking with him, and when the bar bill came and the man went to show his generosity, Julius searched under tables and stools with him and shrugged grinningly. If he was suspected, by that point he was also well-liked. But he doesn't want that sort of thing now. He wants this honest work and the nights playing cards with his honest pay in lighted rooms no cop has swept out.

"You think—" Henry begins. He unwraps the sheet and stands naked by the bed. The pause in his talk a little seduction. Julius turns so that his face is half-buried in the pile of sheets and Henry grins, then turns so his high ass is bared. Two strides across the room and Henry finishes the sentence.

"—that a man is only one person ever, no matter where he is or who he's with?"

"We got a name for that. It's called talking out both sides of your mouth."

Julius sits up and watches Henry as he walks over to the bureau and turns to face him again. Julius feels a swell of boyish dislike for Henry's bright face, that cruel feeling after sex. Henry has not asked directly because to ask directly would be an admission. But Julius knows what he wants. From the bureau Henry takes a crumpled Strikes package and finds the last cigarette there.

"What I'm asking is, say you did tip those players off. But it was your job to see them in the first place. We're up there every night, looking down at men doing exactly what we do when we're not up there."

"I don't cheat and I ain't going to make a habit of cheating, so whatever you're seeing ain't me."

"Now I'm not saying cheating, I'm not talking about that. Think of it more agreeably than that."

"If you mean there ain't no difference between cheating and not I'd say you're crazy."

"What I'm trying to say if you'd listen is that this place, where you can take another man's money off him like that and get rich doing it and also catch cheats and watch a bomb go off all in the same day, is exactly the kind of place where the line gets blurred."

"Between right and wrong?"

"Sure. Or between real and not. Or legit or not."

"I still say it matters."

Henry smokes thoughtfully.

"I ain't seen that particular cheat before, but I have heard about it. You know what they call it?" he says.

Julius shakes his head.

"'Spooking.' Ain't that applicable."

Julius nods but doesn't smile, which is what Henry wants him to do. He thinks of men in fashionable ties pinned neatly to their white shirts, other men in three-inch boots made of dyed snakehide. The great variety of men he's known or watched. All of them with something meant to identify their place in the world. A thin-brimmed hat tipped back, a rolled cuff. Always some talk, these days, about who or what they should be, and in this talk was frank ambition. A sense that there was nothing more important, or more interesting, than themselves. Julius knows about the nights Henry spends at twenty-one with other men and the money he makes at those tables. He's known it from the beginning. Henry moves toward the bed in a sexy walk meant to shake Julius from his coolness, then sits on the edge.

"You have people, though," Henry says, as if this is part of the same thought.

"What are you talking about now?"

"You do though, huh?"

"Just my brother and his wife."

"That's enough. And they love you probably, they wonder where you are."

"I don't see your point, friend."

"I'm saying they know you."

"They don't know anything."

"They know more about you than anyone knows about me. I've been dead a hundred years, you ask my father or the fine citizens of Maricopa."

Julius makes a face.

"Well hell," he says. "Ain't that too bad for you."

"It is. It is too bad for me," Henry says.

"Look, bud, you're getting me mixed around. Whole point you ask me is, we get to be legit here. Play cards all night if we want to, and keep the game statutory to boot. What's my brother's wife or your self-esteem got to do with that?"

Henry laughs at him. He reaches out and takes a hank of Julius's hair and pulls him forward and kisses him.

"What I'm trying to say is, there are nights sometimes when I look down through that glass at the game below and I half-expect to see myself," Henry says.

Then he moves in next to Julius and pulls the sheet so it catches under him and Julius rolls to one side to let it loosen and Henry slips under the freed corner so they're arranged again as they were.

"How would that be, to see yourself in the world?" Henry says into Julius's prickly unshaved neck.

"Could be a kindness. Could be disappointing."

"Maybe you did the right thing with those cheats, but maybe it don't matter. Maybe trying to be good or right is just a chore they set up to keep us distracted from the real point."

Julius wants to move the conversation into another register. He reaches into the bedside drawer and pulls out the Bible and opens to a random page. Henry leans away from him so the sheet tightens between them and without looking at the page Julius quotes a verse from memory.

"*Those who guard their ways preserve their lives.* See now, Henry, the Lord says we ought to go one way and not another."

"I'm not sure you should treat the good book that way. You're asking for bad luck."

"Seems to me good luck and bad luck start somewhere far beyond Gideons."

"How is it a believer like you stays put every Sunday morning?"

"I'll tell you what, you ought to spread it around. Play something else besides twenty-one or the bosses will think you have a specialty."

"I do have a specialty."

At this Henry smiles and Julius pulls the sheet and with it Henry's wiry ruined body and the two men make the kind of love that follows an unfinished dispute of some importance.

Afterward, as Henry sleeps, Julius rises and showers, then returns the Bible to the drawer and steps out into the dark parking lot to smoke. He'd like to take his boots and his hundred-dollar bill and his bonus and walk down to the train station and wait for the dawn train out. But to leave Henry would mean leaving his real job and his house pay, and the feeling of repletion he had. Across the lot he watches the streetlight click through the colors and the bright line of the horizon that even on the darkest nights is visible as a blue vein against the mountains and the glow of the city. He walks through the lot without turning around and spends the early hours playing slow stud with some tourists. He doesn't sleep, and when the light comes and he knows Henry must have woken alone he gets up from the table and tips the dealer. In the bathroom of the Frontier he washes his face in the sink, then he eats a bit of breakfast and goes to Binion's Horseshoe where they've set up a table for Kansas City lowball, and in this way he has the feeling of leaving, without the act.

THE NEXT MORNING after work he plays the seven-card table at the Mormon joint and loses his bonus in four quick hands. He tries again at Binion's and wins awhile but then he tries too hard. It's late afternoon when his money's gone so he wanders through the downtown bars but sees no men or women alone or amenable. He sits for ten minutes at the Lucky Strike but no one turns to him, and when the barman starts his long walk over Julius stands and steps out into the day doubly brightened, the neon spill of the lights over Fremont and the sun low and stern. He walks several blocks from downtown, where the dealers and the pitmen and the waiters gather in the low-end bars. The string of short buildings has a regimental air, like a barracks, and Julius dislikes the sight of it. But he wants some company that has no taint to it, he wants, for a few hours, to be no one's lover.

At an old tavern called the Cave, where the servicemen drink, Julius turns off the narrow street and sends a glassy flare of sunlight into the room when he opens the door. At the bar, a half-dozen men who don't really know him but recognize him by sight; along the dim walls many others. Julius slides in next to a man drinking alone, older, dressed in the uniform of a custodian, his collar still buttoned all the way up. Julius does not look at him but orders a beer and when the bartender brings it he tosses a nickel on the bar; the custodian turns toward the motion and the sound, then looks away again. As Julius sits, he lets his attention drift until the man says what Julius needs him to say.

"They say drinking alone is the first sign of trouble. Too bad us."

Julius glances at him sideways, as if reluctant to abandon his privacy, but then he says, as pitifully as can be believed, "Usual state, tonight or any other."

"You oughta go back home, then. We all ought to."

"Not sure I'd be entirely welcome."

"Oh surely now."

"I was a navy man, misfit me for any life in Kansas."

A touch of pride in this partial truth, as if, were he simply to tell it right, such a story might sum it up. He knows what will happen next and that the man will stack him two or three beers and that Julius will offer his company in recompense. In Los Angeles he drank this way whenever his pockets were light.

"No fooling. Army here. Different war than yours, though, I'd venture," the man says.

"Korea. By way of Japan, like everybody."

"Oh, you'll like this then," the man says and turns on the stool to hem in toward Julius. Julius turns to meet him. Easy friendship of remote places, of early mornings.

"Here's a story: Two nights ago I was at the Desert Inn and in the clubroom they've cleared out all the tables but one and set up something with tiles, look like dominoes."

"Pai gow," Julius says.

"You got it, but don't ruin the story."

Julius nods and sticks his nose in his glass theatrically. The man laughs.

"That your last nickel?" he says, and nods toward the bar.

"Just about."

The man signals the bartender who hauls another two beers and the man pays. When he's downed half the pint and wiped his mouth he says, "So I'm at the bar waiting for a five-card call. I'm no real five player, but no one plays seven-card too well around here, perhaps you've noticed."

"Just this morning I sat through twenty grim hands down at Binion's," Julius says.

"Sure, you can play at Binion's if you're touched. Anyhow, a bunch of Chinamen in suits file in and they sit for some time, playing that pai gow.

I get called for a place at poker and play in and more or less forget about the whole thing. But then some hours later I'm leaving—" And here the man looks meaningfully at Julius and Julius sees the smallness in him, his grand scale of address, and what is surely coming next, a story about his bigness, veiled by detail. "Real flush, mind you, had some luck at that table, and who's coming out but those Chinamen, and I can hear the game breaking up in the cardroom, the sound of all those tiles being swept off and the scrape of chair legs. Might've heard a gong too, swear it."

The man pauses, raises two fingers for another round. Julius knows already that this kind of man will thrive on a bit of enmity, lightly offered. He is tall and wiry and high-cheeked, good color up to his temples, old enough to be Julius's father. Julius counts in his head how many beers the man might have in him and subtracts that number from the price of loneliness.

"So I stop and watch them pass, and with them are three hardnosers, casino men you know, acting almost conciliatory, and so I'm thinking: What would a bunch of Chinamen be doing in one of our great cathedrals? You think there's an opposite to communism, it's gotta be the fucking clubroom at the Desert Inn."

"Sure enough," Julius says.

"But then I think, and to my amazement: This place we've got here, these casino runners, hell, they can just set a spread for Chinamen to play any foreign game. Who cares who's watching, middle of the goddamn day? What a thing is progress."

The man leans back into the room and scrapes at his chin with the butt of his hand.

"I'm not sure I catch your drift, friend," Julius says.

"Look. I won't say it out loud, I don't know a damn thing about you except your service in the Far East, which I believe by the shivering look of you. But you know who runs these casinos, without my saying it."

"I guess so."

"You guess so. If you're so green how'd you end up in this joint with the rest of us dumb fuckers?"

"I ain't so green."

"No shit. Look, all I mean is, you got your regular business types, your Henry Kaisers and your Sears and Roebuck. And then you got Moe Dalitz and Wilbur Clark, and who says that's not business?"

"It's business, I can see that, I get some relief from that fact."

The man lowers his chin and looks at Julius. The door opens and throws a wedge of light into the room and across the man's face. He nods.

"That's right. But what I'm saying is, we got business here without all that bullshit of right or wrong. You don't have to believe in nothing to run a casino, not even democracy. It ain't like war. You can let in whoever you want, throw out whoever you want. Ain't no House Committee on fortune, poor or good."

"You're getting me a little worried now, friend," Julius says.

The door closes and the room again grows dark. Julius straightens his shoulders and sits up and brings his jaw tensely forward. It might be the edge of this town and dark as night and every man in the joint drunk and soaking in his own misery but he doesn't want the association. The cops who cleared the cardrooms and the men's hotels in L.A. said they were all reds, working against decency. Julius thinks he'd be smart to change the subject.

But then the man says, "Oh hell. I'm just like anybody. I pay my taxes—" And he gestures in a wide arc meant to take in the whole room. "It's 1957. McCarthy's dead. I thought we got to talk differently now."

He signals the bartender again and Julius thinks he ought to end this small con and pay his own way. He tosses a dime on the bartop and the man flicks it back to him.

"God in heaven, Kansas," he says and makes a pitiful face. "Your very last nickel huh."

"I told you just about."

The beer comes and the man lifts his glass and contemplates it, then sets the glass down and purls it in the ring of condensation. Perhaps the conversation won't survive. The drinkers in the corner extend for a moment a raucous energy, which both men turn to acknowledge. A light scuffle, a few raised voices, then one man is lifted under the arms by two others and dragged to the door. Julius and the man look at each other and decide in that glance not to intervene. The shaft of daylight as the door is opened, men's voices, then the darkness again as the door is shunted closed. The mood changes between them.

The man says, "So here's a story. I had an old uncle, right, who spent his good drinking years in Europe, with our fine army." Again he waves across the grim room. "He told the usual stories about it, women and booze and English cigarettes tasted like mud. But in the years after—" Here the man takes a long drink of his beer and Julius keeps his eyes on him, though already he's tired of this story, he's tired of every army story. "In the years after, my old uncle got religion and wanted to make amends. There was another private in his unit, cave-chested and not a hair on anything, including his eyelashes, and the other men used to pummel him and play jokes on him, the way men do."

The door opens again and an elevator man walks through with his uniform jacket off and draped over one arm. Another crow of voices from the back corner, and as the man crosses the room the other men gesture and begin the story of what has just happened. Between the door and the lintel Julius sees the street outside growing dark.

"So my uncle gets it in his head that he'll find this guy and say he's sorry and all that. Like maybe an apology would turn this guy's life around. He remembers he's from Omaha, which is about a half-day's drive, and he figures there can't be too many fully hairless men in Omaha, though with the way this country's going who knows. Anyway, he drives down there, and finds a phone book and gets the guy's address, but when he goes by the house the place is run-down and when he knocks on the door the woman who answers has never heard of the guy, so he goes to the VFW and asks around. And wouldn't you know of course *they've* heard of him, and after a couple beers my uncle knows everything he needs to know."

The man raises his hand again and Julius makes a feint for his back pocket and the man brushes him off. Now he's plowed, warm flush in his cheeks and crotch. He's hanging on to this story by a thread but still he's pleased to be drinking. The man's earlier comments have faded but not disappeared.

The custodian continues. "What my uncle learned was that there was not a thing to differentiate the other guy from anyone else. He was married and had a job and paid his bills and lived the way people do. He'd even moved to a better neighborhood and every week he came down to the VFW and told his little war story and listened to the others and when he left no one breathed a sigh of relief or was sad to see him go. Seems he'd gotten a wig or something because the others knew him by name but would not have guessed this hairless bit about him. My old uncle saw no sense in apologizing to a man that plays with house money. That kind of man is just fine."

The custodian lets out a long and resolute breath and though Julius understands the story as a weight cast against the man's own lonely life he's not sure he understands the rest of it. He wants to ask what the man means about house money but suddenly he feels terribly sad. He thinks of his father in the front yard waving to each person who passed, the factory women in their scarves and flat shoes, the men coming behind them always at a distance, as if shadowing them for some experiment. Those who waved back and called out his father's name, those who laughed openly. The aluminum chair and the cigarette butts and the reticence of his father's raised hand, raised not for attention but out of duty to the Lord, who demanded that he greet every soul who passed. Then he thinks of Henry and his philosophies, half-formed to suit his needs. Moe Dalitz and the cat-faced men and the other illegitimates who run this legitimate city. Julius wants all those men to mean something other than what they mean.

So he says, "Couldn't you say though that *that's* the story? All those VFW soldiers thought he was no one but your uncle knew he wasn't? Your uncle knew he was Private So-and-So of the U.S. Army who got the shit kicked out of him by a bunch of his pals and had no hair and came back and made a nice life for himself without telling anyone about all the rest. Isn't that the interesting part, the part where he doesn't tell anyone?"

Julius lets the image of his father slide away. The drink in him hotly now. The custodian studies Julius as if he had just arrived. The door opens again and the two men return without the chastened third.

"At any rate, here you are telling me his story," Julius says.

"I told you my uncle's story."

"No, I don't think you did. I think I know more about that man from Omaha than I do about your uncle or you or whatever creed you favor."

Now he's far overplayed it, and the man says, "Look, friend, I told you. I served this country like anybody else."

The man turns the stool around so he sits facing the room and unsettles their little camaraderie. Julius knows better than to follow him into this detachment. Inside the dark bar it is impossible to tell the hour and the desert sunlight through the doorway is the same anytime from eight to eight. Next to Julius the custodian wears fatigue around his eyes but now something bitter too, nerve at being challenged too vigorously, the fretful pride common in men of his class and age.

Julius remembers an early morning in San Dimas not long after his discharge, when he'd spent a sleepless night in a marmalade factory. He'd been chased there by two locals from the Community Squad, who caught him loitering in a park. The factory smelled of orange rind and burned sugar and something else like copper, and at dawn a janitor came and saw him and ran him out. That man had looked nothing like the custodian next to him now but he had the same moralizing tone, the same vocational aptitude. Custodians are like spies, Julius thinks, and wishes he'd thought it earlier. The man has leaned his back against the rim of the bar and sits looking out with his beer glass cupped in both hands. Julius thinks then that he'd like to hear his brother's voice, though it's been so long since he's called.

"Got work in a few," he says, and the custodian nods without looking at him but pleasantly, as if avoiding any real feeling, good or bad, about his departure.

"I liked talking to you, sure enough, and I thank you for the beers."

Again the man nods. He turns his face away and his reedy skin catches the light and in the hard-set line of his jaw is some dignity.

OUTSIDE THE SUN has set and the neon drops bold light in the ditches. A sense of chronology returns. On the last block before Fremont Julius passes a bar with a front drawn up like a garage door, and inside he sees the man who was dragged out of the Cave, sitting at a table near the front. His forehead is gashed and blood has collected at his shirt collar, but he sits drinking whiskey and smiling. At the train station he finds a pay phone, but it's occupied by a weeping man in a quilted jacket, so he heels around to walk another five blocks to El Cortez. He passes a few weary men smoking outside the open doors and walks into the lobby, then slides into a phone booth and rattles in a nickel. The call rings out for a long time, the conciliatory trill like a rope tossed out in the dark, and for a strange moment he wonders if he's dialed the hairless man in Omaha. But then the line opens and there is Lee.

"George Lee," he says, and he hears in his own eager voice the old men who knew their father, who pumped their arms in greeting and said their names over and over as if their names were made of sounds they'd never heard before.

"Well goddammit, Julius," Lee says through high laughter.

"Goddamn nothing. I can't believe you're still at home. You get fired or something?"

"It's past ten in the damn evening, been dark a whole hour."

Julius laughs then too. He wishes he could always be a source of joy.

His brother covers the mouthpiece and calls out and Julius hears a woman's voice.

"Is that Muriel then?" he asks.

"I thought she'd like to know you ain't dead."

"I ain't dead."

"Well hallelujah for that, you son of a bitch."

"Tell me all the news then," Julius says.

"Most of the news is that you ain't dead."

"You go first, it's my nickel and I get to say."

"How am I even supposed to start? Good lord, it's been months and I'll tell you I did think the worst."

"Start with the weather then."

Lee laughs and tells Julius that he hadn't predicted the heat and Julius wouldn't believe the wind and when he says nothing more Julius asks him about work and Lee says it's been all right. The silence goes on a long time then. Finally Lee says, "Now, Julius, you should know something," and then he tells his brother that they've finally sold the house in Kansas and bought that land in the valley. He lists these things in this order as if resistant to their hierarchy.

"Well, shit, there's the news," Julius says.

Lee clears his throat but doesn't speak. The phone booth glass is yellow with tobacco smoke and along the sides are round clearings in the crud where other men have leaned. Julius runs a fingerline through the yellow film then turns this line into an X. Finally Lee says, "Pretty soon there won't be nothing to buy."

"I can't believe she let her mother's house go."

"Yeah, she did," Lee says, in his voice a small relief, that Julius has moved the conversation sideways. "I didn't even know about it. She got it all done on her own, as a surprise to me."

"She didn't need your signature or nothing?"

"I guess not."

"What's the point of being married then?"

"All sorts of points. You should find out yourself."

"You know me."

"I do. That's what I'm saying."

"Boy, we loved her mother's place, remember?" Julius says. "Remember them doorknobs? All that brass, so smooth in your hand."

"Seemed fancy to us, but it was just a regular house," Lee says.

"Don't pretend that's how you felt about it."

A long pause on the line that absorbs the tension between them.

"Well, I hope you got a fair price," Julius says.

"Just at seven thousand."

"That ought to do it then, guess you lucked out for sure."

"It ain't luck."

"No?"

Lee lets this comment settle. On his end of the line a rush of traffic. Then he says, "Them big-city contractors move fast. Put in the floors last week. Not a dime left for furniture, but we did get a little car. The place is still a ways out from town. Town's coming though."

"Sounds prosperous, overall."

"Won't have this number anymore, so you'll have to tell me where to reach you. I've tried a hundred times that other number."

Behind Julius a bell goes off in the track of slot machines. He waits through this noise and then the silence after.

"Brother, I haven't seen you in more than a year," Lee says. "Last time was in Okinawa, and after that—"

Lee doesn't finish this sentence but Julius knows what he's thinking of. He remembers the last time they met, in that sailors' bar. Lee had been so stout then, and so happy, though the night had gone terribly in the end.

"It all turned out just fine," Julius says.

"It don't necessarily seem that way to me."

"It wasn't nothing, really, I told you that."

"Why'd they send you home then?"

"Why are you asking me now?"

Lee doesn't answer.

"I think they figured they could just dock my pay and get some money out of it," Julius says.

"Out of what?"

"I told you, just a card game. Bad luck I got caught is all."

"That ain't what I'm saying and you know it."

Julius closes his eyes and lets the silence stretch out between them.

Finally Lee says, "You've been three hours away all this time and couldn't even jump a train."

"What would've been the point?"

"I guess I'm saying you can't be mad."

"I didn't say I was mad."

Julius cradles the receiver and fishes for cigarettes and comes up with an empty pack.

"I'm doing all right now, though," he says.

"But you ain't in L.A.?"

"Got too crowded there."

In his mind Julius sees the little house in the valley and the river running by. Muriel standing in the kitchen like a prairie vignette, shovel propped by the door and a bucket of wash water on the porch, though surely the view behind is treed and without clouds and crisscrossed by powerlines and the white contrails of military planes headed out to the coast. He sees himself there as a child but he can't see himself any other way. His brother is there in his enlisteds, ironed flat as housesiding, and then their father on a Sunday playing checkers with the board they'd made from shingle. They had everything now.

"I ain't in any trouble. Got a real good job at the moment, good little thing going."

"Well, I'm glad to hear it but that don't change what was supposed to happen. It don't change that you didn't call."

"I just wasn't in no position to."

"There's a damn phone every ten feet anymore."

"It was you all went on ahead."

"How long you think we'd wait, huh? Not like you had any discharge to contribute."

The operator comes on for another nickel and Julius presses the hard plastic of the receiver between his cheek and shoulder and wiggles his pocket and finds one more coin there.

"Got just one more nickel, George Lee."

Julius drops the nickel, then neither speaks. The argument sputters out. He imagines Muriel's house and her hissing radiators and how they'd all been together there.

"She doing okay then? Muriel?"

"Oh sure," Lee says, and in the pause that follows Julius senses some discord. He thinks about her eager voice on the phone.

"I can't get her too excited about this new place, but she loves that little car," Lee says. "And that's fine, you know, women need things they can't explain. The whole world is different to them."

"True enough," Julius says. He makes another X in the glass. The floor of the booth is covered with black shoe scuffs and cigarette butts left by other lingerers. He thinks of that night he and Muriel talked so long. He'd been standing in a phone booth much like this one, on the corner of Fourth and Alameda, in the hour between when the produce train headed east and the railway post headed west, rattling past the flimsy apartment where he was staying. He recalls her voice as a gentle intervention in that window of silence, a silence that had come to unnerve him after so much regular noise. He'd never spent any time at all talking to women and it felt luxurious to him. He'd imagined her in pegged pants and a man's shirt, the way women were sometimes in movies, just laid or about to be laid, at ease in a world that desired them. It is not just Lee's voice he wants then, but the sound of both of them together.

"Is that her calling you now?" he asks his brother, though on the other end is static.

"I don't hear nothing," Lee says, and Julius can sense his confusion, his slight unwitting concern.

"Should you holler back just in case?"

And his brother agreeably does, and there distorted by the door and the hallway and the many miles is Muriel's voice calling back to Lee, though Julius can't make out what she's said.

"She says hello and it's about damn time."

"Well, hello back then. Hello back."

The slots go off again and a man's voice calls out and Julius wonders who he is and if he's won or if he might be searching for someone. No voice calls back and the slot-bells jingle and the casino is quiet again. Julius says, "You know what, tell me where you'll be. It's time I sent a letter to you now."

A moment of silence on the line and then Lee says, "If that's your price," and gives Julius the new address.

"I'm going to sit down this very afternoon and write you," Julius says.

Then the operator is on again and Julius leans against the wall of the booth until the call drops. For a moment he stands there listening to the hum of the open line.

Outside the lobby a half-dozen tournament men are breaking up, walking in different directions down Sixth, two of them slipping through the alley that lets out onto Las Vegas Boulevard. Julius tries to imagine Muriel's face. He wonders what it would be like to walk through the streets of any town with a beautiful woman and be seen that way. What it must feel like to his brother, to be given that chance.

Next to the phone booth is a cigarette machine. Julius steps out and nudges the machine but no loose packs fall through. He stands in the lobby looking out, then follows the tournament men down the alley and back toward the station. The evening train has arrived and the newcomers take the first steps of their pilgrimage. Signs going up on the corners for another detonation in a few days' time, this one called Galileo, smaller signs claiming sightings of the Russian satellite, which no one has confirmed. Then Julius sees Henry at the curb in front of the Golden Nugget. He is leaned into another man who stands counting chips in open view. This other man hands half the stack to Henry, punches him lightly on the shoulder and walks away. Henry pushes back his hair and glances around. Julius waits for Henry to leave and then waits a few minutes longer before he turns away.

Back at the Squaw the room is empty. Julius lies on his back looking up at the ceiling, thinking of his brother's new house. His brother sleeping beside his wife while outside the cypress trees stand in their custodial lines. He tries to imagine Henry there. He recalls a moment at the beginning of their affair, Henry standing naked in the middle of the room, half-hard, the light from the bathroom covering his brown skin and recasting it bronze, the withered arm like a remnant not of the past but of a whole other existence, as if he had borrowed it from someone older and more knowing. Somehow his injury never made him seem hurt. It lent him instead an air of placatory misfortune, as if he had taken someone else's trauma out of pity. Henry looked at Julius so intently that he thought he might die waiting for Henry to touch him. *You go on home, Joey, and grow up to be strong and straight,* he said. He held the good hand over his heart.

And Julius said, *Shane, come back*. Henry lifted his hand and aimed his finger up at the ceiling like a movie outlaw bringing down a bank. Posed like that, a figure straight out of a western but the kind of western they never find to watch, one in which the lens follows not the sheriff or the boy but the dark bandit, across the mountain and back to the hideout, inside the curtained room where he undresses.

SOME DAYS LATER Julius sleeps late and wakes with Henry beside him. He buys two cups of coffee in the lobby and he and Henry sit drinking them on the bed while the television plays a football game. The plaid bedspread pulled up and tucked into the space between the wall and the mattress, pulled slick as the back of a knee, ashes in the embroidery. Julius's other shirt hung to dry in the shower, his jeans folded on the chair with the wallet still in the pocket. Henry in his white undershirt with his legs planked out and crossed at the ankles is a picture of honest manhood. The two men look at each other, amused by the light domesticity of the scene.

"Yes, ma'am," Henry says.

"Go, Rams," Julius says.

Outside Sunday morning quiet, the peculiar hour between the all-nighters and the all-dayers, when the sidewalks are empty on Fremont Street and the gritter boys come out for dropped change. In this quiet Julius can hear, from six blocks away, the alarm calls of slot machines and the barkers with their coupons for free pulls and buffets. For a while they sit without speaking while the television plays on low. They do not touch or sit close enough to touch, but in the conjugal spirit of the morning they begin to talk of the places they're from. Henry tells him again of the parks and plazas of Tijuana, where he spent the years after the war.

"I hate to say this to you now, given my feelings. But a man can earn a good living down there with all the sailors and the husbands from California, who can't find love in the northern cities no more."

"Oh I'm sure of it, they've got all those cities copped up now, from San Fran to San Diego."

"I had a bit of time in San Diego too, but I'll tell you there's a city doesn't want no greasers."

"You ain't no greaser."

"You tell that to the cops."

"They run you out?"

"Worse than that even. I had a decent job there but I messed it up."

"How so then?"

"Like you want to know."

"I do."

Henry snorts. He uncrosses his legs and recrosses them and smooths the thighs of his jeans.

"They only let greasers do two things and that's row crops or horses."

"So it was cotton then."

"What makes you think I don't know horses?"

Julius laughs.

"Well, a third thing, if you count billiards," Henry says then.

"I never saw you hit a pocket."

"Then you know it ain't billiards."

Julius hips over and reaches for his jeans on the chair and takes a fold of bills from the back pocket and peels off a dollar and snaps it.

"I'll take you a quarter a game over at the Silver Palace."

"You got it, bud."

Julius drops the dollar on the bed and leans back, but the joke doesn't last.

"There was just the one place in San Diego, when I was there," Henry says. "The Chester Hotel. You never went south that far, huh? Just as well. Fine old building though, right by the ocean, and back then you could find just about anybody there."

Henry lights a cigarette and pauses a moment before he says, "I wouldn't be surprised if that place is burned to the ground by now, though. They raided it practically once a month. It's an easier time in Mexico. In Mexico even I look pure American. Brings a premium with the husbands."

Henry glances up at Julius to see how he reacts to this. The room seems to hold his revelation like a draft. On the black-and-white television comes an advertisement for color televisions. The woman selling them wears a dress shaped like a conch, lipped at the top around her shoulders and darker than the background. She gestures toward the tower of new televisions like a witch.

Finally Henry says, "This is better than any damn hotel or husbands, I'll say that. Having a real job and being here with you."

"You ought to consider playing cards somewhere else, you want to keep that job," Julius says, though he's thinking something else.

"I hear you every time you say that."

"There's that tournament at El Cortez."

"Hoo, now there's an easy time," Henry says. "You want your dollar, go there. It's all tourists who saw blackjack in a movie."

"So why you need a left-hand man then?"

"Who says I got a left-hand man?"

Julius doesn't answer. He thinks of the rent boys he'd known in L.A. Their sharp division between sex and love, which they seemed always willing to revise for the least tenderness, and their clear satisfaction in the disappointment that followed, as if it proved all over again the line they'd drawn between body and soul. How they'd looked when the cops gathered them or they took some other beating, not sad but exalted. Not for the first time he imagines Henry among them, though now there is this other thing, which he had not been sure of before.

"All I mean is, you got me. You don't need to play partners with no one."

"I got you in this room but nowhere else," says Henry. He pushes back his fine hair and wets his lips and waits. Then he says, "I was at the Boulder Club the other night and they got a new dealer, sits facing the door. When he thumbs up that hole card you could see it from a hundred feet away."

"That ain't something you should know."

"But I do know it."

"You oughta be playing chuck-a-luck with the wives, you want an easy hand."

"Well okay, I'd do that if you came along, friend."

"You'd be just as likely to get me to church."

"Well then I'll try that, too."

Julius nods gently. Henry rises and checks the pocket of his trousers and then the bureau drawer and then Julius's jacket draped over the chair. His own jacket hangs from the bathroom knob and he searches those pockets and finds a cigarette package and a matchbook and a handful of other things. He lights a cigarette and speaks through the exhale.

"If I ever went back to San Diego I think I'd last about a day. I couldn't stand to look at another damn palm tree, and in them flops you have to sleep ass to elbow. Ain't even no good cardrooms. No, I'd go back to Mexico. I can tell by your look you've never been there and never thought of going. But I'll tell you, you meet all sorts."

"Got all sorts here."

Henry sifts through the items in his hand and dumps the matchbook and some coins on the dresser. He squints against the lipped cigarette and turns to Julius. Then he uncoils a short block chain and regards it.

"I might pawn it, what do you think? Hardly good for anything."

"You do what you want, though it does lend you a bit of seriousness, which you need."

"I bet you never thought a person could win such a thing in a trick-taking game."

"Certainly not in a game meant for women," Julius says.

Henry lets the chain fall straight from his open fingers. At the end of it is a tiny pistol. Henry told Julius he'd won it in a game of pitch on the way to Sioux Falls. The chain is dainty, rubbed smooth; the pistol no larger than a thumb and dry as paloverde.

Henry points the gun at Julius and says, "Pow."

Julius clasps his hand against his heart and bolts backward.

"You're a fine shot," he says.

Henry puts the gun on the bureau, stubs out the cigarette, and comes back to bed.

"The thing with money is, it don't last if you spend it. Always got to have more."

"Now there's the truth."

"A man will do more for money than he will for love."

Henry rolls to him and Julius waits a long moment before rolling too.

The erotic taste of the other man's breath released into the space between them. For ten minutes, longer, they lie this way, their knees threaded together, chests touching, kissing then stopping to look then kissing again, neither man willing to move the game forward. Julius feels not sexual jealousy but something more complicated. He imagines Henry as a younger man, a jockey's groom at some two-bit place or a picker in a hot field, boot hitched up against a fence or a truck, then further back, a child playing stickball on a dirt road. Henry in his small existence with no awareness of Julius, Julius somewhere with no knowledge of him, two hands chasing each other on a watch face. Julius taking a shower or having a drink or shoveling snow while two thousand miles away Henry's body was engaged in some other act, unrelated but simultaneous. In this magical overlap a sense of Henry's childhood as part of his own, a sense of owning too that boy in the golden city with his ready mouth. The man who tricked with men for money once a child always fated for that.

Finally Henry pulls away and bends around to glance at his watch.

"Now what do you say, huh," he says. "That Boulder Club table clears out this time of day."

"Honey," Julius says and the word pleases them both.

"Honey what."

Henry kisses Julius again and Julius thinks of his father and the times he'd gone with him to church, near the end of the man's life. Before his reformation he had been the kind of man everyone wanted to please. And by simple paternal alchemy Julius had been left with that reservoir of energy, that desire to be visible to the single person whose pleasure mattered. He knew his brother was this way too. They were in the service when their father died and there was no funeral and no mourners, just a notice in the post. Their little house was razed and they never went back. He thinks of his brother's new house, the fine turn his life has taken.

"You know what, I'll play just to shut you up," Julius says finally.

"There's my boy."

"I'm telling you, though, keep it simple. I ain't no cheat at heart."

"You won't even have to do nothing but win."

Henry kisses him again. Julius smells the hot smell of him and then both men leave the bed. Together they dress and tuck in their shirts and pull on their boots and step out into the still-warm day, the sun beginning its drift down into the valley. They walk without speaking past the rooming houses and municipal buildings and the little half-stocked bodegas, the stuff of real life not meant for tourists, toward the lights of downtown.

IN LAS VEGAS it is not possible for any man to forget where he is. Often Julius has considered this. Perhaps on some mornings in winter, or late summer as it is now, when the light comes in low but just as instantly, a man might wake on the tenth floor of some hotel and in the still-dark room confuse for a moment the walls or the slant of light for the white plains of his youth. But such confusion could happen anywhere away from home. As soon as his head returned to him he would see the lighted figures against the hotel drapes, the names of casinos and the price of a buffet dinner. And if he stands to part the drapes he will see the far mountains shadowed into landscape, the clouds cast down onto them, then the once green expanse of the ancient meadow that gives the city its name, then the strips of buildings and their peculiar grace. He might eat, he might work, he might find a store and buy a pack of cigarettes, but he has no need of other things: booze will be offered to him, and sex, and he won't need a toothbrush or bar of soap. In other famous cities of the West, with their own famous geography, their memorable architecture, a man might go about an ordinary day and never think about where he is, because he is too busy trying to get what this other city gives up willingly.

For two weeks Julius and Henry spook the blackjack tables at the Boulder Club an hour at a time. Julius sits at the sloppy dealer's table and Henry sits at the table behind the dealer's back. Henry watches as the dealer corners up the hole card and then he judges the other cards on the table and the money in play. He drinks and laughs and sends Julius signals and Julius plays accordingly. Sometimes there is little to win and sometimes the tables are too crowded and in any case they do not stay together long. As they learn the cheat's intricacies they run things quietly, cashing out no more than thirty dollars a night. Of course Henry could make more with another, more daring man, but this is the delicate agreement they've made.

Each night Julius worries that above the tables a man in a catwalk watches them sit across from each other, that he studies them for palms and marking, for playing two sides against the men to their left, who will draw after them. But Henry's little gestures, the small differences in his laughter—these are things only Julius knows. After a week they have two hundred dollars between them and they each buy a coat and tie and Julius has his boots shined. Henry hails a cab on Fremont Street and hands the driver a twenty to take them all the way to the Aces High Casino in Boulder City, where they eat steak on an open terrace overlooking the dam. A piano man plays loose ragtime and all around them are couples and businessmen and old women in lace gloves drinking champagne and they are among these people as birds are among trees.

After dinner they walk across the dam on Route 93. The lighted roof of the Aces High rises behind the wall of stone. The sky is so dark it plunges into the massive lake and all the way to the bottom like a cataract. Julius imagines that the stars sit among the bones of men there, on the lake bed. He and Henry stand a long time looking from east to west across the canyon where the concrete is pressed by the rock into the curved shape of the dam. It seems to be held there by pressure and nothing else.

Henry says, "It almost looks like it's been here forever."

"And will be forevermore," Julius says.

They look at each other and like lovers everywhere take such claims about the world to be their own fortune. Henry glances around and moves back into the shadow of a penstock where the darkness is complete and Julius moves into the dark with him and kisses him. And though both men pull away then and leave the shadow one at a time, there is still some victory in it. Back at the Aces they dance and drink until the dawn starts to leaven the vast desert.

Once home at the Squaw they bounce the bed so hard the manager comes around the corner and knocks at the door and Henry calls out in a convincing falsetto that he ought to go to the pictures or get himself a Gulch lady if he's so hard up for love. "At least my loneliness don't make no noise, girl," the man hollers through the door and Julius and Henry laugh behind their hands until he leaves.

In the new quiet demanded of them they touch slow and easy, but inside Julius is wholly gone. If he could turn his love into a noise it would be the noise of a bomb in the far desert, one that reaches the city in delay. The dawn sight of the cloud drawing up is the spectacle and the miracle but still at its distance could be a mere trick of the eye. Sometimes whole minutes later comes the convulsive thud, as if the sound was the sound of time passing and could not be rushed, and only then is the bomb real. No man could make that sound and no man could stop it. It is the sound of time itself coming forward and catching them where they stand.

AT THE END of the third week Henry says they ought to run the outside table at the Nugget, where they've added two tables tight together with new dealers and high limits. The house stands at seventeen and the splits are twice as good as the Boulder Club and they could make a grand in ten quick deals. Julius refuses and makes a point about working there and in that way being known and Henry says they can keep playing for nothing if that's all Julius wants. He lets his eyelids sink beautifully and Julius knows that thirty dollars a day was never going to last. He tries to kiss this knowledge away and when that doesn't seem enough he lets Henry stack him at the Boulder Club for an extra hundred and when the chips are cashed he turns his money over and he feels weak and lonesome but he's bought them time.

Another night they work the peek together and when they switch sides Henry grabs Julius by the collar and kisses his neck and Julius pulls away and scolds him but then lets Henry kneel and take him in his mouth and when a noise in the stairwell sends them away from each other the feeling is of great and reckless dread. Back in the room they argue and Julius throws a glancing punch that leaves a mark and then he has something to apologize for. He does and they make up and the next morning play slow stud at Binion's and don't cheat at all, but that evening another argument sends them sprawling. Henry takes the night on the town. When he returns at dawn he is drunk and contrite and for a long time they sit side by side on the bed not knowing what to say until finally they have dry and disconsolate sex that makes them both come at once.

When the sun rises they give in to sleep. Julius dreams of nothing and when he wakes the room is hot and he gets up and opens the bathroom window and stands a long time in the small breeze it offers. He thinks of the ride from Tokyo to Inchon and the men leaned against the bulkheads naming off the things they loved and would like to have again: peanut butter, sex, American beer. They prayed for these things and not for their own lives. Julius had thought not of objects or pleasures but of his father. He'd wondered abstractly if the love of God and fathers was so lasting because it could be neither denied nor consummated. It was always on its way, the way Inchon was, and heaven, the way money and chance outpaced you and did not end. He could keep refusing or he could give in but neither would protect him.

Now, he has nowhere else to go. There was Kansas and Los Angeles and the long gray slice of Asia and in all those places he'd been a petty thief and a faggot and alone. Outside his window is the noise of the city moving toward darkness and Julius leaves the bathroom and wakes Henry with his mouth and the night goes by sweet and quiet, and after work they sleep and wake together in the desert morning to birdsong thin as reed outside the covered windows of the Squaw.

SOME NIGHTS LATER Julius works the peek alone. The catwalk has lost the dusty heat of summer and he watches through the windows with his jacket buttoned all the way up against the chill. Below him nothing much. All rules and pure luck on the floor, as if the games of craps and faro were simple acts of trade. Cigar smoke blown politely up and away from the wives. But when he checks the northern glass he sees below the shape of Henry's ears and shoulders. From above the top of his head is dark and strangely unfamiliar, like the picture Julius had seen of the earth from space, that fragile and that abandoned. The table is half-full and Henry has a nice stack. It is two A.M. or nearly. At the far end, an old-timer in a corduroy jacket plays by the book; at the table behind are two men, one dark-eyed and brunet, the other with honeyed hair slicked back. Both with their hats on their knees, playing loose and mean. Julius stands watching and for a few unremarkable hands sees nothing unusual. He thinks Henry must be waiting out the lonely night for Julius's shift to end. A warm and anticipatory feeling, then another thought comes through and darkens it. As Julius watches, Henry fails to hit a low draw and leaves the dealer with a ten that busts him out. At the other table the blond takes a five and clears the pot and winks at no one. Julius watches more closely. Another few hands like this, Henry standing low and busting first the old-timer and then the dealer. Behind, the blond smiling and clowning, touching his ear and then his nose. From above Julius thinks with clear and sudden terror how easy such a game is to spot, when it's your own game.

Henry's dealer cracks the deck again. Julius wonders if the blond is older or younger than Henry and where he might be from. Of course Henry knows that Julius is above tonight, he has come to be found out. It's a bluff, or something like it. Julius thinks of the few things he knows about his lover, the little biography. The larger things that lovers know, which have to do with essence or hurt. He thinks of what he'll say later, if he says anything at all. On the next deal Henry hits a seventeen and steals an eight that would have made the old-timer's hand, busting them both. Henry flutters his chips in a short stack. Behind, the blond hits a nineteen with a deuce and hollers out his pleasure and Henry regards the blond so levelly that Julius sees everything he fears.

Suddenly a man in a black suit appears. He stands by the sports book a few feet away, watching Henry's table. He lights a cigarette and waits. Julius knows who this man is. Not his name or his specific story but his role here. Behind him the sports book is empty except for a single man on a telephone leaned halfway across the bar. The sign above the bar reads, in ironic script, *We are as close to you as your telephone.* The man in the black suit taps his ash onto the floor.

Julius leaves the window and descends the stairs and in the back room finds the cat-faced men sitting across from each other, one man's feet on the other man's chair rung, one passing another a copy of *Life* magazine. They don't look up at him and when he tells them a blond is spooking at the new high-limit table they merely nod. One slaps the magazine closed and says, "Who's his man then?" and Julius blinks but does not answer. He sees the way it all might go and it hurts him to see it, to think about doing it. To consider what it might solve for him.

The man looks over the magazine at Julius's hesitant form and finally Julius says, "Seems like the geezer, in the corduroy coat."

Both men stand and Julius climbs the stairs again. Back at the glass he watches. He'd like to make a noise or hold his lighter to the window to make Henry look up and see him, but he knows Henry will know what he's done. The cat-faced men emerge into the pit. Above them the round globes slick their hair in white light. The sports book is empty now and the man in the black suit has drifted past its edge. The cat-faced men smile slow and wide and for a moment Julius almost loves them, as he has loved other men who carried some part of his fate. The way he loved sergeants and preachers. Henry sees them coming and looks up and though the glass above is black and indifferent Julius tosses down a little wave. Henry jerks his pretty chin and closes his eyes but the men do not raise him. Instead one man takes the old-timer by the elbow and the other leans to whisper something and the man stands obligingly and is walked away. Across, the blond stands and takes his stack and is met at the edge of the pit by another suited man. Henry stares ahead and plays another round and then another and finally he stands and moves out of Julius's view and Julius does not see him again.

Later, back at the Squaw, Julius undresses in the dark. Shadows on the inside of the drapes. He waits for the knock and when it doesn't come he climbs under the covers. The sun is rising. He thinks of other men he's busted and the confederacies he's sniffed out and he knows where the blond is headed now. He feels a vindication that sickens him. He waits a long time. Sleep hovers close and he thinks of Henry tipped far back, spine concave, over the edge of the table or bed, nipples like dimes, until his shoulders disappear and his face disappears and his body is a boy's body, sweet belly soft and unmuscled, brown nipples flat against his chest. It feels like another childhood, this moment Henry's face disappears into their lovemaking, the inverse exposure of it, a chance for Julius to see him as he might have been before he was marked off as anyone, before he even had a name. In his waiting and his valor Julius tries to imagine a grateful scene. He tries to imagine the door opening and his lover entering, but he falls asleep and wakes alone.

THE NEXT DAY he looks for Henry in the rooming house behind the Moulin Rouge and at the clubs on the edge of Glitter Gulch, and when he doesn't find him there he goes back to the Squaw and waits. The day drags on strangely and he begins to worry. After work he drinks at the bar until noon and stumbles drunk through the white streets and sleeps with the door open. He is woken by shouts from the vacant lot and he rises and stands in the doorway in his underwear and watches as the streetlight clicks through the colors. He bathes and pulls on the same clothes and goes to work again and comes home after and watches *Gunsmoke* and does not sleep. When again it is afternoon and Henry has not appeared, Julius leaves a note and rises and walks toward Fremont. At the Mormon joint he goes on a tear so profitable it is a form of violence, and with pockets bulging and fists clenched he is asked politely by the pit boss to find another place to play until his luck passes. Instead he stands and walks to the roulette table, lays everything on red and loses. He stares at the boss squarely and returns to the faro table. He smokes so many cigarettes his eyes twitch. He sits so long and so alertly that he believes he can tell which type of liquor is being poured at the bar behind him by the smell and the sound of the liquid in the glass, by the clink the bottle makes as it is removed from the shelf.

The next morning after work he returns to the Squaw and bolts the door and pulls the chain across. The week's sheets are gray with dust and skin and hair oil but he will not strip them to place outside for the maid. In the dirty curl of bedclothes is evidence that Henry has slept and woken there. He flings off the bedspread and shakes it and then he pulls out all the drawers and dumps them and there are Henry's shirts and socks and a bale of bills totaling sixty dollars and his lover's best jeans and the watch fob. He kicks apart the shirts, then gathers them and throws them in the corner. Then he lifts the fob and holds it in the lamplight. The gun is slightly larger than his thumb and rounded at the handle like an umbrella, the trigger a loose button on the side. He slides into the grip and thumbs back the hammer and presses the trigger with the tip of his middle finger. He holds it to his temple. Henry would not leave it, no matter how angry he is. He might leave his socks and his jeans but not the money and not this. Julius sees again the men coming toward the table and the blond being lifted. He sees Henry stand, but after this he cannot find him in his memory; he disappears past the edge of the glass. Julius presses the button and the hammer clicks softly and he feels the firing pin coil out and tremble the metal against his skin.

THAT NIGHT IN the back room the two cat-faced men are waiting for him.

"Here's our good man," one says, and together they face him gravely. Both men reach toward Julius and place a hand on each hard shoulder, one man's left and the other man's right pressing him together, so that facing them Julius has the impression of being embraced, of being included in a circle of understanding. He decides to risk the question.

"I guess you ran them out of town, huh."

"Who's that then?" asks the man on his right.

"Them blackjack skippers," Julius says.

"There's a fine car on the dawn train for spooks," says the man on his left.

"The old-timer gave us trouble," says the other.

"Can't take them to the back eighty these days," the first man says sadly.

The men are still hemming him but seem to have forgotten his presence. Julius cannot risk another question and the men's hands are heavy. He sniffs and they look down at him and both smile the way men smile at other people's dogs. They drop their hands.

"Good thing for your steady will," says the first man, taking a roll of bills from his breast pocket.

"What about those others at the new tables, the greaser and the brunet?" asks the other.

"What about them?" Julius asks.

"You knew the greaser, before," says the other.

"Not well. We work together, here," Julius says.

"He played here often. But not with you."

"No, I ain't never played here."

The man regards him but does not answer. He clicks three bills from the stack and puts them in his coat pocket, as if he is compensating himself for the chore before him now. Then he nods to the other man who holds out an envelope. Julius takes it and lifts the flap and sees a stack of chips from the Boulder Club, where he'd played with Henry just three nights before.

"You hadn't played together *here*," the first man says.

Julius catches his emphasis. He shakes his head and lets the envelope flap closed.

"I ain't never taken nothing from here," Julius says, but the men do not acknowledge him.

"I don't expect you'd like to see your friend again, considering."

Julius shakes his head again but slowly this time.

"I bet nobody on the dawn train wanted to see him either, or in the place he got off."

The man snaps his fingers strangely then reaches up to straighten his tie. For a long moment Julius stands without understanding. Then the first man steps forward and holds open the office door, and when Julius walks through it both men follow him across the casino floor and through the front doors to the sidewalk, where they wait until he reaches the corner. Julius turns back once and sees them there, watching him. As he walks the full meaning comes to him and at Carson Avenue he breaks into a run.

At the Squaw he collects his old shirt and boots and the jacket and tie. He fishes a hand through the bureau drawer for underwear and socks. When his fingers catch Henry's gun he pulls it out. He shoves the fob and the envelope in his pocket and rolls his shirt and razor in a motel towel and leaves the room key on the television set. He takes the rolled towel from his busted boots and slips it under his arm, then leans against the doorway to pull the boots on. Then, with the good jeans and the jacket tossed over his shoulder and the good boots in his hands he leaves the way he came, on the evening train headed north.

In Pahrump he waits for the mail train to Indian Springs and pays a dollar for the open coach. When he arrives it is nearly noon. He takes a room on the second floor of a hotel downtown. Inside the room he locks the door and pulls the chain across and then sets the single chair against the knob. He turns on the television and dials through the midday news, which shows a mockup of the Russian satellite, and he moves past this channel to a black-and-white western. He rolls the volume knob all the way down. On the screen a pair of silent cowboys plan something across a barroom table. Behind them the walls of the barroom are gilt in punched tin; in black-and-white they look like snowfall.

Julius goes to the window and fingers the curtain back and stands looking out at the little town. To the south the long pull of the desert and to the north a hem of mountains. Just across the street a sign that names the town. He remembers a long way back, to the man from Iowa. For a moment he sees himself at the bar with that man the day he arrived. He wonders how long the cat-faced men had known, and thinking back through the weeks of play with Henry makes him cringe with shame and longing. Worse, the men had made a fool of him. They had let him come down with his reconnaissance and his little half-story about the blond and the old man, and they let Henry play on until Julius left the peek and then they made Julius wait three days in suspense. They hadn't dropped him from the roof or knifed him in an alley, but they had made their knowledge a kind of torture, and now even though he's out of their proximity he is not beyond the reach of this knowledge, and this makes him more afraid than love does.

He closes the curtain and turns back to the television. He slips off his boot and finds the Iowan's bill there. The ink is gone from the edges and the folds worn to lace, but it is spendable. He needs to think and to sleep but he worries that sleep won't come. In the room beneath him another television plays the same program but with the volume up high so he hears the music and the cowboys' dialogue as if damped by water, while on his own screen the men in profile ride through a landscape like the one outside his window but a hundred years ago and brighter than any city.

THAT NIGHT JULIUS dreams that he is inside Henry's dream. That wherever Henry is sleeping, in a rooming house in San Diego or in the county jail, his dreams are of Kansas, of Muriel's mother's house. In the dream Henry walks through arched vistas of bluestem and foxtail barley, grass so tall and gently blown it is like a sea churning, waist deep, lighter than water. Julius doesn't know if this is the past or the future. Henry enters the house and goes up the stairs to the room where Muriel used to sleep, and Julius sees himself inside this dream, lying in bed in the middle of the day. All the windows open and the breeze blowing through. Birds flying through quick as fingers snapping. They are both aware of the passing sky above them, a rain coming fast. Julius turns and the sheet falls back and he is naked. Henry moves toward the bed. The rain begins, first a few noticed drops and then a thousand more. As Henry knees up onto the bed he glances again out the window at the barley and the unkempt lawn, the silvery boundary between them, the graying sky behind them, the grass merely a stage to play out this moment. Say it's billiards, Henry says, say it's horses. He whispers this to Julius inside the dream, and to the sleeping Julius on the edge of the dream, while outside in the yard the rain fails on the upward-straining grass.

IN THE MORNING Julius goes downtown and finds a pawnshop where he sells the good boots and jeans and the jacket and tie. He adds all this up and he needs three or four times that to get even a few days away from Vegas and the cat-faced men, and a hundred times more to find Henry, if what he knows about Tijuana and hustlers is true. He hates that this is true and that he knows it and he hates the only option he has. He asks around and the locals thumb him north and he hitches a ride to a ranch some miles away, sprawled out among the scrub and backed against a ledge of orange rock. It is a cheerless operation, a few lilting buildings with tin roofs peeling up in the heat, a split-rail fence weathered a dilute gray. A man with an eyepatch and shoulders as broad as a doorway—much broader than the man from Iowa, who, when he slept, curled his thin shoulders forward like someone anticipating a blow—waves to Julius from a sagging porch.

Julius approaches him. "I heard you had horses. Mustangs."

The man thinks this over. He looks at Julius and then scans the horizon, his hand shielding his one good eye, which is blue as a jay. Julius sees only four horses bent over a trough some distance away, and across the rock and scrub in all directions he sees nothing else.

"Sure," the man says. He stands and bangs his boots against the porch to get them fully on again. They walk toward the little group of horses standing in the scrub. There are two gray horses and a spotted one with a rump raised high and only a patch of tail. At the end of the trough is a ewe-necked mare, mane long and blonde as hell.

"Which one you want?"

"Those are mustangs?" Julius asks, thinking maybe the man hasn't understood him. The man shifts between one short leg and another, so slow it seems impossible, as if the entire weight of his considerable breadth were moving from one place to a wholly other one. He blinks once, then again.

"Yeah," the man says.

He can't show up empty-handed and he can't turn around. He likes the one with the blonde mane, haunches like tractor tires. She might be enough for his brother's forgiveness, for what has already happened and for what comes next. He thinks about the house and his brother's prosperity and he knows where his brother would keep a dollar.

The man exhales mightily. "Oh, that one," he says, and shakes his head a little, looking at the ground. "That one's wild as lightning."

Julius looks again at the golden horse, who stands there eating.

"All the better," he says.

The man shrugs, quotes him a price half what the man from Iowa told him, and Julius feels the whole thing is fated. He hands over the hundred-dollar bill and the man hands him back the remainder in dented fives. In town he buys a third-hand truck and a trailer for a song and drives the bouncing mess back to the ranch to collect the horse, who balks at the ramp but obliges after a switch from the man, who leaves the rest to Julius. In the cab Julius waves back his hair and flicks out the legs of his jeans. He thinks of the man from Iowa with his woman's back, his little choking cries into the pillow, before this the lonely phone booth and Muriel's story of the horses and the money in her letter. He'd spend a day in San Diego and eat a hot meal and see his brother and his brother's wife. The decent and natural fact of their lives.

He drives slowly back through town. He worries he won't make it, that the horse will bust loose and run down the highway like the wild thing he wants her to be, that he will lose this moment and the mistakes that brought it to him. A few cars pass him and honk, but it is not so far and he is young. He thinks of Henry's pink lips, then his shoulders, then his body. That the one-eyed Mexican was not Mexican at all, that the horses were fed by trough in the desert scrub, makes no difference to him. Between the pickup and the trailer and the golden, wet-eyed horse, he'd paid a hundred dollars for an enterprise worth less than half that, but it feels necessary to him. It feels necessary to start again in just this way.

II.

FIVE

The bluffs

The days shorten and in the evening the wind comes down the river and blows the leaves from the trees so they settle in heaps against the new house. Lines of smoke band across the northern sky and anyone outside or near an open window can smell the burn of the freeway site, inside it the brackish hint of the river. Lee and Muriel spend their days at work in town, then evenings in the new house. They bring the card table from the apartment and buy two folding chairs at thrift. In a coffee can they save their wages toward a real bed and a Naugahyde sofa and they still have a long way to go. In the backyard Lee sows grass seed, though the season is late and the men at the dry goods tell him it will drown in the rainy season, that winter crows will peck it until it's gone.

One afternoon they are in the front yard breaking up dirt clods with a garden hoe and re-spreading the dirt level to the curtilage. Across the road another house is going up, the frame is straight as teeth against the vista. The adjacent lot is still unsold but the next two are graded and mapped out for foundations. At the edge of their own lot a line of trees has been left and marks the northern edge, behind the house the river runs low and soft. Against the setting sun Muriel slants her hand to her forehead and squints. From the direction of the city comes an old GMC pickup with a trailer, barreling through the dust it makes. The pickup slows to a crawl. She looks at her husband and he steps forward. The truck turns sharply into their drive and stops, the trailer jacked at a sharp angle, one set of tires still on the road, and from the cab Julius emerges without turning off the engine.

"I'll be damned," Lee says.

Julius walks toward him and shrugs his shoulders, as if he too disbelieves his presence there. They meet in the dusty yard and Lee takes his brother in a hard hug and thumps him on the back with the flat palm of his hand and says again, "I'll be damned."

Muriel watches this without moving. She is wearing a pair of old canvas pants and a workshirt tied in a quick knot at the tails. She thinks she must seem like a country housewife inured to beauty. Over Lee's shoulder she catches Julius's gaze and returns it.

"Look what you've done," Julius says and waves to take in the house and the lot. "How about old Dad, huh? Wouldn't he be choking on this. You got a whole acre here?"

Close to him now Muriel can see the squareness of his chin and his wide ears, and though she would not have been able to remember them precisely they are as familiar to her as grass. A new feeling then, something like disappointment. She sets her face and her shoulders coldly against this feeling.

"Not even a postcard, to say you're coming?" Lee says.

"You can count on me for surprise," Julius says. His voice is cheery but it rings against his teeth and comes out pitched too high. Behind them the truck still idles, halfway on the road. Lee looks across the front yard at the truck and then up at his brother. Julius traces a light circle in the dirt with the toe of his boot, the sound of the engine ringing against the tree line. For a moment the silence between them is heavy enough to stand on.

"I might pull all the way in, if you don't mind me parking this heap in your fine yard," Julius says.

"Oh, sure thing," Lee says. Then, "You bet." He turns to Muriel with a look so open she sees the child in him. They watch Julius back the truck out of the drive a few feet to get the trailer straightened out. He pulls forward and the truck wheel digs into the descending bank of the drive and spins dirt out in a trough.

"That's a horse trailer," Lee says to Muriel.

She cannot reconcile the fact of Julius's presence with her long anger that he had not arrived and never would. She hears the animal make a wet noise of complaint, the trailer creaking like a bad ladder. Julius backs up again to take the turn a little wider. Behind the truck and the jackknifed trailer the sun is setting over the bright city. Muriel pulls at her shirt, unties the knot and lets the tails drift. She reaches up to touch her hair. Finally Julius backs all the way out and gives up and parks the truck two wheels in the road ditch. He cuts the engine and steps out of the cab smiling.

Lee calls to his brother, "You win a bet or lose one?"

Julius comes to stand by them again. "Mustang. You wouldn't believe the story."

Lee waits but his brother says nothing more. Muriel notices the dirty legs and seat of his cuffed pants, the boots worn so badly he appears to be pushing forward on the balls of his feet to keep from falling back on the ground-down heels. One sleeve of his shirt hangs in a bell, the seam flayed open.

"Look at this," he says again, as if he had arrived only to witness their prosperity. He raises his arm and makes again the broad gesture that takes in the trees and the river and the house still unpainted but set straight as a church, and in this second wave is a certain anxious filiality.

He seems taller, much older than before, older even than Lee, who stands next to his brother like an antidote to something, all clean cheeks and hands.

"I guess I had something a little more country in mind," he says.

"I can see that," Lee says, and nods at the horse as if in apology.

"Where in heaven did you get a mustang?" Muriel asks.

Julius pulls a wounded face and she realizes she had not yet spoken. He does not answer her. She feels suddenly a powerful resentment, a frustrated resentment like children feel when their lies are disbelieved. It has been nearly two years.

"How far you haul it from?" Lee asks.

"Little town in Nevada. North of Las Vegas, which is where I've been."

Julius fingers his hair back then shoves his hands in his pockets and takes them out again. He takes the sides of the flayed sleeve and twists them together so the fabric sits in a ball behind his elbow.

"Can't keep it in there all night, surely," Lee says.

"Her," Julius says. "She's a mare."

The three of them move out onto the road and stand behind the trailer. Muriel can smell the horse and it is a smell she knows. Julius frowns, then moves toward the trailer and pulls the bolt closure back. Then he flings the doors open. The horse snorts, her rear to them, dusty and round as an apple, but otherwise does not move.

"Call her a wedding gift. Or . . ." Julius says, rubbing his palm along his forehead. ". . . housewarming," he says finally, as if he had invented the word. And then he does invent one: "Horsewarming," he says, and at his own joke he smiles.

"Now, it's a fine idea, Julius, but you said yourself—"

"Since when are you the kind of people who couldn't make use of a horse?"

Julius looks at each of them in quick turn, in case they might have become those people in the time he's been away. Muriel thinks again about their long phone call, and the secret she'd told him about the races and wonders if he believed her after all. A moment's excitement at this prospect, and then a sharp worry.

"But we've got no fencing, Julius," Lee says finally. "Seems like something necessary, don't it?" He looks at Muriel sternly. She moves closer to the trailer. She can smell the stress of the horse and the dirt on her coat and in her poor hooves. She looks back at Lee with all the puzzlement she can muster.

"Only necessity is salvation, anyhow," Julius says brightly.

Lee's stern look turns parochial. "I never did get why Dad said that," he says.

"I think he thought only the needy get saved, not that getting saved is all you need."

"Well, that sure would be like him."

Together they watch the horse ignore them. In front of them the light spreads in gauzy colors against the low-lying clouds. Muriel wants to reach out and touch the horse but she worries she'll startle it. An insular threat beats between the men as they talk this way.

"Our old dad would be the type to muddle up the whole issue of salvation though, in the end," Julius says.

The horse is a foot shorter than a racehorse, the color of dry sand, ewe-necked and too long in the hip. Muriel watches its dark eye turn back and glance behind and for a moment catch Muriel in its vision. Muriel can feel herself caught and considered there. The horse snorts. Then it looks away and is still and silent inside the dented trailer. Muriel can see now that it's no mustang or thoroughbred but a simple palomino nag, the kind of fat girl used in the pit for cooling runners. Probably once called Holly or Peaches. She might wait in that trailer until she dies.

"Well okay, I guess we're real Westerners now," Lee says then, and at this he takes his brother in a tight sidearm.

Julius ducks his head as if Lee had gently cuffed him and clears his throat and spits onto the dirt. The horse moves her ears to locate the sound.

"Let her be a while and she'll come out. We didn't come from too far but it took some time on these roads," he says. "I bought some apples on the way, so I'll put those around and she'll be sure to come for them. If you've got a jug or barrel, we can water her a little. Until then I'm wasted for a drink. Afraid you'll have to invite me in."

THEY GATHER AROUND the card table in the kitchen with a bottle of port wine. Muriel takes one chair and Lee the other and the men bring in a wooden stool from the yard where Julius sits and heels off his boots. She looks around the house. An empty house, a house without a dining table or wallpaper, feels haunted by the future imagined for it, which has not been this future, all three of them together. The kitchen seems to wait, to hover between being lived in and not. Julius sits on the stool with his knees spread wide and his missing canine tooth like a little hole in the story he is telling, about a woman who rode up and down Fremont Street on a bicycle.

"You'd see her out there any day of the week, in any weather. Of course no one asked but the overall sense was that she was plying her wares. You ever see a working girl on a bicycle? That's the kind of town it is and I'll tell you I'm glad to have seen it now. One afternoon the rain came sudden like it does and there she still was, riding up and down. Must've thought she had the market cornered, since all the other girls had gone inside to save their dresses and whatnot. And wouldn't you know it, here comes some old blackjack stiff with a newspaper tented over his head with one hand and trying to wave her down with the other. And that's when we all realized the drawback of such a method, of riding on a bike and not just hanging about, when even on an empty street in the rain a customer had to make such an obvious gesture to get her attention."

"Ain't it legal there?" Lee asks.

"Believe it or not it ain't. Rest of the state it is. Vegas, they banned it."

"Well that's ironic, huh," Lee says, in an indulgent tone. Julius frowns.

Muriel notices again the poor state of his clothes. In the bright overhead light of the kitchen the skin at his neck is rough and red, as if he had shaved in the dark. She remembers him as fresh and young, not this man before her now.

Julius plays down two face cards and a nine of spades. But Muriel has two kings and a jack, and she slaps these down grinning on the table.

"You didn't pick up any of that on the draw. What were you waiting for?" Julius asks.

"Your confidence," she says.

She cups the dimes they're using for ante and pulls them in. In Julius's tone, in the crass story, an unease that widens out over each of them and over the house. As if Julius's presence distorts their respectability. Muriel senses this and it excites her, it draws away her feeling of apprehension, though the brothers play as if burdened by it, as if they might rather do something cruel or reckless.

"Well, I'd tell you the end of that story but it hasn't ended, I bet. Somewhere that girl is still riding that bicycle, and that's the moral right there. Nothing was going to stop her."

"You'll remember sometimes when the Sunday Dorcas ended and there on the street were them edified women of North Topeka, handing out leaflets," Lee says.

"Good lord, those women in their terrible black shoes! Only Lutherans would let women that frigid have meetings."

"That's about the closest we ever got to the kind of thing you're saying."

"Oh God, Lee, that might be the funniest thing you ever said," Julius says, but he doesn't laugh. He palms the deck and starts to shuffle in the elaborate way of movie cowboys, the bridge cracked upward and downward, the deck split with the heel of his thumb. Lee asks Muriel if the store just off the county road is open past seven and if they need milk for the morning, and she hums a moment before answering. Lee rises and takes the coffee can from the counter and fishes a finger through the bills inside. Julius glances up from the cards and looks at Muriel then at the coffee can. Here a small intrusion of the domestic life they had assembled without him, the familiar, logistical talk of married couples.

From outside, a wet snort near the kitchen door. They all three start, then their laughter erases the retreating edge of Julius's odd look.

"I guess she came out, then," Julius says.

He stands and walks to the kitchen door and opens it onto the yard, bluish this hour past dusk, and pokes his head out. Lee rises too and when he's halfway across the kitchen the horse passes by the open door and Julius jumps back. The horse turns her great head in and sniffs. Julius moves behind the table and Lee laughs, still moving forward, and reaches out one hand to the curious face. To everyone's surprise the horse necks in under the lintel and pulls back her black lips. Her teeth are flat and even, the color of church piano keys. She steps slowly in until her withers and neck are even with the cabinets and Lee touches her huge jaw with the flat of his hand.

"Well hello there," he says.

The horse lowers her head and accepts Lee's touch and then she throws up her proud snout and Lee scolds her lightly. She snorts in happy consanguinity.

Muriel stands. Julius holds still behind the table and as she moves close to the horse he says, "Careful, girl."

The horse leans further in and clops toward Muriel until the horse has all four feet on the linoleum. This close, she is chinked in vein and bone and smells of grass. In these last months Muriel hasn't missed horses or the track but she misses horses now. Now that one is here. She reaches out and the horse bows and Muriel touches her in the bony cleft between her eyes and looking down the horse's eyelashes are thick as terry. Muriel has never touched a horse before.

From outside the planate slap of wood dropped from height, at the tract up the road. The horse jerks and neighs and Muriel moves her hand away and Lee steps back. Julius claps once and then again and the horse moves swiftly backward in the way of cultivated creatures, a perfect awareness of the space through which she's passed, gait low and competent. Lee follows and says, "That's all right, honey, that's all right." The horse leans away from Lee's reaching hand and fully out into the yard. Julius skips over and closes the door and shuts her out. Lee says, "Hey now," the way he might reprimand a child.

"You don't want no wild animal in your fancy kitchen, now do you?" Julius says.

"That horse is just fine," Lee says. "Though she could use a hosing off."

He opens the door again and the horse is still there but a few cool steps back, one eye casting back the twin image of the house, the other of Lee's head and shoulders. Seeing her round eyes there in the doorway, Muriel remembers suddenly one of her mother's men, who lived next door to their apartment and across a vacant lot. He'd made a lovers' telephone from tin cans and a curl of boater's string and he drew one end across the lot for her mother and kept one for himself. The day they moved out of that apartment Muriel saw him standing in the lot forlorn with the telephone in his hands. When he saw Muriel watching him he pressed the cans to his eyes so he looked like a minnow and grinned at her. She never saw him again after that, though he had been so sweet and childish, he'd had the nosy fortitude the horse had now, interrupting their card game.

For a moment Lee stays in the doorway, between the kitchen and the horse, until Julius moves behind him and bangs under the sink for a coffee can. Lee turns toward his brother. They smile at each other in some mutual remembrance and Lee shuts the door and goes to his brother and takes the empty can and holds it out and his brother dumps the ashtray in. Julius dusts his palms against his jeans and lips a new cigarette and pats his pockets until Lee scuffles a drawer for another book of matches. As they perform these small tasks the energy in the room shifts back to them, they are brothers again. They had been vigorous children, Muriel knows, the way boys without mothers, with unsuitable fathers, were given to mischief and high emotion. She can see, in their dance around the kitchen, how they must have held themselves apart from the world. For a moment it is as strange to be with these men as it would be to wake among starlings.

They play a round of spit and drink the last of the wine, and then Lee stands, peers out through the window and spots the horse by the tree line where Julius has dumped the apples. He pulls a coin from his pocket and looks at his brother shrewdly.

"Tails," Julius says.

"Predictable," says Lee, and with his thumb flips the coin high in the air. When it lands on the floor the men lean over. Julius claps his brother on the back.

"We'll go up together. You can give me a ride in that fine car," he says.

Lee stands and takes a few coins from the coffee can.

"You know what I wish?" he says, leaned against the counter looking at his brother, the drink running ruddy up his neck. "I wish I could've been a kid for all this. Those builders took just eight weeks. You remember how long we spent trying to fix old Dad's place. I'd come out here after work and I'd look at the house all clean and new, just wood and angles, and think, now here's a place that makes sense to a kid."

"We ain't kids no more," Julius says.

"I'm trying to explain it to you."

Lee looks at Muriel as if she might help him. She knows that during the building he'd come out after work and climbed to the raised wall of the bedroom and looked out over the valley, because he'd told her so. She might say this to Julius now and allow him to see his brother this way. Most evenings Lee sat with the plans at the card table in their apartment kitchen, narrating them to Muriel, working his dreamy way through the rooms, names etched in their boxes like countries: CLOSET, BATHROOM, DEN.

"I wanted you to be here then," Lee says. "To see that it was possible, even for poor nobodies like us."

"I'm here now."

"Sure you are. Sure you are."

For a moment Lee stands with his hands folded below his beltline.

He says, "We waited a long time for you," then he turns in the doorway and steps into the hallway beyond. The sound of the bathroom door pulled shut. Julius looks around the room and up across the ceiling and out the front window. Silence in the kitchen, the slow wind through the trees.

"Nobody's fault is it," Julius says, and drops his feet from the table and lets the front legs of the stool knock solidly to the ground. Inside this sudden intimacy Muriel doesn't want reproach, but she can think of no other way to speak to him. She cannot say, *You left me alone.* Nor, *You can see we got along just fine without you.*

He presses his toes against her shoe in a sweet goading nudge. She looks at his shirt with the ripped sleeve, down to the gritty nubs of his discarded boots, tipped now on the kitchen floor so the soles point up at her. She waits to see if he will say anything about their long phone call or the track or the time he has spent away from them and when he doesn't, when he simply holds her gaze, she says, "Doesn't look like you cashed out much ahead."

He laughs amiably and she laughs with him. He reaches out and takes her elbow, then skates his hand down her arm, turns up her palm, and kisses it. She thinks of what he might smell there, dirt and soap and sweat, ordinary things, and somehow this is more exciting than the fact of his touch, imagining what his touch will tell him about her. He holds her hand there a beat too long until the kiss turns parodic or even forbidden, and she laughs to keep the moment easy and pulls her hand away and waves it against his charm. Though he wears still the anguish he's brought along, he's smiling at her. Where his sleeve is ripped his elbow shows and she reaches out and pinches it and he yelps away and she lets this be the character of the moment.

LATER, THE MEN HAVE BECOME DRUNK and drape across the table in their postures of male affection, playing a card game unknown to her and salvaged from childhood, a game whose rules seem to change with each hand in the way of children's games. They've danced to all the songs on the radio and now the station has lapsed into static but Julius keeps swaying and Lee reaches out every few minutes and takes his brother by the shoulder and pulls him near. Conversations she can't follow. The ashtray overflowing and juice glasses rimmed in dark wine and fingerprints. Outside, a scrubbing noise in the trees not far from the house, the shape of the horse visible for brief moments where the trees break open.

In the bedroom she takes off her clothes. She leaves the lamp off and stands in front of the mirror. Through the thin curtains, the moonlight and the citylight cast into the room like faraway lights underwater. With her fingers she waves back her hair and parts it long from one side and tucks it behind her ear so she looks like Dietrich when she tips her hat in *Morocco*. But she is not so beautiful and she knows it and on her the wide part looks matronly but not dignified. She fusses her hair back out so it falls around her face and in the strange light she looks almost blonde, as she was born. She recalls with remorse the story her mother told of their last winter in town, when Muriel's hair had darkened and she'd grown four inches. That spring they moved to Marshall County and her mother was married and Muriel spent the summer not among the rural children but in her room looking out across the fields, so her hair did not lighten in the sun and she was never blonde again. Her mother told this story the way any mother might, to acquaintances and shopkeepers, as a lament for her own youth. That Muriel had been grateful for her new plainness was something she knew would hurt her mother.

From the kitchen she hears the music of the radio and the men's laughter. She pulls her hair straight back, pricks her hairline with her finger, and makes a long center part. She tows each half behind her ears and ducktails the back together, which gives her the appearance of an evangelical or a hayseed, so she fingers it back over but keeps it balled at her neck, and here is something closer to what she wants. With her palm she lifts the front so it arches softly up and away from her forehead. She looks bold and almost masculine, but something in her posture or her eyes gives her away as herself. She steps back from the mirror and looks at full length. Her own body is a thrill then, her breasts and hips below the tomboy hair, and she slides her hands flat along her sides and down her thighs and feels the warmth of her skin in the dark room.

She gets into bed without dressing and sleeps easily and dreams of horses across the fields of her childhood, though in life she never saw horses there. Much later she is awakened by a sound in the room. Lee's body next to her is heavy and hot. She turns toward the door and as she nears sleep a shadow passes by the doorway. She drifts off and when she wakes again Julius is in their room, by the window looking out, and she thinks first of her nakedness and then of the hour. She thinks she must be dreaming, though his smell is in the room. The figure rises and comes toward the bed and it is indeed Julius, his face calm and pale. He leans over and kisses her forehead and she stirs and lifts her chin toward him. She says his name. He holds a finger to his lips and turns and leaves the room.

For a long time she waits without sleeping. Then something occurs to her. She rises and steps to the mirror. She lifts it from the nail and turns it, and there is the envelope with the deed to her mother's house and the receipt from the tax board and a letter back from the Carters, saying all is well. Inside this envelope is another, smaller one, folded tight with the rest of the money, two thousand dollars give or take. She sifts through these things as if in confirmation of the facts. Everything is there. She takes this as it is and soon she sleeps and when she wakes she thinks she must have dreamed it. That the wine and the horse and her own long waiting had entered the night and made the shape of him.

THE NEXT MORNING comes in warm and bright. Muriel rises and finds the men already dressed. The kitchen is disordered and on the back stoop the radio plays country-western from twenty years ago. The brothers stand at the back of the yard looking up at the house. The horse has slipped away, off among the trees to the east, and Muriel watches as the men split off north and south to bring her back. The mood between them is tense, this she can tell from their heavy strides and the bolt of impatience she feels from Lee, who disappears inside the morning shadows. The horse hears them coming through the trees and steps tall into the yard away from them and the look on her long face is weary, as if this game is one she's played before and she knows the odds. Across the river the pinpricked valley, a few houselights on in the early morning. The moon is still up and looks cold but bright as brass.

Lee steps out of the trees and whistles and lets his hair fall across his eyes, like a weekender freed from work in town. They've draped a blanket over the horse, but when they come close she moves deftly away and the blanket falls onto the ground. Lee sidles up and touches her flank and the horse tilts from him but does not run and he steps carefully forward and his brother sneaks up to steady her from the other side but she sees him long before he is parallel. She stands thoughtfully between them. Neither man will step in front of her and she seems to sense this small respect, this memory of her power. She moves straight forward and her march draws dust which rises motely around her and again she slips off into the trees, toward the vacant lot to the north.

Lee turns to Julius and says something Muriel can't hear. The men confer lightly, then Lee sits in the center of the yard and laughs. In his defeat he becomes a man she hasn't seen in some time: a little Midwestern boy laughing at his own failure like only failure suits him.

Julius stands a moment looking at his brother, then comes to Muriel on the stoop.

"We've got a little wager going here," he tells her. "Who can mount her and stay."

He sits beside her and lights two cigarettes and hands one over.

"Looks like you're just trying to catch her, let alone ride her," Muriel says.

Julius smiles and hollers to Lee in the yard: "Even your wife says that mare's got too much blood."

Lee looks up into the coming daylight and does not answer.

"You all aren't going to get very far with this," Muriel says to Julius.

"It's good you're on my side," Julius says.

"It isn't just the horse that's holding you back."

She takes a long drag and smiles but Julius is working through some feeling. For a moment they smoke in silence. The mist snakes from the river below and crawls into the tree line where the horse stands, then burns off to nothing at the road. The horse is reddish in this light but her mane is nearly silver, split across her wide brow in leaves so her eyes below are numinously dark.

"So this is paradise, huh," Julius says.

His voice is rough and strange and he radiates frustration.

"Something like that."

"Just like that."

"You all had a party," she says.

"My brother still has some vinegar in him."

"Well he must've got it from you."

She nudges him sweetly and he lets her but she feels his distance. She thinks of his face in the night and his small touch and these seem like gestures from a film in another room. She had drunk too much and imagined it, she feels sure now. Lee sits cross-legged in the yard and the horse stands some distance away, chewing the new grass.

"You want double or nothing?" Lee calls to his brother.

"You couldn't get no bookie on earth to take that bet," Julius says. He turns back to Muriel.

"What was it you told me about them horses?" he asks.

Muriel is surprised.

"What do you mean?"

"Those fellas where you work. The racehorses."

"I didn't think you remembered that," she says.

"I remember lots of things," he says.

"That was just a lark," she says quickly.

"The horses, or telling it to me?"

"The horses. Both, I guess."

"So what happened?"

"Nothing."

"Uh-huh."

"What do you mean what happened?" she asks.

Julius doesn't answer. He leans back and stabs one boot heel on the toe of the other, and in his length and his posture is someone naive and recently hurt. She remembers him sitting just this way in her mother's yard, but he had been young and wild then. He had known far more about the world than she did. Now in his filthy jeans and his ripped shirt he is vulnerable, receptive, as if these traits have been drawn out from some isolation. This surprises her and she looks away from him. As she does the damp surface of the new grass catches her motion. The few clouds also catch there and the surface is like the lens of an eye. For a moment she watches the light sift and break up these images. She is not sure what to make of his questions, coming now so late in the story.

"Must've been hard, letting go of your mother's house," he says.

"It was."

He flicks the cigarette into the yard and it hisses out in the damp grass. She pokes hers out and wipes her fingers on her dress and leaves the butt ledged on the stoop. He watches her closely. She looks back. She feels wary of him now.

"You remember that card game we played?" he says.

"We played lots of card games," she says, but she knows the one he means.

"We played it the night the weather finally cooled. Maybe it was Christmas Eve," he says.

"It was."

"And Lee got railed and slept on the table, and you and me placed bets on what he was dreaming."

"He was dreaming about cleaning heads midship."

"Girl, he was dreaming about you."

Muriel shies. Julius's teasing shove is an act of affection but he brings it too hard and knocks her sideways.

"There was something you said then, about how your mother played cards. I was trying to remember it."

"On your honor?"

"That's it."

He lights another cigarette. His fingernails are clipped tight and clean as if he's managed them carefully, though at the ridges they are dark as pitch.

"That was her rule. If you're playing for coins or matches or something and you run out, you get one more play," he says.

"Yeah, but she always said nobody ever won on their honor."

Julius lifts one finger in sudden understanding and his sleeve falls back and his gentle wrist is exposed. Through the trees the river drifts by and lends its sound to the fields beyond.

"Your honor ain't something you want in the pot," he says.

"That's what she thought."

"Smart woman."

"She'd like you saying that."

Muriel remembers the way her mother played cards and misses her terribly. Though her mother never cheated she made everyone think she had and in this way charged the game with vengeance, and often those playing against her tried to call her out and lost by playing too meanly. It was a strange kind of bluff and Muriel wonders if Julius would have fallen for it. He holds the cigarette out to her and she takes it and drags and keeps it. This feels a little better, this camaraderie, the shared memory of their time together. Placing him and her mother together in her thoughts. She thinks of his kiss the day before and the smell of her palm and wonders if they might return to that moment and go on from there.

"I told you, I remember lots of things," he says.

A lea of clouds passes over and catches the sun. The ground beneath them darkens. In this new light the yard seems burned at the edges as if the ground had sunk there hot and all at once and then filled through the night, not with dirt but with groundwater, seeped up from the earth the way gold was said to in the book of Daniel. The horse steps out of the trees and into the strange light. She walks with high-footed humor past the rim of the grass and Muriel thinks how horses love drama, even if they are old, even if they are overmatched.

"Where have you been all this time?" Muriel asks.

"I told you."

"Before that."

"You know I was in L.A. some, other places up there too."

"Why didn't you ever come here?"

"Did you really expect me to?"

She hands the cigarette back. The horse stands bathing in the bright sun. She looks toward Muriel and Julius on the stoop and snorts. This look goes on for several beats and is touching in its seriousness and then the horse turns sharply away and begins to move along the tree line toward the river.

"What'd you spend that sixty dollars on?" Muriel says finally.

"You wouldn't believe me if I told you."

"You bought a horse, is what you did."

"I bought that horse with someone else's money," he says and leans back again on the stoop.

"And what did that someone give you the money for?"

He laughs amiably but when he looks at her his face is tired.

"Not for horses," he says.

"There's my point."

"Here's the thing about money, it don't really belong to anyone."

"That sixty dollars sure enough belonged to me."

"Did it now."

She doesn't answer.

"My philosophy . . ." he says. "And don't make that face, I just got the one. What I think is, you can give somebody something, but once you give it that somebody gets to use it for whatever he wants."

"So what are we supposed to use a horse for?"

"Anything you want."

She looks out across the yard and the river. Lee has reclined in his infant grass and spread his arms in a posture of beatification and is not listening to them.

"Okay then," Muriel says. "You remember so much. You remember that story you told me? About the man who sold rabbits?"

"God yes, I forgot about him. What a—" Julius says, but does not finish his thought.

"You said he was handsome," Muriel says.

Julius smokes hard and looks away from her. The darkness he brought with him darkens further in the cold morning and turns to fragility.

"You said he seemed just like a rabbit," Muriel says.

Julius nods and smiles but then, as if arrested by another, more urgent thought, he turns to her and says, "I had a friend in Vegas. I've seen a lot of things, but he had something I ain't ever seen before. Tiny little pistol on the end of a chain, supposed to connect to a pocket watch or key fob. I don't think it works at all, but it looks a little menacing. He would say, Julius, what a thing *seems* like is all that matters."

The horse starts in to the yard toward Lee and Lee sits up. Julius sees the horse too and stands and scrapes the dirty seat of his jeans with both hands. He looks down at Muriel and says, as if to conclude his previous thought, "I remember I asked you if you'd ever been in love."

"You did ask me that," she says.

He stomps his boots rigid and hands down the cigarette. Muriel reaches up for it. They are commensally arranged then, Muriel can feel this in the angle between them, the long-legged man with his moody brow throwing a serrated shadow along the grass, below him her sleepy figure, her hair still stiff from the night before. She thinks of her afternoons at Del Mar, the hour she'd spent at the Radford Hotel. That brief interval in which she might have chosen anything, the seductive anonymity of the room. She had been so angry at Julius then, for disappearing, but she doesn't want him to know that now. She wants him to see her as she had been, with money heaped across the bed and all her bets come winning, not as she is now, a woman on a stoop in the suburbs.

"I remember what you said, too," Julius says.

"Oh yeah."

"But maybe you just had the jitters."

Muriel smokes the cigarette out and pinches the cherry and drops it and Julius kicks dirt over it with his dirty boot.

"You never told me how you knew that man," Muriel says.

"What man."

"The rabbit man."

Julius smiles sadly.

"I've been lots of places, like I said."

Julius looks at her and she looks back and for a long moment they hold this look between them and Muriel can see in his tired face some yearning or perhaps the opposite, perhaps a desire to be left alone. She wonders what he sees in her face. Then Lee says in a sweet and placating voice, "Okay then, girl," and the moment is broken. Muriel and Julius turn away from each other and watch as the horse stops in the center of the yard twenty feet from Lee. Lee rises and puts his hand out for her to smell, as if she were a dog. He approaches slowly and she lets him. He strokes her mane and flank and asks the horse how she feels about him.

Julius calls out to him, "She thinks you're about as smart as a brick." Then he says softly, almost to himself, "Man said mustang. That was the whole idea."

Lee presses a hand to the horse's flank and walks forward. The horse follows. Julius lets out a low whistle. At the edge of the yard is an upturned bucket and when the horse is close beside it Lee stands on top and balances. The horse does not move away but looks at him and seems to nod. With both hands on the horse's wither he swings one leg wide and jumps off the bucket with the other, and though the horse sidles he manages to land and lean over her neck. The noise of this maneuver is absorbed by the trees. He bends full on the length of her and Julius stands and stares. The horse walks to the scrub along the bluff and then turns back to the house. Lee whistles through his teeth and then lifts slowly from the mare's back. He raises an arm and waves an imaginary hat. When the horse steps forward again he slides perilously then rights himself. Julius watches all this with mild annoyance.

"Who you want to call wild now, huh?" Lee calls out.

Julius turns away and spits. Muriel looks at him and sees his hunched shoulders and disappointed face. Why had he brought up the racetrack? What he might know seems suddenly menacing and dangerous, and though she cannot quite read him she knows he is afflicted by something. She might think money or revenge or her long-ago disclosure, but she had spent her childhood with a beautiful woman and so she recognizes what she sees in him as heartache. It amazes her to see it. She thinks of the rabbit man and the man with the tiny pistol and a thought begins to form and she can almost catch the tail of it. She senses inside his trouble the sharp contours of her own.

The horse stops in the center of the yard and Lee slides from her. When she doesn't move away he palms her long neck and leans his face to hers. Muriel watches this romance and next to her Julius takes his hands from his pockets and stretches his arms and shakes them loose.

"Let's see about this then," he says, and moves toward his brother and the horse.

Lee steps away and Julius takes the bucket and upends it. He finds a position near the horse's belly and presses as Lee did and throws his leg over. The horse whinnies sideways but does not bolt. Julius nickers at the horse and she moves forward. Her hide trembles and she snorts and Muriel thinks of horses she's seen and bet on and how from far away they seemed smooth as plaster.

Lee comes to stand by Muriel and takes her hand and says, "Sorry about this."

She shakes her head.

"My brother never let nothing go," he says.

"You're the one who said he'd never come."

"I never have predicted him, in the end."

"I guess not."

"I don't see you complaining."

"I'm not complaining."

Lee brings her closer. He softens his tone.

"What's going on with your hair then?"

"I just slept on it wet is all."

He nods remotely.

"Except I'm not at all sure what to do with him now," he says.

"Did he say how long he'd stay?"

Lee laughs. "Well, he can't leave that heaping truck on the road all winter," he says.

A silence between them. The horse stands stock-still in the center of the yard while Julius digs his heels to nudge her forward.

"Can you believe this horse," Muriel says.

"I can't."

"What a thing to do."

"I just don't see the reason in it."

"You never wanted a horse?"

"Well, sure, what kid doesn't? But we ain't kids."

"He's saying he's sorry to you," Muriel says.

"Oh. I guess."

"You don't think so."

"I think he could say it another way."

Lee frowns as he watches his brother.

"You seem to be having an okay time," he says to her.

"So do you."

"Oh, we're all having fun sure enough."

Suddenly then a flat noise and a cry and there is Julius planked on the ground, both arms out and his legs spread. The horse has run him into the low-hanging branch of a tree. He reaches up to touch his forehead. The horse clips off toward the road. Muriel covers her mouth and Lee laughs openly and from his supine post Julius says, "I guess no one has any worry I'm dead then."

"Got over that worry the last time," Lee says.

The horse looks back when she is some distance across the yard and stares a funny moment. She snorts hugely. At this Julius throws up his hands in frustration but does not rise and Lee laughs with his palms on his knees and his black crown of hair shaking. Julius laughs too but not happily. He lies still looking up at the sky. Lee stands over his brother and sends down a hand but Julius waves him away.

"Would you say I won or Lee did?" Julius asks Muriel.

"Oh, who cares about that," Lee says.

"You cared before."

"That was before I won."

Both men laugh then. The horse is moving across the yard and as they watch she crosses the road into the walnut orchard beyond. Neither man moves to chase her.

"I told you she's wild," Julius says.

"And I told you we ain't got no fence."

Julius nods, winces. "You'd not think it," he says to distract Lee, "but you can actually see some stars." He points up at the sky and calls his brother to lie down next to him but Lee is still looking after the horse and does not move. Under his boots the ground sinks wetly.

"We got real troubles, catching that horse now," Lee says.

"Your wife'll look at stars with me," Julius says to him as if he had not spoken. Then to Muriel, "You look then."

Muriel cants toward him but does not lie down.

"You hear they're making a Sputnik cocktail?" he says.

"Who's they?" Muriel says.

"Two parts vodka, one part sour grapes."

Julius crosses his arms over his chest like a dead man. Lee scowls over him.

"It's just a bluff, all the thing does is circle. Them Russians are just trying to scare us," Lee says.

"A bluff still has some truth in it," Julius says.

Lee stands with the river black behind him and his face caught in the sunlight.

"You said you saw them bombs," he says. "Now *that* ain't no bluff."

Julius sits up and finds a clump of folded winter grass and pulls it. It comes away in his fingers and he lets the blades drift. Then he sweeps one arm out the same way he did when he arrived but this time the gesture seems to dismiss his own appreciation and the very fact of the place.

"Can't have everything, hey. Not people like us," he says, and the simplicity of this seems to comfort him.

LATER THEY SET UP thirty-one and the brothers tell jokes and sing along with the radio. The strain between them has lessened. When the hour grows small Muriel showers and steps into the bedroom which is cold and smells of wood dust. She lies a long time without sleeping. In the kitchen she listens to them laugh and joke until something shifts between them. A chair scuffs back and something knocks against the table and she hears Lee tell Julius that he is free to go, then Julius's voice thick with drink and the late hour saying Lee has misunderstood. She worries about what will happen next. She listens as she had once listened for the moment the record scratched off in the living room and her mother stopped laughing and the house grew very quiet. Just the sound of wind or night birds and her mother would climb the stairs with a man often still wearing his boots. Muriel could see the morning star through the window facing east and on those nights she curled toward it, away from her door and the hallway, when her mother passed. She would remember what they'd been told one Sunday, that it was the devil who rose first, because he had been God's most beautiful creation and then he had fallen, so as the earth turned past the night it was the devil first up from the ground. *Good morning, devil,* she thought as she looked at that star.

In the kitchen Lee says, but softly now, inviting, "I wish that had mattered, little brother."

"I guess I thought I'd see old Dad again."

"It always seems like there's more time but there's only so much."

"You act like it don't matter to you."

"Wasn't nobody could save that man."

"We might've tried harder."

"I'm telling you, Julius."

"Well, I guess you had other things you wanted."

"So did you."

"Without him here you ain't so beholden to me," Julius says.

Then their voices lower past her hearing and she drifts to the edge of sleep until they rise again.

"A year and a half is too long," Lee says.

"Hell, you don't want my company. Look at you two, married and settled and all that."

"I said I wanted it. How many times I have to say it?"

"You just want to keep me in line."

Lee does not answer.

"I'm right, huh," Julius says then.

"Well Muriel surely wanted you to come. You should have seen her."

"What do you mean?"

"I honestly think she was counting on it."

For a long moment no one speaks.

Then Julius says, "But you convinced her otherwise."

"Seems to me you did that yourself, by disappearing."

Silence, then Julius again, "As soon as you got that letter from her you'd had it with me. You saw your chance."

"Why'd I bring you along then, that Christmas?"

"'Cause you thought you had to. 'Cause you worried what I'd do all alone."

Lee says something Muriel can't hear and then Julius speaks too in agreeable tones and for a while it seems their argument has ended. Outside she can hear the river pulling gently. She recalls a night early on, when they'd driven out to the house to drop off the table and some clothes and dishes, and rather than drive back to town in the dark they'd slept in the empty house. Next to her husband on the living room floor with their coats covering their legs, she heard the river running as it is now, but through the walls and windows and the blank space of the yard it had sounded like a mere breeze. She had made a wish that night, that the river would rise and come into the house and take them. She missed her mother and her own house and the low plains from the bedroom window. She had missed the familiar smell of wheat. Before the day she won so much at the track, there had been only the secret and its own pleasure. It might have been horses or bridge or anything capricious, or anything merely new. But after she'd gone to the bank and posted the envelopes and lied to her husband the secret and its source were the same, they were commensurate. She'd liked having a secret, but she did not like lying. Lying had erased her from everything.

Suddenly a chair scrapes back and Muriel hears it fall onto the kitchen floor. When Lee speaks his voice comes from a distant corner of the room, as if he's moved very far from the table.

"Well that's just fine. I saw how well you got along in the service, on your own."

"That was nothing."

"I know that ain't true. And that fella in Okinawa, in that village bar."

"I told you I didn't know him."

"Then why did you fight him like that?"

"He insulted us."

"Maybe so but it ain't like you."

A glass planted on the table, the ashtray rattled. The radio still on but dampened to susurration so through the wall and down the hallway it sounds to Muriel like a secret.

"You going to tell me the rest of it?" Lee asks finally.

"There ain't no way to say it, George Lee."

Their voices drop again and the night deepens and soon the valley grows quiet and slips into its full pastoral and Muriel lets sleep come.

SOMETIME BEFORE DAWN she is awakened by noise from the road. She rises and walks through the empty house and stops in Julius's room. He's folded the blankets and stacked them in the corner. The rest of the room is empty. She goes to the kitchen. The radio is on and plays low. She looks out the back window and sees nothing. She tries the window over the sink. A line of dust hovers at the road. Then she tips the coffee can and sees that it's empty. She walks back to the front room and opens the door and the truck is gone, though the trailer is knifed on the roadside and unhitched. Hoofprints deep onto the road and disappearing north and away. The sky has leavened a snowy yellow. She knows all at once what has happened and she is not surprised, though she wonders if she should be.

She turns and passes back through the kitchen and the front room and down the hallway. In the bedroom Lee sleeps soundly. She moves to the front wall and again lifts the framed mirror and turns it. She peels the envelope from the backing. One envelope is gone and in the other Julius has left the deed to her mother's house and the tax receipt and the letter from the Carters. She unfolds these items and reads them. Inside the folded receipt she finds another slip of newsprint and she unfolds this and sees the names of horses and jockeys and the odds laid out by post order, in the margin a few notes in her own hand. She folds the form into her pocket and puts back the rest, then peers out the window to the drive and the road beyond, cast up in thin dust where he's driven the truck through and away. Again she sees the prints on the road and thinks of the places a horse might go and how far away those places are.

In the bed Lee is solid and perfectly shaped. She recalls the snags of their argument and starts to piece it together and then another thought arrives: If Julius didn't believe her that night on the phone, about the horses, he does now. He'd seen the deed and the letter and the tax receipt, perhaps the racing form, too, and surely he could find the story there. She thinks of his dark shape in their bedroom, two nights before. The conversation on the stoop and the heartache she'd seen in him. She is sure now that he'd come to steal from them but this is less important than the redemption she's begun to feel, that has begun to sneak into the day. She thinks, *I have been found out.* And that fact brightens all the months before and renames them.

SIX

Tijuana

When Julius crosses the border it is just past dawn. He passes through San Ysidro without trouble while men in guayaberas and felt hats cross the elliptical archway above carrying sacks of fruit and grain, some with shoes tied together at the laces and slung over their shoulders, others with cardboard suitcases mended with tape. Once through the border the signs switch to Spanish but the landscape is still dusty and gently rolling and dotted in creosote the color of mint. For a while he drives along the main thoroughfare with the river running between the lanes bright and flat as a mirror.

He thinks not of Henry exactly but of the white heat of the Squaw in the afternoons. Next to him on the bench seat is the little pistol and eighteen hundred dollars from the envelopes Muriel stashed behind the mirror and a hundred more from the coffee can. The money will last a long time if he is careful, though how long it will take he can't say. A mile into the city he turns off the broad avenida and drops into the tourist section where the buildings are low and plain, but each has a lighted sign erected in a wing high up and out over the street. Above him the tangle of letters and scaffold seems to arc across and meet in the median like a bower. Along the curbs are cars parked nose to fender for many blocks ahead, though it is still only seven in the morning. On the sidewalks are fruit merchants and mariachis in sombreros and charro suits so dark and studded with gold they catch the morning sun and appear to wave, and wandering through these figures are tourists and sailors and women in broad-brimmed hats like movie stars.

He takes Agua Caliente east and away from the thicker traffic. He pulls into a parking lot attended by a man in a green jumpsuit too tight in the shoulders and crotch.

"Five cents to park, ten cents to leave," the man tells him through the rolled-down window of the truck.

"That's the very definition of getting you coming and going."

"How it is," the man says.

Julius pays him the nickel and parks the truck in the corner of the lot in the big shade of a tipuana. The sun has risen without his notice. He steps out and looks across the city, which is bigger than he thought and cleaner. On the street are flower sellers propping up their stalls and canopies, ringing them with dried asters and ristras coated in polish as if preparing for some sacrifice. In their aprons and sniptoe boots he sees them as stage dressers against the ragged prospects of this city, and the moment feels unreal to him. A sorrow he remembers from years before, looking at the first green coast of Asia, when he learned how small his childhood had been. He had not known he was clumsy and vulgar and unimportant until he'd seen new places like this, and men with other languages, and cities with their toothy skylines. Just across the border another world.

He walks out to the street and finds a hotel and pays for a private room. He's already lost a week and thinks he should look for Henry right away but the room is so quiet and clean and he is afraid. He washes his face and neck and arms in the bathroom down the hall, and when this doesn't seem enough he runs a few inches of hot water in the tub and drapes his clothes on the toilet and sits with the water just over his hips. He hears footsteps on the landing and someone passes the door but does not open it and then another door opens and slams shut. He leans back in the water and closes his eyes but his clothes smell rank and the tap drips and he can hear the pipes laboring in the wall. He empties the pockets of his jeans and the breast pockets of his shirt and dunks the clothes in the water and scrubs them together. When he lifts the jeans the water is grainy with dirt and he twists them and hangs them back over the tank, then drains the water and scoops the silt toward the drain and runs another inch. He sits again in the hot water and wrings the socks a second time. He recalls a night at the Squaw when the heat was broken by clouds from beyond the dam and he sat in the tiny hotel bathtub with his shoulders out of the water and his knees pulled up to his chest. Then Henry woke up in the other room and came in and sunk down in the tub across from him, and for a few minutes they sat in smiling silence with their soft cocks blurred and floating, half-hidden by their updrawn knees, as Henry scooped the cooling water and tossed it over his face and head.

Julius thinks through the little part of the city he's seen and wonders where the cardrooms are and the hustlers and where he might begin. The sliver of soap is as blue and useless as skim milk and breaks in his hands, so he washes his armpits and crotch with one sock then hangs them both over the spout. He sits in the water until his shoulders prickle. Outside the sound of rain starting and stopping, the faint draft of the sea. He dries with a washcloth thin and pilled as carpet, then sleeps through the day and all night, and only when he wakes does he think of his brother and Muriel and what he knows about her now.

EARLY THE NEXT MORNING he walks out into the crowd of flower sellers and ambulantes again preparing for the day. In the parks and plazas he looks for young men alone in the shadows or spread out deliberately among the pines, but he does so with a tourist's soft eyes. All along the fringes and among the ravaged trees are Indian women in serapes and young boys selling gum and loose cigarettes. The only men he's likely to find in the morning light are pickpockets and bail bondsmen in their wide-bottomed slacks, but he considers Henry's early rising. When he enters a park somewhere in the Marrón he sits a moment on a cement bench and rests on the heels of his boots. There in the corner, under a canvas tarp sagging between a tree and a scarred statue of a bull, are three men standing cocked, dark jeans pegged at their ankles and their bootshafts uncovered. One wears a slouch hat in a dun color like hay. Behind them and across a narrow street is a bodega painted silver, with a corrugated awning bent back at the edges and showing rust. He feels their gaze drift toward him. He looks past them to the shining silver front of the bodega, which reflects back the men's shapes in a wave, their jeans blurred gray and their dark hair. When he feels their attention turned somewhere else he slides his gaze across them long enough to see that none is Henry.

Along the edge of the park early pigeons catch sunlight in their wings, tossed up occasionally by passing handcarts covered with fraying tarp, pushed by men in heeled shoes. A man and a woman walking slowly without speaking. Between Julius and the three men runs a cement path embedded with green stones and oblong pieces of glass, as if to evoke a river draining slowly out to sea. Julius looks up again and sees one of the men coming toward him. The man sits next to him on the bench. He wears furiously clean boots, each stamped on the toe with the image of an eagle.

"Five or eight *dólares*, depend your interest," the man says.

He rolls his eyes up so far his chin follows and the effect is of violent dislike, of Julius or this work or the day itself. The clean bronze of his neck is like a lathe. Julius finds a ten and whisks it in his fingers. The man smiles. He inclines his head toward the alley and Julius know this is where he will be taken, should he name some pleasure. He smiles back at the man to buy himself time. The two men underneath the tarp share a glance. One holds out two fingers. The other scrapes a cigarette from his pack and the first man lips it and leans forward for a light. The rest of the park is empty except for the pigeons and from a distance Julius hears the bounce of an old truck and a sound like chickens squabbling. Next to him the man in the eagle boots is waiting.

"I'm looking for someone," Julius says finally.

"Bien. We have lots," the man says.

He nods to his compañeros and they drop their cigarettes and move out of the shade slowly. One slackens his gait into a showy twirl and smiles.

"Someone specific," Julius says. *"Específico."*

The man frowns.

"Como todos. That is my fate," the man says and though this is a question and not a statement Julius laughs carelessly at the way it sounds. The man holds up a hand. The two compañeros stop in frozen motion, each with one foot hitched back off the ground midstep and their arms bent in a running posture. Then they smile stupidly and let their bodies loosen.

The man says, *"Maricón,* no worry." This is a term Julius knows. The man says it like a statement of fact, not a threat, but it still makes Julius bristle. If he can't find the words he will be asking for sex and this is the transaction he most wants to avoid. If he wanted trinkets or cigarettes he could get those now, but not this new thing he's after, this particular other person. He can smell the man's shower, hard soap, tooth powder. He imagines a room sparsely furnished but clean as sunlight. A fire escape, flowerpot for butt-ends along the rail, the man with his smoking hand out the window. Julius is sure of these things, or their equivalent. But he does not know how to say what he needs to say to find that part of the man. He cannot simply ask about Henry as if he were a brother or cousin, nor can he lie and say that Henry is either of those things. Differentiating brotherly from romantic love is an industry in such places. He might ask for a young Mexicano with a wounded arm but beside him the man radiates impatience.

"No hay problema, lo siento," Julius says, and when he says nothing

more the man stands and moves in front of him and looks down. Julius looks back at him and then around the empty plaza. The two hombres are standing at an occupational distance and speaking closely to each other but Julius can feel their attention. He thinks of the men who robbed him in Torrance and the other men he'd seen lined up against hotels and along the alleyways. The power men lost in such transactions and the dignity he'd lost, the two cat-faced men, their hands on each shoulder holding him. He thinks again of Muriel and it occurs to him suddenly that she must have won hugely to pull off what she did. She had gone secretly to that track and placed her eavesdropped bets until she had enough for her own private life. What a trick she had pulled then. What fantastic improbability.

The man in the boots whispers, *"Como todos. Está bien,"* and Julius knows he should go now, that he will not get what he needs this way.

"Lo siento," he says again.

He leaves the bill on the bench so he won't be followed and rises and says, *"Muchas gracias,"* and slips between the man and the bench. He takes a long route through the plaza and back around to the main street where the shopkeepers have started rolling out their awnings. At the corner now is a wooden oxcart hitched to a donkey painted in broad stripes like a convict, the man beside it small as a child and wearing a burlap maize sack cut out below the armpits. In the cart are hothouse roses the color of the sky above. As Julius walks away he looks behind to catch the man following, but no one seems to move at all in the lengthening daylight. Glancing sidelong at the faces in the trees and doorways he sees no one he has ever seen before.

THE REST OF that day and through the night he walks. He will not risk the street peddlers or the hustlers, though this leaves only children and women and tourists and the slow drawn policeman on the take. Along the thoroughfares he stops in parks and cantinas, hotel bars decorated to look like the parts of Mexico the tourists will not see, jungle motifs and hacienda blues, papier-mâché masks hung from the vigas and ristras on the lintels, and in these places he parses out the money for information only middling and wryly offered. The tourists know nothing of anyone or anything and the cantina owners smile like Eddie Cantor and roll their eyes. Walking alone he is marked repeatedly by Indian boys dressed like rustlers who offer to take his photograph among the drooping palms. If Henry had taken the train or hitchhiked from Barstow he would have arrived four or five days ago, at most. Of course it's possible that he has not come at all.

When the day opens the streets fill with navy men taking the sidewalks four across. When one group of sailors meets another they slow and walk deliberately and sometimes one group fans aside so the other men can pass and sometimes they hold the path. The panhandlers and hawkers watch this cautiously. The pigeons keep their margins and when the men have passed they peck back to the sidewalks and the hawkers resume their calling. Julius finds a few small bars packed with local men and drops nickels for weak beer and peanuts. He does not ask about Henry but instead waits, watching the doors and corners.

At dusk he joins a card game in a hotel lounge and finds the men there playing Mexican Sweat for two-dollar antes, a version of poker in which all the cards are known and there are no raises or bluffing and the men wait for a trump to turn and decide their fates. He plays in for twenty minutes, but the absence of bluffing makes it difficult to suss anything out. He loses twenty dollars and no one speaks to him.

"I sure wish I knew where a *norteño* might find a better time than this," he says.

None of the men look up from their cards. Another few minutes pass and Julius begins to feel the prickle of the men's attention. When he rises to leave, one of the men half-stands and his hat falls from his knee and he gestures with one arm in a wide arc toward the door.

"Basta," he says, *"adios."*

All night he walks through Centro and Este and down into the Cacho by the old casino, where the gridded streets give out to curving lanes that cross each other at narrow unmarked intersections. In each of these places Julius peeks in windows and through tilting trees and waits on benches near where men have gathered. He sees the men leaned against the cinder-block walls and squatted on their heels. Some are men like the men he saw that morning and some are the sons of dust bowl migrants down from the denuded hills across the border. Loose-legged Okies with their fat combs and their hair ducked back and their big self-conscious laughter. By midnight the small open lots in among the shops and the bars are lighted with fires in painted drums and the shadows assemble around in postures of organized danger. The fires shoot fetters of sparks into the night.

On Jalisco he passes a hotel built like a prison tower and he stops in the lobby for the toilet and a drink of brown water from the tap. He is hungrier than he can remember being. The walls and floors of the lobby are cold gray cement and the elevator door stands open but inside it is empty and dark. All the shabby chairs are unused except one by a narrow window, up high like a jail, where a woman sits alone. She is dark-haired and not young and does not appear to be waiting for anyone, though she presses one thumb under her chin and curls her first knuckle to the side of her mouth as if anticipating some insight. The window casts down a providential neon from the street outside and colors the woman's face, streaks of green and red wheeling across her nose and chin like a pinion. For a long moment Julius stands watching her. He feels very tired and hungry and as the woman sits detained by the light he thinks that he'd like to be touched by her, perhaps held close. She does not look like Muriel but she has Muriel's bearing, and he feels that if he called out to her she might turn to him with Muriel's face. A strange, urgent thought, but another thing he cannot ask for.

Then Julius thinks of the simple landscape of Henry's body, his moments of concentration, and Henry and Muriel and this woman seem placed one over the other like slipped film. These are the mysterious things he knows about his lover, as much as he knows about this woman or his brother's wife or anyone else. He might look in every bar or hotel lobby and find such traces in the presence of others, and even if he stands for weeks in this very spot he might not wait long enough for Henry to catch up with this thought of him. In twelve hours he's spent two hundred dollars and he is nowhere. The gray walls of the lobby emit no sound and Julius hears his own breathing. In some park where he has been the hour before, Henry might be standing among the palms, never knowing that Julius has passed through. The woman reaches out for a glass on the chair arm and moves slightly forward, revealing her face through the light, and the spell is broken. Julius hears a clamor in the stairwell and walks back through the lobby doors, out into the everlasting city.

The sun is at seven in a cloudless sky. He looks across a street bright with flags and finds that he's walked all night in a circle. To the south the crumbling minarets of Agua Caliente, to the north the tourists' Bel Airs, and beyond these things the fringes Julius has skirted, that he thinks he's found the edges of. Then he thinks of the fob in his pocket and remembers Henry standing with an elbow propped on the dresser and knows suddenly what he will do.

He finds the alley as easily as men find anything in cities where they are looking, past the streets downtown where the shopkeepers are sweeping and rolling out their carts, into an older part of the city. Across the street a bar emits the low sound of laughter and music. The men out front stand smoking and teasing one another. He will have to navigate their dawning sobriety and the clarity it brings, but he knows also that the men who are left here have not found what they wanted, or they would be somewhere else. That sadness, that unmet need, will be useful to him. As the men began to clump together at the sidewalk's margin he knows there is only a slim chance that any of them has money left.

Inside, the bar is full. The jukebox in the corner plays a country ballad; the men sway and clap each other at the chorus, which must remind them of something they are substituting this long night for. Julius elbows up and orders and pays with a new dollar. Then he stands at the end of the bar waiting. Behind the bar a cheap mirror kinked at the center and curled with smoke. The room gives off the odor of damp cotton. The back wall is covered in catalogue tear-outs of women in girdles and suspender belts, advertisements for toreos and weeklong fiestas at the coast, a map of the world as it was in 1840.

He allows a thought of Muriel to gather at the back of his mind. He'd not slept that first night and before dawn he pulled his boots on and drank a silty cup of yesterday's coffee, then stepped out into the blue chill of the grassless yard. He walked down to the river bluff and stood watching the brown water while he pissed into the scrub. From the bluff the new house was white and clean and quiet. He thought of the envelopes and what he'd found there and he could not make sense of it. Why she would still have the deed and the tax receipt to a house she didn't own. Perhaps they were only souvenirs, he thought. But when he zipped and turned back he saw her through the kitchen window, standing at the stove. The propane burner fluttered a weak blue and caught under the base of the kettle. Her hair was strangely plaited and combed back like a man's. As she stood there waiting for the kettle she placed both palms at the counter's edge and pushed back so her arms straightened and her back arched. She looked then like paintings of trees he had seen in Japan, the ken painters had in that part of the world for bowed or windblown shapes, the way the trees or waves or cliffs or fields exposed the constant motion of the earth. A moment later Lee entered, and she stood upright and lengthened her neck and dropped her hands from the counter and turned toward her husband. Julius saw the gravity of her mood dispelled by the simple adjustment of her body, and he knew then something true about her and about his brother's marriage, though it was another day before he really understood it. He wished then that he could go back to their earlier conversations and listen again but harder this time. He had thought that his brother had it all, and realizing it wasn't true shook something free in him.

Finally then he sees the man he needs, at the rear of the bar. From the slant of the man's round chin toward the room Julius can see the weakness in him, the want in his arm thrown loosely across the back of the chair. Julius waits for the man to feel his attention, and when he does Julius looks back at him. This look hangs between them long enough to answer its own question. When Julius finishes his beer he orders two more and carries them to the man's table and raises one glass. The men at the jukebox have awakened from their thin daydreams and play now the rancheras they know from movie westerns and draw pantomimed pistols on each other. One man narrows his eyes down the sight of his finger and out the front door.

The man says his name is Ralph, though Julius suspects it is not. He gives his own name honestly and the man smiles. Up close Julius sees that he is older, light hair cut just a day or two before. On the back of his chair is an Eisenhower jacket coated in dust, one corner of the collar unraveling, belonging first to an uncle or brother. The kind of jacket a man past a certain age would wear to honor another, better war. When the man offers the empty chair, Julius sits with his elbows looped around the back and his hips curled under his waist, knowing he seems younger and less shrewd this way. They speak then of ordinary things, the price of a Corona and its general flavor, the dark women on the Avenida Ensenada, and at each turn in the conversation Julius asks a question meant to seem artless and naive. As they talk, Julius studies the man's hands to see what risks he might be willing to take, the same way he'd watched gamblers from the peek above. His own hands he drapes lightly at the ends of his arms. The music of accordions and vihuelas like a bed being bounced.

Finally Julius says, "Night's full over and it's too late now for anything good to happen."

"Not so, friend," Ralph says. "Days don't work the same here."

"You ever feel like that, though? Like there's just this narrow window of time when what you want might come to you? I feel like that all over right now."

And at this signal Ralph does what Julius needs him to do. He leans forward and lowers his voice. Between them the smudged glasses like a story about what happens next.

"Listen, I know a place we could have some fun, before the day is through," he says.

A few simple looks and first Julius rises and then Ralph after him. Out front the man flags down a cab and they are driven through the gilt winter dust. When they are dropped at the gates of a park Ralph pays the driver and steps stiffly out and strokes the dust from his sleeves and snaps out his collar. They are somewhere at the northern edge of the city, near the border. Bright blue cinder-block walls etched with the park's name and its founding—Santa Cecilia, 1898. Across the street a puzzle of chabolas made from particleboard and broken brick and glass bottles, each shoveled into the next, the roofs thatched in tree limbs and plastic sheeting and bolts of cloth, all of it held up with ropes attached to iron crosses and bits of fence. From the mass comes a cacophony of human sound, laughter, pots banging, the cries of young children, somewhere near the street a slide harmonica. Above all this a pall of woodsmoke, waiting crows along the eaves.

"The mother of invention," Ralph says.

For a few minutes they walk toward the center of the park as if they had not yet agreed on anything. Inside the blue wall the sounds of the slum dissipate. The trees open into a small meadow planted in struggling crabgrass. In this country light Julius sees that Ralph was once handsome, that in many places he still is. Through the branches above, the late morning sun falls into soft shadows that texture the grass.

Julius sees no other people, though along the edges of the meadow are a few solitary shapes, a hint of habitation. Ralph leads him through the open space and behind a stand of ash, near a low stone wall.

"You're here from the station," Julius says.

"You've done some service, too, I see. You're of that age."

"Sure enough, so we're even on that score."

Ralph unbuttons the dusty jacket and puts his hands on his hips and lets the jacket open over a white silk shirt embroidered at the shoulder in faint roses. The buttons are pearlescent and feminine and strain against the man's broad chest.

"I don't need to know any more about you as long as you don't ask me."

In the man's clean and hopeful look is something Julius doesn't like. He thinks of the men and their wives below him in the peek. The ease of their beauty. He thinks of his own brother and his ignorance. He lets Ralph come forward and he slides one leg between Ralph's legs and pulls him by the belt so their noses come hard together. Julius kisses the bottom of his laughing mouth and almost forgets himself.

"Been too long then," Ralph says.

He takes the loose fly of Julius's jeans in his fist to bring him closer. In the heat of this moment their cheeks press together and the dim light of the tree cover dapples them sentimentally. Julius drops one hand to dig in his back pocket. Over the man's shoulder the regular daylight falls bright and unbroken inside the low wall of stones.

"This can be very easy," Julius says, the little blackened nub of the gun in the loose flesh under the man's jaw.

Ralph cuts his eyes and sees the gun and laughs. Julius presses the muzzle hard. Then Ralph frowns, reaches with one hand into his pocket, the other hand raised in mock surrender, and Julius laughs too, because of course the whole thing is ridiculous. The tiny gun a kind of joke about violence, like a stick of dynamite in a cartoon. Julius pulls the gun away and steps back.

"You know I've been hustled in a dozen cities," Ralph says, handing over the bills he's pulled from his pocket. "Cost of doing business." He makes a smacking sound with his lips, rubs the butt of his thumb across them.

"Good to be realistic," Julius says.

The man leans against the low wall of stones and softens his look.

"Is that it then?" he asks. "Awful lot of trouble for a few dollars I'd planned to give you anyway."

"I'm afraid that's it."

Ralph rubs one palm down the hard front of his pants and the gesture is not lewd but somehow tender, as if he were smoothing a lover's hair. He stands and steps forward and Julius holds the pistol straight out.

"I ain't no hustler. That ain't why we're here."

"Fine, if you say so. If that makes you feel better."

Julius dislikes the man's tone but he's never robbed anyone so openly and he does not know how to leave this interaction.

"There can be more. Take off your jacket and shirt."

Ralph smiles and the tip of his tongue presses through his square teeth. He unbuttons the top button of his shirt and then stops. His face loses its flirtation and he glances off as if considering all this for the first time.

"I'm going to let you keep that stupid jacket, but I want the shirt."

Ralph shrugs out of the jacket then unbuttons the shirt and takes it off one arm at a time while he switches the jacket between hands. He tosses the shirt and Julius catches it and flips it over one shoulder and levels the gun on him again.

"How big are those boots?"

"Listen, baby, you're getting away with plenty here."

"What size?"

"Twelve."

"Keep 'em."

Julius runs out of the forest shadow and into the coastal autumn light. He crosses the green expanse where a few old men have arrived with dominoes, then back into another grove of ash. He watches as Ralph emerges from the trees in the jacket buttoned tight to the throat. Ralph sees the old men and nods lightly and stands a moment in the clearing looking around. The men look at him and Ralph looks back and when one of the men begins to stand Ralph turns and walks out the way they came. Julius waits for ten minutes, then twenty, until he is certain Ralph will have found another cab and is back on his way downtown. Then he rolls the silk shirt into his pocket and leaves the cover of the trees and walks through the meadow and back out to the street.

Once, he had stolen a woman's pantyhose when he could find no money in her bag, and he kept the hose for some weeks though he had no use for them. He never told anyone that he had taken them, not the rent boys he knew or the card players whose talk was droll and vicious, any of whom would have laughed and liked Julius more for this pointless act, as if it proved his authenticity as a thief. To tell them the story would be to enlarge it, to unlive it. To share a moment of such intimacy would make those hearing the story more important than he wanted them to be.

But now he needs the story shared. He thinks that if Ralph tells the right person about his foolish mugging, about the young man with the souvenir pistol, that word could travel pretty fast. The best stories and the harshest cautions took only days to circle in Los Angeles, through the streets and the poor neighborhoods. Such efficiency made it both dangerous and easy to live there. No privacy, but no surprises either. Julius feels sure that Ralph is the right type but one never knows; a man can become any type at any time. He walks around the perimeter of the park as the day begins to warm, and as he does he makes a mental map of the places he'll return to once the sun has set.

THROUGH THE REST of that morning Julius sleeps in the cab of the truck, curled, bootheels caught on the edge of the seat and his toes hanging. He wakes shivering in the cooling afternoon. He opens the door and steps out and shakes the stiffness from his arms and legs. The sun is lowering in a long cut of light and he follows it to the edge of the lot and stands looking out at the skyline of the city. He thinks of the work ahead of him. He pulls the envelope from his pocket and thumbs through the money there. In his head he adds this money to the cost of the old Ford, then to the price of the lot and the plans and the lumber and the labor. He had never won that much at anything, never known anyone who had. It was the kind of luck that made tyrants of men and yet she had given it away. She might have kept the money for herself along with the house in Kansas but she had bought the house for Lee and let him have his dream and his fantasy and hidden the rest. He tries to imagine any reason for such a decision and he thinks again of the night in Torrance and the way he'd lost on purpose to protect himself from harm and he sees the edge of her choice but not the thing entire.

He peels off his torn shirt and puts on Ralph's, which is nicer and cleaner and smells of the man's aftershave. He leaves the truck and walks up the broad street back into the denser part of town. There, to pass the remaining daylight, he steps into a movie house showing a cabaretera. He pays a quarter for the movie and another for a lukewarm beer and sits in the darkened theater in the back. The few other men there sit far away from each other and slump down so that only their hands and noses are visible, their shiny foreheads. On the screen before him the ficheras flirt with the practiced ease of women who have never loved romance, who have always understood it as work, as a myth to make work tolerable. The machotes wear mustaches and wide-collared jackets, and when the ficheras uncross their ankles or sweep their long hair forward to cover their breasts the theater fills with sighs and then the furious sound of trumpets from the speakers hung low along the banisters.

Under the dim orange lights the men are all one color, a sameness that turns the theater into something nascent, like a perimeter of heaven, though some must be sunburned or pale as the plains or dark-eyed and brown-skinned. When Julius sees his hands around his glass or his faint reflection in the black wall he sees that he too is the same—the color of dusk across a mown lawn. Below him a boy sits alone, nine or ten years old, a souvenir Tom Mix hat covering half his face. From the side and above, Julius can see the boy's slender frame, his chin and broad nose. On the screen the fichera is sitting in a crowded bar across from a fat man whose scrutiny is stupid and vulgar, and when he asks her to dance for him she pulls out her falsies and hands them over the table, then stands and slips off one strap of her bra. The frame cuts off her waist and her legs and her arms below the elbow, but the movement of her shoulders suggests she is reaching under her skirt to remove her panties. The camera holds her gaze as she does this. The boy raises his chin and presses the hat back with a finger and Julius sees the wide-eyed, nectarous youth in him. He feels his own gaze filtered through the eyes of the fichera, her excitement at the possibility of revelation, the mutiny in it, as she undresses for the man, for the boy in the cowboy hat, for Julius, for the theater. In the cinematic trick of perspective the fichera's gaze falls on everyone equally, and Julius can almost feel the silky tug, the slippery freedom of undressing, as she is revealed. She is a saint preparing herself for some ceremony. In the darkness of the theater Julius's mind is refracted as his sight is pulled first through the woman on the screen, then the boy below him who is not quite old enough to understand, then the other men scattered around the rows. He feels, all at once, what each of them might be feeling, watching the woman undress. He thinks of the man Ralph and his freckled shoulders. He looks down at his empty glass and shakes his head at this strangeness. Through the tinny speakers the sharp drums of the bolero plunk and circle. The fichera begins to dance, and the men in the theater groan back in their seats. The boy's tall hat dips down until it covers his whole face; he is a peasant sleeping in huaraches and pantaloons, a stubborn parody of the border. He slouches into the seat until he disappears.

When the dance is over and the shot cuts away to a landscape of dirty mountains against an ocean flat as paper half the men in the theater rise to leave. Julius watches the end of the movie and the scattered feeling subsides. As the credits roll through a manic cumbia, he works his way down the aisle.

Outside the theater he follows the boy up the block toward the Zona

Norte. Evening now, the infinite winter blue dropping between the buildings and across the hat brims of the tourists and the mariachis, emotional in its contrast to the darkened theater. Julius shakes out his arms and stretches his neck and keeps soft eyes on the periphery. The boy makes his way to the Plaza Viente de Noviembre, where he joins a group of men selling cartonería dolls and wooden coins. Julius walks past them toward the center of the plaza. As he does the boy draws a finger pistol at the men and they fall back laughing, hands up. The oldest among them leans forward and flicks the brim of the hat so it sails off the boy's head and drops to the ground.

Across from the merchants, a man in a guayabera unbuttoned to the navel weaves in and out of the flow of tourists. As Julius passes he sees what the man is selling: the sight of his own heart, knocking visibly against the skin of his bared left breast, rolling up and down in a knuckled ball. Julius stands and watches a moment without believing what he sees. Those around him do not respond to the sight, as though the man has been here for some time and is no longer a shock to anyone. His heart beats fussily, perfectly there and heart-shaped as if it might soon break the skin. Some tourists avert their eyes, a few toss pesos, and the man plays for them either way, showing his impossible heart and holding out his hand. Julius waits and watches for wires or seams in the man's skin but he finds no deception, though a heart so close and defenseless is unimaginable. The man disappears back into the crowd like a rumor.

Julius returns to the lot and starts the truck. At the entryway he pays a different man the dime and sways out onto the broad avenida. He finds the park again by memory and leaves the truck along a side street where there are a few knitted chabolas set away in the trees. Then he walks to the back corner of the park, where he removes the shirt and twists it under the slow-running water of a fountain. When he shakes the shirt open he sees that the water has rusted the fabric where he and Ralph have sweated, along the collar and the armpits, and he scrubs these sections with the flat nail of his thumb. He wrings the shirt out again and puts it on damp, then combs water through his hair. The moon is out and a few pale flecks of starlight. In the grassy center a half-dozen shadows have begun to assemble. He lies down in the grass with the fob coiled in his fist and the damp back of the shirt letting through the cool softness of the ground.

Two nights ago now, after he found the envelopes, he'd sat in the kitchen wondering what he should do. He thought about what Muriel told him on the phone, and the money she'd sent, and both things took on new and surprising meanings. The tax receipt and the deed and the letter from the neighbors were easy enough to parse, and the racing form gave them provenance. The words she'd written on the form were familiar to him somehow but he couldn't say why. He sat in the kitchen a long time considering all this. His reflection looked back at him from the window like an image on a movie screen, as crisp as that and as distant. It was a kind of double exposure, he'd thought. He knew if he told his brother that Lee's heart would be first broken, then adjudicated, then dialed back to its small expectation. The strangeness of the crime might be enough to salvage things. Yet it would be the lie and not the money that injured Lee: The lie would confirm something his brother could not admit or name.

Yet, more troubling was Julius's sense that he too had betrayed his brother and that he'd wanted to. Whatever he had hoped for by coming to them and by bringing the horse dissolved inside this fact. He had learned Muriel's secret because he had come to steal from them, but long before that she had tried to tell him about it. He'd stayed on the phone that night a long time because he'd wanted her love and her disclosure, he'd wanted something his brother did not have. He wanted to be known by her and he suspected she wanted to know him but he had no way to say what he meant. In the dark window of their kitchen he was no longer handsome or tempting. He leaned his head on his brother's table, wanting to weep but unable, and felt his decision taking shape in the cold morning. He might have left the hundred dollars in the coffee can but he needed the cruelty of it, the retribution his brother's hurt would bring to him. He could not tell his brother and he could not keep a secret with his brother's wife and that left only thieving, only his own exile.

Often, as a child, he had imagined the crucifixion—not the abstractions of sin or death or eternal life but the actual bite of the nail. During a sermon in the small church where his father had tithed, Julius dragged there some morning in summer for something he'd done, the pastor told the congregation that the nails were driven not into Christ's palms, as everyone had believed, but into His wrists. Julius watched his father ring his hand around his own wrist as the pastor spoke, as if he had just been released from some rope or cuff, and Julius understood for the first time that his father had feelings.

In the trees above him a bird takes off in the direction of the city. In the winter trees the birds move in dark flutters like waving hands. He thinks of every dead thing as a bird in the air. He remembers something then, a little fold in time. He sees himself at eleven or twelve holding a hedgepost while Lee digs around it, bare branches like those above him now, cast against a cold sky. He remembers no more than this, just the feeling of that moment and the pastel white of the sky, the blank arms of cottonwood and oak stretching across the view.

Now, perhaps right now, Ralph is sitting at a bar playing pop-cap or freckles with some hard-up kid, and as the kid leans out of his practiced reserve and lets some intimacy open between them Ralph begins to speak. He tells the kid he was approached, just that morning, by a darkhaired man in a dirty shirt with a missing button, a man with broad, unlucky hands. He is careful here to keep his shoulders square and his voice low, not to affect any toughness but rather a posture of masculine delight, the body arranged to mask its desires, to create a friable distance between the story he is telling and the way he really feels about it. In his boastful voice he tells the kid about the tiny pistol, his lost money. The young puto, vocationally aware of the man's tastes but inexperienced, pockets this story to use later, as a cautionary tale, or as foreplay. He tells it first to his lover in a noisy café, to avoid talk of where he's been, and then to the other kids at the plaza where he works. The story will roll out into the street where men gather, down into the Zona Coahuila and back out to the place where Julius lies now, imagining it. By then the story will have changed but one salient detail will remain, and it is by this singular item that Henry will know, when the story reaches him in some motel or bodega or alley, and he'll begin to trace it back. And it will not matter that Julius betrayed him, that the decent work of the casino has been lost to theft and wandering. When he hears the story of the pistol he will come to Julius and Julius will be forgiven for all he has done wrong.

IN THE DEEP WINTERS of their Kansas childhood Julius and his brother found work among the farm boys, kept busy through the fallow season clearing snow for county maintenance, salting sidewalks and thawing stock tanks. They were gathered in the dark at the corner of Ninth and Topeka Boulevard in a repurposed school bus shared by the maintenance and sheriff's departments, fitted inside with bars like towel racks for attaching handcuffs. The bus was unheated and the boys smoked with the transom windows popped out, admitting a flange of road salt and snowy mush. The city in those days was a single laid-out line of brick warehouses narrowing to the southern horizon, with the residential districts scattered out like henpeck to the east and west, and on such dark mornings the boys could see the early stars reflected in the blank panes of windows.

Julius's memory of the bare branches and the hedgepost is from one such winter, soon into the thaw, nearly spring. He and his brother had been hauled up Burnett's Mound where an ice storm weeks before had downed trees and flopped the fence that marked off a dirt path from a copse of cow oak. The fence had a moral purpose—to keep teenagers and servicemen from parking there, those who might reveal to young women the city lights and the western sky and the thorny work of romance—and their task that day was to restore it. Julius was just twelve, his brother nearly fourteen, old enough to have forgotten almost everything about their mother, who had been dead ten years, though something in the regular morning tasks still brought her perceptibly near, her smell and shape and warmth, a loneliness that reached out for some meaningful form so that they might name it and in that way snatch loneliness back from the general world.

On Burnett's Mound they watched the sunrise from the top of the hill. They lifted the fence six feet at a time and dug the posts into the holes, through the top layer of frost down to where the earth was moist and workable. While two or three boys held the fence upright, another came through with rich new dirt and tamped the posts back in. As they worked, the day lighted slowly around the distinctive lip of the earth.

As was often the case, inmates from the county jail worked alongside them, and no one in authority prevented their interaction, though the hired boys were told not to let prisoners bum cigarettes or anything else, on penalty of mutual prosecution. On this day the inmates worked down the hill some distance, clearing branches and tossing them into a burn pile. By ten they had peeled off their square coats and moved about in the canvas pajamas that marked them as prisoners, while the guards stood holding their rifles. The men cast gloomy looks up the hill at the boys, who did their best not to look back.

Julius and Lee had reached that age and time when one of two things happens to brothers. Their father had been dunked in the Kansas River wearing only his nightshirt and since then had adopted the habits of pious men, with all the zeal and shortcomings of the converted. Julius and Lee each learned to negotiate this change differently. On weekend days Lee hauled the wash water from the street-spigot and made the coffee and kept the fire going while Julius disappeared into the vacant lots and the maze of winter trees by the river. The extra work they took on Fridays was the only time they were together now, except at night when they slept in the parlor by the woodstove. When, in another six months, their father stopped working and the electricity ran out and then the firewood, Lee quit school and Julius soon after him and both took jobs on factory row and came to separate conclusions about things.

But on this day they were still brothers. As they worked the prisoners started to loosen, to enjoy the outside world, and though they did not speak to the boys an air of attention began to drift between them. As they worked one of the men began to sing a little gospel song, about the river running headlong to the sea, and as he sang he lost the tune and began to hum inchoately until the other men laughed at his forgetfulness. Up the hill the boys stopped a moment to listen. Then a second man began another bar of the hymn, getting the words right this time, and the other prisoners joined in, and for a few minutes the tune carried along. The sun was fully up by then and the little frost had melted and the wet ground sucked at the boys' boots as they moved between the posts. When the men reached the final verse no one could recall the words and the song fell apart in the field.

But the prisoners had invited the boys and anyone else to be aware of them. The guards had relaxed their watch, chatting with one another as they looked down idly at the men. Julius, whose sweet voice hadn't changed yet, nudged his brother and began to sing, still holding the hedge-rail and keeping his voice soft. "Shoo fly don't bother me, 'cause I belong to somebody," he sang, rising up a fragile octave to mark the change in mood. The men down the hill stopped their work and looked at each other and then up the hill at the boys. Julius caught the eye of one prisoner who nudged the man next to him and pointed up at the singer and Julius felt a pleasant surge of fear. The guards quieted their chatting then. Lee saw the man pointing at Julius and moved closer to his brother. Even then Julius knew how to stand in a way that pleased other men like him, one hand in the back pocket of his jeans and the collar of his jacket popped up, though his youth was a disguise he would wear a long time. Lee started to sing along as a kind of protection, and Julius clapped the heel of his hand against the hedgepost while the guards looked on, until a voice rose up from below, then a few other prisoners' after. Because no one knew the verses they sang this first line a few times, until finally the song died away. They went back to work until one of the boys drew up another song from the radio, which everyone knew, and the prisoners and the boys together sang through the song once and then again, while the guards watched. The guards did not settle back to their ease but they did not stop the singing either.

When the light began to fail the boys were gathered and put back on the bus. Through the windows they watched the men come forward one by one to have their hands cuffed in front of them. The man who had pointed at Julius stared through the dirty transom window, and as he was cuffed he winked at Julius, who winked back. His brother, already preoccupied by their return home and what they might encounter there, did not notice this. Julius stared a long time until a guard butted the man with the rifle and he turned and walked down the road toward the second bus. Julius could feel it, the freezing bite of those handcuffs, flung closed in a stirrup. The boys had been hauled there to do work for pay that grown men were punished by doing, and this seemed the progress of things, the vista a boy of that class in that time might glance warily toward.

The boys' bus followed the prisoners' bus down the hill and to the flat south end of town where the feed stores were shuttered and a few men stood outside in the cold, smoking and talking. When they were well away from the site the buses parted ways, one toward downtown and the other out to the county jail. Later the city scraped all of it off—the cow oak stand, the hedge fence, the side of the mound itself—to pull through the new turnpike from Oklahoma to Kansas City, past towns that came to mean something by proximity to it, so that a man might take his wife down to the Granada in Emporia on a Friday night just because he could. But by then Julius was long gone, and Lee too, though if they'd opened a map they could still have pointed out the place they'd worked and where their father's little forsaken house had been, along with a dozen bars and shops along the turnpike route, the razed shingles and bricks sent on to county salvage to be made into asphalt.

When the boys were let off, the foreman waited at the door to hand them each two dollars in coins. Julius and his brother did not stop for day-end popcorn at the hardware store or bread for Sunday as they might have on another evening. When they turned the corner where the neighborhood gave way to factory bars and the chain-link fence collapsed under thistle they saw that their father was not in the yard. Since it was Friday he might be at church reciting Vespers and in fact he was, and though neither boy said anything the relief was palpable between them. Inside Julius found the Hills Bros. can and shook it and when he heard the sound it made he tipped the can over into his brother's cupped palms and fished out the cigarette butts their father kept there, along with a few coins. Then Lee wiped the coins one by one on his jeans and put them in his pocket with their wages and Julius tossed the butts in the woodstove.

They found a Mason jar in the cupboard, dabbed it out with a rag, and set it on the stove to warm. Lee took a pint of milk from the larder and poured this into the warming jar. For a few minutes the boys sat by the fire with their boots off and talked about what they might do next. The larder was empty but for the milk and the wood was low. If they didn't hide or spend the coins their father would give the money to the church, as he had many other necessary things. The window frames gaped and the roof was caving. When the milk had warmed Lee took a long drink, then handed the jar to Julius.

"Ain't nothing going to fix all this," Lee said, and his brother nodded.

"But you have to do something, don't you."

"I guess."

Lee covered the jar with the rag and set it back on the stove, then held his hand near the flue collar, which leaked heat.

"I'll get another five this week if I work two shifts on Wednesday," Julius said.

"Just don't spend it where you ought not," Lee said. Then he stood up, turned the aluminum chair over, and kicked through the base with his foot. The seat was covered in a peeling vinyl and Julius asked if it ought to be burned.

"Who cares," Lee said and cracked the cheap base over his knee and when it didn't break he used the little woodaxe by the stove and split it. He fed the pieces to the fire, which burned the vinyl in a puff of green and then settled. The brothers looked at the second chair, which they thought they remembered their mother using in the evenings, though probably they had only imagined this.

"Not that one, not yet," Julius said and Lee agreed, though it would have burned the whole night.

"We'll wait for when we really need it," Lee said. They took the chair to the small mudroom off the kitchen and covered it with a blanket and shoved it in a corner. Then Lee took the woodaxe and carried it through the backyard and past the factory fencing to where the river trickled levelly and from the fallen branches there he gathered what he could carry.

The next morning they turned back their blankets and rose and before they fed the fire they checked in on their father, who was still sleeping, and then in the mudroom for the covered chair. When their father woke he waited several long minutes at the table and when Lee brought him hot coffee he said nothing. But when he had finished his coffee and set the cup down on the table he made with his hands the shape of a chair, though not to Lee or to anyone else. Then he went outside and sat directly on the cold ground and waited.

All that day their father sat in the yard, though it was nearly freezing and the wind funneled down the street between the tall buildings and past their house. Only a few people passed in the weather and their father waved to each of them and wished them God's blessings. At midday Lee coaxed him inside with cold ham sliced the night before and muddy coffee warmed on the stove, and as he stood at the kitchen counter to eat their father thanked them for observing the Sabbath. For an hour he slept in the parlor with his arms crossed, and when he woke and went back outside Lee took out a horsehair blanket and a hot-water bottle and said this was all they could do. Soon after, Julius left for downtown, where he could make a few coins shoveling sidewalks and then take those coins to the bar where they let him play monte, and he does not remember a time after that when he spoke to his father about anything of note.

IN TIJUANA, anyone who sees Julius in the days that follow might think he is a man on a call from the Lord. If the stars fell on him he would have acted surprised but not been. Along the Avenida Ensenada a litany of sights: Girls from San Diego in dresses above their knees kicking their heels straight out to the music of the vihuela. Sailors easy in their peacetime rest. He sees more men like the men he'd met the first day, in ironed jeans thick as canvas and cuffed above the ankle, and their female counterparts in the backstreets, high-rouged. Along the avenues shell-gamers with folding tables and three-card monte played with an eared deck and boys in graceful poses and other boys kicking rocks through the alleys and girls on the fire escapes watching these boys for no reason they can name except that they are discouraged from looking elsewhere. The man in the Plaza Viente de Noviembre with the peculiar condition that makes his heart roll outside his ribs—ribs that must, Julius begins to realize, be missing—works each day as the twilight falls. In the absence of anyone dear, each stranger is a vessel for his anticipation.

At night he walks the parks and plazas and exchanges glances with other men while the night knits thickly, then in the strange hours between midnight and six he drives back to Santa Cecilia park, where he has discovered obscured thickets and cinder-block toilets and lean-tos of corrugated tin tilted back into the shrub. Here he finds willing men but not Henry, though he gets as close as he can to the leaning figures to peer at or proposition them, waiting for them to speak or reach out. Sometimes he takes money and sometimes he doesn't; sometimes he takes a jacket or a watch and these he leaves at the edges of the slum, where he imagines they will be pawned or put to some ingenious use. In each case he flashes the little gun at the man he is robbing and says his own name clearly. If he is tired, or if the man he's chosen seems dodgy, he might move away and into the open. If he finds a man particularly young he might walk up to him with a hand held out gently and offer some advice about the night, a word of warning about a thief known to work this northern section with a pistol the size of a woman's thumb. Those boys might laugh at him but he knows they are listening. When the light begins to lengthen and the park fills with early risers from the adjacent neighborhoods, he stops to make casual conversation about the weather or the coming holiday, and if the tone is right he might ask if anyone has heard of the man with the pistol, or of another Americano much like himself, the way one might ask a stranger about the outcome of a race.

In the daylight hours he drinks or plays cards in the many bodegas and navy bars, or he sleeps in the cab of the truck with his shirt rolled into one side window and his pants rolled into the other to block the light. He is not recognized and only twice does he see a trick again, from a distance, and then he ducks away. From the squat shops and piled garbage it is clear to Julius that this city, once bright with joy and life between the wars—when there was no booze or gambling to the north—is now decaying. It seems to Julius that Tijuana is the future that awaits all their steady surplus, that American luck will run out eventually and when it does all the cities will look like this. He thinks about telling his brother this and how Lee would sigh at him. There is some comfort in knowing he would not be believed.

One night in the park he finds a man sitting in a lean-to with his legs crossed like a schoolboy. In his lap an open magazine and though there is no light he bows his head as if reading.

"You got X-ray vision or something?" Julius asks.

The man does not start but looks up slowly and it's clear he'd seen Julius some time ago. He circles his fingers and holds a hand to each eye like binoculars.

"You been waiting for me?" Julius asks.

"Searching for someone," the man says theatrically and scans the clearing from left to right then settles on Julius again and adjusts the pantomimed lenses. "May as well be you."

The man smiles and lowers his hands and sets the magazine aside and rises. At his full height he is much taller than Julius and in another circumstance Julius might back away into the open field. But the man's boyish gesture suggests not danger but something wilder and sweeter and Julius lets him come close.

"I just hauled in this evening, from the coast," the man says.

"What were you doing out there?" Julius asks.

"Lordy, you ought to go. That's where the real fun is."

"What kind of fun?"

"A fella's kind, good American kind."

"Then why ain't you there instead of here?"

"Gotta come to town sometimes, to cash your checks."

The man smiles and pats his back pocket.

"Ain't I in luck then," Julius says.

Even at this distance it is too dark to see much about the man's face. The man lights a cigarette and waves the smoke from his eyes though the stillness of the night settles it again just above his shoulder. The trees are motionless around them and the smoke hovers as if held by some force and both these things add to the odd feeling of detention.

"My name's Julius."

"I don't need to know that," the man says, not unkindly.

Julius says, "What's your pleasure then?"

"What's yours?"

"I asked first."

And like other men in the preceding weeks this man reaches for Julius and cups his neck and kisses him. Julius digs in his pocket for the gun and brings it out and touches it to the man's cheek. But the man does not pull away. Julius stops kissing him and pokes the gun into his ear and this catches the man's attention finally and he leans out of the kiss. This close Julius sees that he is gray at the temples and blue-eyed.

"Oh well," the man says.

Julius backs up and opens a few feet of space between them and points the gun and the man sighs. He looks at Julius as he finds his money and makes a curious face and something changes then but it takes Julius a moment to register it.

"What kind of round does that thing take?" the man asks.

"Twenty-two," Julius says, and the man laughs. He hands Julius a thousand-peso note and a bar-cap and unholsters an imagined pistol and points a finger at Julius. Julius says, "Pow," and the man turns his head as if a bullet has whizzed by him. Julius bangs the little pistol-butt with his palm as if it had misfired and regards it and then he laughs too.

"You'd have to shoot me right between the eyes to kill me with a twenty-two," the man says, and Julius registers the change for what it is. He stops laughing. He sees what's underneath the man's boyishness and it is not sweet or wild.

"If you say so," Julius says. He glances around for openings in the trees. His best route is behind him. But then the man turns his back and leans beneath the tin awning and retrieves his magazine. Julius moves a few feet away but when the man turns back he has no violence in him and he walks out toward the park. Julius breathes deeply and shakes his hands to get some feeling back in them.

"Nothing ever goes the way you think it will," the man says as he passes.

"You can count on that," Julius says, and watches as the man leaves the trees and disappears.

That night Julius sees a rumbera in a movie theater on Revolución, where the beer is fifteen cents a pint. He chastises himself for his poor judgment, for failing to intuit the blue-eyed man's true character. He worries he is not himself. The rumbera is less risqué than the cabaretera he saw some weeks before, more inventive, the women do not undress or feign undressing. Instead there is dancing, buoyant music, melodrama, and Julius finds it cheers him with its gritty confidence. The story itself is familiar: A young campirana, gifted with beauty and *cara*, lights out for the city. There she finds betrayal, fame, danger, modernity. She finds a man, then loses him. On the other side of this adventure she is gorgeous and shrewd, she is beyond help, she lives dancing on the edge of ruin.

The movie is a double feature. The rumbera is followed by an American western dubbed in Spanish. Julius stays through the western, which is funnier in Spanish but less romantic. The two films are not so different in kind, and together they make bearable the long interval of evening. Together they make their own story: The mujeres led to perdition in the bright city, the men hauling out for the bloody plains, as if the girls in their volantes had driven them there. A little parable, Julius thinks. A little truth about the world, played out in the murky theater.

AT THE BEGINNING of the third week he steps out of a spitting rain and into a mercado at the northern end of Revolución. It is just dawn. Two days of drizzle and one of ominous wind have dropped great brown palm fronds and left the plazas empty and the streets skidded in mud. Julius drifts through bodies packed and steaming in the warm rain. Three nights in a row he has seen no one at the border in Santa Cecelia except the domino players at dawn, dressed in long dusters the color of barley. His back and legs hurt from squatting all night in the trees and his clothes smell of rain.

He returns to the truck parked along the Avenida de los Insurgentes in one of the pay-twice lots. Inside the truck is cold and damp so he starts the engine and lets it idle and runs the heater. He peels off his damp shirt and jeans and hangs them over the dash for the heater to dry, then takes the little gun from the back pocket and a wad of wet bills and lays these on the seat. Under the seat he fumbles for the envelope. He straightens the wet bills and puts them together with the others, then counts out the amount. He has stolen less than he's spent and too much time has passed.

The heat unfogs the windows and outside it is still raining but lightly now, and to the south he can see a break in the clouds. While he waits for his clothes to dry he buffs the pistol with the tail of Ralph's shirt until it is buttery and even. Then he floats through a light sleep, sitting upright in the cab, until the heat grows stifling even in his underwear. He wakes sweating from a dream about Henry and his brother and knows he won't sleep again for a long time. He takes a handful of dollar bills and a twenty and the buffed gun and he slats the dollar bills along the bottoms of his busted boots to keep the rain out. Then he kills the truck engine and steps out into the late afternoon drizzle.

In a cantina down Revolución he sees two women sitting alone at the bar. He ponies up next to them, and when a few minutes have passed he lets some attention open between them. The women order another round of drinks and raise their glasses in a toast to each other and then to the stranger to their right. Julius raises his glass back to them and swivels on his stool and the women introduce themselves. They are housewives on holiday, here with their husbands, who are shooting pool in the back.

"This weather," the first woman says. She is brunette and wears a pale lipstick the color of champagne. She looks so much like Muriel from the side that when Julius catches her at this angle he draws in his breath.

"We'd be missing this rain in Bakersfield," the second woman says.

"That's the only thing we'd be missing," says the brunette.

"Not over, they say. Even worse on the other side of Friday."

Beyond them, bottles on crude wooden shelves serve as a barricade between the bar and the street. Through the bottles Julius can see the low wet curb where mariachis sit smoking in a rare moment of silence and leisure. He watches the men, outlined all at once in unfaded life, sitting and joking on the curb, as if in their rest they are suddenly visible. The women talk of the hawkers and the little boys with their Chiclet gum and the donkeys painted like zebras and the ficheras that play the bars up and down the Zona Norte.

"Now there's something," the brunette says. "The men buy caps from the bartender and the caps pay for dances, but then they buy the woman a drink, too, which you never see them drinking."

"Everything here is for sale," Julius says.

"And what are you selling, mister?" the second woman says and raises three fingers for another round.

"You ever hear of a Sputnik cocktail?" he says and when the women laugh he tells them the punch line.

"At the very least it can't see us here. No one will bother to look at a place like this," the second woman says.

"It can't see you," Julius says, and as he does the brunette also speaks. "It isn't looking at Bakersfield either, I'd say."

"It ain't looking at nothing," Julius says.

"And how do you know that?"

"I know about looking is all."

Straight-on the woman's face is nothing like Muriel's but she does have Muriel's aloofness. He wonders if that's the right word. If it might be instead a kind of patience. It would have taken extraordinary patience to do what she'd done. It would take patience to live with the result. He thinks again of her stretching posture through the kitchen window and her slicked-back hair. Christmas Eve so long before when he'd asked her if she'd ever been in love. He recalls very little about that night but he recalls her answer.

When he is loosely drunk he reaches past the brunette to clasp the hand of the other and asks plainly, touching the second woman but eyeing the brunette, "Would you ever marry a man you didn't love?" and both women laugh.

The second one says, "Oh ho! You think those are the stakes, love and romance?"

The brunette says, "I'm not trying to marry you, if that's what you're after."

Then both of them smile knowingly at each other and then turn smiling to him.

"You know what, pal?" the brunette says. "Maybe you get to go around here without anyone watching, but we could never do that. We'd been sitting here less than five minutes before you showed up."

"I don't have any interest in you that way," Julius says.

"That may be, but what if you did?"

"I've got enough of my own troubles now."

"I can see that clear enough."

Then she reaches out to trace the faint rose at his shoulder, sooty and stiff with rain. He reaches up and covers her hand with his own and they touch that way, both their hands at his shoulder. He feels her attention turned behind to the billiard table. He could take anything from her and it would not change her opinion one bit; she has already decided about him. To him that is a freedom that will not barter for virtue. It is the way he recognizes tenderness.

So he says, "You remember how McCarthy used to talk, about fairies and reds."

"Sure," says the second woman. She looks at his hand touching the brunette's and frowns.

"One has secrets and the other traffics in them, and there's a bad combination," says the brunette.

"That was the idea. But McCarthy didn't see the irony in it, did he," Julius says.

"And what's that?" asks the brunette.

"A whole great majority of Americans had never heard of fairies or reds until McCarthy and Cohn got them in the craw. And now everyone has to wonder if they've met one. So do you all."

"Well, hasn't this turned bleak," the second woman says, but he can tell what's dawning on her.

"Here's the thing," he says, and catches the eye of each woman in turn. "You don't want people's secrets, do you? When you're someone with secrets that means you're either very good or very bad, and neither one seems to me much to hope for."

"Things I learned in Tijuana," the brunette says.

Both women look away and through the tilted bottles to the street beyond. Outside the mariachis have lifted their instruments and stubbed out their cigarettes and stand tuning for evening. They are transformed by these acts. The rain falls inside the trumpet bells and the rims of their sombreros and along the neck of the vihuela. A strange confusion of causality, whether the mariachis have changed to or from something. The rain on the tin roof of the cantina sounds like teeth grinding.

The brunette turns back to him and says, "You ought to be careful out there."

"You too," Julius says.

"Out there is where everything is though, isn't it," she says.

She slides her hand from his and pats it gently and lifts it from his shoulder and places it neatly in his lap. The other woman has not looked back and now she stands and turns toward the billiard table and says, "Mary Ann," and shoulders the brunette who stands too.

Julius leaves them then and walks out into the rainy street. He walks through the plaza where the heart man works, but the heart man is not there. The vendors have returned and the rain comes lightly and Julius buys a glass of corn chicha and drinks it as he stands by a statue of Flores Magón, then buys another and downs it, and when the vendor shakes his hand to indicate a third glass Julius toasts the statue and pays the vendor another nickel and crosses the river toward Los Insurgentes with the sour cup. By now he is maudlin drunk and he knows it. He returns to the truck and pays the man the dime and rolls out onto the street, then turns again on Padre Kino and past the federal highway headed toward the border.

Several blocks from the border park, Julius stops the truck along a covert of trees and waits for full darkness. He tries to recall the day, sorting its elements into a simple order. He thinks of the men he saw, then their wives or children or lovers or bosses, then the women at the bar and their husbands, and he tries to count who might have seen him or might be told about him. He imagines Henry circling the same bars and plazas looking for him, an hour or two behind, perhaps now buying a glass from the same man by the same statue. It had been so long now and he doesn't want to walk again into the soaking park, but he worries that if he does not keep his routine he will become remote from the workings of history. That what is left after history is merely fate. He says very quietly, *please*, then he closes his eyes and says it again. He doesn't have anyone in mind when he says it yet it does not feel unheard.

He tucks the shirt in tightly and brushes the roses with his fingers. He stamps down on the bills in his boots to make them flat again. Then he leaves the truck. The slum is quiet in this twilight hour and the gate to the park stands open. Inside the meadow is silky with rain. He watches the wind animate the grass and the small pools of rainwater, and as he watches a shadow emerges through the trees by the stone wall where he'd been weeks before, with Ralph. The shadow edges and takes shape against the branches and in the fading light between them, a figure like a man behind a lectern or altar. The shadow does not move closer but stands there with the square of darkness in front, then the figure raises his arms, hands open like someone asking not to be shot or blamed. Julius moves across the meadow and the figure moves toward him. The man stops and Julius keeps coming and in the slant of light he sees the man in more detail. He is tall and lanky and short-haired. Julius thinks of Henry's grim laugh and his courtesy. He narrows his eyes and smiles and thinks the same thought many men have had looking at the dimming sky—that the dark universe is lighted by human will.

But before he can cross the wall the man vanishes. Julius steps over the wall and into the shelter of trees. Inside the half-tumbled stones he sees what he'd missed before, with Ralph and on the nights after when he'd stuck to the tree line, an opening in the ground that hints at some depth beyond. It seems impossible that he has not noticed this but when he bends down and looks he sees the earth cleared and a set of wooden doors swung open. He is looking at a root cellar.

He steps through the squat doorway and the darkness is purple and gray, influenced by the pocks and open spaces above them where the rock has fallen in or a tree root grown through. Fifteen feet down, the hardpan gives way to black, fragrant dirt, and it seems there should be tombs but instead there are stone arches held together with mud and moss, the bottoms crumbling and shifted. He smells a wheaty cologne and then he sees the man's shape. He calls out.

"Henry?"

The man does not answer. Instead he pushes into Julius and kisses him and Julius knows at once that he is not Henry. In the dark of the tunnels Julius can see only the gray outline of the man's shoulders and chest. Their belt buckles clank together. He is not Henry but he is someone and Julius's desire and his desperation allow some confluence. He runs his hands through the man's lacquered hair, the feeling between his fingers like tar-slicked weeds on the side of the road where he once worked off a probation. He had been so young then, caught stealing cartons of engine oil from the back of a gas station. Hot summer on the plains, drinking beer afterward with the other men, fingernails black with tar. One man lighting the tar on his hands with the end of his cigarette. Why should he remember this now?

The man untucks his shirt then reaches for Julius's and Julius helps him lift it. Still he cannot see the man's face, though the smell of his cologne is deep and grassy and he thinks that he will remember it forever. He unbuttons from the bottom so his shirt tents open and the man can touch his bare skin. How quickly and how fine.

"You know me," Julius says.

"I don't know you, darling, but I could."

The man's voice is sudden. It is casual and even and it could be Henry's voice.

"You do—you know me."

The man's body is so yielding and expressive and he touches Julius like it might be the only thing left in the world that he can manage. He kisses Julius's neck and collarbone. Julius thinks that he has disappeared from himself and not been replaced by anything. He has been lifted out of time and the body left here now in its blank pleasure is like the light delay of stars.

"You've been out to the coast then," the man says.

"What coast now."

"That's where I come from. That's how you might know me."

The man pulls him forward again so they crush together chest to knees. Julius stumbles and the man catches him and he remembers that he is drunk. He reaches down where the man is hard and lovely and the man touches him in return. The man makes a noise of languorous assent and kisses Julius again. Then the man kneels and takes Julius in his mouth and he gives head like a saint and very quickly Julius comes. The man stays on his knees and finishes himself and calls out in Spanish in a high fragile voice that Julius likes the sound of. He pants a minute and Julius lowers too so their knees are touching and he puts his arms around the man. The man does not pull away but lets his shoulders sink into this embrace. They hold together against the cold wall until Julius lifts his face away and makes a space between them.

"What coast," he says again.

"You're looking for a certain man, you go there," the man says in his new faint voice.

"What makes you think I'm looking for someone."

"I've seen you here. If I've seen you here others have too. You mustn't linger."

"When did you see me?"

The man does not answer. The cold of the tunnel is suddenly boundless, and in the silence Julius can hear the tapping rain above. He feels the man's heat and cannot imagine kissing him again, though between them still the sweet camaraderie that came from their kissing. The man touches his cheek and Julius squints but sees only that the man is clean-shaven, his eyes are brown or dark green. He turns his face into the man's touch so his chin and ear are cupped and then he turns again to press his lips to the man's palm.

"You need more than this place, to find someone, is what I'm saying to you," the man says.

Then he rises into his kneel and kisses the top of Julius's head and then he stands. He clamps the waist of his pants together and turns and ascends the stairs without saying anything more. Julius watches him until he disappears.

Then he too stands and buttons his shirt and jeans. He feels the unevenness in his boots and stomps them tighter. He thinks of what he's heard about the coastal towns. Then he flicks open his lighter and lifts it. He moves to the back of the room where the mud walls have been tamped smooth in some bygone procedure. In the earth are scratched figures of men swimming or running, animals with human heads, trees scored in the soft grain as if made from a single line, the trunks lifting up into branches. Along with these images are swirls of graffiti, men's names and Spanish slang he doesn't know. He walks with the lighter held a few inches away from the wall and swung top to bottom. Hispanophone names and hands outlined in mud. A dozen hearts drawn in their crude dimensions, two curved lines reaching up and apart then meeting at the bottom. Because he has spent each night in this park he has the unsettled feeling that this place has sprung suddenly from some distant imagining, that it was not open to him until now. The way that insights and charms were withheld from men who were not ready to receive them, though those men wailed in their rooms. On the ground the indentation of the man's knees and the white trail of his cum, other knees and other cum like maps to the need that had led them here. Only longing itself would bring back the thing their touching has stood in for, it could not be named by the ordinary world. And though Julius has never seen ancient art carved in stone or drawn on brittle paper, he does not need history or paintings to know that yearning takes these bright forms. Here were the archetypes of human dream, and they marked the very end, the great finale, of love. Every man who ever lived had been here. It would take less than an hour to reach the coast and in the rainy dark he might be seen as these marks are, only by other seekers, and with this shape and these new eyes he would find the man he loves.

SEVEN

The cliffs

The day after Julius's departure Muriel stands behind the bar smoking and waiting for the evening. The afternoon is gray, remorseless, a cold and hesitant rain falling straight down between the buildings and onto the parked cars. The lounge owner has pulled the plantation fan from its mounting and angled it in the corner on a drop cloth. Above the horsemen the ceiling is a lighter color in a broad shape that matches the fan's arc. Without it, the horsemen's cigarette smoke and her own and the smoke of the other customers draws in a flat cloud from one corner of the lounge to the other. The low winter light and the gathered smoke lend everything a pallor that suits her mood. In the corner the fan has the forlorn look of scrap.

The horsemen complain of the smoke and the stale air, and when someone points out the resting fan the men look around and above as if hurt by some repudiation. Someone says, "Was that always there?" and another man replies, "Who notices the ceiling?" In its absence the fan is finally needed and here is an irony that pleases everyone. The lounge owner sends the men a round for their trouble.

The day before, a horse had gone down at Del Mar. The man with the mustache recounts the story as if the other men had not been there to see it.

"It was that huge buckskin and Artie Cleaves was bailed up on it and just after he got free the buck went down at the turn and when the stretcher came there was Artie by the tunnel crying like a girl. Like a *girl*."

The other men nod sincerely and do not let on that they know the story. Of course Muriel has not been to Del Mar since that day, months ago now, when she was so touched by luck. But hearing the man tell the story she feels a proximity to it, as if she'd watched it in a movie. The man describes the buckskin dropping into a kneel and then down, the jockey Cleaves pressing both hands flat on the horse's head and leaping over and off, the sound of all this like a car stopping hot on gravel. Such things happened but she'd never seen it.

The mustache says that anyway Artie Cleaves always rode like someone trying to win back his heart and when he pushed the buck along the rail everyone there could guess what was coming. The race continued and the downed horse did not panic and this at least was a blessing. The ambulance bounced out and after the horse was carried off the men in the boxes stood and threw balled cups and tickets at Artie Cleaves. As the mustache tells this part of the story the other men at the table break into triumphant laughter, as if their lives were charmed by this accident or by the retribution from the boxes. Muriel sees on their faces the unmistakable relief of the exonerated. She had seen them this way before, once, when the man Gerald died.

The mustache continues: "Because anyway the whole time Artie'd been riding that buck like a man in the process of escape. Pressed back into the cantle like that. And when he wept and those raffs threw their beer down on him! Well, I can't condone that but I can't blame them either. That's how it is in winter. Not one of them real turfmen. Dumb cousins not even wearing hats or wristwatches, and they get the horses and the riders they deserve."

The others nod and this concludes the story. The mustache leans back in his chair and for a while sits silently while the others lodge their smaller complaints: meager train schedules, falling ticket sales, the general providence of men like them, set out here at the ends of the earth to tend some rich man's field. Someone brings up Las Vegas and one of the men says, "Damn university now, out there."

"What subjects they teach, you figure?" someone else says. "Wire fraud? How to get elected to Congress?"

"We get that Kennedy kid on the Rackets Committee he'll shut down the interstates," says another.

"Only after they finish the interstates, that's the law now. They pull the 15 down to Tijuana, we'll be watching cars zoom south out of here and then zoom back with absolutely fuck-all."

"If you can even get out. There'll be houses from here to San Ysidro, now they've annexed it."

"Better learn how to say coat-tugger in Spanish."

"Even downtown, huh. They'll clear out the junkies and the queers until the whole thing looks like the Garden of Eden."

Silence then, as if someone had let slip a dark secret. Muriel looks up from her tasks and sees the men leaning forward and lifting their glasses and drinking guiltily. Then someone says, "Ain't that true, Rosie."

Rosie crosses his arms then uncrosses them. He doesn't answer.

"Hey, I'm on your side," the mustache says. "They don't just raid down there for fun, you ask me. They're going to run out them hustlers and put up apartment buildings."

The other men turn toward him. Muriel remembers the day that man Gerald was buried. It was Rosie who knew him, she'd written this down, along with the name of a place by the sea where men gathered. This was just after she'd won so much but before everything that happened next, and now the money was gone and Julius, too. She thinks of

Julius on the steps and the heartache she'd seen in him, the story of the man with the watch fob. The kind of place he might go next.

"That's the sad fact of things," Rosie says. "Nothing to do with morality."

"You don't think it has some moral implication though, additionally?" the mustache asks.

"Oh sure, like you're planning for the coming of our Lord."

The men laugh. Another man, a bookmaker younger than the others and always in better clothes, says, "Listen, gentlemen, here's what I'll tell you," and then he leans into the table, where his voice dissolves. As he talks the others nod for a moment and then move marginally back, eyes cast elsewhere, as if the man's ideas were scandalous. They glance at Rosie like boys hearing sacrilege and Rosie rises and drinks the bottom out of his beer and sets down the glass. He turns his head and spits on the floor and then he leaves the lounge. The others watch him go.

"There's a solution if I ever saw one," one of the men says.

"What a goddamn disappointment progress turns out to be," says another, and the men bloom out laughing, slaps against their wide thighs.

Muriel thinks she knows what all this means but she is not certain. Wherever he is, Julius might once or twice come through a place like that. She feels somehow that she needs confirmation. That she needs to see the place they'd named, the same way she'd needed to see the horses.

THAT NIGHT AFTER DINNER Lee rises from their silent table and opens the kitchen door. Muriel watches him as he goes outside and makes a round along the tree line and through it to the bluff and halfway up the road. When he comes back his cheeks and hands are red with cold. He shakes the empty coffee can, fishes a hand through it, plunks it down again. He picks up a hammer and a box of nails, sets them down, then takes up a measuring tape and scouts the walls and cabinets, making small marks and scratching them out, until finally he sits again at the table.

The radio lists farm prices and then the weather, its ecumenical tone a structuring music. Muriel does not try to comfort him.

"You know what," he says. "We was in the service when our father died and it was me that got the notice in the mail along with his wedding ring. Julius didn't like it was me that got the post, but of course it would have been because I'm older. They had to tear down the old house, it'd gotten so bad. The county sold what was left and sent a check for seventeen dollars to the station in Japan and I signed that over to Julius and he lost it at cards the same night."

He picks at the frayed ends of his fingernails. Muriel thinks of the argument in the kitchen two nights before. Lee does not act like someone overheard or like a man betrayed. But his hurt is fresh and implacable.

He says, "It ain't like this never happened before. And he feels bad about leaving here like that, and about taking the money from the can, I guarantee you, though feeling bad won't do no good to anyone. That night in Okinawa, on R and R, he jumped this other fella, out of nowhere. That fella said we were too poor for the navy and should've been grunts at Camp Casey, hauling out the army's trash, but men say things like that and worse when they're drunk and they're in some fucking war that's never-ending. But I think Julius believed him. I think he might've agreed. He couldn't ever see how much luck he had, in getting to live like he does."

"Like how," Muriel asks.

"Like there ain't no future."

Lee stands then and walks through the front door. Muriel follows him and stands in the doorway and watches as he hauls a bag of grain from the trunk of the car and shoulders it and carries it to the tree line. He opens the bag and edges its contents from one end of the lot to the other. She presses out of the doorway and goes to him.

"I'm just bribing the old girl now," he says.

His voice is not bitter or angry but oddly buoyant. She wonders if he's always been this way and she hadn't noticed until now. As if, without

Julius's trouble, without his own gentling proximity to it, he is no one. She thinks of those first months they were together in San Diego and how walking home after dark Lee had linked his arm with hers; the feeling was not romantic but protective, as if he were leading her in blindness. She had liked this feeling more than any other in their marriage and she realizes she has not thought of him this way in a long time. Perhaps Julius had been right, and she had needed someone to tell her what to do. Hiding her mother's house and giving Lee her winnings had changed what she expected of him, and though she'd wanted him to have those things she isn't sure she wants to share them. Sharing is a debt she had not anticipated.

Lee looks up then and squints into the sky and points.

"Hey, there it is," he says to her, and suddenly there is joy in his voice. "Not clear as day, but you can tell. It looks just like a beach ball to me."

Lee nudges her and she searches for the satellite in the sky and finds it, just closer than the stars and slightly larger. She knows from photos on the news that the slick hull is pierced by antennae whipped back from the body, but she can't see them. She can see only the bead of it, like a copper tack, doubled in her vision so that she almost feels she can track the satellite's motion as it circles above them.

"I just can't imagine it," she says.

"It's right there."

Lee points again.

"No, I can see it," she says. "But I can't imagine it."

A noise in the tree line like a man walking on stones. Lee turns toward the sound and looks and waits, and when nothing emerges he turns back to Muriel.

"We ought to name her," Lee says. "Maybe she'd come back if she had a name."

"I was thinking Peaches," Muriel says.

"What about Delilah?"

"God no."

"Or maybe Patsy."

"George Lee, those are husky broad names and you know it. You want a horse for a girlfriend, you might have got a younger one."

They both laugh and for a moment it seems like everything might work out fine. The wind sends down a shiver of rain. Across the empty lot next door comes a dark gull gliding and they both watch it until it's gone.

That night she lies awake a long time. The moonlight cuts across their bedroom and over Lee's masculine resting form and she thinks again of Rosie and the other horsemen teasing him. She remembers Julius standing in the bedroom and how she'd said his name. He had not taken anything from her then. The next day he'd asked about her mother and the game they played on Christmas Eve and he'd told her about his friend. Then he'd quarreled with his brother about their father and the service, and sometime that night he did take the money, which surely he'd come for. In her husband's ignorance and in Julius's theft she should find her own widening guilt, wider than the house and the money and further back, all the way back perhaps to the night she stayed up turning cards at her mother's table. She might also feel relief or gratitude. But she does not feel these things. She rises and slides her hand behind the dresser and pulls away the newsprint taped there. She unfolds it and reads the name of the place and where to find it. In the moonlight Lee's shoulders quiver and the room is heavy with his breath. For a long time she watches him sleep and she feels the wild feeling of someone pardoned, the way women in movies felt about the men they left behind. She remembers mornings during her childhood when she woke too early and could hear down the hall the sound of her mother also waking, a man shifting in the bed then standing, the noise of a belt being lifted from the floor and threaded through. It was always the first thing she knew, the distinctive chiming sound of the belt buckle, a sound all men seemed to make. And though the sound itself was particular it never differentiated one man from another, so she would have to wait and see who he was when the coffee perked.

Those mornings, her eyes closed in her own room on the second floor of her mother's house, she experienced an anticipation much like the one she feels now. She would hear the buckle, then the slow rough sound of bedding being drawn away, the unoiled headboard and the floorboards. She might have been anyone in that constellation of forms. Of course she was herself, down the hall and thus outside the ritual intimacy of waking, dressing lovers, but through force of allegiance she was also her mother, one arm below her head and the other draped over the edge of the bed in a suggestion of escape. But then she saw her mother from this angle, as if from across the bed and above, the way the man must see her, his belt looped through and not yet clasped, the ends hanging outward and down, both menacing and vulnerable in his half-dressed, standing silhouette. Later, her mother might touch that man as he sat drinking coffee, she might lean to kiss him on the head, and Muriel would feel herself transposed again, the smell of cigarettes in the man's hair, her mother's lips against her own child's brow, quick, domestic, like a key in the door.

THE NEXT DAY, the horsemen come early and stay late. In the corner the owner has pressed two tables together and covered them with a drop cloth. Ten days to Christmas and all the other tables are empty except those by the front windows, where a half-dozen men have spread themselves along the benches as if waiting to meet people other than themselves. With a taping knife the owner strips the fan of residue left by months of smoke. The smoke makes a film in the bevels and seeing the owner peel this away is like watching the restoration of a lung.

After lunch Rosie rises from the table and walks out the door trailing cigarette smoke. For a moment Muriel watches the owner at work on the fan and when he doesn't glance up or even sigh Muriel follows Rosie out to the street, where the light rain has drawn up the smell of engine oil. For a moment she stands in the glowering afternoon. She watches a group of men walking along the street on the other side. To her left two women laughing, a single man following behind. Rosie crosses the street against the light, his hands in his pockets as he picks up speed and brushes past the group of men and on ahead. If he turns uptown she'll duck back inside. If he crosses Eighth toward the sea she'll follow him, because that way is where she wants to go. He turns left and Muriel waits. He disappears past the corner.

When the light turns, Muriel rushes across and trails Rosie at a distance. When he crosses again onto the small street that runs a block from the ocean, she does the same. He turns to walk south along the line of cafés and small bars hemmed in by cottages and beach houses and the ferry landing to the north. Then past the Hall of Justice and a square block of project housing and a city park paved over with bitumen. Muriel has no watch, but the courthouse clock says four-fifteen. They cross Island Avenue and then J Street and Rosie dips down an alley and out onto K Street where the sea rises out of the cement at the vanishing point between the buildings. He turns left and Muriel waits a moment then follows down the alley and when she turns onto K he is a block ahead. The rain has nearly gone and the clouds above cast shadows along the sidewalks.

The neighborhood changes quickly then. Rosie passes a Chinese restaurant three stories tall and wrapped in cracking neon; across the street is a bar with no sign, boarded in blackened plywood. A block away is a plaza marked by tilting palms that Muriel can see in pieces down the alleyways, and two other buildings boarded up. The concrete margins are lined with struggling trees set in cages and the discards of pleasure: playbills and keno tickets in the gutters, glass bottles broken and filled with rain. Cars rattle by on the wet streets; along the streets men walk alone or in pairs. There are no women. Four or five young men, filthy with dust, ride by on the bumper of a dump truck. At the bus stop, two old men watch this display. The truck blocks her line of sight, and when it passes, Rosie has disappeared. In the place where he was standing a narrow door stands open to the weather. Her eye follows a fire escape to the second story, where a figure leans through an open window and drops a peach pit into the street. Across the street three boys lean over a window-well with their asses in the air. She does not know if this is the place or not, it looks like a half-dozen others. Music leaves the doorway in pips and bass notes and she can hear men's voices and the clink of glassware. It does not seem like a hotel but maybe the Chester is not a hotel at all. She loses her nerve. She turns away and takes the same route back to the lounge, where the owner is still scraping at the fan and the rest of the horsemen have gone.

SHE LETS A DAY PASS, then another, and on the third day she tells the owner she's taken ill. She strips off her apron and dabs her forehead with it, then presses it with both palms to her abdomen to suggest female trouble. The owner reaches out and looks away as he pats her shoulder. Outside she ducks into an alley, pulls the hat and the scarf from her purse, and dresses there, resting the purse on the toes of her shoes. She takes the same route and when she crosses Broadway she lights a cigarette. She finds again the darkened doorway and the fire escape above. For a moment she waits. If she is the only woman, her hat and scarf will not disguise her. She pulls the hat brim lower and she is afraid. Then she thinks of the first time she went to Del Mar and the money she won and the way she felt afterward.

Inside, the bar is dimly lighted and crowded with bodies. She recognizes turfmen and a few radiant youth who must be sailors and the tense jaws of workingmen and a few suits in the back. In the corner are two men talking close. A waitress and another woman by the open door and a third woman in a fine coat at the edge of the bar. The woman in the coat is talking to two men and when one turns toward the door Muriel sees that he is Rosie, cheek unshaven and red with drink.

She takes a seat at the bar so that Rosie is behind her, and when the bartender comes he looks her over and stands without speaking. She orders a Stinger and tosses a quarter in the ashtray. He doesn't reach out for it.

"It's all right," Muriel says.

"Is it?" the bartender says but he takes her quarter.

The mirror behind the bar is kinked in peeling lines and cracked across the top. She hears Rosie behind her and then the second man. The woman in the sable coat has a light accent and a voice rough from smoking. Her reflection in the mirror is watery and sedate. The bartender returns and slides the glass to Muriel and watches her take a drink.

"Okay then," he says, and turns away.

Behind her the second man has gone. Someone puts a dime in the jukebox and plays a song she's never heard and the two men in the corner cheer and sing along.

"Sounds like bad luck," Muriel hears the woman say.

"Sounds like no luck," says Rosie.

"You can't get much from a color breed, is what I've always said."

They are talking about the buckskin and Artie Cleaves. Rosie's voice is brighter and louder, and the woman's laugh suggests she relies on him for such forceful opinion. In the mirror beyond, Muriel sees Rosie shake his head. The woman turns away from him and looks cautiously around.

"You think he'll show?" she asks, without looking back at him.

"I think it was a one-night thing."

"You're not over Gerald."

"Gerald was a bastard," Rosie says, and the woman laughs. Rosie laughs too, but his face in the mirror is grim.

They talk for a while longer about the accident, then about the Sunday races. Muriel finishes one cigarette and lights another. She reaches up to loosen the hat then thinks better of it. She is not sure what to do next. A phone rings at the end of the bar and a man picks it up and doesn't speak but after a moment he presses the receiver to his shoulder and calls out to the room, "Irish Chimes, Mistress, Loose Talk, nine-two," and

Muriel understands that there is gambling here and worries she's made a mistake or reached a dead end. Cheers go up in a few corners. Rosie's voice is drowned in the cheering. In the quiet after, Muriel hears the woman say, "Too bad for the stable. They paid some money for that buckskin." To hear a woman speak this way about the horses she's come to know is like hearing a woman broadcast the news.

"I did think he'd show, to tell the truth," Rosie says.

"I know that," the woman says.

"This world's too small."

"Tell that to Fred and Ethel," the woman says, and gestures to the two men in the corner.

Rosie laughs.

"You hit that one on the nose," he says.

A rough jostling behind and Muriel brings her purse around to her lap and links one arm through the strap. If this is just a gambling den and nothing more she should stand and leave and hail a cab. She feels stupid and alone and not at all sure what she thought she was doing. When she looks up again she sees no one in the mirror beyond, just the vague shapes of men and her own blurred reflection. For several minutes she hears neither Rosie nor the woman, and when she risks a glance at the room she does not see anyone she knows. She finishes her drink. When she feels a presence at her side, she turns away to hide her face, and in her periphery is a woman in a dark coat that carries with it a punky smell of hay. When she speaks, Muriel knows it is the same woman.

"You're waiting for someone."

While Muriel thinks how to answer, the woman speaks again.

"I don't mind that. They turn up, I'll skedaddle."

The woman slips onto the seat next to Muriel and shrugs the coat off and over the backrest. Her hair is dark and fragrant and loose around her face. She wears silver earrings in the shape of coins. She dips in her handbag and pulls out a cigarette case and tips it toward Muriel, who shakes her head.

"So, who is it then? The person you're waiting for?" the woman asks.

"Just my husband."

Tension at being spoken to this way, this odd and instant familiarity. She wonders if Rosie has seen her and sent this woman as his emissary. In the mirror Muriel sees the woman's pile of hair and the little shining dots of the earrings but no other features. The woman's face in the mirror is blurred and pale as sand.

"Personally, I've stopped waiting for mine."

The woman wants this to be a leveling fact. But her tone is quarrelsome, defeated, and before Muriel can say anything else the woman has looped one arm around the back of the stool and leaned against it, her face tilted at a childish angle.

"Do you play the ponies?" she asks.

Muriel thinks immediately that she ought to lie. "Not me."

The woman lifts her glass and regards Muriel over the cold lip of it but does not drink. Her close smell makes Muriel light-headed. She leans into the bar for support. She feels suddenly very frightened. The wind off the sea presses the rain flat against the dark front window so the outside light is serous against the glass.

"What's this place called?" Muriel asks, and sees the woman watching her cautiously. Before she can answer, a noise from behind makes both women turn. There in the corner the two men stand facing each other. One man has a beer bottle held out and downfisted, like an awl; his rival stands dumbly with his hands upraised. What prompted this is unknown, and the other patrons are not sure if they'd like to see blood or be heroes. For a moment no one tries to intervene. Then a third man comes in from the back and stands between the fighting men and some conversation ensues. The man raising his hands is very young and wearing a new shirt buttoned to the neck and wrists, as if after all this he intends to go and find an office job. Muriel watches with disquiet. The man with the bottle seems not angry but despairing and finally he is coaxed to sit. The younger man leaves through the front and trails with him a sorrowful draft.

"Goddamn men," the woman says and turns back to the bar. She raises a finger for a drink and when the bartender comes over she points at Muriel's glass and Muriel says she has to go. She worries the woman can see her trembling. She looks around for Rosie but does not see him in the crush of people.

"But what about your husband?" the woman asks.

Muriel shakes her head.

"It's only a spat. You know how fragile men are," the woman says, to Muriel and to the general air.

Muriel pushes off the bar ledge and moves toward the door. On the front wall above the windows is a carnival racing game, one-dimensional horses snugged into green lanes of serrated plastic, each affixed with a number and jockey in silks. Three men in the front corner gesture largely and one lifts a billiard bridge and spreads two of the horses forward from the pack and as Muriel walks past them they laugh. Outside on the street she pulls off the hat and curls it brim to brim and shoves it in her purse. She lights a cigarette and smokes it as she walks back toward the lounge.

THAT WEEK THE RAIN comes in earnest. For several days Muriel does not go back downtown. The evenings draw long and the house is gloomy and grayly cold. The horse does not return. As Muriel washes up she glances through the kitchen window with some hesitation, as if the horse's absence is a trick played by a child. As if, when she turns away, the horse will emerge through the door and frighten her.

One night Lee drinks too much and says, his hands palmed together as if in prayer, "I remember this girl from town. She had two men. One was a kid Julius ran with, pool hall kid, even shorter than you are, boy could he hit a pocket. I played with him once and it was like basic training or worse, I was dead on the ground inside three minutes. The other guy, he was a college kid none of us knew. He ran the sand mill across the river and wore the tiniest knot in his tie, like McCarthy. I don't know how they met each other. He wasn't the kind of guy any of us would have known personally."

Muriel can feel the marine layer passing into the valley as a moist draft through the window, stealing the remnant warmth of the kitchen. She's heard this story before but she doesn't interrupt.

"It went on this way for a while, and the girl—her name was Sally, I want to say—she spent her afternoons with Julius and his friend and then went to dinner half-tilted on Hamm's and in a better dress with this other guy, and then she'd come back late to the pool hall or wherever they were and get right back to her short man, who knew where she'd been and didn't care. Baffled me, when Julius told me about it. And he said it like it was a thing anyone would understand, though six months later she sat the short man down and told him it was over, and in another month there was her name in the engagement section and Julius was just outraged."

Muriel knows Lee thinks of this story as a parable about money but she can't help thinking he's sending her some message, though the distance the drink has made in him is his own distance. When she leans closer to him he leans into her for comfort.

"You must have known a dozen guys who lost out this way," she says, to placate him.

"I did. And Julius did too, but I do think he was more upset about it than his friend. I think Julius hated that she picked what wasn't real, honestly. It bothered him to no end that she hadn't chosen what he thought of as love. That would be something that bothered him."

"Would it."

"And I guess I thought that too, but really I didn't know her, so who was I to say."

She leans into his shoulder. This is a new version and she watches his face as he works through it.

"I guess maybe he thinks now that I'm on the other side of that story," he says, and there is sadness in his voice but pride too. She thinks that, in the time Lee waited for her to sell the house, he had begun to think of himself as an actor in a narrative of stuttering progress, challenged by trials of love and spirit for the sake of some greater victory. Maybe that was always true of him, though she hadn't known it. And it suited him, this sense of himself as outsized, as protagonist, and not simply because it was a comfort against his small life but because it was the burdened way he made meaning.

"That's what time does," she says.

"What's that?"

"Change which side of the story you're on."

Lee laughs kindly and low. "We're gonna have to get cheered up, huh?" he says and kisses her cheek.

She thinks again of her lost money and the hotel by the sea. She recalls that first winter at Del Mar, when she had begun to lose. After months of terrific reliability, losing had been hard to understand. Later she would realize just how much losing had to do with winning, but she didn't know it then, and her days had been occupied by a careful attention to everything, as if somewhere in the inflection of the horsemen's voices or the color of their ties she might find a clue to her small fate. She watched the weather and the shopkeepers and the men walking along the avenues and the ragged stray cats. She worked through every sign and pattern she knew, for insight into her trouble. She wonders what Julius is doing and if he has spent her money already and if someone has left a dark scent along his collar. Still no anger comes forward, only a sharp, familiar desire to be where he is.

SUNDAY MORNING, she is awakened by a knock at the front door. She hears Lee answer and then a woman's voice. Lee comes in the bedroom and pulls on his boots and jacket.

"Neighbor saw her up the road," he says.

"Saw who?"

"That damn horse."

He leaves and the front door closes hard. In the kitchen Muriel starts the kettle and walks first to the front window and then the back but sees only the rain and the scrim of light as the sun rises. When the kettle boils she makes a cup of coffee and sits at the kitchen table. Soon the front door opens and Muriel expects Lee's voice calling out but a woman walks into the kitchen.

"No dice," the woman says. There in the doorway is the woman who gave her the olives months before, dripping on the linoleum. Lee comes in behind her.

"I'm going to try something else," he says.

"I'm not sure you're going to have much chance in this rain," she says.

Muriel sees that some disagreement has already passed between them. Lee nudges by the woman and into the kitchen. He gathers a wilted head of lettuce and an apple and two winter tomatoes, then opens the breadbox and finds a last slice of pie. He looks at Muriel.

"It's all right by me," she says.

The woman turns to him as if to speak but doesn't. She looks at Muriel and shrugs.

Muriel says, "Is she by the river?"

"Walnut orchard," the woman says.

"She was eyeing it, before," Muriel says.

"There's walnuts. Who could blame her?" the woman says.

"You go ahead and get warm now and then I'll take you back up," Lee says to the woman. He pulls the lettuce to his nose and regards it, then tosses it on the counter. He puts the tomatoes in his pocket and holds the pie flat on his hand like a jewel. With these items he leaves the kitchen and Muriel smiles at his broad back.

"I don't think he'll catch her," the woman says.

"We've been looking for her a week now."

"Well maybe, then, if she's not had her fill of nuts. You can get a horse to do most things for food, even come home."

The woman takes a step into the kitchen and holds out a cold hand and says, "Sandra."

Muriel recalls the moment, months ago now, in which she might have asked this and didn't. Sandra wears a man's flannel shirt with the long tails folded over and tucked, the sleeves rolled so the fabric sits squared above her elbows like straps. Her hair is pulled back in a single plait and curled under. Everything wet from the rain. She looks around the kitchen as if she is accustomed to entering spaces meant for others, or in which she might be unwelcome. For a moment Muriel stands dumbly staring. Then she holds up a halting finger and finds a towel in the hall closet and comes back and hands it over. Sandra leans against the counter and squeezes the water from her hair and wipes down her arms, then drapes the towel over her shoulders. Muriel hands her a cup of coffee.

"Did you try to tie her before?" Sandra asks. She looks at the coffee and frowns.

"Wouldn't take it."

"No surprise there. What you need is a rope bridle, get one without any brass in it. Then you can tie her up or lead her by it. She ain't going to like being ridden or corralled, at her age." She turns to the unpainted wall and with a finger draws the long outline of a snout, then a quick half-circle around it and two lines up and behind the ears. The wet tip of her finger leaves a faint trace on the Sheetrock. "When you catch her, that is."

"You know horses," Muriel asks.

"If we're talking relatively, the answer is yes."

Sandra goes to the window and fingers the curtain back and looks out. Muriel stands beside her and together they stare out into the rain but they do not see Lee or the horse. The ash trees are freighted as if by the heavy clouds above. Muriel wonders if she should mention their meeting or if the woman even remembers her, but then Sandra turns away from the window and drains her cup. She backs against the counter and looks at Muriel.

"I didn't know this was the lot you wanted. I used to play down here. Before the levees, the water rose to the top of this bluff in spring and rolled down to make a pool where the road meets the edge of your drive—there was no road then—and my father and I fished for bluegill here, down among the rushes and small turtles and snails the size of your pinkie nail."

Sandra turns her face up, grinning. A little spur of history that connects them.

"You haven't been here long," she says then.

"As you can see, we're not finished."

"You will be soon though."

"So you've lived here your whole life," Muriel says, to talk of something other than the house.

"I was gone some time, actually. Then my father died and I came back."

"Why did you go away?"

"Same reason anyone does."

Muriel pours the coffee and sits at the table. The woman nods to the empty chair.

"You're not from here, though," she says.

She wipes her face and neck again. Above the oven range, the clock ticks off the time. She hopes Lee will catch the horse, but below this hope is another strange and surprising one, that they will have to keep looking forever.

"Kansas," she says.

"Long ways."

Sandra flattens the towel over the seat and sits. Across the table she seems very small. Perhaps Lee had spoken to her roughly, perhaps it was only the weather.

"Why would you ever leave the plains?" she asks.

"Have you ever been there?"

"No."

"Well then," Muriel says.

"Now wait. I went to Idaho once." She holds up an enlightened finger. Muriel smiles at her. Sandra speaks as men often do, and not the way women usually speak to each other.

"I had a friend who moved there. I only went to see her the one time though," Sandra says.

"I'm not sure Idaho counts."

"They have sand dunes in Idaho."

"There you go."

"My friend loved it. She dreamed of going there her whole life, though honestly it was hotter than hell and full of church people. I guess we all take what paradise is offered us."

She says this without bitterness. Muriel nods and lights a cigarette. Outside she can hear the faint whine of a car out west on the paved road. Sandra reaches across the table and raises her eyebrows and Muriel passes the cigarette to her. She brings it to her lips and blows the smoke out thickly without inhaling and hands the cigarette back.

"I've given it up, you see."

Muriel laughs and some tension is broken between them.

"You think he'll catch her?" Muriel asks.

"Well, she isn't fast. But she's had a lot of years to learn."

Sandra leans in as if in conspiracy and lowers her voice. Her pleasure at what she says next expresses itself in a blush.

"I guess his pouting worked then," she says.

"Or your olives didn't," Muriel says.

"You should've got García's olives, like I said."

"That's not what I remember you saying."

Muriel looks up at the ceiling and then out the window. Outside the light gutters as the trees blow across it and from far off she can hear sirens and the slap of the river against the bluff.

"Why'd you get a horse if you have no fencing?"

"My brother-in-law."

"He gave it to you?"

"He hauled her from Nevada in that trailer." Muriel nods her head toward the tree line. Sandra laughs. Muriel passes the cigarette again.

"All these cowboys, but this whole place will be a cul-de-sac by next year."

"Surely not so soon."

"Mark my words. I ought to sell out myself."

"He thought he was getting a bona fide mustang," Muriel says. There is a guilty pleasure in this, holding Julius up for ridicule. For a moment she has made him harmless.

"Didn't he ever see Roy Rogers?"

Sandra takes another parochial drag and passes the cigarette back. Muriel holds it a moment and regards the ash, which has crumbled to the table. She licks her thumb and presses it away. She likes this woman's self-possession. She suspects it developed in another, harder time and had been abandoned for solitude.

"I didn't think I'd see you again," Sandra says.

"Well, here I am."

"You ought to come up for dinner sometime."

"Me and Lee, we work late most nights."

From the front room the sound of the door opening and Lee appears at the threshold as if by evocation. He's soaked and dripping and across his jacket front is a smear of blueberry. Muriel stands up.

"Well," he says. "I think you can see how well I did."

"Did she get any of that pie?" Sandra asks. She rises and lifts the towel from the seat and drapes it over the lip of the sink, then sets her cup on the counter.

"Snatched it and ran," Lee says.

"You might say that's progress."

"I guess if you think so," he says.

He snaps his pant leg out and shoots mud across the room. Muriel senses his need to posture for the woman. She sees something else too, which she had not been able to name before. She recalls the moment the horse necked in under the doorway, Julius leaping to turn the horse away and Lee rising calmly, not in fear or apprehension but in joy at being surprised, at the simple presence of the horse. He wants to be thrust into peril. He doesn't like that the woman might see this pleasure in him or that she might join him in it.

"The tires rotted on that trailer?" Sandra asks.

"It ain't in great shape, but no."

"I've got an idea."

The three of them walk outside and up to the road and Sandra tells them what she means to do. Lee looks skeptical and tries to argue but the woman simply walks away and begins to rock the trailer to test its weight. Lee stands watching her while the rain falls on his shoulders. Finally Sandra stops and turns to Lee and explains again and points to the tree line and speaks in an appeasing voice. Lee nods and shrugs and finds a shovel in the garage and digs out the trailer tires where the mud has slung against them. Then he pulls the trailer by the tongue while Muriel and Sandra push from the back, and together they wend it through the yard and angle it alongside the stand of ash trees where the rain is dampened. They lash the door open and then Lee goes again to the front and takes the tarp from the pile of backfill dirt and drags it across the wet yard. He hands one end of the tarp to Sandra and she stretches it between two trees. Lee ties it there, and then they tie the other side through the trailer vents, making a shelter as wide as a bedroom between the tree line and the trailer.

"Now who wouldn't come back for that," Sandra says.

"If you say so," says Lee.

"Get some dry hay, too," Sandra says. "You gotta give her something to come back for besides cold shade. And then when she does, you'll need a fence."

The woman looks at Muriel a long moment and her look is a request for something. In the rain she is dark and young, the way rain turns people back to children.

"Come on then, let's get out of this weather. I'll give you a ride back up," Lee says.

"That's all right."

Sandra stomps into her own cold boots and rolls down her shirtsleeves. She turns back and says, "I can spare a little feed. I'll put that around and between us we'll get her." Then she walks back out into the druid morning.

THE WEEK BEGINS under light drizzle. The hay molders under the tarp and Lee sets out a bucket which fills with rain and inside the trailer they dump a dozen apples sliced open for the scent. Muriel sleeps poorly. As always she dreams of horses, but also of heavy rain like a screen across the winter fields. She dreams of the Radford Hotel and the empty room and the money on the bed. Each of these dreams presses forward through the day and brings along a portentous feeling.

At the lounge the men suffer and despair at the weather. Dusk comes early and with sudden force. One night Muriel is woken from a dream of Artie Cleaves, whom she has never seen. In the dream he is small as a child, wearing pink silks, and he is kneeling over the fallen horse while the cups and ticket stubs drop from the upper boxes. Against the fine buckskin hide, the jockey's silks appear translucent. Inside the dream Muriel sits in the grandstand, and as she watches, the buck begins to rise. Artie Cleaves stays kneeling on the track until the horse is all-fours again. Then he lies down in its place, between the horse's legs. The horse passes lightly alongside the jockey's small body and keeps going, stepping in high action down the fairway. The ambulance comes and the doors open and out comes the woman in the sable coat, from the bar. She looks into the stands and catches Muriel's eye and grins.

THE NEXT DAY Muriel calls in sick and drives the car as far as State Street and parks under a streetlight. Again the day is gloomy and the sea seems stirred by some offense. Muriel goes into the bar and sees Rosie talking to the same woman. The woman's back is to the room, but the coat and her dark hair are unmistakable, and as Muriel enters she lowers her chin among the rough shoulders of the other patrons and sits a few feet from the edge, where the bar curves back toward the wall.

She orders a drink and covers one side of her face with her resting palm. For a long time Rosie and the woman talk of the track. They are beyond the edge of the kinked mirror and Muriel cannot see them. In the other noise of the bar she hears only pieces of their conversation but she won't risk moving closer. She is not sure what she means to do next. She thinks of that first day at Del Mar when she'd taken the bus all the way around and sat for an hour at a diner. She had known nothing then. At the races that day she watched the sailors in their heavy slacks and the piqued horses as if she were new to every worldly sight. Rosie and his friend are engaged in the same kind of speculation: the health of jocks and their weights, the horses rumored to be up at claimers. But the horsemen's grim prediction is replaced by Rosie's untempered joy, the woman's clear low voice.

Rosie says, "And maybe that's no winning choice but you can't help but see the future in it."

"I suppose I could help it, but I don't want to," the woman says.

At the front now are men in cuffed pants and misshapen hats, young and able, playing some game with the carnival horses. One man presses the horses forward with the billiard bridge while his companions uncover dominoes and call out the numbers. There seems to be some wager on this contest: When a number is called, a horse moves forward, and one man celebrates while the others scowl and pull pennies from their pockets and toss them onto the table.

More talk covered over by the noise of the room, the woman's voice lowering and then her laughter rising, until Muriel hears the tones of departure. She feels Rosie move behind her and when he's passed she turns to watch him. She thinks suddenly that she could make him see her, that she could call his name and when he turned toward her voice she could smile and stand, and ask him where she might find the Chester Hotel or if she is already there. And when he balked or tried to turn away she could ask him about the time in Tijuana when half the pit ponies got rainscald from being boarded uncovered in the monsoon season. Or the time when his mother called to tell him she'd taken up with a no-name trainer from Snake River and did he want to come ride in the Indian relays for a bit of cash. Rosie would look, and look again, and see finally his brown-haired waitress with the Midwestern build, and he would know how long and how carefully she'd been listening.

But when she turns back to find her purse and her cigarettes, the woman has again taken the seat next to her. She orders a drink in the same low voice, then turns to Muriel.

"You're back then," she says.

Muriel watches Rosie duck out the door. The woman's perfume is dusky and masculine. Next to her, Muriel thinks, she must look as friendless as an apostle.

"Now you *must* be a gambler," the woman says.

"Still no."

"Your husband then? Absent again."

The woman tosses her coat on the bar and shakes out her bangles and sighs. The wide lapels of her blouse come together low, suggesting some regal affect, though Muriel can see the open back and the tender skin under her arm. Muriel would never wear such a thing, though her mother had worn peasant blouses in bright patterns that fell off her shoulders in summer.

"Maybe you don't gamble but surely you read the news," she says.

"I suppose."

"That poor Russian dog died."

"They knew that would happen, didn't they?"

"What gets me, first creature to go into orbit and it's a terrier."

The woman's face is exasperated and seeking, the way men's faces sometimes were at the Heyday, when they were feeling righteous.

"Better a dog than a—" Muriel begins, but the woman interrupts her.

"Russian?"

The woman snorts.

"I just imagine that dog," she says. "I don't know if you know dogs but I've known a lot of them. And I can see that dog clear as day, giving exactly no goddamns about space. You can count on dogs for that. They are not ambitious."

This time when the barkeep comes Muriel accepts the woman's nod, and when he returns with two cool glasses she tips hers up.

"Hey, Tony," the woman says to the bartender. "What are we calling this place nowadays?"

The bartender tilts his head. The woman grins at Muriel.

"'Tony's,' same as always," the bartender says.

"There you go," the woman says, and drains her glass. Then she looks at Muriel again and Muriel tries to smile but she's disappointed, though if this little bar had been the place she sought that would have saddened her, too. She tries to imagine the form of the question, if there's some way she can ask about the hotel without telling the woman anything about herself. There must be an art to searching, but she does not know what it is, only that it is not as simple as listening. Now the question seems naive, and too small to hold its own implications.

"You know they ran a book on it?" the woman asks.

"On what?"

"The dog."

"What about the dog?"

"What would happen to it."

"What were the odds?"

"Twenty to one the dog would make it into orbit, hundred to one he'd come back down."

"What about dying?"

"Nobody wanted to pay out that bet."

The woman raises her eyebrows and Muriel laughs the scrupulous laugh the woman clearly wants, that aligns Muriel with her. The woman smiles again and winks.

"It used to be enough to lay odds on the one outcome, win or lose, but now you can speculate about how long it will take for the mail to come, or whether John Foster Dulles prefers oranges to apples," she says. "You could get half the population to bet on a race between raindrops."

"Why do you suppose that is?" Muriel asks, and she really wants to know.

The woman takes a thoughtful drag and drains her glass.

"Oh, who knows. Suddenly you care about something you'd never thought of before and never would care about, just because there's odds on it."

The bartender plunks two more drinks in front of them and gestures to the corner, where a man in a clean white jacket sits drinking alone. The woman pushes both cocktails onto the bar mat and shakes her head and the bartender leaves the glasses there, but turns to the jacketed man and shrugs. Then the woman looks back at Muriel.

"Though I'd be more inclined to say it's because it heightens the suspense."

Muriel pats her purse and reaches for her cigarettes, and before she can find her lighter the woman has clicked hers open and reached out. Muriel dips to light the cigarette.

"It bothers you that it's a terrier in particular?" she asks.

"Terriers are hole diggers and rat killers. Terrestrial. You want to send a dog into space, send something that howls at the moon."

The woman turns her head slightly and looks over her own shoulder, as if in Muriel's sight line were the rebuttal to this sad assertion. Then she turns back and laughs and waves her hand and returns to herself. Muriel likes the slight tilt of her head, the bright consideration in her face. Suddenly Muriel does not want to lower herself to ask what she's come to know. She wants instead to simply sit here, with this woman in this place. She beckons the young bartender over. "Don't let any man buy us anything," she says. "If anyone asks, explain that our husbands are coming any minute. Say they're merchant marines, or ex-cons. Elaborate at will." She slips the corner of a five-dollar bill under the bar mat. She had seen her mother do this once, when Muriel was young and they were waiting at a restaurant bar for a man Muriel no longer remembers. She suspects that the bill means less here than it did in Holton, Kansas, but she likes the gesture of it, the way it confers to the woman her full attention, as it had once conferred her mother's.

The woman turns toward Muriel and closes the distance between them. She shakes the ice in her glass, then reaches in and plucks one piece out. For a moment she holds the ice in her fingers until it wets her palm and then she pops it in her mouth.

"How long until he shows?" the woman asks. For a moment the ice stalls her voice, then she cracks the ice and swallows.

"I can't say."

"Marriage is a lottery, isn't it? Maybe not for men, though more than it used to be," she says.

The need to stop talking this way floats between them. Muriel lifts her glass and lets the ice click against her teeth.

"Gail," the woman says.

"Muriel."

They talk a little longer about the dog and the satellite but the mood has shifted between them. They remark on the weather and Muriel tells her about the house they've built on the river bluff. Soon their glasses are empty. Gail does not mention the man Muriel is supposed to be waiting for and Muriel doesn't either. When Gail insists on driving her home

Muriel does not protest, though she'll have to double back to retrieve the Ford. Gail collects her coat and the five-dollar bill and leaves a ten in its place. The five she hands to Muriel, who folds it back into her purse.

Gail drives an old Packard the color of slate and inside it is creamy with warmth though the day has chilled. For a moment they sit in silence as the engine wakes and idles high, then Gail pulls out onto the coastal street and drives north with the windshield wipers fanning.

"What did we do before cars?" she asks, and she means everyone but also specifically them.

The woman drives her back the long way, through neighborhoods opening out in narrow vistas along the shore. In the barrio Gail turns a horseshoe across the centerline to head back south and asks if Muriel minds a scenic route. Across the vista the sun lowers captiously and Muriel nods and Gail smiles and cuts across the midway and onto Catalina Boulevard and up the cliff and there pulls neatly to the side of the road. There are no streetlights and the sea is visible as a white fringe that stretches into gray at the horizon, the sunset pouring down over it, a little too fine for the mood between them.

"Look at that," Gail says. She turns in the driver's seat so her back presses against the door and she can stretch her legs out from beneath the steering wheel. She does this so quickly the move feels self-protective. Behind her head the dramatic reflection of the sunset, the feeling between them of standoff or threat, which Muriel dispels by looking out toward the ocean. To a woman from the plains, the sea from these cliffs is too much. The heart leaps out for it, a reluctant pragmatism draws the heart back.

Gail says—with the candor that seems her trademark now, cultivated like a trademark—"Funny. I never meet anyone."

And Muriel sees clearly the opening this stranger has made. She is not certain what it means, but she knows it is there, that if she is going to ask she must ask now.

"I heard you talking."

"Oh?" Gail's lips turn the sound into an embrace.

"I'm looking for a place," Muriel says.

"Aren't we all." Gail leans forward.

"A specific place," Muriel says.

"Not Tony's?"

Muriel shakes her head and Gail laughs. For a long moment neither speaks.

"It's a hotel. I don't know if it still exists or not," Muriel says finally.

Something odd and refusing enters Gail's face.

"And how did you hear about it?"

Muriel doesn't answer.

"Why do you think I would know?" Gail says.

"You just seem like you would."

A beat of silence as Gail considers this.

"What brought you to Tony's then? If you're not a gambler?"

"Only the rain."

Muriel considers the foolish hat and her damp hair. She is not sure if she feels exposed by Gail's scrutiny or embarrassed by her own plainness, but either way she is out of her depth. This matters much less to her than what might happen next.

Gail leans toward Muriel conspiratorially and her face changes again.

"Do you really know what you're asking?"

"I think so."

"How'd you find that bar back there, really?"

"I asked around."

"You did not."

Muriel wants to lie but she feels sure that Gail will call her out.

"Okay," she says. "I know someone."

"Who do you know?"

"You've probably met him. Gambling type. Carries a little pistol on the end of a chain."

Muriel pantomimes smallness between finger and thumb.

"I've met no such man, and I know all the gamblers."

"Well," Muriel says.

"Such a thing seems hardly useful." Gail's voice is flirty and low. The sound of the engine is a humming breath in the quiet of the roadside. Gail rests her chin in her hand and looks past Muriel to the sky beyond. Muriel can smell her hair which is dark and loose and the pitched sweetness of her perfume, which has caught the smell of the rain and changed slightly, into something softer. They hold the moment between them like a shell.

"Well, maybe you can introduce me then," Gail says.

Muriel can't believe what is happening. In her beige sweater and practical dress she feels for a moment like a churchgoer, left with mild rapture in the pews. She leans forward. A look of disbelief on Gail's face, which turns to clear amazement. Muriel tries to imagine closing the distance and leaning into Gail's fine mouth. In her life Muriel has kissed only her husband, though she has witnessed hundreds, perhaps more—kisses her mother delivered or accepted, moments at the lounge in which a couple parted or reunited or met that very night. Young women and their cowboys in the movies. Somehow she can see all of these moments at once. From this catalogue Muriel draws up one she remembers well: Ingrid Bergman's index finger hooking Cary Grant's ear in a film about murder, the sea below and behind them, draining away along the smooth endless curve of the shore, the city also arched in tall buildings and hotels, much like the scene below Muriel now, in the quiet western sunset of Point Loma. But in the absence of love and of any man the movie kiss takes on the atmosphere of comedy. Ingrid Bergman laughs the delighted, vulnerable, slightly cruel laugh she is clearly suppressing for Cary Grant, the laugh that is ready for his sudden distance. In Muriel's mind Ingrid Bergman laughs into the anticipating circle of Gail's pert mouth.

"Maybe," she says, to both Gail and herself.

Gail leans forward and their noses are nearly touching. The question of the hotel has not been answered but another has been asked. Muriel rises on her palm until her chin is against Gail's lips and her mouth at the tender skin at Gail's temple. Gail's coat falls away from her upraised shoulder. It is only a touch and can be taken back and Gail's fingers behind Muriel's ear might be easy enough to forget, too. They both know this and that the boundary is receding. That to touch any further than this would mark out a confession. Muriel lifts her chin and brings her mouth to Gail's mouth. She hopes Gail will resist. Her resistance would give Muriel power, would make Muriel feel certain, in control of this. But instead Gail lowers that slow inch and presses her mouth to Muriel's and the kiss is tender and long. Outside there is no sound and no cars passing. The bench seat of the Packard sets them at an odd angle and presses their faces together but keeps the rest of their bodies apart and because she wants something else now, she wants the woman closer, Muriel hauls onto her knees in the seat and wraps an arm around Gail's shoulders and draws her in. Gail leans her head back and laughs. Then she comes forward and kisses Muriel again and her palm finds Muriel's breast and brushes Muriel's nipple which hardens and sends down a line of heat and both women make low noises of surprise, but then the sound of an engine knocks against the cliff behind them and a set of headlights condenses on the road. Muriel's desire slows all of this, and when Gail pulls abruptly away she doesn't understand at first. She has forgotten her search and the time and the time of year. She feels suddenly very much like a woman.

The car passes and the moment has changed. Gail retreats and pulls her coat closed and seems frightened. Muriel would not have thought she could be frightened.

"I can't stay out any later tonight," Gail says.

"Me either," Muriel says, though she wants to and she could.

Gail pumps the brake. The brake lights hit the cliffside behind them and cast back at them like fire.

"But I'll meet you tomorrow, in the place you mean," Gail says and rights herself in the seat and pulls away from the curb before Muriel can get her knees unbent. Gail drives back up the isthmus and past the bar they'd left and down two more blocks by the sea. The sun has set and a fine purple rim of light floats along the horizon. Near darkness along the road. Past the plaza, Gail pulls neatly to the curb.

"Meet me here," she says, and points to an old building with boarded windows painted black, once grand and stout and now cupped a little at the eaves. Just beyond the building the sky falls heavy across the rising tide. A man stands at the doorway in a lowered hat, watching them. Muriel knows that she is looking at the Chester Hotel and her desire expands inside this fact and turns into something new and terrifying.

"Okay," Muriel says, and Gail turns and reaches across the seat and touches Muriel's chin with her thumb and the gesture is both sweet and coolly final.

Then she pulls away again and Muriel points out the turns without thinking until she's directed Gail to the Heyday Lounge. Gail does not ask about the house on the bluffs and Muriel does not explain why they have not driven there. Muriel collects her purse and hat and opens the car door. Along the city street the blue winter night feels less dangerous than she'd like. She leans into Gail's open window and thanks her again for the ride and though she means to say more she does not. The windows of the lounge make squares of light on the pavement, so distinct and inviting they seem to Muriel like openings to the world below.

Gail backs all the way to the intersection, turns onto the cross street and disappears. Muriel walks past the Heyday and past the cafés and the little houses near the sea. At State Street she gets in the car and drives toward the river. Against the darkening sky the city has a reproachful look. She takes the long way home, through the park and under the freeway and through the orchards. She feels dizzy and wanted. The orchards flit by in the darkness and appear to move. In Kansas she had driven with her mother at twice this speed through farmland on Sunday afternoons, and the wheat in any season rolled in the same peculiar way, the endless rows seeming to undulate as she drove by. Though she understood this as an illusion, she had been captured by the trick of it, as if the car itself brought the fields to life. In the cradle of the headlights she catches a dim shape. She pounds the brakes and the golden horse crosses the road at a clip, through the orchard and past the irrigation ditch and up into the field beyond.

In her own driveway she checks her face for flush and shoves the hat and scarf to the bottom of her purse. In the kitchen she finds Lee sitting with his eyes closed and his chin tipped back. Built like a catapult, Muriel thinks, but sweetness in his posture, too, the way men were so vulnerable in their sleep. He starts at the sound of her footsteps and rises from the chair, his hands fisted, and for a moment Muriel sees him as he perhaps most wants to be seen, as a man ready for anything. She tastes Gail's kiss and their parting has another taste and for a moment she might tell Lee everything, just to take this readiness from him. But then he sees her and laughs and opens his hands and presses his hair back and the feeling shifts. She watches him the way men watched women when they cried or sang. As if her husband's pleasure at her return were something that required assuaging, as if there were terror underneath it. She moves forward to greet him and he asks about the hour and she drops the keys on the counter and says she had a fine day.

EIGHT

The border

One summer night, back when they were working the peek, Henry arrived with two plastic jugs of water frozen all the way through and a couple of frozen hotel towels around his neck, plastered down inside his shirt. This was late August and the heat had returned after two weeks of storms in the mountains that kept the meadows cool and the sun vitiated by long clouds passing over at great height. The storms came through town, heavy rain falling in broad daylight, and dissolved into sunshine over the valley. The weather made everyone downtown feel homesick or lonely or worse. Men were caught with their attention flagging or drawn toward the horizon, and many lost more than they could afford and had to scrape together change for the train. Julius spent much of that time at the Mormon joint or sleeping through the gray mornings at the Squaw. There had been two stabbings in the wasteland off Fremont and a stakeout at the Hotel Apache that sent a half-dozen card counterfeiters not to jail but to Mesquite, where they were shot on an airstrip by men no one would name. The city was not panicked but it was unsettled.

Now summer had come back violently and the peek was a hundred degrees or more. Julius walked the eastern section with his boots off and his jeans rolled past his calves. Below him the floor of the Golden Nugget was half-empty. The heat was keeping the Angelenos away and many others in their rooms, and those downtown that night played with cautious intensity, as if recent events had frayed not their nerves but their ability to imagine themselves removed from ordinary life. When Henry arrived he walked through his own section of the peek to find Julius on the other side and draped two cold towels over his neck and shoulders. Julius asked where in hell he'd found a freezer and Henry smiled and did not answer. He walked away and Julius felt the cooling weight of the towels and sighed and Henry turned halfway around and blew a kiss over his shoulder. Julius did not like romance on the job but he let this display charm him, because the night would be long. He turned up his sleeves and adjusted the towels and watched the men at craps below, who seemed to play as if the whole game had been revealed to them, as if they understood the way the rolling dice obeyed the universe, and this was not a comfort. There was no cheat in them, and Julius grew bored and sleepy and thought of other things.

The hour stretched late and below a piano man played songs they knew from the war, "I'll Get By" and "Don't Fence Me In," songs Julius heard in the factory bars of his youth. In the hot stillness of the peek he could catch almost every word, and on the other side he could hear Henry pacing. Then, in a break between songs, Henry started to sing "Wishing Will Make It So," the way Ray Eberle sang it, with his keening tenor, pitched too high. When the men at craps below raised a noise, Henry's voice was vanished. A moment later the piano man started up again and Julius heard it was the same song, and when the man started singing about the parted curtain of night, a sweet quiet passed along the scaffold and Henry laughed. For a moment Henry's laughter caught along the edges of the peek and hung there, and then both men started walking toward the center, and when each came into view of the other they stood a moment still smiling. Then, because this odd prescience made them both feel exposed, they did not come closer but simply waved, as if between them were an invisible barrier that crossing would make permanent. Julius thought of the night they first touched, when the heat was even greater and Henry shirtless and young. While the piano man played they mouthed the words to each other. When the song ended, they both heeled around and returned to their posts.

Later, after work and an hour of blackjack, Henry came home to the Squaw smelling of well whiskey and sweat. In the small room he took Julius in a vaudeville waltz across the tamped carpet and sang to him, *Wishes are the dreams we dream when we're awake.* By then the morning had broken and both men needed sleep, but the heat was coming back and with it a sense that something was fleeing, having just been named.

IN ROSARITO BEACH Julius wakes from a dream about that night, in a rented room on the sea road he'd paid two and a half dollars for. He'd not slept so well in a month or more. He rises and pulls the blanket across a twinned cot like the ones they had in the service and leaves a nickel for the wash. Next to him another three cots are laid out with blankets, unmussed. He washes his face and neck in the bathroom down the hall and remembers why he's come, and the words of the man in the cellar, who sent him here, who told him it was time to move on.

Downstairs the proprietress stands dishing cold paella into Mason jars. He nods to her and leaves the key and does not say he'll be back and she does not ask. Along the walls of her small dining room are paintings he hadn't noticed the night before in the rainy dark, when he'd arrived in search of Henry. In each of these paintings the same motif, a solitary boat out past choppy surf, floating at the horizon line. They are not accomplished paintings but they have, in their faulty perspective, a compelling narrative. Julius nods again to the proprietress and gestures to the empty tables in the dining room and asks if she serves dinner or supper and she holds up the paella spoon and points out to the sea and says, *"Camarónes. Después de las tres."* Julius nods and pats his pockets and finds there everything he owns and steps out into the gray afternoon.

The tide is coming in high and flat. Though it is past lunchtime he sees no one along the road or on the beach except a fisherman in hip waders far out on a sandbar. Somehow his troubles feel light and amendable. Past the rooming house and a laundry and the small hotels, the town gives way to landscape. In the low hills to the east are two-room houses and restaurants and a few awnings stretching across the roadway. Beyond these the shell of a plant or factory half-finished against the green mountains to the east. The rest of the afternoon he walks the edges of the town and in a cross through the center. The town is so small he does this half a dozen times without seeing anyone except shopkeepers and children hauling refuse to the street. One park he passes holds so many gulls it seems to be another sea, pushed inland. The rain does not abate but falls slowly, as if through the pocked lid of a jar. He feels Henry's nearness, formless and light. The great pleasure of having seen him, even for the briefest moment, in his dream. He thinks that perhaps the man in the cellar sent him out to the coast just to sleep one good night in a bed, to open up the space for the dream to enter. Otherwise the coastal town seems empty and useless and Julius knows he will have to wait for night, when the gamblers might come out and the other wayward men.

In a shop at the eastern edge of town he buys a hot champurrado made with Nestlé syrup and sits drinking it by the fogged window. The sun is setting. Outside a pack of lank dogs in reservation colors, red and brown, with mismatched eyes and of various sizes, trot past shops and hover in doorways, greeted by the shopkeepers like visiting relatives and sometimes tossed scraps of fish. Julius worries about how much money he has left. He remembers that most of the money is Muriel's, and where it came from, and the charitable feeling of the day wavers. He watches the dogs bend in their distinctive way over some carcass while the bunting overhead sends trails of water to the curb.

As he sits in the shop, he remembers something else about that night in the peek: that during the strange stormy weather, after the break-up at the Apache, the cat-faced men had moved in a table for a new game called canasta, which was like rummy but played against the house. The game was too complicated to be popular and because each hand took a full ten or fifteen minutes to play the stakes were steep, and for several weeks it sat empty in the middle of the pit like a weird invention. But the night Henry sang the song, two men sat playing for several hours. Because the play at craps was honest and perfunctory, Julius stood for a long time at the window above the canasta table, watching the men suss out the game and each other. They were good-looking men, near in age, and though they did not seem to know each other they played with a polite deference to one another's skills. But at some point in that long hot night a deal had gone around that made the men angry first with each other and then with the dealer. As the men stood facing one another across the felted table, the dealer did as he was trained, folding one hand over the other on the bumper and waiting for the pit boss. When the boss came, the card players followed him quietly and Julius walked down the catwalk to the adjacent window to watch. The two men and the boss stood making hot gestures until something shifted, and all of the men began laughing and then clapped shoulders and went on their way. The next day Julius found the dealer and asked what the problem had been. The dealer smiled and said it was the damnedest thing: Both men had been dealt exactly the same hand. When Julius scoffed at this, the dealer explained that canasta was played with a double deck, and that while such an occurrence was unlikely it was not, strictly speaking, impossible. The men had suspected some foul play on the part of the dealer or the Nugget itself, but then it had dawned on them what magic they had seen. Because Julius had witnessed so many men raised from the tables and taken away, he knew how powerfully this affected their allegiance, and that while they might never see each other again those two men would think of each other forever, whenever they felt alone.

Now the darkness is falling quickly. Julius counts through the weeks. It must be mid-December or later and the longest night of the year is coming. When he looks out the window at the coast road, he sees men's shapes on the beach and under the awnings. In the other direction a cantina is lighted and beginning to fill. He leaves the shop and walks down the road toward the water. He sees a lean-to made from a wrecked pier and a sheath of aluminum siding, a few men assembled there. He'd hoped for such a game and this is a good place to start. If he plays in a while he can drop a few canny questions and find the places in this town where men gather. When he finds that place he might run a hustle or show the little gun like he did in Tijuana or he might just wait for what the night has to offer. The dream and his memory of the canasta players and the words of the man in the cellar have left him with a deductive certainty. As if all those things are arrows that point in the same direction.

He walks toward the playing men and pats the envelope and the gun in his jacket pocket. Toward the surf line a fire reaches up to meet the coming night, the shapes of the men cast into shadow against the ombré blue of the horizon. They are playing a form of stud poker Julius knows from the Mormon joint, sometimes called Telesina or Shifting Sands, here called Stud Loco. The community cards are faceup and weighted with thimbles on a cardboard fruit box. Around the box the men kneel or sit against piles of sand palmed into chocks. Just beyond them and toward the surf a second group of men sit on an overturned boat half-buried in the sand.

Julius stands by the playing men and when he's noticed he gestures respectfully and one man nods and then another. Julius sits with his back against a fallen soffit, the sand cold but dry beneath him. The gathered men vary widely in age, some are Americans and some aren't, but each of them watches Julius as he sits. Two young men, one blond and one freckled as July, have the penumbral look of card cheats; Julius sees in them something familiar, though he cannot place them anywhere specific. Two others are older locals in bright wool jackets with wide tooled leather buttons. The last man has a severity about him that Julius suspects comes from the service, that and his wool coat and his double-buckle cuffs, worn open and folded over so the brass rings in the wind.

The blond is dealing. He says they're playing lowball in honor of the Christmas holiday, and when Julius raises an eyebrow the blond explains that Jesus was a communist, that getting the most of anything should not be the goal of any God-fearer, American or otherwise, that's what the old cat Himself had said.

"The meek shall inherit the earth," the blond says, and in turn his freckled friend raises his glass. "The meek," they both say, and their drunkenness is callow and convenient.

Julius says he'll watch a hand to learn the scoring. The game is played like five-card stud poker, with three cards laid out faceup for everyone to use, and two cards dealt to each man. At each round the betting is called or increased, until the last card is revealed. The man with the army boots, the wool coat buttoned to his throat, claims victory with a low straight finished on the final card.

"Playing straights and flushes then," Julius says and nods to be dealt in.

He plays for a while with the men, winning a little but mostly watching. The two boys sit shoulder to shoulder and are clearly playing in cahoots, and because none of the other players try to stop them, Julius assumes they are terrible at it and soon this is confirmed. As they play Julius learns their names are Dick and Chrissie. The man in the wool coat wins nearly every other pot and Julius suspects he is marking or dealing from the bottom. If he can catch him at this he might gather some advantage though what he might use it for is still unclear to him. The other players do not seem disreputable and soon the two older men wander away. In another circumstance Julius would rise and thank the men and be on his way. Cheats and drunkards could not be played against grandly. But something in the boys' faces, the quiet intensity of the man in the wool coat, holds him there. The night settles while past the fire and the surf line the darkness competes with the remnant light on the water. Julius accepts a cup of wine, which tastes of milkweed and the sea, under that a rage of alcohol, and he turns the cup into the sand to keep it upright. Such a game is exactly the type Henry might find.

The man in the wool coat antes and then Dick and Chrissie ante in turn. Julius pops a dollar in the pot. He's got most of a high straight. Dick and Chrissie confer like women playing Kemps and the man in the wool coat shrugs openly. Then he raises a dollar and Chrissie calls his dollar and raises another dollar and Julius folds. The man side-eyes Julius's cards and calls Chrissie's dollar and deals the final card. As he does Julius watches not the top card but the man's thumbs, which he might use to press the bottom card forward for the deal or to slide the card back into his palm. Instead he does something Julius hasn't seen, sliding a card from the center of the deck by pressing in a long thumbnail. He deals this to Chrissie and then a card from the top to Dick. He does this so easily that Julius thinks it might be a joke. Then the man deals himself from the top and lifts the corner. Chrissie turns up his last card and says, "I'll be motherfucked," and counts out sixteen damp pesos and tosses them in the pot. The wool coat calls him and turns up a straight flush. Chrissie turns up a useless two-pair and the wool coat pulls in the pot.

"You're tits up then," Dick says to Chrissie.

"I'll be motherfucked," Chrissie says again, in a somber tone.

Julius risks a glance at the wool coat. The man doesn't look back but smiles from the side of his mouth and says, with a voice surprisingly light and ecumenical, "Haven't seen you here."

"Just arrived," Julius says.

"This place ain't on the way to anything."

"I'm on holiday."

"From your office job," the man says, but his tone is friendly.

The men on the periphery start to roughhouse until their playful voices are shouted down and someone's porkpie hat is blown off and catches the inbound wind. The hat lands between Chrissie and Dick like a wish and Chrissie picks it up and twirls it onto his head, then pops it off with his forefingers and looks around as if for some specter. Dick does not smile but nudges him seriously. It's Chrissie's turn to deal but he seems to have forgotten this and when the man in the coat starts to shuffle Chrissie does not call him out. Dick leans back in the sand and seems no longer willing to play. As the wool coat shuffles, he sleds his thumbs along the edges of the deck and does the same trick with the center card and fingers one out and deals it to Chrissie. He looks at Julius who does not look back and then he starts to speak.

"You all know the story now, don't you, about how this game got invented?"

Chrissie smiles in his new hat like a fish. The hat is too big and the boy tilts it down and cocks it sideways so all that shows are his full mouth and the very tip of his nose. He says, "It don't matter to me how anything got invented, if it was invented by the man, as is likely," and Julius sees how very young he is.

The coat says, "That's fine, because the thing about stud poker—or any game—is that you can play it without knowing any real thing about it. You know the rules, you can play, even if you don't know why the rules are what they are."

Julius feels this little speech could be for him or for the two boys or for the dark night itself. Dick has found some small awareness of the world and he sits up and takes his cards. He watches the wool coat and twists a dull smile. Despite the drunkenness and the ragged clothes and the coarse talk, Julius is sure the boys don't know that there is a lower floor to losing than they've yet seen. The wool coat calls for bets and Dick folds, but Chrissie tosses in another ten-peso note, then lifts one hip to dig in his pocket for a dime. Julius meets the raise and stands, and then the coat deals out the next card as he talks.

"A cold night in Texas in the last century, there were four men playing poker the old way, with all the cards hidden," he says, "and as the deal went around here comes a ruckus from outside."

Chrissie pricks up the card he's been dealt and makes a face so beneficent his fate is obvious. The wool coat sees this and the side of his mouth curls up. He continues: "One of the men at the table gets up and runs outside toward the noise, and while he's gone of course the other players take a peek at his cards, like anybody would."

Dick has turned to look at the surf or perhaps at the stars beyond and the man in the wool coat smiles openly. Chrissie is so intent on his own good fortune that only Julius sees this bit of pleasure from the man, and that pleasure makes him fond. He smiles back and feels the man's attention drift toward him kindly.

"The other players are still laughing about how stupid the man was, to leave the table like that with his cards sitting there, when he comes back in leading a stallion by the bridle. Well, they really laugh then. Apparently he'd raised the horse up from a yearling but he hadn't gelded him because he was worth quite a bit as a studhorse, and the noise outside was that studhorse trying to rear up on some old infecund mare."

Chrissie tosses in another dollar and Julius follows and raises and the wool coat calls. The two boys are distracted by the story and the night and whatever the man has dealt them and do not see the man wink at Julius. No one in any attic above them to witness this fleecing, either.

The man says, "So now there's a stallion in the bar, which isn't all that unusual really, because this is the olden times—" And here Chrissie laughs cynically, perhaps at the way the man has spoken or at the idea of a time before this one. "But when his owner sits back down he realizes the mistake he's made, by leaving his cards. He's got money in the game and doesn't want to lose it."

Chrissie is paying careful attention to the man's story and has not glanced again at his hand. Outside the firelight the beach is uniformly dark, but now a figure steps into the light carrying a wooden crate and

Julius hears the clink of bottles. Julius watches the figure over the top of his cards and something about him is familiar. He is tall, with pendant cheeks, his skin the color and texture of cantaloupe rind.

"And you can't blame the other players, really. You couldn't even call it cheating. So the man with the studhorse says—"

The coat pauses and looks at Chrissie and nods for his wager. Chrissie comprehends and lifts his cards. He pats his pockets and shrugs, then pretends to find a ten-peso note he'd forgotten, in the band of his sock. Then he leans over and nudges Dick who checks his pockets and then Chrissie throws in his money and the rest of Dick's, then he takes off his boots and tosses them in with the money.

"He says, 'Listen, gentlemen, I see what's happened here and it's my fault for leaving sure enough, but let me propose something to you. Let's say we all turn up our pocket cards to make it even steven and then we'll each take one more card on the draw and we'll wager on that. There's a bright idea in that kind of game, it makes the math more interesting, you have to admit.' And when the other fellas look skeptical the man walks over and pats his ungelded horse and says, 'To make it worth your while I'll raise the bidding with this studhorse here.'"

Chrissie is watching the wool coat carefully now. A few of the men on the periphery have turned to listen to this story. The tall man steps forward into the firelight. Julius watches him from the top edge of his vision but does not look up or around.

"Why would that man bet his horse? That ain't going to turn out," Chrissie says.

"You're catching on," says the coat.

The tall man stands still at the edge of the fire but comes no further. The firelight throws his shadow long and angular across the sand. His chin casts a shadow over his neck and shoulders, so he appears dark and without particularity. Julius looks with soft eyes at the man's shadow and tries to bring him into clarity. He thinks through the men he met in the Parque Santa Cecelia and others in the low-rent Cacho bars and he can't find this man among them but he knows the man was there somewhere. The man takes a long pull of wine then turns with the bottle and heads back toward the coast road. In the streetlight he has the lean and single-minded look of a match-head. Julius tries to imagine the form of the question and where this man might lead him and if Henry will be there. The dream and the canasta players and the easy way he's found this game: all seem to Julius the kind of fate that states itself clearly. That is, in itself, absolution. He cannot stand in the middle of the wool coat's story or leave this hand of cards to follow the tall man but he watches as the man walks toward the lighted cantina and Julius knows where he will look later.

Finally the wool coat thumbs two cards from the deck and deals the last cards to himself and then to Chrissie and when Chrissie turns up his card he has lost spectacularly. The wool coat drags in the pot on a low straight then he finishes his long story:

"And whoever won the pot that night in Texas—for a happy ending let's say it's some old miser with nothing to his name but a scrap of land with no oil but a decent fence, who could make a far better fate for himself with a horse to stud out—that man teaches this new game to someone, and then that man teaches it to someone else, and so a whole system of risk is born, and forever after we play poker that way, with the hole cards up, and call it stud."

Chrissie frowns and says, "Now wait," and Dick calls up from the ground, "Because *stud* poker. Because of the man's horse."

This conclusion clouds Chrissie's face and then lands fully. Chrissie laughs in his ratty way and says, "Oh that's good, huh," and elbows his reclining friend. The boy's bootless feet are bare and filthy and Julius thinks how young he is. Then, as if he heard every day the origin story of the world, Chrissie shrugs and sprawls out next to Dick and together they look up into the sky and the clouds strung across it. The stars come through only here and there, and the moon is partly covered to the east.

Julius thinks the boys must come by money like mistrals or daylight, that it means nothing to them.

The wool coat gathers the pot and holds Chrissie's boots by the heels and regards them, then tosses them back toward the boy. He puts away his money and stands to go though Julius senses in his posture a continued attention. He senses the man's desire for him. Upwind the low tinkle of a steel drum; just above the beat a flute plays "Singin' in the Rain." A few of the men run shouting toward the cold surf. Julius leans over and picks up the hat and tosses it next to the boots but Chrissie doesn't notice. The two boys lie on their backs in the sand sharing the intimacy of the sky and for a moment they are not lost or squabbling but perfectly together and Julius feels a fondness for them as if for his own childhood. He thinks of Henry and nights they reclined and watched the lights of Fremont and the headlights of cars cast across the ceiling of the Squaw.

Julius stands and turns to the man in the coat and thanks him for a fine game. The man holds out his hand and says, "Jack Dunlap. My folks always called me Jackie." He laughs as if his name is a joke he dislikes and Julius sees two things in him, the service he'd done and his predilections.

"Maybe you ought to offer me a drink," Julius says.

Jackie narrows his eyes and nods. From the heavy sound of Chrissie's breathing it seems he's fallen asleep.

"You've been a real good sport," Jackie says, but without menace. Beyond, Julius watches as Dick points up the road toward the cantina.

JULIUS OPENS THE DOOR to the rooming house where the lobby is warm and smells of coffee. The dining area is empty but one table is dirty with dishes and two others are set for supper. The proprietress is sitting behind the desk reading a book; a turntable turns with the needle rested, making no sound. When she sees them she spines the book on the desk but does not stand. Julius says, *"Gustaría comer, si está bien."* They take the table by the window farthest from the door and the woman does not ask them what they want but brings two cups of coffee and a plate of grilled tortillas too hot to touch. Julius sits with his back to the strange paintings and Jackie looks them over but makes no comment.

"I won't say nothing if you tell me how you learned to rig like that," Julius says.

"Rig what now, friend?"

"Don't get savvy or you'll miss out on this fine spread I've brought you to."

"You could've called me out back there."

"My heart wasn't in it."

Off the dim beach and the shadow play of the fire the man is Julius's age, fine-looking but with the dark brow and stare of a curate.

"You got a good eye," the man says.

"I wouldn't have seen you if you hadn't let me."

The man laughs.

"That was fun though, wasn't it? Taking home those little cousins," he says.

"I didn't have nothing to do with it."

The proprietress returns with two flange bowls of paella and a plate of shredded meat and another bowl for their shrimp tails and yet another bowl with some milky soup the color of robin's egg. She brings all of this stacked up one arm and when they're settled she returns to the desk and plies the record needle and picks up her book. The record is a sonata on twelve-string and sounds so rich and forthright Julius feels he is hearing a prayer. For a while they talk of the game they've played and the fire and the music of the beach and each feels good and light and they laugh without expecting anything from each other. Jackie's hands are wide and the fingers long and tapered and perfect for the work he's chosen. If Julius had seen him below the peek he would have watched him a long time. They eat until the shrimp is gone and most of the meat and the woman returns with more tortillas. When the song ends she pulls the needle back and plays it again.

Then Jackie says, "You've been overseas."

"Yes, Japan and that, Inchon before."

"And you stayed after."

"I did, a bunch of us was still enlisted and owed time. I was navy and Inchon was just about all they had for us to do in that whole war."

Jackie nods.

"It's all airmen's wars now," he says. "I was army but it was like you couldn't tell. Where we were along the coast we played pinochle and took in the wounded but it was the hero aces who landed and fucked all the women and ate all the bread. They'll drop those bombs too. That'll be on them."

Jackie pauses.

"It will—all of it, everything—will come from there now. From the air. No great need for the common man."

Julius hums his agreement. Jackie pushes his plate to the side and lifts the sleeve of his wool coat and wipes the table before him. The woman sees this and clears his plate, and Julius gestures for the rest to be taken though she leaves the bluish soup and their coffee cups. Then Jackie brings the cards out and cracks the deck.

"What's true about that, though, is our worse chance of being alone. Those satellites or whatever they call them. Flying over and keeping an eye."

He lays out three cards from the top of the deck like street monte. Julius glances at the proprietress who has rolled up the sleeves of her sweater. She sees the cards come out but doesn't seem to care. Jackie gestures to Julius, who taps the leftmost card, and Jackie turns it up and shows it to him. Ten of spades.

"You know the story of Pan? The flute on the beach made me think of him."

Julius shakes his head. Jackie scrapes up the remaining cards and with the ten packs them back into the deck. He cuts the deck a few times with his thumb and lays down three more cards. Julius taps the middle card this time and Jackie turns it up. Queen of diamonds. Through all this Jackie keeps talking.

"He was a god, but if you see paintings of the devil chances are you're looking at Pan. Goat legs and horns and cloven hooves, but a man's face. His whole deal was nature and mirth and lust. These boys—" Jackie points his thumb behind to indicate the beach where they'd been. "They think Mexico is some wild pasture filled with pink flowers and wine where no one can see you and you can do as you like. Like there's no culture here and no time, just one long night in the garden."

Again Jackie performs the procedure. Julius is listening but he's also watching the trick. He's already seen what a story can do to a card player's attention, and though there's no money on this game Julius thinks there might be some other reason to play it. He's waiting for the right moment and he'll know it when it comes. Jackie shuffles but this time he lets Julius cut. From the top of the cut Jackie lays out three more cards and Julius picks the middle again. Queen of spades. The bedpost queen.

"But the thing about Pan was that, when he fell asleep, he shouted and carried on because he had terrible dreams. We get our own word from that, *panic*. He'd spend his days in the green pasture fucking and playing the flute, but at night he'd wake from nightmares about those very things. And it was that—his bad dreams and the way they brought memories back to him—that gave him his best idea."

As he talks he fans the whole deck out and lets the cards sit there a moment. Julius has pushed away the soup and set his coffee cup on the edge of the table, and when the proprietress comes back around he holds it up. Jackie covers his own cup with his hand. Outside the darkness has come fully and the rain with it.

Jackie says, "Pan could do lots of things, but the most important thing he did was make people forget. That's what he wanted most, to get away from those dreams. Then you got your garden and your romance and your flute and perfect empty sleep."

Julius, knowing stories of this type if not this one, says, "But surely there's some cost to that, huh? Something you've got to give up for that."

The fan of cards on the table sits like a footnote to the story and neither man reaches out.

"You know how a god ain't supposed to be able to die? Well, Pan dies. And when he did, so the man says, Jesus Christ was born," Jackie says.

"You're a believer then."

Finally Jackie slides the cards back together and shuffles and breaks a few times, then drops the deck on the table except for a few cards left nipped in his palm.

"Nope," he says. "That's just the end of the story." He lets the nipped cards fall by spreading his fingers and they land facedown. Julius reaches out and separates the cards and turns them up, then laughs and picks up the rest of the deck and fans through it.

"Now, how'd you do that?"

Jackie is still holding up his open hand. On the table the ten of spades and the two queens. He says, "In the service I think we felt free but we shouldn't have. We came home and cashed in our leave and then it turned out we were supposed to live in the world we'd protected."

Jackie's face is serious and heavy but his voice still holds the pleasure of his trick. Julius understands what he is being told, though neither man will name it directly. He thinks of Dick leaned back in the sand and the flat forlorn face of the man Chrissie. Jackie had taken nearly a hundred dollars from those boys. Eventually, when they sober up, they might care about their loss. Jackie shifts in his seat so his shoulders frame the window and his legs plank out into the room. In this dimmer light Julius sees how Jackie might be handsome to someone. He sees what another man might love in Jackie's pointed face, his wide eyebrows and tiny ears.

"But say it's true, about Pan. Then you got to think, this time of year, that what we're celebrating is the end of pleasure and history."

Julius holds his breath a long moment and looks around and sees the proprietress far back behind the counter and the turntable louder than the rain and decides to risk the next question.

"Did you get caught ever, in the army?"

Jackie waits, looks over his shoulder to locate the woman himself.

"I did not, but I knew others who did."

Neither man speaks. Julius leans against the chairback and then leans forward again.

"You did though," Jackie says, and Julius nods.

"I had two months left. Can you believe that?" Julius says.

"What'd they do?"

"Let me off pretty easy, really. General discharge, no leave and half-pay."

"That's lucky."

"I saw the man again though. The man I got caught with. That was the worst part, really."

"What do you mean?"

"I was with my brother when I ran into him, a last R and R before they put me on the boat."

"What'd you do?"

Julius looks away and doesn't answer.

"I'm sure it's all right," Jackie says.

"Well I must not have killed him or I wouldn't be sitting here," Julius says then.

Jackie nods and both men look away from each other and stare out the window.

"I've only seen my brother once since then, though," Julius says.

For a long time neither man speaks.

Finally Jackie says, "What about when you got back?"

"They had started raiding the hotels and such. Some Negroes were killed, some other men."

"I was in San Francisco for a while and it was the same there," Jackie says.

"They crippled people, or they sent them to jail. Lots of guys never turned up again, and some women, not many. Who knows what happens after that. Same as anything, probably. The bars and hotels will come back, or they won't."

"But you didn't go to jail."

"No I did not."

Here Jackie turns away from the window and looks at Julius directly. Julius has never had a conversation this intimate with someone he'd not slept with, with whom he had not shared that mutual confession. Before Jackie can ask him anything, Julius says, "I did go once, to jail, but not for that."

"Then what for?"

Julius shrugs.

"Just your basic theft," he says. "My father was sick as hell, and we were just kids. He gave everything to the church and the house was falling in and it was winter."

"How long were you in?"

"A few weeks. They let me run probation. When that was over, my brother got me and we joined up."

"So what happened after that?"

"Same as you, I reckon."

"No, with your father."

"What he wanted, I think. He met the maker he so admired."

Jackie leans back in his chair and looks up at the paintings and along the walls of the dining room and shakes his head. Then he laughs. "God. Are we all criminals, then?"

Julius mirrors this new mood and laughs in turn. "Not much we can do about it, you ask me," he says.

"Well, there's the truth."

"I guess I tried once but it didn't take."

"No use in seeking praise from this fucking world."

"You sure you ain't no believer?"

"No use seeking it anywhere men have been, is what I mean."

A long silence between them. The rain braids against the window and the song ends and the woman does not turn the record. Julius lowers his voice.

"So you don't know those others, really."

"The unfortunate blond?"

Julius thinks of Chrissie's sullen face and laughs. "Or the others. By the boat. That tall fella who brought the wine."

"Only by sight. They got philosophies, you know. Live down here across the border because the laws are better for them. If I were you I'd just steer clear."

"What's their game?"

The man eyes him a moment. "I got no part in it, so I'm not going to say."

"You must not have played with them but once or twice before, or they'd have sniffed you out by now."

"No, just been here a few days. Won't probably last a few more," Jackie says.

"You ever meet a fella named Henry? He's Mexican but down here he may not look it."

"I've met all sorts of people. I don't remember any Henry."

Julius waits.

"I'm sorry," Jackie says, and shrugs.

"There's a cantina up the road. I saw it lighted. You think there's other men there?"

"Like I say, it ain't my business."

Jackie tents his fingers together over the deck of cards and it is clear to Julius he won't say more. When Jackie lifts his hands again the deck has disappeared. Julius thinks of the other cots lined up in the room upstairs and whether they are bolted to the floor or if they could be pushed together. Though he does not want this man he knows that Jackie wants him, and the feeling of another person's body long and warm against him is appealing. Perhaps he could ask about Henry again, after. But he doesn't want to wait. He wants to find the tall man with the wine and the night is already drawing away. Jackie reaches for his back pocket and Julius waves him off and stands and pays the woman for the dinner and for another night in the room upstairs.

"Quién es?" Julius points to the record player.

"Ponce," the woman says. "*'Estrellita.'*" Then as if for the first time she smiles and the lines around her face are deep and charming and Julius nods and thanks her.

Back at the table the talk has drained out between them and soon Jackie stands.

"Hey then," he says. "You got a room here I could show you how to cold-deck, long as you don't try to use it on me." He points toward the stairway. The wool coat is done to Jackie's neck, but one pocket flaps open at the seam and Julius sees the man's thumbnail against the drab olive of the wool where it pokes from the torn pocket.

"I ain't no card cheat," Julius says, and wishes it were still true.

"Well I'll play you euchre for quarters then," the man says and smiles hopefully.

"Ain't euchre for ladies and people with families?"

Jackie laughs and Julius turns his palms up and looks at them and drops them away. Jackie steps forward and reaches out with one finger and touches the stiff collar of Julius's jacket and then traces down the hem of the lapel until he reaches Julius's heart and then he taps once. Julius steps fractionally back and pulls the jacket closed and looks up to find the proprietress. She is staring down at her book. Jackie lifts his hands in a comic gesture of contrition, and all at once Julius dislikes him.

"Might have spent all the luck I've got tonight," Julius says.

Jackie nods and wipes his hands on his coat front and turns and the men part under the veil of this invitation.

UPSTAIRS HE TAKES off his shirt and shakes it out and puts it back on. He washes his face and arms in the sink and stows away his razor and comb. Then he steps back out into the night. The streets both north and south of the rooming house are empty, and for a moment he stands inside the sound of the sea. The rain has let off and the town smells of offing and cooked meat and burned lavender. He walks several blocks north and sees then the lighted cantina and a crowd gathered outside. He can hear music, another flautist or the same one, and steel drums and a singer and a six-string guitar. As he approaches he sees Americans smoking on the patio. The Americans have the look of itinerancy and among them are the first women Julius has seen in Rosarito besides the proprietress. They lack the bold insistence of the American women he met in Tijuana and bear instead some calm defiance, as if their presence is a misunderstanding they might soon correct.

He walks through the group of men and their women to order a beer at the bar and turns in a slow circle around the room. Then he orders another beer and carries both outside. The band has set up along the iron balustrade and Julius leans a few feet from the guitar player. He leans and drinks his beer and waits. The band strikes up an unfamiliar melody. At one table two women sit close and the men across deal cards in a diamond pattern, but Julius does not recognize the game and he can't imagine betting with women. He sees no other card or dice games and he worries he's in the wrong place. Across the street another crowd of locals is gathering outside the cantina's light and he watches them awhile and decides he will wait until his beer is gone.

The band is playing "El Torero" and the flautist takes the high line and it gives the song a hollow lightness like inside of a shell, though below the melody the drums drag along the street, as if the two forces were competing for the souls of those gathered. In all directions the streets are empty and dark, though along the margins Julius can hear the shuffling of night animals and far away the ubiquitous barking of dogs. The band finishes the song and in the quiet interval Julius hears the Americans and the brittle laughter of the women. He wonders where Jackie has gone and if he will see him again.

A few of the women walk off toward the neighborhoods and he wants to call out to them so that they might stay and keep him company. For a moment he wishes harder for that than for Henry or the tall man, but then one of the women catches him looking and pulls her skirt above her knees as if she were walking across a ditch and spits a dark string of tobacco by her ankles and winks at him. In the pegbox shadow of her thigh he sees a penknife and a dark fuzz of hair. It occurs to him for the first time that there might be as many kinds of women as there are birds or men or wind. He imagines Muriel in the stands at the horse track alone and for a moment senses her freedom and her separateness but he can't hold on to this sense. In his mind she turns again into his brother's wife and the guilt he feels is a thin scratch across the dark night and the weeks that brought him here.

Soon the musicians shut away their instruments and wander off hauling these black cases toward the beach. He finishes the first beer and nests the second inside the empty glass. He moves out of the cantina's light and across the street beside the group of men in heavy serapes bunched together along the curb and spilling out into the lane. The men turn to look at him, but none speaks, and Julius sees that they are playing some kind of card game run by a seated dealer. He moves inside the building's darkness and watches as the musicians disappear toward the beach. The globe lights of the cantina flick off and for a moment the street is lighted only by the reflection of the moon on the wet streets and the sea beyond. A brawl of complaint from the patio and then the lights return and the crowd quiets but one woman still cries out and her single voice carries through the silence for a half-second until it turns to laughter.

The men at the curb are playing not pitch or poker but reading lotería cards. A young man in a blue guayabera lays out the cards in a cross, faceup. Across from him another man with a bandaged hand. The young man turns over a card, then speaks to the injured man across from him. The circled figures bow forward in a single motion, as if peering into a hole or grave. From where Julius stands, he can see the turned-up cards over the bowing heads of the men. Each card marked with a figure or object—*la sirena, el camarón*. A rooster, a boot, a soldier, a dandy, the moon.

Julius saw once, in Compton, a woman turn cards like these for money, to tell the fortunes of those gathered. The reading was not private but on a street corner, a crowd assembled to witness each other's fates. Now the young man turns up a card red with a muscled heart, pierced by a fragile arrow. A sigh through the crowd, a ripple of movement, and the men sing out: *No me extrañes corazón, que regreso en el camión.*

The flautist has lingered among the men. He peps a little song from the flute and the high vivid sound seems to travel up the wall behind them and hang there. Most of the men know the song and they sing out a fine melody but in hushed voices, as if hiding from the night. The rain is falling again but very lightly now and the cool air has changed its character as the pressure drops.

When the second man has learned his fate, Julius calls out. "What about me then? *Me toca a mi.*"

The gathered men scoff and shake their heads, but the young man waves him down. Julius finishes the second beer and ledges the empty glasses against the wall, then sits in the center of the men. The man in the blue shirt offers his flat palm and Julius thinks to touch it in greeting but then he understands. He rises and takes the envelope from his back pocket and sits again.

"Cuánto?"

The man holds up four fingers and Julius peels off the bills. The other men horseshoe behind, watching. The man in the blue shirt draws first the open hand, then the tall black boot, then the heart pierced by arrows. Up close he is younger than Julius by ten years or more, almost a child, and his smooth skin against the dark legs of the crowded men has the look of dusk among trees. The boy says, "This is already happen."

Julius nods. Then the boy holds out his hand again and Julius tilts onto his hip and this time offers ten American dollars and says, "That ought to get us at least to the present, hey." The men in the crowd laugh and shove each other. In the moonlight their eyes shine back with something like divine anticipation, the way believers in the Bible were said to apprehend the miracles.

The boy reveals a man holding the world on his back, then the uneasy woman in her hat and jacket, then the unmanned umbrella floating inside a horizontal rain.

"Viene la lluvia," the boy says.

The men laugh. Julius knows the word for rain but not the grammar of the sentence so he says, "American dollars ought to equal English, then," and the boy smiles and Julius senses his power is not deception but the mockery of deceivers, and this is far better than prophecy, because he can never be wrong. On the edge of the group the flautist has stopped playing and Julius can hear the waves and the wooden signs of the storefronts creaking in the wind.

"El gallo," he says, "rooster." He turns over three cards in quick succession and each is marked with the image of a bird. A flamingo on one kneed leg and a parrot on a stand and a songbird stretching toward heaven. The crowd is quiet.

"Esto es todos. Entonces. Everyone is here."

Julius looks at the birds in their line, like some genealogy of flight. He reaches out to touch the parrot with his finger and the boy waves off his reaching hand.

"You wait, please," the boy says.

When he looks down again the boy has turned up a bucket. He studies the line of cards a moment and turns up a final card, marked with a tin star. He rubs his hands together, then opens them palm up, and Julius knows the fortune is completed.

"So it's a bucket," he says.

"No, el cazo. Como—" With his hand cupped the boy makes a scooping motion and brings his hand to his mouth.

"Like a dipper? Like a water dipper?"

"Sí, exactamente. Con la estrella." The boy places the star over the pot and with one finger presses both cards toward Julius. *"Norte.* North-uh."

The crowd laughs and someone says *Americano* and someone else says *adios* but the boy waves silence at them and looks at Julius gravely.

"Están todos en el norte."

"Everything is what now?"

"Every person. In the north."

The boy is severe and radiating certainty but Julius feels this statement is like the rain, obvious and without utility. The cards are wetted with raindrops that lighten the colors but the boy leaves them on the ground as if in punctuation.

Through the legs of the standing men, Julius sees a slim figure walking toward the beach. The man is very tall and dark and has a familiar bearing. Julius stands and holds his hand against the light. The men in the circle look where he is looking and turn back shaking their heads at his impropriety. Julius thanks the boy and the gathered men sing out, *"El caso que te hago es poco,"* and when Julius does not acknowledge this they sing it again, and then a single man calls out without singsong, *"La guía de los marineros."*

"You should not stay here," the boy says. "You should go there." He points with two fingers pistoled toward the northern border.

Julius nods and walks across the street and toward the sea. He could easily run and catch the man, but he doesn't want to frighten the figure away. The man glances over his shoulder but does not seem to see Julius and then he turns north. From the side Julius can see the man's brow and his arm held against his body and Julius's breath quickens. He waits and watches as the figure crosses laterally to the beach, then passes under the old pier and disappears.

Then Julius too crosses Paseo Costero. There is nothing much to the north; the man will have to come back this way, and when he does Julius will approach him. He has waited so long and the waiting feels now like an oblation. The tide is coming in and he sits against the same soffit and pulls his knees to his chest. In the dark sand are prints like comets where the men roughhoused earlier, now eroded and flattened by the spreading waves. When he closes his eyes he sees the four birds laid out on the street and in his mind those birds are the same as the footprints. When he opens his eyes he expects to see the prints lifted and on the wing. He thinks of Henry's story about the little gun and the game of pitch on the train to Sioux Falls. How he'd not believed it because he did not believe any real gamblers would call pitch by that name if they'd play it at all. But Henry had come from somewhere, the gun had come from somewhere, everything had.

Up the beach to the north, three men come into view. In the dark they appear motionless, though they grow as they approach like shadows in the afternoon. A tall man is among them and it might be the same man, it might be Henry. Julius rises from his place under the lean-to and walks out where the moonlight peeks through the clouds. On the other side of Paseo Costero, a woman comes out onto her stoop; one of the men calls her over and the group huddles a moment. Then the woman crosses back and enters the house and closes the door firmly. Then the street is empty.

The remaining figures separate and in the fringe of darkness left by the streetlights Julius can see who they are but not the state they're in. He does not raise a hand or call out and his heart moves down inside him and he listens to the sound of their boots in the sand. He is sorry to have stood and revealed himself, but maybe some chance could be salvaged. He can feel by the pitch of the air that the wind is rising and the tide is coming in. When they are a few yards away the tall man turns to the others and says something Julius can't hear and all three men stop. Dick and Chrissie light cigarettes and stare out into the dark street and then the tall man says to Julius, "Here you are then."

Julius does not answer. Close up the man is wiry and straight-shouldered, with legs like a dividing compass set at a nautical mile, and all at once Julius knows who he is.

"You're looking to shine us again," Dick says, but not confidently.

The tall man spits into the surf. One night in the Parque Santa Cecelia Julius had taken from this man a thousand pesos and a bar-cap and he had tossed the bar-cap over the wall of the slum. He remembers now the man's childish demeanor and the magazine he was reading and his hands raised like binoculars against the setting sun. He had not pleaded or threatened as other men did but instead asked what kind of round the little gun accepted. And Julius had told him .22, though each knew that was impossible, and the moment between them was dangerous. That afternoon or perhaps the next day Julius gave the thousand-peso note to the heart man in the Plaza de Viente Noviembre and felt absolved.

"Your pal here got his boots back," Julius says and his voice is fragile and too high. He nods at Chrissie's feet. Chrissie points one foot out then the other. Dick leans against Chrissie in some approximation of affection. Drink and night have made them nervier and less ridiculous, though still they seem to Julius like two ends of a frayed rope. He wonders how he might escape this and how much time he has to do it.

Chrissie says, "You all have a good supper?"

The energy between the boys darkens. Julius tries to keep his body loose and inviting. He did not imagine being watched, though perhaps he should have.

"Shrimps," he says. "Must've come right out of the sea."

"That's generally where they come from," Dick says.

The tall man has not spoken again. He thumbs his cigarette into the surf and it hisses then sinks.

"You waiting for someone, or you want to play for studhorses this time or what," Dick says. Chrissie stands with his eyes barely open and a dark chuckle shaking his shoulders. He seems too drunk to speak or walk; he keeps dropping his cigarette in the sand and picking it up again.

"Just out walking," Julius says. "Nice night for it, except for this rain."

Dick sighs as if charmed by this banality. Julius glances toward town and then behind him and the street is still empty and it's a long run to the rooming house on dry sand and still the dark figure might return. He thinks of the man's hands curled to his eyes and the way he'd kissed Julius so long even after he'd pulled the gun. As if the tall man can see Julius remember this, he cocks his head and looks Julius over. Then he laughs. "Hello again," he says.

Chrissie finds some string back to the world and straightens up and says, "Say what now?"

The tall man does not explain but looks at Julius mildly. Not disbelief but the opposite, as if Julius has been expected for some time and his presence now is just some touching confirmation. The way Julius has imagined Henry looking when Julius finally found him in some card game or bar. The way he'd felt all that day and night.

"Nice to see you again," Julius says. Perhaps he can be saved by forthrightness the way he was saved before.

"Is it now," the man says.

Julius thinks of the way this man handed over the money like someone making an offering. He'd asked about the little gun with such fond unsurprise.

"You got out of Tijuana then," the man says.

"I didn't find what I was looking for there."

"I don't seem to recall what you was looking for," the man says.

But before Julius can answer or say Henry's name the man places both hands in the center of his own chest and says, "Like I say, even with a twenty-two you'd have to shoot someone right between the eyes, and that weren't no twenty-two."

Instantly Julius knows that he has lost his chance for anything other than what happens next. The coin has fallen the wrong way. The fear of this moment is mixed with the anticipation of it, so much so that it feels almost wanted. The man moves forward with his hands still folded tenderly; Chrissie is barely present, but Dick picks up the whiff of danger. He takes Chrissie's arm and they too move forward so that Julius is hemmed. Julius looks up and down the empty beach. He can no longer hear music or men's voices in the streets beyond. He could run or protest or put up his fists, but none of those things feels like what he's meant to do.

The man reaches out for Julius and takes both his hands in his own and for a moment they stand like betrothed reciting their vows.

"It's all right," Julius says.

"Oh, not a thing's all right," the man says and drops Julius's hands. His look is terribly sad. For a moment he pauses with his palm against his cheek, as if deciding something final, and then he leaps at Julius and both men fall to the ground. Chrissie jumps wholly into consciousness and squats by Julius's shoulder and helps the tall man haul him up. Then all three men come at him and begin to back him down the beach and toward the lean-to.

Julius calls out first Chrissie's name, then Dick's, but neither man stops and the fact that he knows their names will not make them stop. They've been waiting all night and maybe all their small lives for this violence. So Julius says his own name and then Henry's and he tries to tell the man that he's sorry and he reaches in his pocket for his money. Then the man hauls back and strikes him with a closed fist. When he falls, the man kicks him once swiftly in the face. Julius crosses his arms over his head and shouts for the man to stop, he tries to say again that he's sorry, but the man knows everything he wants to know and Julius's mouth has filled with blood and is pressed against the sand. He stands again with his fists up but the boys merely laugh and flank him and soon he is on the ground again and curled protectively, no longer trying to rise. The pain comes and astounds him. And yet he feels the lightest sweetest feeling, that he is in fact recognized and known. In his way the man has carried the story of Julius and Henry, even if he does not know it. Should Julius die in this dark town, from this beating, there is the smallest chance that Henry will know not only that Julius is sorry but that he is loved, and this is the end he's been waiting for.

Julius tries to say, "I can tell you the whole story. I can tell you what it's about."

The tall man does not answer. He kicks Julius once in the ribs and again in the face. For a moment Julius feels his consciousness falter and there is Henry again and this time Julius does not shake him away. Henry behind the man watching, a shadow in Julius's eye, like the aphotic rim of the ocean beyond which there is only impalpable life, which Julius saw on Henry's face that night at the Golden Nugget and other nights before that when he was distant or unkind. Vaguely he feels hands inside his shirt and his jeans pockets and someone pulling at his boots. In Henry's imagined presence a terror Julius knows is not imagined, and inside that terror is a state of perfect understanding. Julius sees the sand and the moonlight and hears the surf lapping, beyond the breakers the soft suck of the trough against the ocean floor, beyond even this the fizz of moonlight on the resting surface.

Then a car turns onto Paseo Costero without its lights on. The man sees it and waits for a moment, and when the car slows and flashes the high beams he kicks Julius once more in the face, then runs across the street. The two boys run in the other direction, down the beach. The man leaps into a yard lush with winter citrus, and as he disappears behind the house a dozen lemons brush off the branches and fall into the shining grass. The driver does not see Julius crumpled on the beach or does not care to get involved and drives by him. Julius blacks out with his boots halfway off and his heels stuck in the bootshafts like slipped plaster and the rain falling into his upturned ear.

DAWN WAKES HIM but he lies a long time without moving, finding the parts of his body one by one until he is sure he is alive. The tide is hauling out and his clothes are wet and stiff with salt. When he opens his eyes he is staring into the wide face of a cat, ragged with rain. The cat opens its mouth in a cavernous yawn, then snaps it closed with a clicking noise that lights the beach. Julius presses up into a sitting position on the wet sand; the cat moves away at this motion and mews, then circles back, and when Julius reaches out he makes the mewing noise the cat has made and finds his tongue is gummy with blood. The cat seems to smile and curls underneath his reaching hand. He sees the false fronts of the shops gleaming along the shoreline and he remembers the bills slatted in his boots. He reaches up and the blood is sticky. He feels a throbbing behind his eye and inside his nose and rain falling coldly in his wounds. He stands with some difficulty and thumps into his bootheels and cups his hurting ribs. As he stumbles up the beach, the cat follows blithely behind.

ALL THAT MORNING and through the day, Julius sleeps at the rooming house. He does not dream but he rises to the surface of sleep and what he sees is like dreaming, the curtain pulled closed and shadows across it lengthening and fusing out. He does not see Henry again and he fears seeing him. He fears that there are only so many dreams he might be granted now.

When he finally wakes it is late afternoon, the final Sunday of Advent, and in the dusty sheets he's left a sunburst of blood. On the next cot, someone has placed two towels and a cup of milk and a hunk of dark bread. He stands and goes to the small window and slips the curtain back. The light that enters is bright and wintry, but by the thinness of it he can tell the rain is coming again and twilight not far off. The blood has caked his hair and one side of his face. The smell is familiar, old blood and dirt, wartime, Kansas summer.

He runs a shallow bath and wipes an arm of steam from the mirror to shave. The cut on his head is long but not deep. His nose has been broken and under his eyes and along his cheeks the bruise is noxious and dark. When he turns the razor along his jaw, the blade pulls away black freckles of blood. Along the rim of the sink a line of ants ambles toward the scrap of soap; Julius lays the razor in their path and for a few minutes watches them traverse it, their tiny bodies doubled by the steel flank, their confusion at its warmth. He leaves the razor there and dresses in his old shirt and throws Ralph's filthy white one in the wastebasket. He pulls on his dirty jeans and pads back to the room in his bare feet, feeling better, hungry. He turns a chair to the window and sits and drinks the milk and eats the bread. The streets and the shops along the coast are decorated in bunting and thin garlands of gold.

Out in the shallow bay a dozen boats are crowded together in a flotilla, connected by lanterns hung from the stemposts. Their decks are packed with men and children and women in bustled dresses white as noon in the lantern light and against the calm sea. The passengers watch as above them fireworks burst into streamers and drops of light. On one of the boats a band plays holy music. Julius watches as a man walks onto the deck of a boat from the southern dock, stepping quickly and lightly from boat to boat, moving among the gathered people as a woman might move through a bar toward the exit, until the bow of the farthest boat rocks under his arrival. The man disappears among the others and the fireworks drip like elm leaves across the sky.

As children Julius and his brother had gone with their father to the reservation north of town to buy fireworks, each year on the Fourth of July. Among the rows of folding tables their father paced up and down, his fingers laced behind his back, studying each box. So little of any luxury had been theirs that they could not help a feeling of attachment to every possible choice, and as their father passed each box of fireworks they leaned on their toes and hoped but knew better than to ask questions. Always their father would choose the cheapest box, as if his long wandering through the aisles had been a penance.

Once back home they waited out the long summer evening for the right degree of darkness. Julius remembers this part as a feeling and not as an event. Trying to remember the particular color of the evening, the time the sun disappeared or the positions of their bodies next to each other as they waited, was like trying to separate water from water. What he recalls is his father's nearness, how painful it was to wait with someone else for something that always happened. The sun setting. The night coming. When the darkness did come they set the small firework on the slab of concrete by the bootscraper and lit it. The small explosion and the reference of the light and the smoke trailing thin across the dusk. Red and blue balls rising fifteen feet then falling apart. Every box of fire a surprise.

Outside the music rises in pitch and a cheer goes up. Julius realizes he has been thinking of his father without remembering that he is dead. The old shirt he's wearing is wet at the tail, and when he lifts it up he sees that he is bleeding. He stands with some difficulty and crosses again to the cot, then lifts the towel and holds it to the gash in his side. He touches his head and he is not bleeding there and his teeth feel sanded but fine. When he takes the towel away he sees that the wound is deep and the flesh aches where it pulls apart. Across his rib cage is a dark bruise in the shape of a clothesiron. He sits again by the window, leans over painfully, and picks up his boots by the shafts. He turns them over and peels the bills out along with the little gun. He remembers how, when the firework was lighted, his father jogged backward and away from the fuse and positioned Julius so he could see the lights but held him so he would not move too close. He recalls his father's hands on his shoulders with all the devotion the man could offer. In the sky beyond, the small bombs were made meaningful only by the darkness they'd anticipated, temporary and without impact, only beautiful, only theirs.

When he tries to locate Lee in this memory he cannot, though his brother must have been there, on the stoop or near the garage, watching.

He knows he was loved more than Lee, in the way that troubled children are worried over and adored. He understands this suddenly. There is terrible joy in this, and a familiar shame, as if being loved is a gift that confers not safety but reparation. His brother must have known this even then, even in childhood, and carried it with him, and no wonder he wanted to marry and build a life without that burden. Lee might have blamed their father's death or the night in Okinawa when Julius fought the man who'd been his lover or the discharge that followed. But now Julius wonders if it was really this inequity, the way love came to Julius and not to Lee, the way Julius spoiled it, though Lee held so easily the other good things of the world.

Julius pleats half the bills around the pistol and puts this damp sachet in his bootheel. The other bills he folds into his pocket and then he presses back into his boots and stands slowly. He sees with the clarity of the failed how ridiculous a thing he thought he was doing. To attempt to be found, or to find someone else, this way. He has almost no money left; the tall man from the park and the two boys have taken it, along with the truck keys. But he thinks of the way the man folded his hands over his heart and how he'd used those same hands to hurt Julius and feels only that something necessary has been amended.

Downstairs the lamps are lighted. The tables are empty and the chairs turned up and resting on their seats. A record is playing and he approaches the desk with the towel pressed to his forehead and corners it up demonstrably.

"Lo siento," he says.

With his broken nose and bruised face he must look like someone back from the dead, but the woman does not regard him with fear or suspicion. She reaches out and taps her ash into a bowl. She has the beautiful dark eyes of this country and a long braid like a single unbroken tress. From the turntable comes a funereal song Julius does not recognize. He pats the front of his shirt and pantomimes an elliptical thread from the buttonhole; when the woman does not respond he pinches two fingers together, drawing them away from his pursed lips, then makes a circle with the finger and thumb of his other hand and guides the imaginary thread through it.

"Button," he says, and points again to his shirt.

"Ah," she says, holding up a finger. She slips behind the curtain and returns with a plastic basket. Raking through bobbins and pins and wax thimbles, she finds an off-white thread and a brown button and hands these to Julius. He holds the placket out and plies the needle through and around a few times, and though the button hangs loosely it holds the shirt closed. He bites through the remaining thread. Through this procedure the woman watches with amusement and though she could surely do better she does not reach out to help.

Then he lifts his shirt and points to the wound there. She frowns at him. He holds out two fingers. She gives him the cigarette and he takes a long drag, then presses the cherry to the needle and rolls it around. He threads the needle again, and with the cigarette hanging limply from his mouth he stabs through the torn lips of his flesh and brings them together. The maneuver makes him cry out and hunch, and the woman comes around the counter and holds the shirt for him so he can use his other hand to pinch the wound closed. He threads through in tight circles. The awful feeling is familiar; he remembers the man in Okinawa and the blue forever of his eyes. When the wound is stitched, the woman leans down and bites the thread for him and ties it off. Julius looks down on the fine part of her hair and the light thrown against it and his pain is significant. He thinks of the milk and the bread and with one hovered finger he traces the woman's part without touching her while she looks down tying the thread. Then she stands with the bobbin and he hands the needle back and she crosses again behind the counter. He folds the towel against the wound and presses it there, and with his other hand he reaches into his back pocket and takes out a few of Muriel's bills. Among them is a playing card and he picks this out and pushes the bills across the table. When she pushes them back he says, "No, ma'am," and walks out into the rainy street.

WITH HIS ARM held fast against the towel he ducks down the alley to the next street over and sneaks along the storefronts, then through another alley to a residential pocket where the clouds cast long shadows over the squat yards. Inside these shadows children move in groups of six or seven, off into the narrow streets, several groups to the north and another to the south, until they have spread in a cross through the neighborhood. At each house they stand ranked on the cement steps, an appointed leader rapping at the door, until it is opened and a grim adult sends them away. This will go on until the dusk is final, until the children are admitted, as Mary and Joseph were, into the warmth and feast of the willing.

At a distance Julius follows the children moving north, along a line of row houses strung eave to eave in green and gold flags. He keeps to the shadows and the overhanging palms, and once he's past the houses he cuts back across and waits where the highway meets the ocean road. A few passenger cars roll by slowly with their windows up; these he ignores. He looks up and down the road and along the beach but sees no one. For a long time he waits for another car to pass and none does. He thinks of very little, though the memory of his father is present and the thought of Henry, and the two combine to make a lonely atmosphere. The rain pings in the cut at his forehead and he holds his sleeve against it. If he meets the boys or the tall man again the daylight might save him, but the daylight is going. He counts the miles to Tijuana. The walk would take the whole night or longer and already he is exhausted.

He crosses the coast road then and passes through a stand of scrubby pine and down onto a pier. The sea comes in so thick and high it is like a forest. He steps out for the nearest boat and is hauled aboard by revelers, and with great effort he walks across the rocking bow. He steps over the waling to the next boat and then again to the one after that. The boat bounces as another man steps onto it and a cusp of gulls flush before him and settle again behind. He sits against a clocher of rope and reaches in his pocket and finds the playing card; he thinks of Jackie's touch after dinner the night before, and realizes that he must have slipped it in Julius's pocket. On the back, Jackie has written a verse from Isaiah: *In the habitation of dragons, where each lay, shall be grass with reeds and rushes.*

He looks out at the sea and the horizon rests like cut paper against the heavy sky. He remembers the day he was finally free and he stepped off the ship in Long Beach and took the woman's booklet and sat and read it. In Isaiah the holy land is the place where heaven and earth touch. Perhaps that means that in every other place there is division, distance, an unnamed thing holding heaven from earth, like the line out at sea that can never be reached. Isaiah did not give this thing a name, but Julius suspects it is tenuous, less a separation than a pressure, like the fine agony of two bodies pressed together, like one man's hand touching another. That the space between heaven and earth is the touch those two hands make.

III.

NINE

Swallows

Morning comes in cold and sunny and the world has not changed overnight. Muriel wakes and makes coffee. Lee showers and they sit together awhile listening to the weather, which promises to be fair past the Lagunas and all the way to Houston, and when the news comes on she flicks the radio off and steps outside and lights a cigarette. Along the tree line the alfalfa has punked, but there are cleared spaces that suggest the horse has come around. Where they've tugged the trailer the sun is dappled by the trees and beneath the awning the grass is dry and dark, like a hand swiped across a fogged window.

They head into town and Muriel drops Lee at the factory and drives on past Island Avenue and over the tracks and onto a green spit built as surf break. It's Saturday and the sailors are out in their white crackerjacks playing catch or lounging. She drives further and finds a clump of sea pine and parks beneath it. Behind her is a rough pier where there were once grand hotels and now squat housing for the naval base and carnival games and tented surf camps. The incoming tide is blue and wild, and out a hundred yards surfers hang in a line. Overhead waves rise from the surface like mountains. The surfers are crouched on their boards as if assembling something delicate and temporary while the waves hold one behind the other, piled miles back into the South Pacific.

She thinks of the Heyday and the owner and the horsemen, and then she thinks of Lee—of him the day she arrived in San Diego with her one suitcase, and long before this of the day she first met him, outside a bar where her mother was drinking. She thinks of Gail's kiss and her long shadow cast by the sunset. For a long time she watches the surfers, until her neck begins to ache.

The sea reminds her, as it often does, of the fields of her childhood. For miles in every direction the prairie grew waist-high in bluestem and Indian grass, sometimes a great elm in the distance too wide to cast a shadow. In the spring the fields were burned north to west in a pattern set by the Forest Service, then in summer the grass returned new and green and then quickly stiffened and paled, until in winter it caught ice and waited heavy as a robe across the vista. In this way the seasons remade the grasslands in their own image. If anyone had told her that one day she would watch the ocean and see the weather and the seasons change it the way the fields were changed, she would not have believed them. She would not have believed any story about her life as it is.

She doesn't have to go back to the hotel or see Gail again. She might turn around and drive home and sleep in her own bed, and when Lee hitched out after work she might stand in the kitchen to greet him. Julius might return or not, and either way they would keep each other's secrets and go on. That was how people lived. She locks the car doors and drapes her coat over herself frontwise. Outside the street is quiet as the waves come in. She closes her eyes and sleeps for an hour, then wakes again and looks out at the sea. The surfers have moved on, though the waves are still coming. She thinks of the moment Lee pulls away during their lovemaking and the way that pause is like a murmur in a heartbeat, a brief interruption in a pattern that might otherwise go on forever. She closes her eyes and sleeps again.

IN THE AFTERNOON she wakes and drives to a gas station, where she buys a candy bar and washes her face in the bathroom and fixes her hair. She strips off her stockings and shoves them in her purse. She's brought her best skirt and she pulls this on over her bare legs, tucks in her blouse and dabs a bit of perfume behind her ears. Then she drives to the hotel with the covered windows and waits. The same man in his lowered hat stands in the doorway and Muriel watches him and the entrance a long time, while behind the sun lowers over the calming sea. By six o'clock Gail has not appeared. Muriel should be frightened but she feels better than she has all day. She hears the train passing at a distance across the seawall and the sound is a comfort, proof of ordinary life.

She wonders how long she should wait. Along a back channel of shrubs she sees a man emerge as if from a doorway, arms at his sides as he looks around. From the south end a second man in a light suit keeps along an untrimmed line of poplars. Behind the branches the horizon seems to sink, the spongy orange light of this city buoyed above the tree line so the men appear as shadow play against the gray wall of trees. For a moment both men wait at this distance. Then they wave to each other and walk toward the hotel and the man in the hat nods them inside.

Muriel steps out of the car and smooths her skirt and retucks her shirt and walks down the street with her arms crossed tightly over her purse. She pauses outside the heavy door of the hotel and the man in the hat looks her over and laughs. Over the boarded inset window is pasted a notice of police raid, but with the edges scraped away and the word *Police* crossed out and *Air* written above it. At the bottom corner, in another hand, the word *Shelter*.

"If you say so, honey," the man says and opens the door.

Inside the hotel is shabby but done up in elegant colors, gold and red damask wallpaper and walnut paneling. The lobby is shallow but wide as a ballroom. Below her a plank floor trod in sand and ash. Past an empty desk a set of armchairs with a table between them, beyond these a string of lights along a banister leading upward.

Already the bar is full of sailors and other young men in cuffed jeans and striped derby jackets. The windows are painted black on the inside, too, and the air is coastal and sticky and gray with smoke. The bar itself is cherry and lacquered and set very low. Muriel sees no other women. She sits at the bar with her back to the door, and when the bartender comes he asks if she knows where she is.

"I'm meeting someone," she says.

"Are you now," he says.

"I am."

"Here I thought every night was the same," the man says.

He coughs and dabs his mouth with two fingertips as if re-creating some tenderness and then he shakes his head. He is tall and handsome and dressed like a porter. She asks for a Stinger and when he brings it she thanks him and he curtsies and smooths his hair back. She sits a long time with her knees pressed against the underside of the bar. Several times the door opens, and in the cut of light is another man and not Gail. The bar and the lobby fill slowly with men dressed in dark clothes. One man approaches her and asks if she is lost but he stands at some distance as if she might be a kind of decoy. She asks him if he knows a man called Julius or another called Rosie, and when he shakes his head she makes a pinching motion and says, "What about a little gun," and the man laughs and says, "Plenty of those here."

Not long after this the lights are lowered and the men begin to come together. Someone scratches on a record. There are no clocks and no windows, so she can't tell what time it is, but she's had three drinks and it must be nearing eight. Perhaps Gail waited outside or perhaps she is still waiting but probably she never showed. Muriel feels hot though her legs are bare, and her neck catches the draft and she wishes for someone's hand at her waist. Soon the men begin to dance and whisper and hold each other in the powerful darkness. A man in a pinstriped suit stands watch at the door; another stands behind the old lobby desk with his hand on a telephone. The man next to her is turned away, telling a story about his father. It is so dark that Muriel can't tell if the man is talking to himself or someone else, and as she listens to the story it could be Lee's or anyone's. Perhaps that's what the darkness has done, turned every story here into every other.

The turntable plays "What a Fool I Was." The men on the dance floor are paired off and holding each other. She might have expected this and she is not surprised but the feeling she has is like surprise. Surprise at the simple candor of it, the fact that her company has not prevented it. A little scuffle travels through the room and then the room is suddenly bright. Globe lights strung along the ceiling drip down and catch the men in their tender poses; then the lights go off again, then on, then off. Muriel looks around and sees the man behind the desk flipping the switch with one hand and with the other holding the phone to his ear. For a moment no one moves. One man in a workman's shirt and heavy boots draws his chin back and yelps recklessly; his partner reaches out to shush him and the first man slaps his hand away. The turntable plays the last wobbly bars of Eddy Arnold. Muriel thinks to stand, but the lights have not come back on and upstairs she hears the pad of footsteps but no doors opening. The next song begins and it's "How High the Moon" and the electric serration of the guitar clunks the room back open but no one dances yet; the song hangs there until someone laughs and then someone else. What had seemed at first like panic then settles into formality and the men start to move again.

A young man turns to Muriel and holds out a hand and says, "When in Rome."

"If this were Rome, I'd be someone else," she says, and knows the drinks have landed.

"That isn't how it works," the man says, and leads her to the floor.

"Maybe if I were someone else this would be Rome."

The man's smile is pitying but gentle, patient.

"All I mean is, shouldn't I be a man," she says.

"You're fine, darling."

They dance to that song and the next and Muriel wonders where Gail might be and with whom and if she'll ever see her again. The man has dark eyes and freckles nearly black against the night, and his cheeks are still full and tender. She leans close and places her forehead on his shoulder. He dances with her the way she'd seen men dance at weddings with their younger cousins, yet when she looks at his tilted cheek and his neck she thinks that from a distance they must look like lovers. She thinks the word, *lover.* She thinks of Julius beneath her window that Christmas in Kansas and she lets this thought widen out until the loneliness she feels seems to involve even the music, whose tones began to lower and slow until every song is an elegy, and the night itself, which now is growing long.

The man angles his face away from her and says, "How'd you get in here then?"

In the dark with this stranger, with these men and their strangeness, so fragile in the dark, it seems possible to say things exactly as they are.

"I'm looking for someone," she says.

"Aren't we all."

"Someone specific."

"Not your husband, I hope."

"No, not him."

"You got a name?"

"Julius."

"No, honey, your name."

She cocks her head at him.

"What's yours?"

"Peter."

He might be no more than eighteen. He loosens his arms and she unspools from him and then he spools her back. The next song is quick and jangly and the crowd doesn't like it. Someone scratches the record off and a long moment passes in silence. Peter leans out of their embrace and lights a cigarette and offers it to her and she waves it away.

"Muriel," she says.

"What do you think is going to happen next, Muriel?"

He smokes with his head tilted back to keep the smoke away from her. It could be a polite gesture, yet the way he does it makes it seem avoidant, as if he wants no part of himself to be touched.

"I was supposed to meet someone, but she didn't show."

"Your first time getting stood up?"

"Yeah."

"Big part of this game."

"Is it?"

"Lots of times this place doesn't even exist," Peter says. He points to the concierge desk across the ballroom and says, "They have a board, if you're really looking."

The music starts again. Two men dancing close lean into each other, then one turns to face the other. One man says, "Not much time now," and the other leans to kiss him. Muriel thinks to close her eyes or look away but she doesn't. The first man's mouth searches out the mouth of the other and the second man gives up his mouth but keeps his eyes open and sees Muriel watching and his eyes go brass and lively. The first man pulls away and catches the second man open-eyed and smiles very softly at him. Muriel feels the kiss transposed over her and pressing her down. She has never seen two men touch each other this way. Something about its nearness, its very newness, hurts her, is outside the world. She thinks of kissing Gail in the ocean sunset and then of Julius on the horse and the long afternoons at Del Mar and the turned-up smell of the turf.

"Lucky them," Peter says.

He pulls Muriel suddenly close and dips her. He bends his knee and her back rests on it and then he lifts her gently up. Another man says Peter's name and comes close and touches his shoulder and Muriel aches for him, for both of them.

"I'm off now, honey," Peter says and kisses her on the forehead.

Then she is standing alone on the dance floor. Around her the beautiful men are dancing. In every man there is a trace of Julius. She wonders what this feels like to them. To be among each other, but hidden from everyone else. She had heard people speak of love as if it was either a salve or a curse. Her mother said that love was worth doing over and over. But what her mother must have felt, she'd seen reflected in every little corner of the world: men touching women in bars, couples dancing, a film in which a man stands yelling in the rain or on a train platform. What to call this place and these men, herself among them? When she'd seen Julius lying beneath her window Muriel hadn't known who or how he loved, or if she loved him, only that his attention fell on her in a way that suggested love could be instant and precise, without desire or consummation but just as ardent as those things. She did not know if her mother had ever felt this or if she'd wanted to, and if not this then what.

Then the record scratches off and the lights come on again and stay on and the men on the floor break apart. No hesitation now. She sees Peter move away from his man and both hurry toward the street. A few take off for the back and Muriel follows them through a side door. Outside, the evening is new and cold. When she looks up the alley she sees the back end of a Continental, but no one around. She turns into the alley and walks toward the street and she is a block past Market before the squad car is visible. It passes the hotel without stopping and the sirens are off and the windows down and the cop has one smoking hand out the window and the other cocked over the wheel.

She walks back up to the plaza and finds the Ford. Inside she locks the doors and starts the engine but leaves the headlights off. Her hands are shaking and she might cry but she feels exhilarated and fully awake. The windows are fogged and she wipes this away and looks out at the plaza where men still gamble and the busted streetlights look like graying teeth in the night. Another police car passes but more slowly and pulls up to the curb across from the hotel. Again she thinks the word, *lover.* Suddenly the word itself seems built to admit meanings she could not have anticipated. Her mother must have known there were such places as this even if there were none in the small town where they lived. She had been to El Paso and Galveston and twice to Wichita. She had known men who sat all night in barrooms playing cinch and come-and-tell-em for more than what they earned. Among these men and others in the factories she must have heard of those who met quietly and very carefully in this way. And her mother might be proud of her for looking, for knowing this, or her mother might be ashamed, who could say now.

It is past nine o'clock; Lee is still working. She drives toward the river through the poor neighborhoods and under the freeway site and down onto the county road. The neighbor's kitchen is dark, the porchlight out. Muriel parks behind the cypress where the car can't be seen from the road. The sky has darkened to a color like damp silk and though the report was for fair weather the rain has returned. As she walks to the door, the rain beads coldly on her neck and arms. She knocks on the door and the kitchen light comes on and Sandra opens the door. A concerned look.

"Hi there," she says.

She broadens and lifts her arms against the doorway. The doorjambs are sweaty with the rain and Sandra's palms against them make a wet brushing sound.

"It's raining," Muriel says.

Sandra's shirt is worn pale at the elbows and along the collar, a peek of skin between her belt and the fabric of the shirt as her body stretches up and across the doorway.

"It is," Sandra says and drops her arms and steps forward.

Muriel can smell the fecund wet of the mud and the fresh rain coming down over it and even the dry quiet of the kitchen beyond which smells of woodfire.

"Are you all right?" Sandra says.

"I thought I might buy some eggs."

Sandra's look is worried. "Okay," she says. Then, "You got seventy-five cents?" and steps back to let Muriel through the doorway.

Inside the kitchen is cold and the fire in the parlor chinked to embers. A single cup on the table rimmed in old coffee and the kettle turned upside down in the sink. Clementine peels on the counter, a shock of feathers across the doorway. Muriel feels exposed and strange seeing these half-done tasks. The gray light through the curtain cuts the room and traces the table and the doorway, making their shapes visible but not their edges. She apologizes for the hour. Above the sink the window lets in the scant moonlight and the trees sway in the arbor beyond. She sits and stretches her legs beneath the table. She wishes she could heel off her shoes and she realizes how tired she is. She remembers she is bare-legged and she must smell like smoke and cologne. Sandra boils a kettle for coffee. On the counter a weather radio catalogues the price of hay and gasoline. When the price of chickens is called Sandra flicks the volume up and listens, then flicks the radio off.

"Those eggs just went up three cents," she says.

"Surely I'm grandfathered in."

"We did make a deal at seventy-five. I suppose that has to stand."

The kettle swoons and Sandra fills two cups but does not sit. Muriel closes her eyes and sees the globe lights flickering and the man Peter's sweet face. Then the men kissing, then the police car. Sandra stands with her back to the counter and she has the keen but apprehensive look of a pickpocket.

"Tell me a story about this place," Muriel says.

The kitchen light casts down on Sandra's black hair and her hair reflects it. Muriel traces the curve of her mouth and then down to her narrow shoulders and tries to imagine what might happen next.

Sandra looks at her and says, "Okay then. You remember I told you before that those lots used to be olive grove, but I don't think I told you the rest. Before that it was all Spanish mission. Before that it was Indian land and before that who knows."

Sandra lowers her chin and looks out as if from under some shade and she is so beautiful then. Muriel lights another cigarette and holds out a second one and Sandra takes it. Muriel pops the match and Sandra leans to her. She lets the match touch only a moment, then leans away.

"Did you live here when there were olive groves?" Muriel asks.

"Oh no, that was my father's time."

Muriel lifts her cup and coffee spills down her wrist and she sets the cup down again and shakes her hand and licks the coffee away.

"But he saw them, and his father before him would have known the Franciscans, the last of them anyway. What my father always said was that they had these big blouses like women or Arabs and they walked out to the river in the morning and fed the fish. That the fish could hear them coming and shaking the cans of feed and the fish would gob up to the surface. Hundreds of them, like trained dogs. The place where they gathered looked from above like boiling water. Of course he hadn't seen that, but his own father told him."

For a long moment neither woman speaks. Muriel drinks the coffee in two swallows and thinks to ask for another cup, but instead she's going to do the next thing. She can hear the next thing like a sound in the room.

"It's funny," Sandra says, "but I think sometimes that I remember that, too. But it could have been something my grandfather dreamed and no one at all actually remembers it." She looks at Muriel levelly and the look goes on a long time. Then Muriel rises and goes to her. She reaches out and touches Sandra's waist and when Sandra does not shrug off this touch Muriel comes closer. Sandra lets her weight come away from the counter and into Muriel's arms. She fingers the hem of Muriel's blouse. Muriel touches the dent of Sandra's lower lip with the flat bed of her thumb, then kisses her. They kiss until Sandra pulls away and looks at

Muriel with delight and Muriel shrugs, as if anything she'd done could not be helped.

"I wasn't sure about you," Sandra says.

"Are you sure about me now?"

"I'm not."

"What else do you need to know?"

"First off, if Idaho isn't the Plains, then what the hell are the Plains."

"I'll show you on a map."

"Not now, though."

"No, not now."

Muriel kisses her again and the kiss goes on until Sandra turns and looks out the uncurtained window and moves to the side and pulls Muriel with her. At first a series of touches awkward in their plying. Muriel's mouth at Sandra's neck, Sandra's hand on Muriel's breast—questions about consent and possibility, answered by other touches. Muriel wonders vaguely about kitchens and the quiet way they take people's secrets but leave them no place to lie down, which is what she wants most to do. As if in cognate feeling Sandra kneels and looks up at Muriel and lifts the hem of Muriel's skirt and twists it to one side and holds the fabric against Muriel's thigh. She kisses Muriel's knees and shins and then the insides of her thighs and Muriel bends one leg onto the chair rung so her body opens. Sandra eases away Muriel's panties and finds her with her tongue and lips, and Muriel presses her hands to the counter edge for balance. From above the sweet part of Sandra's hair and the little moonlight dabbed onto it like paint. Outside the noise of the river and the wind in the trees and the rain falling. Muriel imagines her shadow through the kitchen window and her head leaned back and in that simple motion is the fact of her pleasure, though Sandra would not be seen as its source. It is too much, feeling this and also imagining it.

"I can't stand," Muriel says.

"You can't stand it?"

"No."

But Sandra doesn't stop. Muriel's legs shudder but she holds herself up and when finally she comes she bites through the soft flesh of her lip and the blood in her mouth is a tonic. Sandra rises back to her and kisses her. She tastes the wound and pulls away and thumbs Muriel's lip back gently, and here their lovemaking ends with the bloody echo of its beginning. Sandra goes to the bathroom and returns with a fold of gauze. Muriel sets this inside her lip like snuff.

"You are practical, aren't you," Muriel says. The gauze lisps her voice.

"You aren't?"

Of course she is. But she feels she has just invented something. That she has told a secret that is also an invention. She has bet on horses and been where men dance together and now this. She looks at the peels on the counter and the empty kettle and the wash water left to chill and the coffee cup. A scene like a frontier tableau, the cheerful rind of the clementine, chicken feathers along the baseboards where they've drifted, no light but the dim rainy sky and the lowered fire casting on the walls and ceiling, the reticence inside a house in the late evening. While outside it is 1957. Over her head the unseen contrail of an airplane, the arc drawn by the metal satellite, asphalt and engine oil, rubber, nuclear fission. How delicate she feels. How out of time.

BEFORE ALL THIS, when Muriel was a child. She and her mother were still Catholic then. In the parlance of the day they were called snappers, distrusted perhaps less for their beliefs than for their weekly abstinence from meat. Because her mother was contrarian and aloof Muriel felt she was required to relish such slurs, as if they proved some fixed nobility. The church her stepfather belonged to was Free Methodist, and on Thursday evenings and Sunday mornings the men and women of that small congregation gathered in a Masons hall on folding chairs. Though their aims were virtuous they sang without much feeling, and after attending once Muriel's mother refused to go again. If she wanted an upright piano and grape juice and paper fans, she said, she'd go to a barn dance in Bird City.

The church they attended instead was large and beautiful and at the edge of the old part of the city. In a region so Lutheran and sane the church was an excess more unsettling than disliked, as if its beauty were a mandate on God's own aesthetic. The pews were cherry, stained almost black, and the altar gilded and set high above; the candles left circles in the eye. Above the altar was a window of stained glass, round and red and divided into eighths by iron bars. During the sermon and the liturgy Muriel sat and counted the segments of the window clockwise and then back, a ritual to pass the time. The church was built with the apse at the south and the red window caught the light through the sun's declination, as ancient temples were said to do. To Muriel the window had the presence of an eye, perhaps God's, perhaps the architect's, perhaps neither of these. Often she noted the changing colors of the glass as the service went on. The transepts and the nave were lined with stained glass panels more complex and beautiful, depicting Christ's death and resurrection, one in which He lay with animals of all kinds and another in which John the Baptist held out an imploring hand. These stories she knew. But the red window told another story. In its simplicity it captured best the seasons. In autumn the low light made it burgundy and the high white light of summer revealed the thinness of the glass and in winter there was often no sunlight at all and the window was nearly purple in the candlelight. Yet it was always just there, segmented and still. The light through it varied but the window itself did not. Muriel in her youth could think of no better metaphor for God, though she would not have been able to explain this and could not have shared it with her mother, whose own beliefs were frangible and strange and not easily resolved by the figurative.

All that week Muriel leaves work early and parks behind the line of cypress. Across the ceiling of Sandra's bedroom the light comes in the afternoon, reminding her of those brief years when her mother was married and they drove into town for Mass. One afternoon Muriel turns to Sandra and tells her this, about the window and her mother.

Sandra says, "You were a deep kid."

"I wasn't, though. I was just very often alone."

"But I'm more interested in your mother."

Muriel laughs.

"What happened to her?" Sandra asks.

"Heart attack."

"She must've been young."

"She was."

"You were young. You still are."

Muriel nods.

"Did you get to see her?"

"Only after. She was in another town, with a man."

"You miss her."

"That's how it is, isn't it."

They make love in the full daylight, the only light available to them. They are caught fondly by the sunlight, lengthened and blocked by tree limbs and the dresser and the curtains and the objects on the dresser, which cast long shadows against the wall and bend at the ceiling. Muriel is casual with Sandra's body and with her own. When Sandra comes she is aporetic and rescued and she does not close her eyes. Muriel loves the way this sounds and feels and she works toward it slowly and with perfect attention. After, Sandra runs her fingers through her long hair, untangling the day's braids, then braiding them back more tightly. She does this once, then again unbraids them, unhappy with their symmetry. As she shakes loose her dark hair Muriel smells the well water, the simple soap she uses, the smell of her skin and its many accumulations. Chicken feed and dust and rain and sweat.

ONE AFTERNOON SANDRA SAYS, "It shouldn't be this easy."

"It isn't all that easy," Muriel says.

Sandra rises and pads to the kitchen without covering herself and comes back with a glass of water and the ashtray.

"Lee will be all right. He's got that look about him," she says.

"He isn't your husband."

Sandra sets the ashtray on the bedside table and drains the glass and caves over Muriel, her lips cold against Muriel's neck.

"What about the rest?" Sandra asks and Muriel doesn't answer her. They touch and bring sex close again. Muriel turns them both so that Sandra is beneath her and this makes Sandra laugh and rise receptively.

"I got this place. It's paid for," she says then. She kisses Muriel's eyebrows and the corners of her mouth and lifts her hips against Muriel's hips.

"We may have to leave this house, sometime," Muriel says.

Sandra dips into Muriel's neck and Muriel slides her hand between Sandra's legs and inside her.

"So we won't talk about it then," Sandra says heavily.

"Not right now," Muriel says and brings Sandra's mouth to hers.

ANOTHER AFTERNOON Sandra says, "I saw you."

"When."

"Before."

Sandra twists to the side and Muriel watches her skin catch the light, her quiet spine and the soft dark cleft of her ass. She turns back and sits up against the pillows and lights a cigarette.

"I knew you were there before I chased the horse down. I saw the lumber come. Then once the two of you in the yard. I saw your car go by a hundred times."

"How can you see anything from here?"

Sandra angles the cigarette in the ashtray; she pulls on a shirt and tosses another to Muriel. Together they walk outside and stand in the shadow of the barn, where the yard meets a hill going up into a defunct dairy farm, sold the month before at auction. From here Muriel can see the housing tract and the freeway to the north, and to the east the brown radius of their yard. From this vantage their house seems like a model of a house.

"Did you just stand here then, looking?" Muriel asks.

"Girl, I have work to do. It was just chance I saw you."

"You ever see the horse from here?"

"That horse is long gone."

"How could she just run off like that?"

"Horses don't honor your hopes for them."

Evening is coming and the air is cool. Muriel leans against the barn and Sandra presses to her.

"What if you had gone to García's that day?" Sandra says and kisses her, out there in the open. Muriel turns her head. She thinks of the races and remembers the uncanny feeling she'd had, of intervention.

"It happened to me like that once before," Sandra says.

"Me too."

"Tell me about it."

Muriel knows she should tell Sandra about Julius. But that would mean telling her about her mother's house and the horsemen and Del Mar. And to tell her those things would be like making a promise.

"It wasn't like this," Muriel says.

"What was it like?"

The shadows of the cypress are nothing more than gray plashes on the ground. The sun is setting fast now and soon Muriel will have to go.

"It was like I saw something no one ever told me was there," she says. She kisses the tip of Sandra's nose, to erase the romance of it.

"Why didn't you come up before?" Sandra asks.

"Why didn't you come down?"

"I didn't think you'd want me to."

"I don't think I knew anything about it."

"Cheers to that horse, then, after all."

Sandra takes her hand and leads her back to the house and from behind Muriel watches the way she walks, almost elliptically, her legs bare beneath the wrinkled hem of the shirt.

EACH NIGHT, as she falls asleep next to Lee, the confidence of the day comes apart like paper. She listens to his breathing and the familiar quiet of their bedroom and thinks about what she's promised and what she might do now. She thinks of that day in her mother's house: *Marry me,* Lee says, *and we'll go to California*. The word *California* like an incantation. She hears herself say yes, she hears downstairs the snap of cards as Julius sets solitaire at the kitchen table.

THE END OF THAT WEEK, Muriel returns from the lounge to find Lee standing in Sandra's driveway. She pulls to the ditch and waits behind the cypress. Her heart beats wildly and she covers her mouth and feels her face grow hot. She watches as Lee peers into the walnut orchard across the road and she worries he'll turn toward her and she tries to think of what to say. Then Sandra steps out of the house in a duster and mud boots carrying a length of rope. Muriel feels her chest tighten at the sight of her. Sandra strides past Lee and Lee frowns but follows her and both cross the road and into the orchard. Muriel steps out but leaves the engine running and calls out and both Lee and Sandra turn to look at her.

"She's in the orchard again," Lee says and points and Muriel follows his finger through the furrows and sees the horse, past the small alfalfa field planted to draw pests and water from the orchard above it. Both the field and the orchard are ankle-deep in rainwater along their eastern edges. The horse stands still and appears to be looking out at them.

"Sandra here thought a rope might work," Lee says.

"She can't walk through all that mud but she might try," Sandra says.

"So you say," Lee says.

He takes off across the road and Sandra shoulders the wet coiled rope and follows him. Muriel watches from the road. The sodden ground sucks at their feet and they lift their knees high to escape it and as they come closer the horse drops her snout and steps backward into the orchard row with her ears flattened. Then she turns and starts to hasten away, parallel to the field. Sandra signals to the west with her rope and Lee nods to her. Then she leaves the field along the edge of the arbor, closest to the river, where the water has collected knee-high. Lee moves into the orchard and Sandra drives the horse out toward a berm of dark clay that divides the orchard from the ash trees beyond, below this a falling grade that turns to water among the empty lots. Two had been sold in the last month and Lee pauses, unsure if he should trespass. If the horse slants left or quickens her pace she risks stepping hard into the standing water and the mud below it. Lee flanks north toward the river to cut off this possibility and around the lots and into a row of trees. The branches bower across and meet above the row and drip rainwater so the resting surface below gives the appearance of lace or shelling. From this distance Sandra is small and delicate, and Lee recedes like a boat going out, and seeing her lover and her husband joined in this task makes Muriel afraid but also strangely satisfied.

Sandra has nearly reached the clay berm when the horse finds an overgrown tractor path that rises out of the rainwater. Lee changes tack and marches up parallel, hoping to cut the horse off at the end of the path, but the water slows him. The sun is lowering and the trees cast down reflections of their upper branches as though they've been duplicated in a mirror, both halved and multiplied. Because the horse has not yet been named, they can only call what names they can think of, hoping to coax her as they move very slowly through the trees.

"De-li-lah," Lee calls out.

"Peaches," calls Muriel, from her post by the road.

Then Lee loses her. Muriel can no longer see the horse or Sandra; even their footfalls are lost in the wind. Lee turns back and comes wading toward Muriel, between the wefted irrigation ditches. He stands in the orchard row catching his breath. As Muriel looks out across the rows, the branches seem to fill with fast-moving shadows. Then she looks up and sees a dozen bodies moving and leaping across the bowers. A pause, then more dark shapes advancing. Muriel looks down at the water and sees them in reflection: the feet and eyes and tails of rats, their reflections much crisper than the rats themselves as they leap through the branches in the setting sun.

"Good God," Lee says.

They turn away from one another to look up and to the east, to find the back end of this dark wave. From somewhere across the field, Sandra calls out, "They won't come down, we've just startled—" but the words are ripped away or uncompleted.

Muriel cries out. Lee turns, alarmed by her voice.

"Sandra," she says, and when Sandra doesn't answer she says her name again.

"Just stay still, darling," Sandra calls back.

Lee hears the word and turns to Muriel, his look baffled and strange. He lifts both hands to his cheeks, as if he is remembering something he was not aware he knew. Above them the sound of the rats is feathery and fast as they move across. For five or ten seconds they pass, like pockets of dark water shot through the trees, until silence follows and the branches still. Muriel thinks that Sandra has said it on purpose and she is not sure if she is angry or relieved. Lee does not know what to think. He says Muriel's name very quietly.

"It's okay now, Lee," she says, and points up to the empty trees.

He drops his hands and looks away. The boy he was years before is in his confused look. The trees are still and she can hear the river but nothing moves in the orchard. Then Sandra calls out again, not any word but a slow and bewildered exhalation. For a weary and confused moment Muriel thinks they are in league together, the horse and the rats, that the horse has conjured the rats by some arcane magic to effect her escape, to make Sandra call out. This confederacy seems as logical as anything, there in the altered world. But then she sees the shape of the horse coming through the trees, Sandra leading her by the rope.

"I'll be damned," Muriel says.

Sandra is panting and red-faced and for a moment Lee glances between them.

"This ain't no mustang," she says. "But she ain't no nag either."

"I never believed she was either thing," Lee says. His tone is brutal.

Sandra looks at Muriel apologetically and Muriel knows she is right. Lee takes the rope and walks the horse down the road and Sandra and Muriel are alone. Sandra palms over her knees and pants and her skin is flushed with exertion and the cold drizzle. Muriel watches Lee walk away toward the house. From behind, the horse seems soft as pudding. Muriel cups Sandra's neck and feels the heat there. Sandra sighs and arches into Muriel's hand. When she straightens up she is crying, but her jaw is set.

"I will sell this house and everything in it and I will go with you wherever you want," she says. Then she turns away and crosses the road.

After a moment Muriel goes too. She feels not moved or worried but strangely defiant. The car is still running on the roadside. She stands beside it and watches as Sandra heels her muddy boots off on the porch step and walks into the house. In her head she hears Sandra say the word again. She likes the sound of it but she's not sure if she likes what it means.

Lee skips dinner and spends the night bedding down the horse and feeding her and rubbing her coat. Muriel falls asleep alone in their bedroom, and when she wakes Lee has made coffee and he brings her a cup.

In his kindness and his silence is the heartbreak coming for them. He leans to kiss her and she lets him. He has forgotten or he is willing to forget or he did not really understand. Sandra is the contrail of light left on the back of the eye by the sun. Like so much of Muriel's life she is invisible. Muriel thinks that there is some dignity in that, yet it leaves a life so immaterial it may be erased in a blink.

THE NEXT DAY, at the lounge, the horsemen are mad with anticipation. They've called in wagers on grass stakes somewhere in India, and one of the men has a transistor tuned to a station broadcasting the race, half in a language no one knows, half in British voices hollow and nasal and distant. They can't sit still, and as the morning wears on they stand and pace and gripe at each other. They lean in to the radio as if it might whisper to them, just once, the secrets of the universe.

"Can you believe this," says the man with the mustache, and the others shush him.

He lowers his voice. "India," he says and turns his face up and smiles.

Another man says, "How far away is that even?"

"Eight thousand two hundred miles," the mustache says.

"It don't even seem like mileage, it seems like time."

"It is," the mustache says. "It's nine at night there."

"They race late."

"They race all day."

"Well, good to know they're racing somewhere," the mustache says.

"Now you want to see the world."

"Not all of it, just the racetracks."

The signal lapses. Rosie stands on a bar chair holding an antenna the size of a hubcap. Muriel watches this without caution. He pays no attention to her though she loves him a little now, after seeing him in the bar with Gail. Rosie catches the signal and holds a moment and the men cheer, but then the plantation fan passes back and shoves the antenna sideways. Rosie wobbles on the chair but he does not fall. He calls out to the owner, who is sitting in the corner listening. The owner rises and turns off the fan, then lingers at the men's periphery, as if he is one of them. Muriel is amused by the whole scene, by the horsemen's sudden interest in the world to come, now that they can lay money on it. Rosie finds the signal again and the British voice comes roaring back in.

"What did he say?" one man asks.

"The Queen of England is there," says another.

"I wouldn't think she'd be welcome."

"She can still love horses, even if she ain't got an empire."

"And the empire can still love her."

"Only empire now is ours."

They've laid a pool on a late race, through a bookie no one names. Two races pass and the broadcaster calls them in a voice made for some other event, perhaps a sermon or a fund-raiser. Though they've set no money on them, the men listen to these races carefully. The race slang sits awkwardly on the British announcer's tongue.

"I never did think about a hand ride that way," Rosie says, from his height.

"Only when this fella says it like it's some kind of flower."

"Oh sure, Rosie. You know shit about hand rides."

When their race begins the men shush everyone, the other men at the bar and the cooks in the back. For a moment the lounge is quiet as winter.

"Here we go," the mustache whispers.

The race goes off like any other. The horses leave the gate high and close in and the announcer calls this calmly. The men have money on an Arabian called Father of All. He pulls ahead early and the announcer describes his gait as like a bowstring and says he runs as if he feels himself chased by something always just behind. The men shake their heads at this poetry but Rosie nods as if this confirms his reconnaissance.

He says, "Wish I could see it."

The horse picks up a bit of distance from the pack. The jockey turns the horse the way a child would turn a bicycle, by leaning gleefully into the speed. The announcer describes this in hushed tones. The horsemen stand and raise their arms but do not call out. Muriel can see in their bright faces the race they are imagining. That in their minds the horses are like the horses in their dreams, as if the fact of horses at all is a dream. They have been taken back to the very beginning. Rosie holds the antenna very still and the men hold themselves very still and the horse necks on beautifully and the whole lounge is involved in this drama, halfway around the world.

The mustache says, "We're going to do it." And the whole lounge believes they will. The sound of the horses running and the announcer's voice roll on against the noise of the traffic outside. The announcer pauses—the end is coming. Then, in the last moments, the jockey leans into Father's neck and drops his hands and relaxes his seat so the horse feels his weight and slows. For half a furlong they ride this way, pressed together and losing ground, and another horse comes up along the outside and passes them.

The men cry out.

"What is he doing?"

"Why would you ease there?"

"Goddamn these Indians, don't they know how to ride?"

"Does he just want to keep riding forever?"

Their questions can't be answered. Over the thousands of miles the same noise as any track, people cheering and glasses ringing and the slowing clop of hooves. The horsemen sit dejected. One of the men reaches out and yanks the dial. The radio catches static, then raving jazz, until finally it gives out all the way to silence. Rosie leans recklessly to the side and another man rises and offers ballast and then a third man says, "Just leave the fucking thing, Rosie."

Rosie creaks the antenna one little bit at a time with his eyes closed as if he is searching for something palpable in the dark. Muriel thinks of him making love to a man and how that man would be so much taller and how Rosie might want that, that feeling of subjection. She wonders if Gerald was old or young and how much Rosie had loved him. Then the radio fuzzes back to life. Frank Sinatra's voice enters the room and all at once the tune is obvious.

Rosie calls out, "Hey then, this is better," and abandons whatever else he had been searching for.

The mood shifts. Muriel remembers the song from years before and it spools out into the lounge. The past comes back to the men and Muriel senses they won't try this again, this trick with the radio and the foreign bookie. Rosie sings along. The mustache reaches out to raise the volume. Then all the men sing, *You can laugh when your dreams fall apart at the seams.* The men's voices turn it into an anthem and the great affliction they'd felt seems to change into a sweeter thing, permission for their failure to be admitted without acrimony.

Muriel remembers something then. A Kansas morning, Muriel at the kitchen table and her mother leaned against the counter, while they waited for the percolator. A man upstairs still in bed, someone her mother had met at a wedding the day before. Muriel can't remember his name, it might have been Jim, something brisk and ordinary. The radio playing softly the same song the men are singing now, refracted in her memory by the distance from that moment and her mother's presence in it.

"Been too long since I met someone," her mother had said.

She was confident, dressed in a nightshirt and nothing else. Her hair piled unambitiously. She was not always this way. Sometimes she wept. Thinking of this now Muriel realizes how young her mother still was, not yet forty, still years from it. Outside the summer morning lived with hot breeze and june bugs scratching at the screens. Her mother's shoulders had burned the day before; in the kitchen light they looked delicate and warm and Muriel wanted to press her cheek to them, to feel the heat there.

"I don't want to get ahead of myself, though. You know how these things go," her mother said. She balanced one hip against the counter and rested one arm on the other, holding a burning cigarette upright. A posture as familiar to Muriel as any touch would be.

"Here's a lesson for you, and maybe it seems like an obvious one," her mother said. "People in love want a mirror held up to them, and someone has to be the mirror. It's too easy to let love narrow down to just two people staring across at each other and trying to see themselves. So you have to figure out the difference, which one is really you and which isn't, which one is just you reflected in someone else. Then you'll know if it's love or not."

Muriel recalls this morning all at once. The men sing, *And love is either in your heart or on its way.* The lounge owner has joined in and Rosie's balance is faltering.

Later that same day, as Jim and her mother slept, Lee arrived stinking of diesel and the farmhand's truck he'd driven out in. At the door he knocked politely, though Muriel had already risen at the dead sound of his boots on the porch. He apologized for the silage smell and she let him peck her cheek like a cousin. At the table they drank coffee and talked of the future. Lee would be shipping off the next day or the day after, and he'd come to say goodbye. He brought flowers and a store-bought cake and they ate it with the coffee. Then, over the sound of the radio, came the sound of her mother upstairs moaning, then the low growl of Jim's pleasure, then laughter, the bouncing of the bed. Lee was shocked to stillness. His face turned red and he looked around the room for escape and then up with closed eyes at the ceiling. Another girl might have risen in shame. Someone else still might have relieved the poor son of a zealot by laughing. She knew he had been to Leavenworth then on to Asia and was going back again and had seen many parts of the world, but he was so young and had never had a mother. She sat and held Lee's eye and the commotion rose to its inevitable pitch, and when Lee's discomfort became unbearable Muriel put her elbows on the table and nested her chin in her palms and waited.

What had she wanted, then? Some revenge for her mother's freedom.

For her mother's ease and recklessness and how much power Muriel took from those things but also how much loneliness. Revenge for the contentment Lee offered and the world of men she had lived in forever and would always live in. She wanted love, but not the way her mother had it. She wanted something she'd never heard of before.

WHEN HER SHIFT ENDS, Muriel gets in the car and drives downtown and parks near the Chester Hotel, next to the old streetcar tracks. She thinks of the young man Peter and what he told her. Below the messy curtain of wires stretch the old tracks, which carried first freight then laborers then men in starched uniforms to the bases just north. The iron rails, now sunk into the asphalt, catch in their grooves flattened weeds and rainy smears of oil. A group of sailors in their dark enlisteds smoke under a theater marquee and the door to the hotel is unmanned.

Muriel cuts the engine but does not step out of the car. The sea breeze has blown the clouds in and over the narrow streets and into the mountains so the waning daylight comes through, though from the west another dark thrum, coming in. She steps out of the car and walks up the sidewalk and into the hotel. The bar is empty, the stools upturned, all the lights on. Behind the clerk's desk, a deco lamp with a broad glass shade and a corkboard covered in notes and photos. She approaches the desk and waits, and when no one appears she slips behind it.

The board reaches from the crown molding down past her hips. Some of the photos show men in their dress uniforms or school outfits, but most are notes listing names and phone numbers and dates. *J.R.B. call home*; *Willie we moved to Chico 8/57, you can find us there off the main road*; *Still have your Spot Kenneth, he is eating fine*. The photos seem posted for the entirely missing. In one, a boy not sixteen years old smiles openly; on the white border below his face someone has written *Wm. Boyd, last at station November of '57*. On a few photos women's names in childish letters marked with hearts or stars.

Below all this, at knee level, hangs a General Crane and Hoist calendar from 1956, still open to December. A brass call bell sits on the desk, its clapper knob missing. Muriel turns around and looks out at the empty lobby, walls lined with framed photographs of the neighborhood as it had been many years before, before the war or even the war before that, silhouettes of men in narrow-brimmed hats, bent forward as if pressing against an unseen force. Below these photographs is the brass-railed bar; a gold spittoon by the door holds a single umbrella, turned point-down and dry. Only now does she notice that the boards bolted across the window casings are pocked with holes looking out to the streets beyond. The last daylight comes through them in long tight runnels, like water from a hose.

She turns again and tries to make sense of the collection. On one hand it is simply a set of messages intended for those without telephones or permanent addresses, who might be known only marginally or who might pass through on their way somewhere else. But the photos record some larger loss, not of any single person but of time. The young men's faces are cleanly shaven and confident. In each of these faces the suggestion of some remarkable change, from the pictured boy to the man sought by those who love or owe him. Lost boys who will see themselves on the wall and come home or not. She does not see Julius or any mention of a man like him, though she stands for a long time looking.

Outside, the rain rattles like nails dropped in a can; she hears a car go past, footsteps overhead, the brief sense of habitation made by these noises a confirmation of the lobby's emptiness. In another time, Julius's disappearance and his theft might have been understood as necessary. Not long ago, men were taken away by war, by quests of one kind or another. That it is 1957 is a trick of history. That men now are meant to stay and be loved. That women are meant to stay and love them. Should he come through this place she wants him to know that she understands.

Footsteps across the plank floor and Muriel turns and sees a man in a too-small suit gilded at the collar and the seams. The suit itself is a color difficult to name though if pressed she might have said coral.

"Sad, ain't it," he says. He keeps to the other side of the desk but reaches out to move the bell sideways and with his palm wipes away some grime. In the lamplight he is older but still handsome, though his hairline has pulled back and revealed a tender birthmark the color of wine.

"You someone's wife?"

Muriel shakes her head.

"Just his girl, then?"

"Sister-in-law," she says, though this feels imprecise.

"Well, put up your name anyway."

The man moves to the side of the desk but doesn't come around it. Muriel glances behind and sees the desk affixed to the wall on the other side. There is no paper, nothing to write with, but the man catches her looking and opens a drawer in the desk. He finds a nubbed pencil and hands it to her.

"You know," he says, pressing the thin stubble of his hairline with the butt of his thumb. "This place was built a century ago. You have to be amazed at the number of men and other people who must have come through, though of course there's no way to know. That's the thing hey, no matter what they do to us there's always more."

Muriel moves fractionally back and reaches out for the wall behind her. She does not want to leave any proof she's been here but she knows what she wants to say. She searches her purse and finds the racing form, where long ago she'd written the name of the hotel. She thinks about what happens next and Lee's sorrow and what it might mean to Julius.

She presses the paper flat and turns it over. *Forgive me,* she writes. Then, below this, *Julius*. She pins the paper in a free spot near the bottom of the board and faces the man conclusively.

"There's a sentiment," he says. Again he presses at his hairline and sighs. She looks up and sees the hem of some kind of screen or curtain over the board, as if to cover it like a storefront after closing.

"What people mostly want, I think, is to know that there are others, that there are still people who haven't forgotten you, even if that's not a story anyone tells," he says.

He moves away from the desk and as he does she sees the pull where the suitcoat is buttoned, which makes little pleats around his waist.

"Now, I don't presume you need anything else, not a room or a drink, but if you wanted those things we do have half of them," he says.

"You're right, I don't need those things."

The man dips one leg behind the other in a kind of lateral curtsy and brushes his sleeve across the desk again and then with his other hand wipes away the dust he's collected. Muriel thinks he might thank her now, but for what she couldn't say. Instead he walks back into the lobby, where he sits down in one of the armchairs, slides a pack of cigarettes out of his suit pocket, and plucks one out and lights it. Then he leans down and picks up a magazine and crosses one leg over the other. His face disappears behind the magazine and his smoke comes winding up and disperses in the dark room.

SHE WALKS OUT of the lobby and into the street. On the sidewalk she lights her own cigarette and walks past the boarded windows of the hotel back toward the car. The sea helming has begun to disappear in the clouds. She gets back in the car and locks the doors. She sits in the car a long time without turning the key. Over the street the swallows are swooping in dozens, dropping in curves like the weld on a barrel down to the pavement and back up to the tips of the trees. When the swallows dip and nearly touch the ground then camber up the feeling is of tremendous motion, as if the world has become unfixed.

She remembers something else then, about the wedding where her mother met that man. Jim. The bride was someone's young daughter in a homemade dress. Muriel was eighteen then, almost nineteen. She stood on the back edge of the reception and watched the dancing. The workingmen loosed from their labor, their women absent for a moment from the rough lives of children, who were allowed to run through a field of late summer corn. Once or twice a man hefted reluctantly to retrieve a crying child whose own menace had gotten the better of him. Most of the wives, hardly ever together in one place, sat in their churchy dresses with their ankles crossed and their knees together. In her short muslin dress and white hose, Muriel felt like a visitor to a future in which she was not accommodated. Jim stood among the men in a white plantation suit, the sleeves of the jacket pushed up his forearms and one tail of his shirt untucked. Muriel knew what would happen next and she felt not jealous or displeased but something else, something furious and lonely, there among the wedding party.

The evening darkened over the party and the country house and the cornfield beyond. A flock of swallows dove over the field as the hot air slackened, and Muriel wondered what she might like to do next, now that her life had started. She was grown up and had a job and might have done anything she liked. She sensed that whatever it was she had not yet encountered any sign of it. In the dark the chairs were brought in close and someone scratched the dial through country ballads and Sunday services to find a Kansas City station playing Patti Page and Johnnie Ray, and the dancing took on a new urgency. The following month these same women would arrive at her mother's house with goulash and bottled milk and their scrubbed-up sons and cousins. The same men would stand too long on the porch and inch toward the door. As if Muriel had been widowed and not orphaned.

The young groom danced close with his bride while the party watched.

"Still free," her mother said. "Just a bit longer."

At the young bride's throat, in the hollow prized by men, a gold cross, Protestant, unspecial. The cross sat perfectly still in that hollow while she danced. As Muriel watched she thought of the night to come, the girl laid across a wide bed by her young husband, clumsy farmhand new to all forms of human touch, familiar with trees and the hot undersides of cattle but not with women, expecting perhaps his mother's dense, unforgiving smell, not at all prepared for the softness of the girl, her ready legs, around him in an instant. The girl, too, with no other point of reference, her groom's new bare chest above her own, the only bare chest she'd seen in her dark and pious childhood the flayed nakedness of Christ. Muriel could see with shocking clarity the husband's lips taking up the little cross, pulling it away with his teeth. The wet circle left by his mouth. The sacrilege he would feel at that, the girl moved near climax by it, the single act of transgression left to them in their marriage bed. What a thing to picture. Did Muriel think of this that afternoon with her mother beside her, watching the girl dance? Or is she only thinking of it now, in the cold car, now that she knows the names of so many things?

A month after that wedding, her mother was dead. Muriel thinks of the house now and knows it might be ravaged by vandals, curtains ripped down, windows broken, the neighbor boy pulling out wire for scrap. She thinks of the towns between here and there, of the yellow desert and the mountains and the long flat pull of the highway. She counts the hours it will take and how many nights she might sleep along the way. She wonders if the cake plate in the closet is filmed in dust, if the winter there is bitter or mild. She thinks of what she might ask Sandra to leave behind and what she will say to Lee.

The rain is coming harder now and the clouds seem to involve her in their intentions, strung wild to the east. In the rearview mirror she sees a figure in jeans and boots; she turns, expecting Julius, but it is only a stranger waiting at the curb. A new thought has begun and she can almost reach the bow of it. The soft pastoral of that wedding and her mother's pleasure that night and the next day. The privacy conferred by marriage, the selves remade and distilled by it, the way it was like a cloak thrown over the broadest parts of a life, hiding everything but the fact of it. The way her mother mistrusted this, as if love were a force outside of people's will and thus could be neither consummated nor claimed. As if love were a third party gathered to witness otherwise private devotions: The young bride and her anticipation. Men and boys on the edge of her waiting joy. Sandra's flushed throat and dark braids and all the men who were lost or searched for at the Chester Hotel. Muriel herself there looking. Love was always somewhere outside oneself, it was always improbable. It could happen to anyone and it could happen a thousand times or only once or never. You had to search for it and you had to allow it. To allow it was to be seen by that perceiving force, and it is this thought, finally, that makes Muriel turn the key and drive into the hard-coming rain, where Sandra will be waiting, where everything will be known.

TEN

Paradise

All that winter, Julius works among pescadores trawling for skipjack and yellowtail in the Sea of Cortez. He coils rope and guts and listens to the men talk of the women they've left or might meet. They do not care about his busted face or his sadness because they've had enough of both.

In a wooden doghouse boat they tool from Guaymas to Colima on nights so dark the darkness seems animate, like Japanese monochromes of cloud. In the evenings below deck the pescadores wonder what world they might encounter when the season ends. Some are young, but not all, and the older men remember when the seas were higher and the cities fewer. They have come from the droughted inlands and the hot forests for jobs paving highways and laying cement, but they miss Coahuila and Durango. In Durango there were windstorms and little pacas you could tame and every village had an edge you could ride past and be in the desert alone, and there's nothing like that in the cities. The world is smaller now but the needs of it larger and the hope that any ordinary man might thrive in it decreases as the distance does. They send a word or two his way in English when he doesn't understand but mostly he understands. He tells them often about Kansas and the heavy fields and the emptiness there and this affinity keeps him in their good graces. For these reasons and the dry fine weather, Julius lasts six months with them.

He doesn't know what he wants or what he intends to do next and he knows he'll have to go, but for now the sea is enough; he feels hidden by the water and sky. The wound on his forehead begins to scar and lends him an air of vulnerability. His ribs heal poorly, and when he laughs or coughs the pressure in his chest feels loose and liquid and passable. Where he sewed the wound, the scar is like basting and still itches. He keeps the little pistol down in his bootheel or below his bunk or stows it in the slip, but he finds he can't stand to look at it.

Sometimes he wakes having dreamed of Korea and blue mountains as simple as line drawings in the distance. In those dreams he is not a sailor or even a man but a mere presence in the landscape, like a tree or a roof or a breeze, and below him the green country goes by, men and women on their way to work, children at play in the fields, birds and dogs and other animals asleep in shade or keeping to themselves. There is no conflict, and though he is there he is not important, he changes nothing in the scene below him. These dreams are so calm and beautiful that he wakes from them reluctantly to the noise of the pescadores and their endless work. He does not know what the dream is about but whenever he has it he wakes feeling reconciled to something. As if by disappearing, by watching without interfering, he has been forgiven. When he rises and goes on deck he forgets this dream among the men and the sun and the lack of shadow.

ONE AFTERNOON LATE in June they pass out of the gulf and into the Marietas, where there are sea dahlias among the rocks. They anchor under a rock arch at midday and out at sea a thunderhead rises fifty thousand feet above the horizon. The weather report is read and heeded. The island is small and uninhabited and beyond it are three other islands even more forbidding. Julius suspects they are not meant to stay but to carry on another fifty miles to the mainland. But the report is for storms to the south and west, and the men haul in the nets and ride the shore.

Shoveled into the rocky spit of the bay is an abandoned naval base. They anchor below its crumbling façade and Julius swims in the clear water while the men tow out blankets and carry them by dinghy and cast them along the sand. They are alone, and when the sun begins to set and the water turns inky and there are no other boats and no coast guard the men make a supper of boiled eggs and watercress. They eat while the lights of Puerto Vallarta clutter the distant shore. High up the spit, the abandoned base has the observant but dogged look of someone waiting for a cab. When the darkness comes and the tide rises, the seawater covers the concrete stilts and reaches the wooden walkway, glimmering at the windowsills. By then Julius and the other men are drunk on wine and strewn along the spit in happy clusters.

They spend that inlet night among petrels. Virgo tilts east to west, nearly gone, and the storm passes many miles away. The men make a fire and sing songs in their language. Julius wanders off to a beach upwind and makes himself a bed there. He thinks of the man in Tijuana with the rolling heart and wonders if he's ever seen water this color or felt left alone by the world. He lies on his belly, but when his hurt ribs seem to clunk forward he shifts his weight onto his elbows and lifts and feels the heaviness in his chest subside. He coughs and turns his head and spits into the sand. He thinks it might be time to move on.

Above him the sliver of moon is hidden by clouds and seems blinked out. No wind, no breakers. He rises and strips and walks into the sea. The water is warm and feels thick as milk as he slides into it. He lets the water ballast him and floats with his arms out and his palms resting until the receding tide carries him too far. Then he rights himself and looks down. Just below the surface are thousands of small glowing creatures, crustaceous and ancient. When he trails his hand through the water and lifts it, his fingers are pecked in green light like fireflies. He shakes his hand and the lights fall away and back into the water. He thinks that he should wake the other men but probably they've seen this before or wouldn't care to. He might be the only romantic among them and that is fine. He lets himself sink so the water covers his chin. The clouds pass over and the moonlight cuts through the water and the creatures cling a moment to his skin, then float away.

THE NEXT DAY THE SUN IS BRIGHT, and when the week's catch is held they skip back to Colima and unload. The men cup his arms and shoulders and wish him well and Julius takes his pay in pesos and tuna steak and walks into town. He hitches far north to Hermosillo, eighty miles inland. There he gets a haircut and a shave and stays a night in a Chinese hotel; in the morning he hauls back out to the coast in a livestock truck carrying guinea fowl. From there he takes a boat to San Felipe and another truck to Ensenada. In Ensenada he finds a fishing charter headed north across the maritime and he hands over most of his remaining money in exchange for passage. The charter docks in San Diego late the next afternoon, in the middle of July, almost eight months since he left his brother's house and crossed the border. He changes his pesos at the currency window and pays a dollar for the showers at the marina, then dresses and rolls his money in one boot and the pistol in the other. How he likes these moments, when he holds everything he owns.

He walks out of the marina and scans the horizon, the tall buildings and the naval base and the steam-pipes to the north, the bridges rising just east of them, and follows these downtown. In a few hours he can catch the nine-thirty bus to Anaheim and hitch from there, to L.A. or even further north. He waits in a plaza where a half-dozen boys are throwing dice. For a while he sits at the edge of the game watching and enjoying the boys' English. The rest of the plaza is empty; a seawind catches against a ball of overhead streetcar wires. Clouds coming in to cover the last of the warm and brilliant day. The dice players switch the game so two boys throw together into a circle drawn with the hot butt of a cigarette while a third calls out numbers. Julius asks what this game is called, and they tell him Man on the Moon. He can't get the gist of it, though the other boys whoop and raise their fists, and soon his eye begins to wander. At the back end of the plaza he sees a single stand of feeble trees, paper sacks flacked against the trunks and gulls among the roots. Then he sees shallow figures and knows what the trees are for. He watches the figures move inside the stand. Their motions seem like pantomime or shadow play and some other man might misread them, but Julius does not. He watches until the two men come out of the trees, and when they've passed through the plaza he stands and follows them across the street. The men stop a moment in front of an old building. The windows are boarded and painted black and what must have been fine architrave has splintered through the century. A man in a low white hat nods to the two men and opens the door and the men disappear inside. Above the flat roof of the building Julius can see the sea pressed out to the horizon. He remembers something Henry told him long ago about San Diego. He rises and follows the two men and when the man in the hat looks him over Julius turns in a slow circle with his arms out and grins and the man waves him through without smiling.

It is only eight o'clock, but the hotel bar is full of sailors and gritters and fine boys with long necks. He's never been in this place, but he's been in others like it. He asks for a glass of whiskey and leaves a quarter on the bartop and turns to watch the dancing men. He can hear their shuffling footsteps as they dance and the noise of cars outside. He stretches his arms so the new flesh at his side pulls and hurts and he imagines it breaking open. He wonders if his body will ever feel good again. On the floor of the strange hotel, the men hold each other. None of them looks his way, though he can see in their faces the wonderful fear they feel. He thinks that this fear is the first part of desire. That terror, like longing, is a door one opens—whatever disaster or pleasure arrests one's motion does nothing to dispel one's cravings, which spring back unencumbered, like a hinge. Here is the allure of love and of chance, to give the lie to reformation.

He asks for another whiskey, and when it comes he stands and passes through the dancing men to the lobby desk. He leans over the desk and picks up the phone. He knows how close his brother is, but not what Lee must think has happened, in the time he's been gone. That Julius has fallen in with thieves, maybe, or that he is dead, and perhaps Lee should think these things, perhaps they are true. Then he wonders if Muriel has been found out and what she might have said to Lee. He presses the tongue and stands another moment with the receiver in his hand. Then he sees behind the desk an aluminum hatch like a garage door. The bottom skirt is lifted a few inches and Julius hangs up the phone and comes around the desk and rolls it up. On a corkboard behind are notes and photos and business cards tacked to the board and a few bits of ribbon and matchbooks listing phone numbers or names. He's not seen anything exactly like this but he knows what it is. In the service they'd had what were called dead-letter walls where they posted lost mail. Though they all wore canvas jackets with their names and ranks and every movement was rostered, still there were men who were lost at sea or whose bodies were never found. How often they had stood around on low days and read their love letters aloud and with great solemnity. He feels now as he felt then, that the declaration of love is a gift offered only to the missing. No wives or girlfriends he knew, nor mothers or fathers, would have said aloud the words they wrote to those sons. It surprised him how rarely they found a letter or photo from someone who should not have sent it, a mistress or another boy back home, that the men who died or disappeared were mostly forthright and ordinary. The things their people were desperate to say were the same things people everywhere wanted.

He looks another moment at the young faces, then tips up his glass.

He wonders how long the dancing will last. Then his eye is drawn to a poker chip in the bottom corner and he leans close and recognizes the lettering on the printed felt, from the Aces High Casino in Boulder City, where once he and Henry ate steak and kissed above the great dam. He smiles but the light feeling of coincidence lasts only a moment, because below the chip he sees a slip of paper with his own name scrawled out. Above this a request for forgiveness. For a moment he looks in disbelief. Of course it wasn't he who wrote this, so the apology must be for him or some other Julius. But then, in the corner of the paper, he sees a scratch of words in a different hand, as if they'd been added to the paper without unpinning it: *Im sorry to. Please come back here and meet me.* Below this the letter *H* drawn big and slanted and then an arrow pointing to the chip, which is worth five dollars.

Julius claps his hand on the desk. His empty glass rattles on the desktop. He steps out and back into the lobby and looks around. Still the music plays; no one is watching him. He moves back to the desk and looks again. He lights his last cigarette and tosses the empty pack and the matchbook on the desk as he stares at the paper. He feels a sudden urge to take these things and hide them. He unpins the paper and the chip, puts both in his pocket, and walks out the front door.

He walks many blocks without awareness until he finds himself in a neighborhood of bright craftsmans and small lawns. Out front are men with hoses and women gathering children and the smell of dishwater. He looks down at his dirty clothes and nubby boots and knows he stinks of whiskey and the sea. He turns onto a cross street and walks further south until the houses give out to dirt lots and brick storefronts. He takes the note and the chip from his pocket and studies them. In his own hand these items have a sentience that excites him. The first apology he could dismiss as a mistake, a note for some other Julius and some other absolution, to which some other H responded or which Henry mistook. But the chip from the Aces is unmistakable. Then he turns the paper over and sees on the other side a racing form from June of 1957. He holds the paper out and looks at it from this distance and brings it back. In the upper corner the name *Chester Hotel* and a few men's names and *by the sea* and he remembers this from Muriel's envelope, folded among the other papers there. The whole story slips into place and he can't believe it.

Night is coming blue and heavy now. He looks at the street signs and past these to roofs floating back into the cityscape and realizes that he has walked himself lost. He folds the note around the chip and puts the little packet in his boot. Across the street three men sit outside a barbershop with their knees spread far and several yards up the sidewalk a solitary dog stands watching them. Julius watches the dog and then the men. A half block from these men a child stands alone at the curb. He is blond as wheat and tough-looking and he sees Julius looking and doesn't care. He leans back and throws a rock into the empty street, throws it side-arm as if the street is a lake and he is trying to skip the rock across. He is seven or eight, Julius guesses, that age when a personality emerges but no real sense of will. The boy finds a loose chunk of sidewalk with his toe and leans to pry it up. Julius crosses the street and the boy watches him. He stands with the ball of cement in his hand and Julius waves and begins to speak, though they are still ten yards apart.

"Hey now, can you tell me how to get to the train station?"

The boy nods and reaches out with the same hand that holds the cement and gestures southeast.

"Are we north of the marina or south?" Julius asks.

"North," the boy says. He drops the cement from shoulder height and it breaks into many smaller pieces and he gathers them and holds them appraisingly in his palm and picks one out. He bends his elbow and reaches back and skips the piece of cement across the street and Julius turns his head to watch. It drops in a sink of asphalt and goes no further. Then the boy takes another and skips it and this piece jumps three times across the whole width of the street and then a fourth time over the curb and bounces high near the barbershop.

"Fucking A," the boy says.

"Fucking A," Julius says.

The boy's face flushes with pleasure but he does not let it last. He tosses another piece and it skips and dies away. Julius takes in his crop of blond hair and his dark eyes. The disorienting knowledge that the boy will grow into a man, a man someone might love and, in loving, would imagine as the child he is now, as lovers often do. The strange eroticism of the lover in a past without one's presence, the lover before he is caught in another's sight line. He remembers his sense of Henry, those long afternoons at the Squaw, as a child somewhere hot and dusty while Julius himself was a child far away, his wonder at how they were joined in time. As if the past were simply a story they told to establish suspense.

There is only the one explanation. And while it is improbable, it is only the improbable that gives the ordinary meaning.

"Be careful out there, kid," Julius says to the boy.

The boy looks up but says nothing and Julius walks on and soon the street curves south. The sky has deepened a rich purple and the houselights are coming on; the streetlamps punch through the sea fog in small discs. He crosses a railyard and slips under a chain-link fence and comes up to the station from the back. He asks the stationmaster the fare to Boulder City and it is far more than he has. He asks the man if he can work for the rest and the man laughs and waves him away. Then he asks for fare partway and the man quotes him numbers from here to Barstow and here to Needles and a half-dozen other stops. Julius empties his pockets and sits on the ground below the ticket window and counts the money while the man leans on the counter and watches him through the iron grate. Finally he looks up and asks the fare to Los Angeles—at least he knows where the card games are there, or where he might hustle a five—but he doesn't have enough for this either. He's already missed the evening bus and there won't be another until tomorrow afternoon. He wonders how long Henry will wait, how long he's already waited. He thinks of the terrace overlooking the dam and the way they'd danced and the kiss they shared in the raw desert darkness. The stationmaster points and Julius turns and sees a family standing behind him with their suitcases lined up neatly by size and he stands and thanks the man and walks away.

He walks north along the sidewalk and holds out a thumb and for twenty minutes cars pass him without slowing. Then it occurs to him what he must do and he shakes his head against it. He does not want to see Muriel or his brother this way and he doesn't want more of their money. Already he has taken from Lee his wife's secrets and her love and he doesn't want to take anything else. But she had been there and now she knew and the thought amazes him.

The dark is coming and he is nearly downtown again when finally a milk truck pulls to the curb. He looks in the window and the man driving is middle-aged and clean as linen and husbandly. He tells the man where he wants to go and the man says he's in luck and Julius climbs over the wood-rail ribs of the truckbed and settles among the crates of bottles. They drive through the derelict neighborhoods, then past the great park where the trees drape heavy and pale, and then into the river valley.

At the turnoff Julius taps the roof and hauls out of the truck and waves a thanks to the driver, who heads off in the other direction. He walks a long mile down the road and his chest hurts. At his brother's house there is a truck in the drive but not the Ford and this surprises him. It is well past ten o'clock now. He pauses at the start of the driveway and looks around the yard. He does not see the horse or the trailer he'd hauled her in. The grass has sprouted where the lumber once was, and the house looks finished and new. The driveway has been overlaid in white cement. The porch sills are planted in meager begonias. The front window is uncurtained and he can see through to the room beyond. There a man and a woman he does not know sit on a yellow divan watching television. Julius can hear the program and the sounds of children and soon two towheaded boys come roaring through the room and the man hollers after them. The woman turns to speak to the man and it is clear they disagree about something they know is intractable. The man touches the woman's cheek in reconciliation and she skirts away. Then she yawns and the man watches her yawn and his face darkens. He reaches out and places his hand over her open mouth and clearly he means this comically, but the woman sees the menace in it. They shift away from each other then. For a long time Julius watches them watch the program. The children do not run through again and soon the couple rises and the man turns off the television and they move into the hallway and do not return.

Now it is very late. Julius wraps his arms around himself and walks back up the road. Above him the citylight is delicately held at the horizon. Up the road is another house and he steps onto the porch and knocks. He imagines his knock sounding through the house, and when no one comes to the door and no lights come on he walks around the house and finds a side window and sees through it a pair of mudboots and a box of nails but otherwise nothing at all. He walks to the back and tries the door there and finds it locked but a hard shoulder pops it open.

The house is hot and has not been aired in some time and smells of dust. He peeks around the corner and the parlor is empty so he goes in and reaches up for the light switch and flips it and the light comes on and he squints and turns it off again. Along the walls are moving boxes stacked two and three high. He peels one flap back and finds practical cotton pants in light colors all folded crisply and unfrivolous underthings and white T-shirts. In another are books in Spanish and a family Bible in the name Gutiérrez. He walks through to the kitchen and opens each cabinet door and feels along their sides and under the shelves and then beneath their overhanging width. He finds a few coins and chucks them up. On the counter a pile of chicken feathers gathered in a spindle. He checks the pantry and pockets a tin of crackers and opens an olive jar and eats three at once, then puts the jar back. When he finds nothing else he moves quietly back through the parlor and into the bedroom. Here it is warmer and still furnished, though the bed is unsheeted and the mattress tipped to the wall. He opens the bedside drawers and finds rubber bands and a *Reader's Digest* and a photo of a girl in jodhpurs in a landscape much drier and more ancient than this one. He drops to his knees and flags his hand beneath the dresser, where he finds a single quarter and a matchbook. He palms these and puts them in his pocket.

Then he steps into the bathroom and lifts the seat and unzips. He wonders where his brother has gone and how he will find him. Whether Henry is still waiting or if he's moved on, and how soon Julius might get there. What he will do once he does. When he's finished, he opens the mirrored cabinet and finds a jar of petroleum jelly and a tube of ChapStick and a small pink bottle of perfume labeled in another language. In his palm the bottle has a receptive look, like a muscle. A woman's small vanity. He feels a tenderness for its owner. He lifts one of the plastic shelves and there taped to the bottom is an envelope addressed to Sandra Gutiérrez from a woman in Coeur d'Alene. Inside the envelope is a twenty-dollar bill and a single pressed flower long ago faded brown and no letter. He smiles at this luck and takes the bill and tapes the envelope back. He walks through the house and out into the yard and turns around to press the door flush.

The night is cool but not cold and he follows the valley road where it runs along the river. To the southwest, a narrow cut of light marks the city. He has twenty-five dollars now and some change. The hour has grown very late, but if he catches the morning train to Barstow he can improvise before another night comes. As he walks more slowly he sees new driveways graveled into the lots west of his brother's house. He walks between these drives and a house frame catches the moonlight and he recognizes the shape. It is a few weeks from windows and doors and wall plaster, and when it is done it will look just the same as the one his brother built up the road, where the young family lives now.

Then, at the edge of the yard where the dirt is cleared and flattened, Julius sees first the trailer and then an awning strung from it. He shakes his head. Between the trailer and the trees is his golden mustang. The trailer door is propped open and the floor inside is laid with dry hay. Around this makeshift shelter is a split-rail fence made from hedgewood of varying widths and splintered. He looks up at the house frame again and understands.

He walks across the yard and into the frame of the new house. He looks up through the crossing wood. He grabs an unfixed post and shakes it and dust falls and covers him. The house is lovely and well-made. He climbs a corner post and up into the rafters and sits looking out across the river. From this height he can see the other lots and the farmland to the north. Miles away, an aerosol of cloud stretches through the gray irradiate night. He thinks of his brother sitting just here and seeing the same things.

He remembers the night in Las Vegas, early on, when he climbed to the roof of Binion's and looked out across the desert and watched the fraying bomb. He had felt free then because he had been free of his brother's vigilance. He wonders if his brother has also looked out across this river and this bit of sky and felt free. If beyond them both was a future they could share in this way. Past the bluff and the river, the horizon lifts from the earth in a band of yellow light. Julius thinks of Muriel's secret and wonders if Lee knows all of it now, if they are together or if Muriel is somewhere else. He thinks she must be somewhere else. He imagines her walking into the Chester Hotel and why she might want to go to a place like that and how she'd heard of it. He thinks of what she must have seen there, and what she must have understood to leave a note for him, and how fearless she must be. She had been so lucky but she had not been content to keep only what was hers, the money and the house in Kansas. She had wanted to give something to Lee, even if it was not the truth. And though Julius had stolen from her it was she who wanted his forgiveness and then she wrote his name and made the absolution he could not make for himself, and this might be the only way love ever is. Love might be made of things that couldn't happen or things no one knows or intends.

The train to Barstow leaves at six-fifteen and it must be nearing that now. The road running into town is several miles away and he has not slept in two days. From above, the aurulent horse sways against the breeze. He flattens his jeans and pulls the boots back over them, then climbs down from the unfinished house. He steps onto the split-rail and hauls over and the horse whinnies back against the opposite side. He drops the top rail and kicks away the bottom, making an opening wide enough to pass through. In the trailer he finds a bag of grain and a pail of apples and he slits the bag open and tucks in his shirt and drops apples through the collar and against his chest so they are held on the inside. He approaches the horse and speaks to her. She is pressed against the fence and her eyes are fiery, but she does not move away. For many long minutes he stands talking to her and stroking her poll and muzzle. When he feels she has calmed and deferred, he brings one foot to the rail and plants a hand on her wither and jumps, but the bag of grain strikes her neck. She throws him and he lands painfully on his bad ribs. She steps marginally back, and the ground drifts up in dust and splinters. Half the apples have smashed and spilled, but Julius holds the horse's gaze and says to her, "I don't aim to be no thief this time and if you'd just wait there, girl, you'll see." And miraculously she does.

He catches his breath and approaches her again. She nickers sideways, but he touches her gently and she lets him. Then again he plants his hand and gets one foot on the fence. She lurches sideways, but he has her by the mane now and she doesn't run. He leaps off the fence and throws out his other leg. He gets over, but too far, and he slides off the horse's fat bow and has to wrap his arms around her neck. She bolts then, out of the enclosure and into the yard, and Julius leans forward and whispers nonsense until she slows. At the road the gravel dust lifts and enters the faint light and he raises the bag and tosses forward a handful of grain and the horse trots toward it and leans and eats it. A hundred yards onto the road, he reaches into his wet and stinking shirt and takes an apple and tosses this too.

They ride several miles this way while the sun draws up, on the old county road. On either side the houses are half-finished or without walls or already inhabited. They make swift time. Soon the road gives out to a housing development empty of people and trees, the streets gridded straight as a clock. The change in scenery makes the horse hesitate and Julius leans to calm her. He sits up. To his right, another mile away, the new interstate runs east–west. He nudges the horse forward. She cringes against him and wants to turn back, so he digs a heel into the soft space between her hip and her stomach. He grinds his heel there but she will go no further. He thinks she must be thirsty. He is thirsty. He leans forward against her and scoops his cheek against her neck and calls her honey. Then he dismounts.

He takes the horse by the bridle and she turns without resistance and he leads her down the road and back toward the river and into a copse of trees. He dumps the last of the grain and the split apples and she leans happily for them. She lifts her head and chews and nudges him and pulls back her black lips and he cups her snout and thanks her. Inside the trees she is the color of wheat caught in an afternoon rainshower. He looks up and down the riverbank and sees no danger so he turns away and walks back to the road and when he's walked a few hundred yards he turns back to look at her. She is still chewing with her fine head raised into the morning breeze. She moves slowly among the apples and from where he stands she looks like a sawhorse spread too wide. Her baseball ankles crease and drop; she moves slowly but with great purpose and he admits to himself that she is old, that she was old before he'd ever hauled her toward the sea.

Then he walks the last mile to the freeway, as quickly as his ribs will let him. He stands at the frontage road and cups his knees and catches his breath and then he rights himself and looks around. The sun has risen and the day is hot and cloudless and already there are lines of cars headed west and he remembers it is Sunday. The windows of the slow-moving cars are filled with hatless men and women fanning themselves and little children in their church lace.

Julius looks at the sun in the sky and gauges the hour. The ride has bought him time. He thinks of the Squaw and the Aces High and he sees Henry there and tastes beer and cigar smoke and the desiccant wind of that place. He walks to the off-ramp headed back into the city and puts out his thumb. A dozen cars pass him until one pulls over and he looks in at the family with their brown eyes and their pleasure and he wonders how long their pleasure can last in this reckless century and if he can share it. The man asks him where he wants to go. Julius tells him, and when the driver nods he folds through the door and sits heavily against the seat next to the lovely children. The car pulls away, back out toward the bay and then up the coastal rise, heading through the park toward downtown. They are well into daylight now, the cars leaving contrails behind their fins in the white summer daylight, lit by brakelights and the white sun, so that driving through the city feels like floating, the sea in haze to the west and to the south the mortared bay, the cars in orbit around the open rim of the world.

ACKNOWLEDGMENTS

I would like to thank my parents, Eric and Theresa, for giving me freedom and respect, and genuine love; my sister, Valerie, for completing my world; and Shay O'Brien, for sheltering me and for making my life more beautiful than I ever dreamed.

This book exists because it was supported by very fine people. My thanks to Eavan Boland, Tobias Wolff, Adam Johnson, my wonderful fellow Stegners, and the Creative Writing Program at Stanford University. Special thanks to Elizabeth Tallent, who read every word and at each turn enlarged my sense of the possible. Much gratitude to Helen Garnons-Williams, and everyone at Fourth Estate, for their enthusiasm and care. The amazing people at Riverhead brought this book to life—and created a beautiful object. For all his gambling insights, my thanks to the remarkable James Jorasch. The genius Cal Morgan and incomparable Joy Harris have been this book's brilliant stewards. Thank you.

Finally, I have been taught, from earliest memory, by women of indefatigable will. My deepest thanks to my many teachers, who brighten their great profession with diligence, wisdom, and dignity.